KAOS:
THE STAR
OF THIEVES

[Raw Manuscript] [UK]

Lindsey B. Williams

Open-Eyed Productions

ISBN-13: 979-8-9911598-3-8

Cover design by: Lindsey B. Williams

Dedicated to the streaming giant in bed with the university that made me sick, who is cluelessly satisfying demands from my aggrieved (former?)(potential?) business partner, who's only mad because someone, who was (jealous?) envious of me (i.e. literally trying to be me), told convinced them I was the fraud.

contents

preface

You don't always get what you want.

October 30th, 2023

My dear reader,

You won't believe me when I tell you this: This is one manuscript in a set of manuscripts that are being published under duress.

...Back in the early 2000's a woman tried to sue several folks in Hollywood for the suspected exploitation of her unfinished work "The Third Eye" which, at that point, she believed had been turned into the The Matrix franchise.

...Back in the early 2000's a scandal broke out amongst artists who literally walked out of their jobs at The Walt Disney Company because they found themselves conscripted to produce Disney's The Lion King, which even artists agreed stole from the ground-breaking Kimba, The White Lion series - one of the first televises shows broadcasted in color and dear to their very childhoods. Of course the decision to pursue Disney on any potential claim rest solely on the desires of the creator of

Kimba, The White Lion, who, based on my research, respectfully, had no desire to engage in such a dispute with Disney, whom they held respect for.

...Back in the early 2000's prominent entertainment lawyers were being prosecuted by federal prosecutors for illegally obtaining information against their opponents and using them to "never loose" their cases.

That was then... why does any of it matter now?

Back in late 2003, I was dissatisfied with Peter Jackson's Lord of the Rings films because they hadn't been able to distract me from my, then, troubled childhood. So instead of just becoming a critic that had no sense of what it took to make those films, I set out to create a better movie to "dethrone" him.

They say that you should be careful what you wish for - well... little did I know that this far-fetched goal would become more of a reality than I bargained for.

Fast-forward to 2016, where after a protracted and lingering business dispute with my former employer, who just so happened to be Peter Jackson's studio in New Zealand, I was retaliated against. Why? There is unfortunately too many reasons to speculate over. However these works (the manuscripts I'm publishing) along with the rest of my vault, were hacked so that they could be exploited by those previously mentioned - those will a completely different sense of "creating" content.

I was given the advice by counsel to register elements of my work in Europe, specifically a trademark on my main character's nick-name "Kaos," after it was obvious that one of my foes was illegally importing my work into the continent in hopes of permanently depriving me of it and making themselves famous on my behalf.

How is that possible? Unlike the legal system in the United States, the European legal system will not "undo" certain illegal actions, among them trademark or copyright infringement. So once my foe releases their work, which we both know is intended to take advantage of me, it will unlikely be taken down even if I prevail in court. As you can see, the intent is to permanently deprive me of my work, defame, and probably most-relevantly humiliate me in front of the entire world, forever.

So this publication is not what I wanted. I've had to pull this all together at the last moment to strategically hold onto my rights. There will still most likely be a battle despite all my effort to avoid one.

Most of these manuscripts were not to be read by anyone other than me until after my death. I was building up the technology and skills required to realize the vision I have in my mind's eye when I personally read these works. I never intend to become an author and have spent most of my career as a computer scientist and a roller skater. I never intended to sell this material to any publishing house or producer, which is probably why I've angered a few of them.

But this was going to be my "Star Wars". Something that I could build and create a whole company from. I'd materialize this far-fetched dream of mine, call myself retired, and spend the rest of my days helping other's realize their own works and therefore retire themselves.

I certainly didn't want my work to be the reason I couldn't be hired or be tinged by Hollywood scandal. Just like the creator of Kimba, The White Lion, I had no desire to pursue anyone over claims of infringement.

But just like my foes get to learn: You don't always get what you want.

danger! danger!

This is a raw manuscript.

It has not been edited... (except for *maybe* a grammer and spell check.)

If you think something's off, it probably is.

If you get confused or hung-up somewhere, just keep reading. I'd rather you get the gist of my work than get stuck on the phrasing.

This work was never really intend to be a book, but reminds me of a film/televsion show in my head. I encourage you to use your imagination if a description is absent and be open to those details showing up later.

Future editions and releases are intended for this material to bring it up to "snuff", as they say.

short comings

This manuscript used a custom font for some of the elvish phrases, which I created as a combination of latin and weird rules. This could not be included in this release.

An entire section is missing because it was written by hand and has not been digitized for this release.

daunting | future

The summer's leaves bombarded two boys with streams of orange-pink light. The rivers ran down, glistening their glory until they hinted of true existence, when, like knowing better than wise Mormons, they disappeared before setting foot on the gray grass.

A foot long, wooden icicle leapt through the densely, over grown forest. Leaves and acorns dropped down in the tension of the red-feathered tail that followed. A tall imperial oak, lush in summer's midst, stood heart-stuck with an arrow. The ring of the wire that strung tightly in a hand-made charcoal ebony bow rang though the forest with defiant and un-withering motion saying: 'beware'. The central point; it hung in the most tranquil of hands, of no more than a 17–year-old boy. His dark brown eyes lay on the bull's-eye lit by a spotlight of orange. His hair: jet black among the pink enlightened green was longer than most boy's. It curled up around his ears and his neck as though month after month he hadn't gotten it cut. His dress was no cleaner as his dirt-smudged face suggested, while his facial features were slight defined, and almost picturesque in contrast. It was perhaps all of these features that could remind one of a teenager's desire to break from all traditional human law in appearance while remain sharp and exquisite in ability. The disheveled look and the archery of a well-trained marksman were not just a stigma of a youthful and brash generation, but the remnants of a personality, and a lifestyle that refused to remain consistent with whatever the normality seemed at the time. Farm boys were farm boys and could only swing a sword like a shovel. It was as though the young lads with disheveled appearances and eloquent talents wanted to prove that perhaps things are more than they seem, and that the stereotypes were incorrect and stupid. Sitting on his horse he smirked and his face lit with the light, he blinked. While looking at his handy work, the boy snorted with a laugh at the trivialness of his success and retreated to the shadows once more. The two horses in the small ravine lay blotched and motionless.

"Kaos, how you do it every time bugs me," a short misty-brown haired boy said with remorse as he shifted position in his saddle and crossed his arms. "Someday, I'll be whimpering about how my little brother beat me" Kaos tried to heal the boy's broken confidence, but to no avail. The young boy's expression didn't seem to change and Kaos turned away urging on his Appalachian horse to move from its lazy position. He clicked his tongue twice and the horse immediately strutted regally and slowly towards the tree. The arrow was straight into the tree at a ninety-degree angle, no penetration marks, no skidding. It solitude seemed to suggest that it had always been there.

"If you weren't my brother, I'd think that you're an elf, or something," Kaos' younger brother nagged, simply jealous of Kaos's ability, "We're only two years apart, and you still are unmatched, even when you square off with father." Kaos didn't smile in pride, nor show much of an interest at all. He had been told that thousands of times that he had a knack for archery. The flattery grew old and repetitive, and many times it was with jealously and bitterness, of the type his brother had now.

A loud whistle rang through a mile-wide area. The brown-haired boy's ears perked and his eyes popped as though hearing a fire alarm. Like his brother before him, he clicked his tongue twice and his black-socked bay turned right, heading towards a field and up a small hill. The hill was littered with small trees, and the larger ones usually had enough of an interval for two horses to pass through easily. The terrain wasn't ruff, and only the fall's restorative leaves sprinkled the grassy floor.

"Speaking of father," Kaos laughed staring up into the canopy of the forest.

"Well, we better get home, I'm getting hungry," he whined. Now calm and continued up the hill. The bay's hooves flipped up dirt as the boy left Kaos alone in the ravine. In some rush, Kaos jerked the arrow out of the tree, stuck it in his back sling next to his bow, and turned his horse to follow the bay.

The sun was heading closer to the horizon as the two boys reached the field. The soft orange light lay on the long shimmering blades as fireflies started to arose and add an eerie glow to the place. Kaos stared like a child into its beauty.

"I love this place," Kaos said rather out of nowhere. The boy on the Bay looked back over his shoulder in surprise as they continued through the field.

"We've been here ever since we were kids," he said and he returned to watch the path at which his horse strode. "At least when you're around." The long blades veered before his bay and brushed upon his ankles as they swam though it.

"We still are kids," Kaos laughed. He smiled at the ground, a small breeze blew by and the grass waved in fancy. He stuck his hand out and let the blades tickle under his fingertips.

"Not you Kaos, you have less than a year until you have to leave this place; me, I have over two," the boy stared down at his saddle. His chin popped up and down as the horse continued the tiresome walk. Kaos and his horse came up to his side. The boy lingered with more heartache than even before.

"Come on, I know three months isn't a very long time, but that's why I've been spending most of my time with you. You're my brother, I don't want to leave this place, but I really have no choice." Kaos stared at his brother, as his white teeth peeled over his bottom lip. "Stop, let's have a talk." Kaos shot as he stopped his horse. His brother's horse stopped as well. Kaos hopped off and placed his bow and arrows on his saddle's side pocket. He walked around and grabbed the bay's reigns. "Come on," Kaos whined, as his bother still hadn't moved.

"What about father?" the boy said with innocence. His eyes glanced sideways into Kaos's in worry.

"He can wait," Kaos said smiling he put his hand on his hip. Kaos's brother hopped down and landed in the grass. He took off his bow and arrows and put them in the saddle pocket. "Hurry up, take your horse, Cella's dying to get the bridal bite out of her mouth so she can eat some of this grass." The young boy grabbed the reigns from Kaos's grip and watched. Kaos went over to Cella, who flicked her sand-like tail in anticipation. He rubbed the white diamond between her two deep blue eyes and started taking off her bridal. The moment it was off, she whinnied and skirted across the plain to the far side, parting the grass in her wake.

"Will she come back?"

"Oh yeah," Kaos exclaimed, "All I have to do is whistle."

"How did you train her to do that?"

"I tied her with father's old pony, Dustirg, and she mimicked him," Kaos said. "Hold on," Kaos whistled, and Cella looked up in grief at him with a mouthful of grass. She swallowed and pranced gracefully over to him. Kaos grabbed the rope from the bag and made a loop over Cella's and the Bay's neck. Kaos's brother undid the bay's bridal and the two horses, joined by the neck rope, trotted down to the far side of the field. "Now that Bay of yours shall learn it too," Kaos laughed, "Did you decide on a name for him yet?" Kaos turned to his brother smiling.

"I was thinking something like Draco," he said, still unsure, and wondering about his older brother's opinion.

"I don't think he's the type, personally," Kaos said laughing.

"What do you think I should name him, then?" He stared at Kaos with laughter as well.

"Well, he's responsive, and laid back... I think you shall call him...Frank," Kaos said sarcastically with laughter.

"Frank? Um...let me think about that one...no," his brother said sarcastically.

"Trust me, I'm not any better than you at picking names," Kaos said as he leaned against a tree that lined the field. His laughter and smile eased one onto his brother's face, who sat down next to him.

"Cella, might not be too happy to hear that," he conjured up.

"That name was a miracle," Kaos exclaimed, "It actually fits her personality."

"Maybe it was her name that shaped her personality, not the personality that shaped the name."

"Who knows," Kaos continued laughing. He calmed down and smiled staring at the sky. There was a long silence and Kaos still had a grin on his face.

"Lural, has been looking at you, Kaos," his brother with that gossipy kind of voice.

"What do you mean by 'looking at me'?" Kaos was still smiling and mocking the gossipy talk that flew from his brother's mouth.

"Hey, it's none of my business, but I've been hearing rumors that her parents want to talk to father about marriage," he whispered.

"Marriage? Ah, I hope not. There's no point to it, life has finally gotten interesting." He continued smiling, "Why waste it on a wife and children?"

"No? But really, if you had to marry any girl in the village, who would it be?" his brother asked with some laughter.

"What kind of question is that? I barely know any of them; they don't do anything but hang around the food market or help their mothers with the chores. We invite them to go riding with us but every time they're mothers shoo them inside." Kaos supported.

"Well, that's not their fault," his brother said with agony.

"Yeah, but I'm not going to get married to a total stranger."

"Gees," Kaos' brother put his head in his hand, and surged at his brother's taste. Kaos's laughter dropped like rain in a cloud and rumbled in warning with thunder for the lightning that would follow. There was another whistle across the grass.

"Oh shit," Kaos got up from his seat on the ground.

"Oh no, what?" His brother sarcastically said exaggerating with hand motions, "It's only father, anyways why are you so worried? You said that he could wait?"

"No, the horses stupid, Cella's sprints off at a whistle,"

"Well call her back," Kaos whistled, and on the far side of the field, the two horses cantered into a ravine and headed towards the sound of their father's whistle.

"Oh, god," Kaos hopped though the field trying to catch up with the horses.

"Hey wait," his brother yelped at which, he hopped up off the ground and lunged after him. The two boys ended up walking home on foot through the thick bottom bushes of outer portion of the forest.

"Lural is really nice, Kaos," the boy added as a small lit up out appeared on the horizon.

"Why, you'd think we make a couple?" Kaos mocked the idea of marriage as he said this.

"Yeah, actually," he said firmly. Kaos taken back by his brother's decisiveness flipped around and stopped him.

"When did you become match maker?" he asked.

"My guess is that I've spent more time with Lural than you, and I know her." He said firmly. "You two would hit it off."

"She's so quiet," Kaos added.

"Can I trust you not to tell anyone that I told you this," Tako said softly.

"Said what? Sure." Kaos asked placing a hand on his hip.

"She told me about three months ago that she's been head over heels for you ever since the time we had that big paintball game after the New Year's celebration."

"That was over six years ago," Kaos exclaimed. "I don't even think I saw her that day."

"She said that you dove and took a paint ball before it landed on her new dress." Kaos was quiet. It hit him, he remembered.

"Oh!" he exclaimed and tried to blow it off. "Gees, that's what I hate about girls, you do something nice and they automatically think marriage."

"She said that you also nearly kissed her during the human knot last year," Tako exclaimed with more force. With this Kaos blushed.

"Charad, go under Kaos' arm," a boy yelled. A boy with yellow hair and freckles creped under Kaos arm as the teenagers all stood and squatted in a human knot. Suddenly Charad tugged the knot. Suddenly one after another kids fell, the line fell and kids shrieked as they were jerked forward. Kaos was standing the middle of the knot his head above most the other's due to his height. He was looking over his shoulder at the crowd as it fell like dominos when all of a sudden his left hand was yanked down and he stumbled among his feet. The potential collapse of his knees sat clearly at the precipice.

"Charad, you idiot!" Kaos yelled at him "What the hell did you do!" A little ten-year-old with brown hair who was tearing at the eyes was pinching Kaos' hand down.

"Don't yell at me!" Charad's voice rose in justification.

"Rio," the same boy from before yelled, "Go under Sarah and Rachel's arms." At this the knot's tautness gave. Like in a dance his front knee dropped and his right hand was yanked. The small ten-year old tripped as he wretched his head over his shoulder to see her distress. It was then that Kaos felt a body being pinned against his chest and he look in front of him and found Lural's face, their noses not even and inch away. Charad from some distance laughed as Kaos flushed. Lural was as red as a cherry.

"Kaos?" the interrogator asked again, waking Kaos from his dream.

"I didn't almost kiss her, we just got pinned against one another." Kaos claimed.

"Whatever," he sighed.

"Let's just get home, before father kills me." After walking for an hour they reached the backside of a small hut-like house with a barn, and a pasture. Both horses were gated in the pasture and their luggage, most likely in the house.

"God, we're lucky," Kaos panted as they slowed to a walk. His ankles were scrapped and cut just above the ankle. He arms were scraped, but they didn't bleed. His shorter brother had endured more than he had. He had cuts on his arms and legs.

"Let's just get inside," his bother panted.

"Hey, we're home," Kaos yelled into the house. His flew up the wooden stairs and around the corner to the kitchen.

"Good, Kaos, you're home," a plump woman came around the corner to stare at him with a smile. She wore an apron with tiny embroidered flowers making a scene at the bottom. Underneath was a pale yellow dress that was only worn for special occasions. It had puffed sleeves and white underneath layer that protruded beneath the yellow elastic ends.

"Hey, why are you dressed up?"

"Yaktako, hello dear." She drew her attention to Kaos's brother. "The Tailors are coming over for dinner tonight," she said coming up to them while holding a bowl, which looked like a mixture for bread, "Lural's coming too." She stared at Kaos, who gave her a weird look. She looked at the two of them then stopped, "Oh god, come in you two," the cuts were stinging. She grabbed Yaktako by the shoulders, and quickly added, "Take off your shoes," Tako (Yaktako) did and she hurried him into the kitchen. Kaos took off his and followed.

"Where were you two?" she said with worry and grief as she put down the bowl and washed her hands.

"We were in the north part of the field when father's-," Kaos tried to explain when his father came in and lounged in the doorway.

"When I whistled, Cella tugged Yaktako's Bay all the way home." He stopped and waited for his words to sink slowly into Kaos. "Kaos, did you teach Cella to respond to a whistle?" His father stared down at Kaos with anger.

"Yes," he said quietly with grief.

"I told you not to, Kaos!" his father bellowed. He hung in the doorway in a relaxed and comfortable position, yet his tone reflected more of his true personality.

"But, she doesn't have to always wear her bridle now, she hates -" Kaos pleaded showing his teeth to his snarling father

"Just shut up," his father said with defiance, "You're 17 now Kaos, you are no longer a child, I am disappointed that you disobeyed me and then cause your brother so much pain, now go upstairs, clean yourself up a bit and go put the horses in the barn before the Tailors arrive." Kaos glared at his father but did as he was told. He stomped past them and headed up the stairs. Making a sharp turn left and back walking all the way down to the last doorway. He pushed the door open with a slam on the far wall and then slammed it shut. There were then loud pounding thumps up the stairs after him. His father raced down to the room, scowling. Kicking open the door his father scoped the room for his son. The back window to the roof had been wrenched open and there was a small pat of earth far below. He ran to the window and stuck his head out it.

"Kaos!!" he yelled defiantly. Kaos on the short grass below stopped, "Kaos, get back inside this house immediately!" Kaos squinted his eyes in grief stayed in the shadows. "Kaos-"

"Why?" Kaos yelled.

"We have guests coming over tonight, and I don't want to be embarrassed that my own son wouldn't show up for dinner," he yelled, but taking the role of a parent, not a scowling man. "I know that you're mad at me for denying you the right to train you own horse, but that's it Kaos. I might have been a little harsh, but I specifically told you not to, and for very good reasons," he held his tongue from saying how Kaos put his brother in danger, and then over reacted about the whole thing. "Just come back inside, please, Kaos, just don't run away again." His father panted at the window. The creaking of the side door, made him sigh with relief.

Kaos climbed up the basement stairs into the kitchen, where his mother quickly stared at him: Noticing his face, she quickly flipped back around and continued preparing the meal. The kitchen smelt of baked potatoes, turkey, and homemade gravy. Tako was in the living room watching TV in the dark. Kaos walked slowly through it to the stairs and headed back up them. Gripping the black banister his father passed him on the stairs; they said nothing to one another until Kaos reached the top of the stairs,

"I'm sorry, father," he said quietly. His father stopped suddenly on the stairs,

"Apology accepted," he smiled and continued down the stairs. Kaos went down to his room again and got out some new clothes; Kaki, cargo pocket pants with a long sleeve, black, shirt. He walked back down the hall passing Tako's room, a closet, and then to the bathroom. He hopped in the shower and let the hot water cool his temper.

After he got dressed he toweled his hair off and went outside. The cool crisp air contradicted the afternoon's warm humid weather. He walked to a tall post by the barn and lit the lantern inside. It glowed with vengeance, though only lighting a small corner of the paddock. Turning to the pasture he leaned his elbows on the three-wood-planked-fence. It had been batter with weathering and it dearly needed some replacing, but for now, it would do. The bay on the far side of the pasture didn't care to notice Kaos's appearance and continued eating. Kaos hopped up on top of the fence and continued to watch them swinging his legs in boredom. Cella shifted her weight once, and then again, and finally out of ill conscience walked happily over to Kaos and nudged him on the side of the head.

"Hey girl," Kaos said quietly, happy to see that he had some company. He rubbed in-between her thoughtful eyes feeling over its small patch of white velvet. There were small pitter-pattering of hooves on the dirt road and the slow creaking of carriage wheels.

"Hello there! Kaos, is that you?" a man's deep voice bellowed in delight. Kaos peered around his shoulder, keeping his hand on Cella's warm head. A well-dressed man hung out the front flap waving. Kaos, wanted to just wave back, but he didn't, instead he hopped down from the fence and greeted them as the carriage came to a halt. He smiled and said,

"Hello, Mr. Tailor, did you have a good trip?" Kaos's smile was fake, but truth be told, he had learned to lie.

"That's a fine horse you go there," Mr. Tailor exclaimed as his eyes set on Cella and turned to Kaos.

"Lural," Kaos continued to be kind. He stuck his hand out to her as a gentleman and helped her down the small steps onto the ground. Mr. Tailor smiled watching the two of them.

"How long have you had her?" he said with a clam but serine voice, as though he had wanted to ask something else.

"I've had her practically all my life," Kaos turned to the man. Lural still had her hand grasped around Kaos's. Lural was quite gorgeous. Her hair was a deep and shiny brown. Half of her large curls were tied up in a bun and half down to rest on her shoulders. She wore a plain pale blue pleated skirt that ended at middle thigh, and a fuzzy, white, no-sleeves non-knitted, turtle neck sweater.

"Speaking of horses," Kaos interrupted, feeling a little wary about Lural's hand, "I have to go put them in the barn, so excuse me," Kaos said politely, "The door is just there," he pointed to the front door, "my father and mother are home, and they've been expecting you." Kaos slipped respectively away from Lural and went to the pasture fence and hopped it. He brought Cella over to the gate, opened it, and led her into the barn. He came back out and took the Bay in as well. The bay was rather reluctant to leave the pasture, and slowly he stepped towards the gate, reaching down for dinner when it finished the mouthful he had snagged before. Kaos nudged at his chin and when they reached the gate, the bay quietly agreed. The barn was rather large for just three their three horses; Cella, the bay, and Distrig. There were at least six square stalls and hay filled each of them. Kaos lead the horse down next to Cella's stall, which was the farthest at the end and put him inside. He closed his gate and made sure there was enough water in the bucket nearby. The bay came up t o him at the door and Kaos gladly rubbed it on the nose. Kaos stepped back and looked at the stalls. The horses' tack lay on pegs out of the top left side of their stall doors. He didn't linger long and headed outside and then into the house. Though Mr. Tailor and Lural had watched him take in Cella, by the time he came back out they had slipped into the house. The door made a loud clank as it closed, Kaos took off his shoes and headed into the kitchen, where his mother was sitting at the table. He sat down in one of the other four chairs and tried to relax. Lural was at the stove, which surprised Kaos. She was stirring what looked to be like stew of some sort. There was a bell and his mother got up and went to the oven. Opening the hatch, revealed fresh baked bread, and the excited woman put on two oven mitts and took the pan out and placed it on the table.

"Where's father? Shouldn't he be helping you?" Kaos asked her.

"Well, your father is in the dining room talking with Mr. Tailor, and anyways Lural has been so kind as to help me." Kaos wanted to know what his father was up to. So he got up from the table but was interrupted; "-and Kaos, could you go check on your brother for me, he supposed to be in the living room watching TV." Kaos changed direction and headed into the living room to sit down on the couch with his brother. He had taken the signal not to go into the dining room which really only made him more nervous about what his father was doing.

"I hear that Kaos will be turning eighteen in a matter of months," Mr. Tailor hinted.

"That's true," Kaos's father said back to him with a steady tone.

"Lural also has only a few more months to stay here with us, so I would like to propose something to you." He stopped and fiddled with his fingers. "Lural has taken quite an interest in your little boy, Jonathan. She walks down into Swander's ravine in the early morning hours watching your son canter off through the fields."

"My son doesn't ever get up early," Jonathan said back to him with disgust. Remembering all the times he had to walk into Kaos's room and strip him of his sheets, yet still he stayed sleeping. "He barley likes to get up before noon for lunch."

"Are you so sure, my friend, your boy is the only person in this village that rides a gray horse with white tails and manes, your son *is* riding every morning. I've seen him myself." He assured quietly. "Whether you believe or not I do. I too have taken an interest into your boy. He's a very strong rider, and practically the best marksman in town. And since he's nearing his eighteenth year with no bride, I feel that we should marry him with Lural." He said with dignity. Jonathan sat at the table in deep thought. "So what about it Jonathan? I know that the food hunting might be a bit slowed without him around, but as my brother-in-law there would be no problem setting up for food to be delivered here for you."

"I think that would be a good idea, but…" Jonathan's tone dropped, "my boy will not be bought with the promise of food. He is worth much more to me than just a good meal daily. I would gladly go hungry for him."

"I know Jonathan, but your boy will be leaving you in three months," Mr. Tailor stopped smiling and continued, "Take a few months to think on it, in two, tell me your decision." Mr. Tailor got up from the table and walked into the kitchen and greeted Lural and Jonathan's wife.

"Smells delicious girls," he said with laughter as though the conversation in the other room hadn't taken place. Jonathon remained at the table. "I could never see you as a husband Kaos, not with Lural, not with anyone for that matter. You are so much like me, perhaps that's why this is such a hard decision. Yet then…what would your mother think…" He sighed and put his head in his hands. "Μαρινα I νεεδ ψου νοω."

"Dinner is ready," Lural peeked her head around the doorway to look a Kaos and Tako on the couch. Tako turned the TV off obediently and got up, Kaos rather reluctantly got up. They walked into the dinning room to a long table. There were two end chairs and three on either side. Mr. Tailor and Jonathan took the two head chairs. Tako sat on the right side of Father, and mom on the left. To Mr. Tailor's left sat Lural and right sat Mrs. Tailor. Kaos was told to sit in-between Tako and

Lural. It was nerve-wreaking, Kaos had always sat next to father even when guest had come over. Now Tako sat in his seat. Tako usually sat next to mom and the seat Kaos now sat in was usually empty.

"Let us say grace," mother said quietly and hinted to Kaos to say something. Kaos with a strange look on his face lowered his chin and clasped his hands on the table gently and said:

"Let us give the gods thanks for the food place before us:

Τηοσε ωηο εξχιταϖερυντ ανιμυμ αδ δεασ, Λετ δεατη ϖε νιβυντ ινϖιτα, Αωακεν τηειρ ηεαρτ σ, βυντ αδ αμαρε ετ χα ϖερε, Λετ εαχη νεω λιγητ βυρν βριγητερ ιν αγε, Δυξ τηειρ το υχη αδ φυτυρμ,Μαψ τηε ηοπε ανδ λυξ εξχιπιεντ τυ χυντι□

"That was beautiful Kaos, where did you learn that?" His own mother asked him. Kaos paused in some shock, as did the rest of the group.

"Was that elvish?" Lural asked him turned to his face in surprise. Her face was lit in some startled and excited fashion.

"I ran into the high priest at the Raika Shrine last week and we talked. Somehow he ended up teaching me the small prayer." Kaos laughed, "It seemed a good time to tell it so."

"What does it mean?" Tako asked in wonder.

"It means: Those who waken their hearts to the gods, Let death come un-welcomed, Awaken their heart to learn from mistakes, Let each new light burn brighter in age, Lead their torch into their future, May the hope and light welcome you all." Jonathan stared at Kaos with an enlightening glare and spoke." The group was rather taken back by the extensiveness of Kaos' understanding of Elvish and he nearly blushed in the silence that followed. His father narrowed his eyebrows slightly and focused on Kaos.

"What was the man's name?" Jonathan queried again.

"Cunti taught it to me," Kaos said.

"So you ran into Cunti," Jonathan laughed, "How is he doing? I have not seen him in a long time."

"Really? You know Cunti?" Kaos said in disbelief.

"Yes, we are old friends, I'm surprised he's still around." Kaos smile said he already knew the two had been friends.

"Well, everyone feel free to start eating." Kaos's mother said. Kaos was laughing a little realizing that Cunti had to have been a friend of fathers. Jonathan stared at his son with wary now. "What did Cunti tell you Kaos?" he thought and grabbed potatoes. The night went by with no other surprises. Kaos, Tako, Jonathan, Lural, and Mr. Tailor ended up playing poker that night, and Lural came back with all the change. They left at 10:00 three hours later than they had planned and Kaos saw them off. He walked inside to the kitchen,

"That went well, didn't it Kaos?" His mom was washing the dishes asked him.

"Whatever Good means," he sighed with relief sitting down in the kitchen table.

"What do you think you're doing, come over here and dry off the dishes," Kaos got up and got the dishtowel and picked up a glass next to his mom.

"So what did you a Cunti talk about?" she asked worried.

"Oh, nothing you should be worried about mom," Kaos said and kissed her on the cheek and returned to the glass. Kaos was taller than his mom, practically the same height as his dad. She smiled warmly and stuck her hands in the soapy water.

Kaos walked up the red staircase and peeked his head into his brother's room.

"So, how are you doing?" he said smiling.

"Fine," he closed a book and sat up in bed, "Don't tell mom I'm still up, she sent me to bed almost an hour ago," he pleaded with his brother.

"Trust me, I won't," Kaos calmly retorted. "And anyways I'm heading to bed right now. Mom's still picking up after dinner, so she probably won't come up to check on you tonight."

"Thanks," Tako said warmly, "Well good night then."

"Yeah, good night." Kaos turned, smiling, and walked down to his bedroom. After changing into his pajamas he slipped into bed and fell asleep.

Jonathan woke with a start, and took a deep intake of air.

"What's wrong Jonathan?" his wife lay at his side as he panted.

"I thought I heard something," Jonathan said with a keen eye and then stared at the clock: 3:02 am.

"I didn't hear anything honey, so just go back to bed and get a few more hours of sleep in," she said and rolled over onto her soft pillow. Jonathan didn't move but kept his ears perked, but they heard nothing.

"Shale, I think I'm going to go take a walk," Jonathan said roughly. He slipped out of bed and started changing into clothes.

"Why would you want to take a walk at this hour?" Shale yelled in a whisper.

"You can go back to bed, I just need a little fresh air." Jonathan put on a dark blue sweatshirt and slipped out of the bedroom door into the living room and then though the front door.

The April air was crisp, but frosty. His breath flew up in front of his face in puffs of smoke and he quickly shoved his bare hands into the large pocket of his sweatshirt. He slowly headed around the house and into the barn, in which he found that Cella's stall was empty. The bay stood quietly staring at him with wild eyes, but he didn't really see them and turned around to face another horse: Dustirg. Dustirg was a bay as well, but he had a white blaze that flew from behind his ears all the way down to his noise. He wasn't very young and it showed around his face, but just because he had aged didn't mean he was a push over. Jonathan quickly unlocked his stall and flung the saddle over his back.

"You saw my crazy son this morning, didn't you?" Jonathan smiled and hopped on the back of his horse and clicked his tongue twice. Dustirg immediately responded and the walked out of the barn. They turned left and they cantered up and behind the barn. They traveled for a few minutes until they finally reached the ravine Mr. Paterson had talked about. Sure enough on the far side of the field was Kaos and Cella. Cella cantered around in awkward precision, Kaos was on top nailing arrows in nearby trees. Jonathan trotted though the field towards his son and when within 50 feet he yelled,

"Kaos." Cella immediately stopped and Kaos lowered his bow. "Kaos, I need to talk to you," Jonathan said with some desperation.

"Why are you out here?" Kaos said with wonder as he put his bow on his shoulder and walked Cella over to him.

"I should be asking you that," Jonathan said with a smile.

"I always come out here in the morning," Kaos responded still shocked about his father being out so early.

"Well, that doesn't really matter. Come on son. Let's just take a stroll. He urged his horse into the forest away further from their house. Kaos paused for a moment the rode up next to him.

"What do you want to talk about," Kaos asked him with concern.

"You, Kaos," he said.

"What about me?" Kaos told him.

"How are you doing?" he asked his son causally.

"As well as I can," Kaos said.

"You've grown up quite a bit," he said and looked at the trees.

"Oh, not really," Kaos said.

"Don't be little yourself, you are a great archer." His father said and then rubbed his head, "You've beaten me several times. And your skill helps a lot with hunting. I'm going to miss you when you go."

"I've been gone before." Kaos said.

"Well, that's true," he laughed a little "I was meaning to ask you, what did you and Cunti talk about?" Jonathan asked.

"The old elf and I met during the service and he pulled me over." Kaos laughed, "We talked a little and then he wished me good luck."

"That was all?" he asked with wonder.

"Well..." Kaos paused, "He felt compelled, or at least he said it this way, to tell me something. I have actually known him for some time now – the elvish. I have been learning it in bits and pieces ever since we came back from the trip north."

"What? That was over five years ago!" he exclaimed.

"The elvish certainly came in handy," Kaos smiled, "But what he told me." Kaos paused and looked ahead into the darkness, "I must say is rather disheartening." He paused, "I had suspecting something for a few years now, but was hoping that it wouldn't be him who told me." Kaos dropped his head.

"Kaos," he paused.

"Who is she?" he asked. Jonathan was quiet "One thing I know is that you *are* my father, dad. Which makes things even worse." Kaos sighed, "I could have dealt not knowing both my parents personally, but not knowing only one is rather upsetting. So who is she father?" he asked, "Cunti said it would be a shock, so let's get it over with." Jonathan was quiet.

"I can't remember," he said.

"Hell you can remember," Kaos cursed, "You just don't want to tell me!"

"I can't remember her," he stated.

"I'm sure that the mother of your delinquent son, isn't worth remembering. I love you too father!" He yelled and panted.

"She is worth remembering!" his father yelled out dramatically over the malignant remarks of his son. Kaos had hushed for only a moment, when he saw his father's frustration, but his boiling nerves didn't meet Kaos' punishment.

"Clearly, you don't want to be mature about this," Kaos stated with grief, "I'm an adult, you can start treating me like one."

"Kaos!" he yelled after his son who was walking away.

"Goodbye," Kaos exasperated, "And don't come out here ever again!"

"Please be careful son, a war is brewing and I don't want you to get involved." He whispered to himself. Those were the last few words Kaos heard before he trotted up the hill and across the field to the dirt road. Kaos couldn't really tell what he was feeling. All he knew was that he didn't feel like talking about it anymore. The dirt road was cooler than the forest and down the road a ways Cella and Kaos crossed over a creek, which fogged and smoke rose like clouds. Beyond the clouds was a town: a usual hot spot for an assortment of things. There were stores, inns, and many things to do. Yet, there were bad parts about the town. Ebony's soldiers tended to pass through the place handing out summons, to go join their ever-faulting army. Kaos hadn't been in town in weeks, not even to go to the temple to pray to the Gods which was required at least twice a week. Cella neighed a bit as they passed the first building on the outskirts of the town. They headed into the heart of town where Kaos could meet up with Charad. Charad was the town's innkeeper's son, and a rather sneaky and funny one at that. Clearly the Kaos and Charad had hit it off, not just because their fathers were exceedingly close friends themselves, but that both boys resented their father's for the fact and took the opportunity to be flighty and sharp to their faces whenever possible. Kaos still on Cella walked further into town passing more homes. The houses were all of the same sandstone color, all were two floored, besides the first few. They usually held families that weren't considered of high caliber. They were active and joist amongst their own kind, but they held a thread of deep enmity against all aliens. There were no showers, maybe a few baths, but defiantly not the type of place many would find suitable. The town was not a "pretty" place, and most of the beauty was concentrated in a center portion around the Inn, government buildings, and library – the few places the government dared to treat. As he progressed further into to the scenery opened up a bit, there were trees now and again and a small park lay on his left. Inside were benches and well-trimmed gardens sprouts of flowers and bushes were appearing in the recently jostled up dirt. To his right was the Opun Inn. Cella stopped and Kaos stared at it. The building stood between two well-painted stores, but it stuck out never the less. It was a dark green with white accent trim and shutters. The second floor hung over a building-wide-porch with rocking chairs and benches. In the middle of the building square-in-the-middle, was a yellow sign that read in orange script-like letters: Opun Inn. In front of the porch was a long horse rack or a poll that horses could be tied to. Although there were many horses tied up Kaos hopped off Cella with ease and hitched her to the poll where there was room. He walked up to the inn's front door and pushed on it. The solid wooden door didn't creek, slam, or crack for that matter.

"God, now what do I do for five hours!" Kaos sluggishly went over and sat on a bench. Cella coughed a bit and rested her head on the bar and closed her eyes. "Not a bad idea, especially after this morning."

"Kaos?" A boy's voice was heard on top of Kaos as he lay on the bench, "Kaos, is that you?" Kaos opened his eyes reluctantly and found a pimply face, craning blondish hair and bright green eyes.

"Charad, come back in a few more minutes," Kaos mumbled and rolling over on his side.

"That wouldn't be too wise," He smiled and noticed Kaos had started to slowly shut his eyes," Kaos!" He grit his teeth, "Kaos get your lazy ass up! The solders will be walking out that door any minute. Just come on." Kaos grabbed one of Kaos's arms and lifted him into a seated position. Kaos's senses were still numb, he dazed at his friend not really wanting to return to reality. Cella coughed and the two boys both jumped. The front door slowly opened.

"Hurry just come on," Charad grabbed Kaos and pulled him down the porch and around the corner. He stopped and peered around the corner and watched a man step out of the door. The man wore a thick layer of armor, brown and black scales, it looked like. An ebony cloth covered the crest of his forehead and wrapped around until it protruded the back of his head with two long red tails. His hair was a golden color and his eyes a bright blue. Kaos's mouth dropped when he stared at the man's ears; they were pointed.

"You are holding-" Kaos started to exclaim as Charad's hand flew over his mouth and he ducked his head around the corner out of sight. The man's eyes on the porch immediately flew towards the two boys' hiding place. His eyes narrowed and he stepped towards them, stopped, and turned away towards the inn, having been distracted.

"General, here are your bags," Charad's father had appeared in the inn's front doorway and was holding out a few small parcels.

"I hope you kept them safe," the general ordered, snatching the bag from the man's hand and pouring its contents out in his hand. There were tiny gems of assortments in color, size, and shape. The man sighed with relief, "Good, all is well, thank you sir." The man flipped around and turned to stare at Cella with his mouth a little open. "Before you leave, could you tell me whose horse this is?" The man eyed Cella. Charad's dad clearly deducting that it was Kaos' horse, immediately responded:

"Oh, I allow several people to use my posts to tie up their horses," he said smiling, "They're usually people visiting friends and family, so I never really know who's is who's."

"Well thank you," the man waved and Charad's father closed the door. A few minutes later more soldiers came out of the inn, each mounted a horse. They soon trotted away and down the road and made a right out of sight.

"Good, god, you could have gotten us both summons!" Charad flipped around and stared at Kaos, who still was relativity dossal from his wake.

"Well, I didn't, so just calm down," Kaos yawned and stretched.

"Actually, boys, he might have," a voice came from behind them. Kaos was immediately awoke and stuck a stiff pose. Charad sat frozen stiff, and eyes wide. Kaos slowly turned around; Charad was lucky enough to have already met the man's eyes. "Now whose horse and bow are outside, I'm positive they belong one of you."

"Sorry, general, it's neither of ours," Charad said somewhat shaking. He smiled convincingly and shrugged.

"I know you, you're the servant-boy in the inn, which makes you the owner of that horse," the man's sword pointed at Kaos who remained stunned. "You're not who I was expecting," he exclaimed, "Up boy, state your name," Kaos didn't really budge, Charad kicked him, and narrowed his eyes.

"Get up!" he insisted. Kaos slowly got up with caution. His mind was turning; gears that had sprung shut now slowly inched around. "I can't just stand here and let them tie me around, but what else can I do?" Kaos bit his lip. It had been weeks since he had thought about the confrontation, about the war and what to do. His arrival home, while uncomfortable, had eased his mind out of thinking about these things. Now he needed some. The General was getting restive.

"State your name boy," the general eyed him with interest. Kaos shifted his right leg ready to spring.

"Should I run? Run from an elf? How much good would it do me? My guess is that I knew the streets far better than they did, if I did a lot of turning maybe I'd lose them?"

"State your name boy, that is an order," the general's sword was cold on Kaos's neck. But he flipped soon enough onto Charad, "What's his name?"

"Ka-" that's when Kaos decided to spring. He quickly ran down the porch and swung on Cella's reigns to sit in the saddle. The general didn't make any sudden moves to stop him and smiled as his prediction was right and Kaos took the horse.

"Hey, boss," the voice of a solider came from behind him in a writhed sordid tone, "By any chance can we go get him?"

"Sure." He laughed with a smile.

Kaos ran along the street like running for his life. He cantered Cella in the early morning hours. The streets were just filling in. He passed the cities center point when he heard voice from behind him.

"I love the fools who think they can out run us," a solider laughed. Kaos took out his bow and strung an arrow. Kaos held his breath and launched his attack. It looked pitiful as a single arrow flew towards a horde of men-at-arms. "Wops, heads up," the man Kaos aimed for ducked and the others behind did as well. "Aw," he said sarcastically, "that one almost pierced my back men." Kaos stared back at them while Cella continued, he had missed, and more or less they had dodged. The streets behind the hoard of soldiers quickly lit and windows opened in fright and interest of the large thundering hooves from the horses outside.

"Hold still Cella," Kaos put a hand on her forehead and closed his eyes. Suddenly Cella and Kaos began to haze until two individual Kaos's riding Cella appeared. The two split and went down opposite aisles and the General suddenly reared back his horse with shock.

"Sir?" The general stood frozen. The soldiers' looked at him for aid.

"Split up, follow the one on the right, I'll take the left," he stated, "and stick together, he seems to have some shadow magic training." The general took off after the left and the others took the left. The general caught up as they dased down the alley.

"Boy! You allied with Dartawg? We're going to get you!" he yelled. Kaos panted and made a sharp turn. He threw a magic ball at Kaos, which hit him off Cella. Cella stopped and stood still. Kaos slowly rose and Daragon got up with his eyebrows low. Kaos wiped his lip. "Now you *will* state you name."

"I won't tell you anything," Kaos sniggered. Daragon crossed his arms.

"You're too young," he stated, "I can't summon you to the army, but if you know shadow magic than you are a Dartawg and I will arrest you!" he walked up to Kaos and grabbed his wrist. They he put his hands on top of Kaos and light appeared above them. Kaos looked him dead in the eyes. When the restraints finished, suddenly they grew white. The general looked down in shock and slowly the entire production turned white an shattered. "Who taught you that? Humans are not supposed to use manna!"

"Humans need shadow magic to protect themselves from you." Kaos stated, "It doesn't use manna!" Kaos stood still frustrated and pissed off at him.

"You're not going to fight me?" he asked.

"Fight you?" Kaos lowered his eyebrow, "I'm not out to kill anyone!" he stated. "You're the one who's out to kill me!"

"What is your name?" he asked suddenly. Kaos shifted his weight.

"I'm not fucking tell you," he stated, "You think I'm going to just hand myself over for summons?"

"Tell me your name, I won't summon you into the army?"

"Your cronies stop chasing me?" Kaos asked. The general didn't understand for a moment until he remembered how his soldiers followed the clone that Kaos had produced earlier.

"Yes, when I speak with them I will tell them," he stated with dignity. Kaos raised an eyebrow. He looked the General up and down expecting him to take further action, but he remained still.

"Why are you so interested in my name? Don't you want to kill me?" Kaos spoke roughly, still untrusting the man.

"You're not with Dartawg, I'm interested because you don't seem like the average farm boy," the man commented with a smile. Kaos grew rather suspicious at that.

"Too bad for you," Kaos turned his cheek. In an instant the general grabbed his head in a head lock. Kaos yelped.

"What the fuck?" Kaos exclaimed and held the man's wrists, which were firmly placed around his neck and head.

"You will tell me you name!" he extorted at Kaos with reprehension. The soldiers came running down the alley towards the two of them. Kaos twisted his body trying to escape the lock, when Daragon cursed and threw him against the wall. He placed his forearm flatly on Kaos' chest and pressed inwards

"Speak!" Daragon cried. Kaos remained silent. Grinding his teeth, Daragon put a hand to Kaos' to his neck roughly and muttered elvish.

"Now what is your full name," he asked. Kaos didn't look at him but suddenly felt a large lump in his throat as his jaw began to open. He fought it for a little, but eventually:

"Kaos Bernedict," he blurted out. His eyes were in shock, somehow the General was making me speak against his will. Daragon smiled in his success.

"There we go," he smiled in spite, "Now Kaos, who is your father?" he asked.

"Jonathan Bernedict," Kaos stated unwillingly. The general looked slightly pale afterwards.

"And you're mother?" he shot soon afterward.

"I don't know," Kaos stated.

"What is your mother's name!" he asked frustrated again coming closer to Kaos and pushing harder.

"I don't know," Kaos stated unwillingly and pushing back upon the wall to get away from him. The general looked at him closely at his hair then his eyes and along the contours of his face.

"Who are you grandparents?" he queried.

"They're all dead," Kaos stated. Daragon looked frustrated.

"What are you getting at, General?" one of the men asked. "We need to kill him, now! He's in league with Dartawg!" The general didn't respond to his men but stared at Kaos with frustration.

"General Daragon?" the leading man insisted.

"We can't kill him," Daragon informed, "He's not with Dartawg and he's too young. Now, where do you live?" he ordered.

"Patella," Kaos stated unwillingly again.

"Sir?" the solider asked.

"He is not with Dartwag, we can't kill him," he stated again with even more frustration. His eyes were glaring and a growl nearly came from his throat. The soldiers stepped back slightly at his voice, "Where in Patella do you live?" he asked more specifically.

"Are you planning to bring him home?" one asked weakly.

"Please be quiet!" he roared at the solider, who fell back in line.

"Northwestern fields by the Geregon Forest," Kaos spat he was shaking now, and he couldn't help it.

"Lastly, where did you get your horse?" Daragon asked.

"A gift as a child," Kaos rambled.

"*When* did you get that horse," he stated again, more specifically.

"Since birth," Kaos stated.

"Now, get up on your horse and take me to your home," he stated. He let go of Kaos, who grabbed his neck and panted.

Kaos lead them towards the house. The group traveled behind him, and the General directly besides him. An archer drew an arrow at his back as they went. Kaos couldn't breathe and stood stiff on his back. It was early in the afternoon by the time Kaos and the group of Ebony soldiers reached his house. Kaos knew that Jonathan was out in the fields, so that would leave Sharle in the house and around to bear witness to the trouble he had gotten himself into.

"Get down and get your father out here!" Daragon ordered. Kaos thought that if he wasn't home it wouldn't be a big deal. He was actually glad because his father didn't know about his sojourns to Dartawg or the fact that he could do magic. It was the perfect excuse to not have to speak about any of the subjects. Kaos went up to his own door slowly and knocked at an average rate.

"Mother!" he shouted. Daragon raised his eyes. "Mother, could you come out here!"

"You don't have a mother," Daragon reiterated, "I want your father, Jonathan!"

"Mother!" Daragon grabbed Kaos from behind at his collar.

"You will call for your father or I'll-" at the moment the door pulled in and Sharle was standing there. She immediately saw the General and Kaos snatched by the collar. She looked at the both of them with a smug and crossed her arms.

"Kaos? Explain this," she stated.

"Who are you?" the General asked before Kaos could speak.

"Well, I'm his mother, Sharle." She said smug and nodded her head as she said so to confirm her solid stature.

"Kaos doesn't know his mother," the General stated. He look at Kaos then back at the woman in the doorway.

"I am his mother," she stated, "I was the one who raised him." At that the general stopped her from continuing.

"You raised him?" he reiterated with some question.

"Ever since he was little babe," she stated. Kaos rose an eyebrow in confusion as to why the General was having issues dealing with this.

"Then are you married to Jonathan?" he asked finally.

"Yes? Why is this important?" she hesitated, "Kaos is seventeen, he's still too young for recruitment and I didn't think he expressed any interest in the army." She stated firmly and looked at Daragon.

"I need to speak with your husband," he stated rather calmly and rationally, although he still held Kaos' shirt.

"Well he's not home now," she stated. The General wasn't going to stand for Kaos' apparent excuse,

"Surrow," he indicated to the large man behind him waiting in the driveway, "Take the boy, make sure not to use any manna." He stated. He grabbed Kaos' arm and roughly threw him into the grasp of the man.

"Hey!" Kaos yelled.

"Kaos!" Sharle yelled. "What is this?" she sternly looked at the General.

"Your husband is under arrest for eloping with an elf," he confessed, "And I am here to take him into custody."

"What?" She asked with a higher-pitched voice, "You kidding me? There are no elves in these parts." She moved her arms to her hips. The general immediately went past her and entered the house. He ravaged through the first floor and went stomping up the stairs and into those rooms.

"You can't do this!" she stated walking after him and yelled up the stairs, "This is a private home!" Daragon came swiftly down the stairs and stopped before her. They were just in front of the front door.

"This is the home of a promiscuous man," he stated, "A Human who went too far up stream, and you're his wife." He stated, "I don't even see how you can live with him knowing this." He stated, "and mother a child that wasn't even yours!" She was quiet. He left and Kaos pulled at the arms of the man.

"Leave my father alone, he didn't have anything to do with my decisions!" Kaos yelled. "I'm the one who went to Dartwag." The general didn't listen and walked into the fields. Jonathan was already coming towards them.

"What is all this?" he stated, "Put my son down this instant!" he yelled at the solider.

"Jonathan Bernedict!" the General stated. Jonathan looked at him, "You are under arrest for engaging informal misconduct with a noble," he stated outwardly.

"Arrested?" Jonathan questioned himself.

"You mingled and flirted with a high standing member of the royal family – a crime which will not go unpunished. And-"

"Daragon, this is stupid! That was eighteen years ago, can't you leave us in peace!" Jonathan pleaded outright, "I've left her, gotten married, settled down and had a family." He indicated to the farm.

"Leave in peace, your son for gods' sake!" he cried, "He doesn't belong in this family! He doesn't even know!" Jonathan blushed and Daragon was pointing directly at Kaos. Kaos looked at both of them in shock that Daragon hadn't come to just tell them he had gone to Dartawg.

"You are going to pay for you crime, and your son is being repossessed by us," he stated. Kaos jumped. "He should have been entrusted to us in the first place." He stated. "Sounds so damn like Charles I can't believe it, yet you let him wander around with Dartawg!" he growled. Kaos looked at his father, he hadn't told him. Jonathan froze.

"He didn't know!" Kaos cried out. "Let him go!"

"Kaos, this is beyond you," Daragon stated, and turned to Jonathan "Everyone took great offense that you thought you had the right to come in and imprint Marina like that."

"I'm sorry, we were young, in love," he stated.

"There is no crime in love! But that," he suddenly pointed to Kaos dead in the face, "That is unforgivable! Elves and humans are *not* supposed to have children!" Kaos blushed.

"Don't talk to him like that!" Jonathan charged.

"I'm not punishing Kaos! Kaos never had a choice in the arrangement!" he growled, "It's your fault!" he paused to collect his breath. "And don't tell me that he's the son of that woman you married, cause he's too much like Marina for me to even consider! Now give me your hands." Jonathan paused, he had nothing more to argue with. He looked at Kaos slowly then stuck out his hands.

"Jonathan!" Sharle cried and attempted to run towards her, but one of the guards eyed her.

"Mother! Dad?" Tako came running from the forest on the opposite side of the group and looked at the scene. He saw Kaos in the arm of the guard with his eyes wide.

"It's okay Yatako," Jonathan yelled. Tako looked at him and then General, and began to step back.

"You have another son?" the general asked with distaste. Jonathan was bound by the magic cuffs so Daragon walked up to Yatako, who took another step back in horror.

"Tako get out of here!" Kaos yelled. Tako turned around and began to run. He got a few feet when Daragon lifted him off the ground with magic and snatched his arm. Daragon went down on a knee and inspected Tako's face.

"You're a little younger." Daragon concluded.

"Get off of Tako, you hear me!" Kaos yelled furious.

"For your half-brother you love him, don't you?" Daragon stated and looked closely at Yatako and dragged a finger across his cheekbone, "You're not elvin, not in the least." He stated and stood up gracefully as a dancer and turned around. Tako's knees locked and he fell on the ground. A solider had grabbed Jonathan and Kaos was powerless in the arms of the man.

"What do you want with me?" Kaos growled, "What has my father done to you?" His father was roughly taken into a similar pose as Kaos.

"You're father tricked Empress Marina," Daragon stated clearly, "And they had *you*. So it's not just something he did to me, but all elves by tainting our only pure family."

fortress life

The sun was hot as the group paraded through the dessert; Kaos's shoulders had reddened before the General said anything more to him.

"Here we are Kaos," he said with a wring on his tongue smiling in Kaos' suffering. Kaos picked up his head in weariness glaring at the man for several reasons. He just laughed and continued, "Meseldom Fortress, your new home for a few months." The hungry and thirsty pack walked up to the metal and imperial-looking gates of at least a hundred feet in height; a span of more than fifty across. They were practically the size of Kaos' house. He tilted his chin up to find a decorated door header. A crest lay there, shaped like a shield with two items crossing in the center of it. The first on the right was a wooden staff, with green leaves dotting the top. The second was a sword, wide and sharp, gleaming with glory. Engraved on the crest were the words: 'EBONY' on top, then below on the bottom of the crest: 'Meseldom: the fortress of Theives.' There was a booming clang, and then the two doors parted a small bit towards them. The crack was just large enough for one horse to pass at a time. The soldiers nearest to the front went first, when the line came to Kaos the General went in behind him and a solider in front. Kaos back stood straight a stiff as he entered the fortress with a diligent attitude and a good strong defense of his mind, behind the doors was a large cavity. Wooden boxes and barrels lined the walls, men sat on top of them smoking and drinking in laughter. Kaos stared at the one who spoke first, before he said a word.

"New kid?" he said laughing a bit.

"Yes, his name is Kaos," the general smiled and the pack continued on down the cavern. It reminded Kaos of a ship or the hull of a ship anyhow. The air was cooler now that it escaped the sun's rays. The door was closed when he peeked around his shoulder and soldiers scattered around Cella in a hurry.

"You can all leave him now," the general commanded his soldiers. They were eager to leave and they trotted past Kaos and Cella as though the only thing that kept them from running was the general's words, "I'll take care of him." He stared at Kaos who closed his eyes and drooped his head. The men on the boxes all watched him as though they had nothing better to do. Kaos' neck burnt with pain as he moved it.

"Why didn't you cut the rope?" the general asked Kaos. Kaos remained in sleeping mode, and responded:

"What do you mean?" the silence grew and Kaos finally opened his eyes.

"There's been a pocket-knife in your hand ever since you pretended to fall off that horse." Kaos snorted and felt the warm handle in his left hand. Cella in response backed up a little.

"So," Kaos cut the rope on his rope and showed him the knife, "Why did you let me keep it?"

"I am queer one, and so are you," the general laughed, "Which is why I would drag you all the way here."

"How did you know I wouldn't cut the rope and escape?" Kaos asked.

"I'm an elf, I see more than what meets the eye, and I knew you wouldn't cut it." The elf laughed, "I'll just say that you were looking for a good excuse to run away from something." The man was wise beyond his years and he glared in entrapment into Kaos' eyes. Kaos met them and snarled, but man simply laughed. "Come along, there is much to be done, young Kaos." Kaos followed the man, though sour about his intrusive remarks. The two walked down the cavernous hallway and made a turn right in front of a door. The general put his hand upon the door and whispered:

"Τηεσε ωαλλσ βοω δοων βεφορε τηειρ Εμπρεσσ," his eyes closed and he stated with ill remark. Cella and Kaos trotted up to the door.

"These walls bow down before their Empress" Kaos said staring at the massive doors.

"You know elvish?"

"You could say so," Kaos smiled at the man.

"You are full of surprises," the elf said to Kaos. Kaos did not say anything back but smiled in his glory. The doors slowly cranked open and the light shown through. It cracked slowly and it opened up a whole world. Underneath the rock was an enormous city. The light shown from a star at the highest peek, glittering down light onto the village below. Kaos stared at it like nothing he had ever seen before. It was amazing, like someone had trapped the sun and inhabited a planet in solitude.

"It is the Star of Thieves, it is about the only thing that stabilizes this city, and without it this place would be dead baron." The general looked at Kaos's eyes then turned up to the star. It burned with flames as purple and yellow as flame on a stove. The general shifted position and urged his horse down the dirt road into the town.

"Why do you call it the Star of Theives?" Kaos asked.

"So, interested are you?"

"Yes, very," Kaos eyed the man and got comfortable.

"I'll tell you the story then. It is called the Star of Theives because a man and his wife, named Carta and Mortan followed Aira, the Goddess of the night, to her temple in the sky. There they laid eyes on the star dotted among the others in her temple. Being so entranced by its beauty, during the night, while Aria was out, flying around on flaming dragons delivering messages to the Gods and Goddesses, Carta and Mortan stole the Star out of the sky. Carta and Mortain used a spell to hold the fiery ball, and hid it under a mountain, hoping that Aria would not find it there and punish them for their wrong doing. Yet, Aria the Goddess of night was not so easily deceived. She invited them back to her temple, it hopes of enticing them to steal another star. Because she is the Goddess of the night, she has the ability to see the true intentions of anyone she wishes, thus was something important when wandering in the dark. Her plan worked and Carta and Mortan stole another star, the Star of Reprehension. Yet when the two tried to pick up the star once more, they found that they could not put it down once they reached the mountain. For eternity, their hands remained touching that star. The

Goddess, Aria laughed in their pain as their hands burned and their bodies slowly withered away, yet a magician sent by Sterious, the God of Metel and Presious stones, who had heard of the goddess's torture, came by the star and helped the two with their troubles. He used magic to cool down the stone and turn in into a cold limestone ball. The only problem with this is that their hands still remained cemented to the rock, now covered in ice because of the rock's cool temperature. Although, the present of death no longer presented itself, even Sterious felt that it was a punishment that they should deserve, they wanted the star so bad, now they had it in their hands for eternity." Daragon paused and smiled, "The tale goes on to tell about the ever growing relationship between Aria and Sterious, which turned sour. Aria who had a higher and more powerful dominion ordered that Sterious' ball of limestone become hers in payment of his meddling. He agreed and the limestone ball was sent into the sky along with the stars."

"Yet, if you have the Star of Theives, then what relationship does it have with the Star of Reprehension?"

"The Star of Representation, is the moon, dear boy. It glows in the east of this village, on the outskirts high above in Aria's domain."

"What was the point of Aria getting them to steal another star, she could have just cursed them or done away with the light of the star they had already stolen?"

"Well, because of Aria's sour relationship with Sterious, the Star of Theives was held captive here in this mountain, in Sterious' domains. Yet, because of the star's origins Aria still has some control over it. It burns warmth and light during the outsider's night when Aria lights the stars and is dead during the outsider's day when she turns them out, hence our night." Cella and Kaos followed.

"Now, boy enough storytelling, where would you like to stay? An Inn? Or a House?"

"Inn," Kaos said without thought.

"Why such a quick decision?" the general asked him.

"Personal preference," Kaos closed his eyes, "You did ask me after all."

"They are solider inns, you know?"

"I can deal with that," Kaos smirked.

"Fine, but I warn you most newbies stay at homes first, before they come into the inns," the general said.

"Thank you…" Kaos stopped and looked the general in the eyes, "Could you tell me your name?"

"Yes, I'm General Daragon," Daragon smiled and continued.

"Thank you General Daragon, but I don't really consider myself a newbie to these kinds of things."

"If you wish," he said laughing. The city had wide streets and tall buildings, there was grass and trees as they passed through a civilian place. The two approached an inn in the middle of town. It was much like the Opun Inn, yet dark blue. Kaos got down off Cella and tied her to the post outside. She nayed in protest, but Kaos patted her on the head and followed the General into the Inn. When inside Kaos strut down behind the General and watched. The General walked into a room full of soldiers, Kaos walked by and they all immediately looked up from what they were doing. They passed though, and didn't stay long. They entered another hallway and down in front of a door Daragon stopped.

"This will be your room," he said.

"22a," Kaos whispered to himself trying to remember the number.

"Evenings you have off, mornings, starting tomorrow at 5:00 am: training for battle until 9:00 pm. Go with your roommate. Oh, he seems to be out right now, but when he comes back you'll meet him." Daragon opened the door to an empty room. It contained two beds that were parallel against to walls. "Of course if you had stayed with a family for the first few nights, then the number would have been pushed back to 7:00 am, but hey,"

"Trust me, I do morning hours," Kaos laughed remembering his wacky schedule.

"Really?" he said. "Well anyways, most of the soldiers are out in that hallway we passed, but you're welcome to go anywhere you'd like around the village, but first…" He reached back to his pocket and took out a red thin piece of cloth. He walked over to Kaos and taking the two ends tied it around Kaos' forehead.

"What's it for?" Kaos tightened the tie in the back.

"It's to show that you are my pupil."

"Should I be honored?" Kaos said unimpressed by the thing.

"Yes, very few are direct pupils of their general," he said with some shock to Kaos' rudeness. Kaos did not plan to take any looked of apology, "Kaos if you think that by being ill mannered is going to get you sent out of this camp, then do think again. In the heat of battle those with sharper wits and ravenous tempers, fair the best, and right now you illustrate both of these things." Daragon said with strict order. Kaos ground his teeth and crossed his arms in habit of doing it whenever he felt like sheading something apart. Kaos bared it for his own reasons and sighed. He had to stay here for a little, and gather information, so that he would do.

"I will see you tomorrow then," Kaos said at last.

"In deed you shall," Daragon said with a stern but teacher-like voice. He walked by Kaos with a sharp look on his face but smiled when he got into the hallway.

Kaos shifted position then shifted position again,

"What to do?" Kaos said to himself. The room was small and ill lit a tiny bedside table sat in between the beds, one yellow-light sat there. Gleaming the dark shinny stain of the wood.

The general walked down the hallway and back into the room of soldiers.

"Hey, General,' one of them laughed, "Want to play a round with us?" he asked.

"Poker?"

"No we're playing black-jack tonight," another said.

"Can I speak with Hiarge, for a minute?" A third man at the table smirked as he shuffled the cards.

"Lutenit Hiarge?" one of them jabbed him in the stomach.

"Yeah, yeah, I know." He put down the cards a walked over to General Daragon.

"Yes, general?" he said with a smirk on his face.

"I wanted to tell you that you've got a roommate today. The boy's name is Kaos."

"Did you finally get a new apprentice?"

"Ah, you figured me out, yes," he laughed.

"So I'm guessing that the boy must have some talent for you to take him as your student right away."

"Yes, but I'll say that he has too much going on in that little head of his."

"Clever?"

"Much so, and slippery." He said with worry, "He nearly took the rear of the scouting militia taken into town days ago."

"Why would you ever engage a mere boy in battle?"

"He made the first move, he ran,"

"Ran?"

"Why did you pick a student who didn't even have the courage to face you?"

"I never said I wanted such a student as that. Who wants a pupil who's going to rush into a battle he can't win?"

"Ah, you're so strange, and so is your pupil. It makes sense for one coward to learn from another."

"Cowardice? No. It's strategy. No one wants certain elements of battle against him, especially when faced with already daunting odds."

"You are so strange, that's all I can say."

"But its my strangeness that has gotten me so high up on this latter." Daragon laughed.

Kaos entered into the hallway and backed his first steps and pasted the general and lutenat. He slipped out the door of the Inn and into the early evening. The air was cooler than before as he looked up at the Star of Thevies, its vigor was diminishing. He walked along the almost deserted streets in solitude. This would be the second time he would be sent into a training camp. The ways and traditions were still there, the early morning training and the late evenings off. His body had been used to it by now that he barely ran on three hours of sleep. His eyes fell on a building to his left. 'The Thieves' Library.' Kaos stared at it more than quickly walked up to the door and pushed it open. It was light inside but no person lay inside.

"Hello?" Kaos walked into the front room. Bookshelves started about 6 feet in front of him. "Hello? Is anyone here?"

"Oh?" a small wrinkled face of a short man peered around the corner in surprise. "My, my, a young visitor." He smiled and waddled up to Kaos and stared up at him. "What can I do for you young man?"

"Do you have any books on the Star of Theives?"

"Many, what are you looking for?"

"How it was brought here?"

"Oh, there are many books here for you to look at, follow me." The man hobbled slowly but Kaos followed tirelessly. They walked back all the way down till the entrance door looked like a spec on the horizon. It seemed that it took half-an-hour to reach it but Kaos followed in silence. "Here we are." The man said turning the corner and staring at the book shelves. "All of this side is about the Star of Theives," he smiled and looked at Kaos. Who went up the shelves and started reading the spines: "Morton's version of Carta and Morton by Williams Randough," he continued, "The Children's version of Carta and Morton" "Theives and Reprehension," none really appealed to him. Yet suddenly his eyes fell on a book and his hand grabbed the spine. The librarian suddenly grabbed it as well.

"It must have gotten mixed up with the English ones," he sighed and pulled it off the shelf.

"No, no let me see it." The man not really understanding handed the book over to Kaos. Kaos eagerly flipped to the first page and started reading out loud for he could not bring his nerves to do otherwise: "The Star of Theives originated in Aria's temple in the secluded hill tops of Sargoran, because of its size it is presumed to be over 3 million years old. Currently residing in the town of Theives the star is approximately 12 miles from the ground…" it went on and on with words and numbers. Kaos flipped through the pages wildly.

"Boy, you know elvish?" he said with surprise.

"Yes, I do,"

"You should have said something, the elvish selection in this library is one of the best in the Empire. You can find more specifics in the elfish section."

"By any chance is there a book in this library that would tell me the spell in which Carta and Morton used to hold the Star of Thevies?"

"Looking for a spell?" the man's expression turned from one extreme to another, and Kaos took a step back.

"I mean, if you know of it," Kaos started.

"You spell caster! Get out! Get out! You are not welcomed to scope the walls of this library looking for spells to conquer up and destroy your enemies!" The short man shoed Kaos back into the hallway.

"I'm not a spell caster," Kaos pleaded as he stumbled over a table in the middle of the hallway backing up from the man's hands.

"Sure, you know elfish, you just like reading," he said softly, "you, boy, are flaunting around a band of apprenticeship!" he yelled at Kaos, "A band belonging to the sorcerer Daragon if I recall my colors of the cloth." He bellowed at Kaos. "So, know this well young sorcerer, you are not welcome in my library!" The man got behind Kaos and pushed him out the door Kaos stumbled on the wet ground. "Get out! And stay out!" Kaos rose off the ground which covered in snow. His breath puffed as he yelled,

"What about this one!" Kaos stuck the elvish book out towards the door, but it was already closed and the libraries lights; already off. Kaos panted and stared at the book in his right hand. He rose quickly, his pants wet, they were ice cold. He stomped back to the Inn in agitation. Cella nudged him, but he brushed her off. He quickly walked down to the hallway and passed through only to be stopped by Daragon.

"Hey, where have you been?" he looked at Kaos soaked. Kaos didn't answer him but went by. Daragon's hand fell on his shoulder. "Why are you so upset?"

"You could have at least told me," Kaos whispered under his breath.

"Told you about what?"

"Told me that you were a sorcerer" Daragon's eyes immediately fell on Kaos as he said the word. He didn't' know what to say. Kaos pulled away from his grip and walked to his room. The man was left his hand still fit as though still over Kaos' shoulder. Kaos opened the door with a quick motion and closed it. He hopped on the bed that looked inhabited and cross-legged leaned against the back of the wall. He reached to the tie on the back of his head and pulled it, the band fell off and he caught it in his hands. 'you flaunt around a band of apprenticeship...' the man's voice followed though Kaos' head like an unwilling fly. He held it in his hands and picked up the book. It's black leather cover wet from being dropped in the snow, the edge of its pages yellowed and wavy. He took the red cloth and wiped the book in sorrow. All he could do was sit there and let life unfold. He couldn't do anything but wait, wait for something awful to happen. He opened the book and stared at the pages. Tiny font started and his eyes peeled there but his mind went elsewhere. What was the point of him reading and studying, Dartawg sent him on a mission to discover the spell behind the stealing of the Star of Theives. Why would they need to know such a thing? Why couldn't they just do it themselves? Kaos continued to read, the elvish characters fell on his mind unwillingly, he memorized all he could but it would take a week until he could recite the whole thing from memory. The problem with most of the elvish texts were that they never came with indices or table of contents for that matter; so when looking for specific things it was necessary to read almost every word. The elvish texts didn't have what we call sentences, nor did they have things like paragraphs. Most were complete thoughts, separated by large spaces. He slipped to the next pages, 'nothing' there was nothing there on the page for him to use. He passed the words quickly like a machine search engine, looking for a hidden file. Suddenly the door to his room swung open. He stopped reading and slammed the book shut.

"Daragon?" he said with some shock.

"Kaos, what are you doing?" he said with concern.

"Nothing much,"

"Nothing much made you jump when I came in the room? What do you have in your hand?"

"A book,"

"A book?" he asked, "May I see it?" Kaos didn't want to seem like he was hiding anything to Daragon so he handed the book over to him. "Reading more about the Star of Theives I see," he paused, "Did the librarian kick you out because of the band I gave you?" Kaos had to think how to respond, the librarian had kicked him out when he had asked to find the spell of Carta and Morton. Yet, he had been let in with the band on. "I'm sorry Kaos, I should have warned you about that old man. For some reason he doesn't take well to sorcerers or anyone capable of doing magic."

"Why?"

"Something happened a long time ago, a magician showed up in his library and searched through his books looking for a spell. The man found it, and used the spell to cause chaos among the town. Since then, the librarian has blamed himself for the entire thing. Saying that if had not allowed the man to find the spell nothing would have happened."

"It's no wonder…" Kaos said to himself yet then quickly continued the thought in his head, 'it's no wonder when I said I was looking for a spell he automatically kicked me out.'

"It's no wonder what?"

"Oh, it's nothing," Kaos said to him, not wanting to say it.

"Fine then, enjoy your book," he handed the book back to Kaos, "Just remember, training 5:00 sharp."

"Yes," Kaos nodded accepting the book with pleasure, hoping that he didn't have any suspicious thoughts. Daragon left a closed the door after that and Kaos went back to surveying the book. Yet, for a second time he was interrupted, but no longer fearing the lie to be told he continued reading although someone entered the room.

"Already studying?" His voice was friendly. His eyes peeled on Kaos with intrigue.

"No, not studying," Kaos said quietly skimming the pages.

"For fun?"

"Sort of something to pass the time," Kaos said as he reached the last page and closed the book disappointed.

"Heard, you got kicked out of the library in town?"

"Yeah,"

"Hey, you managed to get away with one book, pretty good." He said with pleasure.

"It's not the book I wanted." Kaos said with aggravation.

"Sorry," he said.

"Oh, it's not your fault." Kaos barked.

"Well, if you aren't busy, but bored…do you want to come play black jack with us?" He stared at him and Kaos' mouth turned to a smile.

"Duces wild?"

"If you'd like," he laughed. Kaos got up and plopped the book on his bed as though it was worthless. The man turned and waited for Kaos to come up to his side. "I'm Lutenant Hiarge, and you are?"

"Kaos Bernedict," Kaos said.

"Pleasure to meet you, I'll be your roommate for a time."

"You too," Kaos said and continued to follow next to him in the hall. They quickly reached the hall full of soldiers for them to talk anymore.

"Hey, boys," Hiarge yelled walking up to a table of five men holding hands of cards, "You want to add a new player?"

"Player?" the man who held the deck mumbled and his eyes fell past Hiarge to Kaos. "Who is he?" At this Hiarge walked around the table and whispered into his ear:

"He's Daragon's new apprentice, his name is Kaos,"

"Well, now, Kaos do you know how to play black jack?"

"Yes,"

"Then come sit down boy," A seat was removed from under the table and Kaos went over and sat in it. Hiarge sat down in a seat next to the dealer. "Now let me explain the rules…no cheating, which means, no peering at people's hands or sharing cards beneath the table, that includes with the use of spells." His eyes fell on Kaos, "We are going to be playing duces wild. Kaos and Hiarge you got to use your own money, this is real, not just some kids' game." Kaos cringed, he didn't know if he had much in his pocket, all he had was probably a few dollars. Kaos took out everything in his pockets it turned out to be only four dollars and fifty cents.

"That sucks," the man next to Kaos remarked looking at the few bills.

"If I would have been warned I was being drafted then I would have brought more." Kaos told the guy.

"Oh, I understand," he said with a smile, "Just a few days ago I was drafted, you'll just have to get lucky to earn up more."

"Now, it's a buck on every ante, if you want to add any you can without a limit. If no one can match you then you automatically win the bet." He shuffled the cards and handed them around. Kaos reached for the five cards and picked them up: a Queen, two, three, five, and six. They all were of different suites. So far he didn't have a bad hand. If he used the two to his advantage he might be lucky enough to get a straight.

"Jonah," the dealer said to his left, "Cards?"

"Actually no," Joanh said with a certain smile.

"I'm sure he's just bluffin, he always does," Hiarge commented.

"Cards?"

"Three,"

"Never to lucky are you Shain," Joanh commented this time and the boy named Shain smiled after looking at his cards,

"Who knows?"

"Kaos cards?"

"One," he said and handed his queen across the table.

"Someone's Lucky," he said. Kaos didn't' respond but held his poker face.

"Cards?" he went around the table until he got to himself. "I'm taking two," he removed two from his hand and then replaced them. "Jonah start the betting,"

"Raise one," he placed in a dollar more.

"Call," Shain said and matched him.

"Call," Kaos said and put in one dollar.

"Call,"

"Call,"

"Call,"

"Call,"

"Call,"

"Match and raise one," the overall feel after the dealer had said that was perturbed yet it went around the table again and everyone betted and called. Jonah was the first to put down his cars.

"Straight," Kaos cringed.

"Two pair,"

"Straight," Kaos put down his hand.

"I only had three threes,"

"I had a pair,"

"Flush," the dealer said ad Kaos' heart dropped, Jonah's face dropped too. He had a flush of hearts. "Not bad Kaos, but not good enough," Kaos was rather upset, he just lost three dollars and his supply was dwindling. The night went on and Kaos did manage to win one, but it only managed to keep him alive. Hiarge and he walked down the hallway.

"You did well," Kaos said to Hiarge.

"Oh, you did pretty well too,"

"At least I didn't lose any more than fifty cents."

"Hey, at least you did that." Kaos stuck the rest in his pocket and they walked to the room. The door opened and Daragon was sitting on Kaos' bed.

"Hello," Kaos said shocked.

"Kaos, I need to talk to you," Daragon said in a very serious tone, "Hiarge, could you please step out for a moment."

"Sure," Hiarge said quietly and closed the door behind Kaos.

"Kaos," Daragon bellowed but in a teach tone.

"Yes Daragon,"

"From now on you will refer to me as master," Kaos though reluctant.

"Yes," Kaos started, "master." Daragon tossed Kaos the red band from before.

"You must wear this all the time," he said, "It's part of my apprentice, it lets the other's know who you are." He paused, "I went and I talked with the librarian, although he did not especially talk to me, but he's rather upset that you stole his book."

"I didn't steal the book," Kaos said, "the man pushed me out the door before I could give it back to him."

"He also told me that you were looking for a spell, the spell of Morton, may I ask why?"

"I was interested," Kaos lied.

"But you didn't know that I was a sorcerer till after you were kicked out of the library. And what would a mortal do with such information as that?"

"I was simply interested," Kaos tried to be innocent. Daragon paused and crossed his arms.

"Fine then, but you will return that book tomorrow,"

"I will?" Kaos said agitated.

"Yes, you were the one who stole it so you must go and return it to him," Daragon rose, "And you better give him your sincerest apologies for stealing." Daragon opened the door. Kaos mouth opened.

"But-" Kaos said with rage, yet was easily shut up by Daragon's presence.

"No buts will come from my student, now go to bed! We'll have hard training in the morning. I'll guarantee that you'll regret staying up this late," he said a closed the door on an agitated Kaos. He walked away with a grim expression on his face.

"Reprehending is the hardest part of the job," Hiarge said from the other side of the hall.

"You can go back in now, he shouldn't be too fired up," Daragon said quietly as he passed Hiarge.

"You're right, he probably won't be the type to fire up so easily," Hiarge commented, "But be prepared for him to let loose his rage one of these days, it happens to each new solider that ever steps here."

"I'm usually well prepared." Daragon smiled finally and walk down the hallway.

"You said that he was special," Hiarge commented, "Special in a dangerous way, so don't get yourself caught off guard. The last thing we need is a raged sorcerer."

Kaos' mind raged, he couldn't put his finger on what he hated so much about Daragon. He just didn't know what it was just that his insides tightened up and his instincts just told him to run like hell whenever he was near. Kaos hopped on the cot, faced the wall, and smacked it with his knuckles. He only received the pain back and he sighed. Hiarge finally walked into the room. He didn't say anything but got changed into his pj's and hopped under the covers, when Kaos intervened;

"What is training like?"

"For you? I don't know," he said honestly, "If you come with the rest of the group it starts out with some archery then we spar with each other with swords."

"Why wouldn't I go with you?"

"Daragon might want to do some personal training with you since you're his pupil."

"What kind?"

"Magic, what I can presume.'

"Oh," Kaos said.

"Oh? You're his apprentice, don't you want to learn magic?"

"Sure," Kaos said, "what else is there to do?"

"Nothing much," Hiarge revealed but in some pickle about Kaos' response. "Why didn't you stay in a home, like all the other newbies do?"

"Oh, it's all the attention, I don't really like it. Then the family starts edging into your personal life when you hardly know them. They give you those looks of pity when you reveal your family life. They just aren't worth the trouble. "

"Do you miss *your* family?" Kaos didn't say anything but hunched his back and thought.

"I guess from what I feel like now, I feels as though I never really had quite a family. They just seem like long lived friends. The kind that you trust and care for but if you're around them too long you get agitated."

"I'm sorry,"

"Sorry about what?"

"That you don't have a good relationship with your parents."

"Well, you'd be quite right about that. My father, oh how he's relentless."

"What's your mom like?" Kaos didn't want to say it. His mom, or is mother. "She's great," he said.

Kaos closed his eyes, Hiarge was already out cold and snoring. (Hiarge was human, Daragon was an elf.) He dozed off in weariness yet woke up with shock as a buzzer went off. Kaos flipped out of bed. Hiarge was already changed into his scales.

"Good, that time it actually woke you up." He laughed, "I've hit the snoozer twice just to see if you'd wake up to the buzzer."

"Gees," Kaos smacked the thing off and put his feet on the side of the bed.

"5:18," Hiarge smiled, "Bright and early. Now hurry up and get dressed in some new clothes, breakfast is going to be served soon." He pulled the scales over his head and set them aside. Kaos changed quickly, but on the red band Daragon gave him, and went outside into the hallway. Soldiers scurried by him and Kaos turned back to Hiarge.

"Are we going to go or not? I'm getting nervous with all these soldiers running by."

"Done," Hiarge came out dressed in red under armor. He had an earring in his left ear now, in the shape of a golden upside down pyramid.

"Then, lead the way," Kaos backed off and followed Hiarge. The two walked down the hallway, Hiarge took rather quick steps for being in armor and quickly reached the end. They swung open and door and walked into a room with two large tables. Daragon sat at the head of one of the tables and was signaling to Kaos to come.

"Better go," Hiarge whispered to Kaos and pointed out Daragon. Kaos left Hiarge and made his way down to the back of the room where Daragon sat.

"Sit next to me Kaos," he said dignified. "Sleep well?"

"Pretty well,"

"A little late getting up I see,"

"Hiarge said I didn't really wake up when the alarm went off." Kaos laughed and so did Daragon.

"Well, eat well and save strength, you're going to go with the group today and they're no push overs, especially with swords."

"Oh," Kaos said a little nervous. He had heard lots of rumors about the sword holding soldiers, and never really faced up against one of them before. He had fought with archers and other spies, never really on any battle field of any sort.

"Have you ever held a sword?"

"No," Kaos laughed, "I can't say that I have. I've used daggers, but no swords."

"Oh, well then, it should be quite interesting." The tables filled and women came out with dishes. The food was quite good. Yet, at the end of the meal, Daragon made an abrupt movement and stood up. The soldiers stopped eating and turned to face him.

"Enjoy, and rest, my soldiers. Out fights will halt for a time. Rest and Rejuvenate for I have brought you new comrades." He stopped and the faces of soldiers lit up. "Aragon Squire, Saragari Fishing, Micheal Mortain, Ceri Ungom, and Kaos Bernedict. May you all rise to identify yourselves?" Daragon said this and then stared down at Kaos. Kaos didn't want to get up and be embarrassed. A few other the other's stood up, their faces flush with embarrassment. Kaos got a strange look from Daragon than quickly stood up himself, giving the group a grim expression, but still they all cheered.

"Yeah, newbies!" one solider yelled. Kaos couldn't help but crack a little. He sat down with a smile and took a sip of the water in front of his plate.

As the crowd left, a hand grabbed Kaos' shoulder and pulled him back. A whisper in his ear was from Hiarge's mouth:

"Come on, we have to go get your horse a bow," Kaos nodded and was dragged against the crowd back into the room. Daragon was sitting there as usual keeping his eye on Kaos.

"Cella's in the small barn just outside," Daragon said to Kaos. Hirage bowed and dragged Kaos though the doors. They jogged over to the stable.

"Now which of these babes is yours?" he said and wandered down the corridor. Kaos quickly stepped in front of him and went over to the noisy mare who stood rather lazily in the corner stall.

"This is her," Kaos indicated. Hirage came over and with some envy commented;

"She's yours?" he asked, "She looks like one of the royal colts up by the place," he exclaimed.

"Gees, thanks," Kaos said.

"Here, let's get her out."

customs | of
| bondage

Kaos looked around wildly never before had he seen such happiness. Kaos stopped his horse, and had to comment.

"How come this place is so peaceful, the rest of your empire is crawling with horrors?" he said rather spiteful.

"I'll agree with you on one thing, this place is perfect, but there is a reason for this," Daragon stopped, "There will always an abundance of soldiers in this place. Veterans, generals, and newbies like yourself take up most of the people in this city, with their families and children's children take up most of the rest. Then there is the elves, they live here too. As you can imagine, this place is the pinnacle of perfection. Kaos stared at the beauty. His heart sunk as he thought.

"Life isn't ever meant to be perfect," he whispered. Daragon's next words flew through his ears empty. The place reminded him of everything he didn't have, peace, a home, a safe place, ease, serenity, and the un-dynamic life that he used to wonder through with boredom. Jealousy and interest filled his mind, but the fact lingered in his mind as a hunting memory reminded him. His family was gone, he was going into war, and here he was looking upon a world without either.

"Kaos?" his voice was concerned. His eyes were wide looking at the place. Something flew below Kaos' skin like a small flaw on a gorgeous diamond that made the entire thing sour and worthless. The scratch on a glass vase that made the entire thing look dirty and fake. The crack in the floor that made everyone trip. The small thing that ties everything back to reality, the imperfect world of reality. Good came with Bad, and bad came with good. The small warm breeze fuzzed into the panting breath and the pounding of joy children playing in the field hummed faster with the beast of one heart. It wasn't natural for him to be here, he didn't belong in this perfect place. "Kaos, are you alright?" he said concerned.

"I can name one thing wrong with this place," Kaos lifted up his bow and the general's ear, "Me. I'm the last person that you'd want to bring to this perfect place, and you played right into my trap." Daragon hung onto his horse's reigns in silence.

"Are you really going to kill me?" Daragon said, "Would you stain your father's name with murder?" Kaos pulled the wire back farther.

"My father, ha, he's betrayed so I've betrayed. They build up on one another till adding even one more doesn't make much of a difference,"

"Oh, that's right, you denied all traditions and common law. You waste away your days playing around with people's feelings. Yet, you do this for one purpose, to put what your father did to you on to other. You don't even know who you are anymore," Daragon said with spite, "You don't even know your own mother." Kaos threatened and put the arrow tip to the mans head, "Your father lied, how you like to stain his name, how much you'd like to just die and kill all the strange customs of this Empire. But, you can't. Your brother lives on you and you alone, the guilt and spilt soul of yours is searching for a way out of it all. Act in revenge and destroy his name, your brother's future, your mother's respect, and your innocence. She'll just laugh." Daragon narrowed his eyes. They drooped and the pupils shrank in relaxation, "You wanted reasons…didn't you?" His bloody limp fell down on his horse's neck. Kaos' bow wire shook with fright. People on the street stopped and stared at the first horrid act in their perfect world. Kaos sat straight as the elf bled from the head on the dirt street. As horrid as it was, he felt a rush, the rush that his heart had finally reacted, and he didn't ignore its call. He had actually made a difference in the war between Ebony and Dartawg. His mission, he had completed and with a bonus. A sharp pain filled his head, with a pulsing and high pierce sound filled his ear and he fell of Cella, smiling.

"Wake Up!" Kaos cheek stung as he was slapped across the face. He stat on the floor with his wrists crossed somewhere above his head. A man's unwashed face was in his. A brown beard brushed Kaos's chin. Kaos woke up with disappointment. "Spy, what is the next move?" Kaos closed his eyes and hung his head. Tears welled up in his eyes.

"I want to die," he whispered.

"Well, you're not gonna," Kaos got kicked in the stomach. It stung as Kaos coughed. "Think about that for a while, I'll be back." Kaos's stomach growled and his throat was dry. He opened his eyes to a cell covered in mold. The floor blood stained and full with heartache etched in tallies on the wall. Kaos heaved once with sadness and he dropped his body to hang on his wrists. His mind was wild, and filled with horrid thoughts. He shouldn't have got such a rush after killing Daragon, he was turning into a monster. "I was horrid," looking back on his actions, "I slaughtered, with a smile and slime. Killed an elf, something that represented high society." He was pitiful trapped in this cell now, with all but one completed mission in his entire lifetime. Death lay before him the cell itself pungent of lies and betrayals. Childhood memories of innocence and pleasure were nothing but dust in the wind. He was now a prisoner of war, he was to die the next day, or until his life and information became worthless. Then they'd take him out and behead him or let his body wither away in a cell till hunger and thirst drank all life from within him. He sobbed and finally fell asleep again. He woke once more to be faced with the same solider.

"Now that the drug is in your system I suggest you start talking. Do you come from Drawtag, boy?"

"You know, I was thinking about it," Kaos smirked. He got snacked across the face.

"Rebels like you should be taught a lesson," Kaos dazed and his eyeballs spun.

"North Passage, East forty-three degrees, head on towards sunset till you reach a "u"-shaped valley," Kaos said quietly.

"So you are a spy!" the solider grabbed Kaos by the neck.

"Father would banish me, if he knew where I went when I ran away." Kaos smiled, high. *(Scene cuts off.)*

"Empress Aysil, here is the boy that murdered General Daragon," the solider from before pointed to Kaos asleep in the cell.

"He's just a child, a human boy couldn't take General Daragon so easily," the courageous green eyes stared at Kaos in disgust.

"He is a spy sent from Dartawg," the solider said.

"How do you know he isn't lying?" the empress said, "I have not heard of any government entrusting a spy-job with a mere boy," she paused in shock, "What were his duties?"

"Refuses to say, specifically. Yet, his job was to gather information, not commit any murder."

"So, you mean he was presented with a perfect situation to take a bonus of murder?"

"It appears so," the soldier said.

"Where did the murder take place?"

"In the center of town,"

"He must have been within close range, which is an action very rarely taken by spies."

"Undercover?"

"Probably, if anything."

"Yet what role did he take?"

"The Gatekeeper said he was taken in as a recruit."

"That would figure, right age, he fits the profile well. Too bad that he had already been taken by the other side. He seems quite talented." She held the bars and stared at him closer. "Does this boy have white hairs?" the solider peered at Kaos.

"A see a few miss. Why?"

"The first heir to the throne, has not appeared yet."

"Not appeared, Marina your sister has a son, he is the one. This damn rebel of a boy just has horrible genetics and anyways, the boy is probably nothing more than a farm boy. No heir to the thrown would be a farm boy!"

"I will come back in a month," she said with defiance, "I like to ease all suspicions, do what you wish with him, but don't kill him. Drug his meals." She said and she walked down.

"There are suspicions, Empress?"

"They are none of your business, I suggest he be alive by the next moon, or I'll have your head."

"Assassin, open your eyes," the solider said staring at Kaos. Kaos woke and did so, "Although I think otherwise the Empress pardoned your death sentence for now. Daragon was one of my friends, know that you will not go unpunished for your deed." He took a knife out and the fetters around Kaos's wrist were loosened and Kaos brought his blue hands down to his knees. "You must live for a month, so that the Empress is satisfied, eat," he carried a tray and placed it before Kaos. He left and Kaos ate the food. His heart pounded in his head and he felt like he had been drunk. He fell asleep.

The day's routine changed, Kaos woke with a shock as he pulled sharply against the fetters. His wrists were sore with all the hanging they had to endure. His body had felt the fuzziness come off and on so many times he was surprised that it woke him this time. His survival, didn't matter he was living in a drugged world, where the same object took several shapes. Hair hung in eyes, white, black-tipped hair hung in his eyes. It ran along each strand as though the white slowly crawled up through his roots. The drug in his system probably was doing it, he figured not having any other explanation for it. He had spent the first few weeks crying nightly, but it did him nothing and used up too much energy. His wrists hung over his head all day, and were only released for meals. Where his hands would finally warm and stop shivering. His back was stiff, his legs tingling in sleep as though he still sat in a dream.

"Can you hear me?" a voice rang in his ears, he didn't see anyone in the cell.

"I can't see you," Kaos said calmly.

"What is your name poor boy?" the voice was familiar. He dropped his head.

"I can't remember it," Kaos said lying as he was taught to do.

"Are you sure?" the woman's voice was sweet which made him conjure up fact.

"Kaos," Kaos's voice was softer as he said his name, "Kaos is my name."

"Kaos," she paused, "Where is your family?"

"Mine?"

"Yes," she said assuredly.

"I don't know where they are?" Kaos' voice was distant and soft, as though he told the first thing that came to his mind.

"Where is your home?"

"What home?"

"The place where your mother and father raised you?"

"What such place. I don't have a mother."

"What about your father?"

"Father…" he said with aggravation.

"Did something happen?"

"Father has disowned me."

"Why?"

"I murdered, I denied marriage, and I have done it all against him. I have ruined my father's reputation. "

"How does your father know?"

"He…" Kaos' eyes opened to true reality and there was a woman's soft hand on his forehead.

"Madame, get back," the solider, "He's woken up,"

"It's okay," she said she removed her hand slowly. Her voice was soft and motherly Kaos stared into her face. She had dark hair and brown eyes and pointed ears.

"Dame Marina, may I remind you that this boy is a murderer," the solider said, "A spy sent by Dartawg."

"Marina?" another woman said in the door of the cell, the Empress, "Is this the boy?" she said with her arms crossed.

"Yes, your highness, this is the boy I was talking about," she said with tears.

"Release this boy's fetter's immediately!" the woman said.

"Why, your highness! He has committed murder of an officer, the highest offence in this Empire. He is a spy if we let him go he will only return to Dartawg and lead them to this place."

"Be careful what you say! You have tortured the King's first heir!"

"This rat?" the solider exclaimed. The empress put her hand in front of the soldier's face, a wind veered from her hand and the solider instantly disappeared. Kaos was drunk or high, he stared at the attack and closed his eyes. He felt the tension on his wrists snap and he fell onto a woman's lap. He didn't struggle, he didn't have the strength.

"My poor boy, I'm sorry to hear your troubles," the woman said close to Kaos' ear.

Kaos woke up in a soft bed. Several pillows lay under his head and he was covered in a red puff and blankets. He stared up at a red transparent canopy above him. The bead was round and set in a room fit for royalty. The hangover made his stomach spin, what it was a hangover from he couldn't really recall. The torture had turned to servitude, where did the lies end and where did the truth begin? He peeled his body up. His arms ached with every movement, but they hadn't been cut. They felt odd though, they hung at his sides which seemed invalid because they were supposed to hang over his head. He rubbed his forehead in light of the situation.

"Oh, God," he rubbed the back of his neck and tried to crack it. The bed sat it a complete white marble room. A high ceiling sprung up a good thirty feet. Widows lay in front of him, lining the wall with greenery. A balcony door lay meshed between the full length windows with decorated white trim and panes. Now that he looked at the bed with fully awaken eyes it had much more than just red. Oranges, Teals, and lime green pillows, all having some small design tiled on them, littered the bed in some ornate fashion. He slipped out of bed and wondered over to the windows to see if he had any idea where he was. The glass was crystal clear, and revealed a landscape much unrecognizable. A large grassy field weeping willows and dogwoods filled the outskirts. The small balcony was edged by to pink dogwoods that stood tall. In the distance was another building, a castle like structure, with a spiral tower and stone walls. His hand fell upon the balcony door handle, and he pushed down. The knob didn't budge, the door was locked. He turned around in disappointment and fell upon a wall of mirrors. The entire back wall was a mirrors with pillars separating the ever clean reflections. His eyes fell upon his own reflection, which had changed dramatically. His hair now grown nearly double its length was nearly all snow white. It was all besides a inch of black that lingered of his old reflection on its tips. His skin had darkened to a summer's tan, seeing as the sunburn he had received on his trip had healed. His body had leaned further and he had no more of the little baby fat he carried around, he sighed. "I wonder how long it has been."

"A long fifteen years since I last saw you," a voice echoed in the room. A woman appeared though the glass. Her small frail form floated through the mirror into the room.

"So, then," Kaos stared at her, when she sat down on a old-fashioned three-person-couch. Depressed eyes laid down on her as he said, "you are my mother?"

"Yes, Kaos," she said with dignity.

"Then who is my father?" Kaos tested her.

"Johnathan Bernedict," she said with a smile, "I remember him like it was just yesterday."

"So you two were in love?" her eyes sprang on him as he said this.

"Yes, very much so," she said. "But your father is a human and I am an elf, the marriage would have never been allowed under Ebony law." There was a long silence and Kaos looked into the mirror and slowly closed his eyes.

"Being half-elf explains a few things," Kaos grudgingly said, "Cunti said that my mother would bring a great surprise to me, but I never thought it to be as much as this."

"Did Cunti tell you who I am?"

"Cunti doesn't have to tell me who you are," Kaos stated rather overwhelmed and stared at her. He turned his shoulders to be parallel to her and got down on his knees.

"Please don't-" she shot with grief before he fully bowed down. Her voice returned to normal, "You are my son, please come sit down." She said motherly and beckoned him to come sit next to her. He slowly got up and plopped down next to her. "Kaos look at me," Kaos' eyes met her with the order.

"Oh, Kaos," she held out her arms and fell on Kaos's shoulders, "I can't apologize for what I've done, I've made your life living hell, and I can't do anything to fix my mistakes. At least let me, Kay, help you though your life right now. Let me help you through this change you'll be going through. Your body is changing, your mind will be too. I've seen it happen to my brother so I can help and guide you through it too. How I can't bear to see those who don't deserve to look down on you. Please give me a second chance to be your mother," She sobbed and hugged him tighter around the shoulders. He moved his shoulders and hugged her too. His mind was wild but his body lay serine, he whispered to her:

"It is granted." A moment of relief and revelation burst from Kaos' mouth. She let his shoulders go at ease and she kissed him on the cheek,

"Thank you Kay," she smiled warmly and Kaos said.

"Well now, that was a little dramatic," he laughed, wiped tears from his eyes, and got up from the couch.

"Yeah, I guess you're right," she wiped her tears with her silk sleeve and smiled at him. She got up from the coach with a jump. "Want to give that hair of yours a trim so you don't look so awkward for tonight's dinner?" Kaos stared back at the mirror at his strange black tips.

"What kind of dinner is it?" he said.

"Formal,"

"Then it probably would be a good idea," he said with a laugh.

Marina snipped above Kao's left ear and said,

"Done," she stared at the mirror, "That looks much better." Kaos stared at his reflection without the black. He felt like he was looking at a stranger.

"Mom?" he said, his mind gave a weird tinge.

"Yes?" she said turning back to him.

"Why is my hair white?" he stared at her. She paused in thought and stood in wonder for a few minutes, "Well, I mean, my hair was black and I didn't think that I was that old for my hair to being going white and-" she put a finger over Kaos's lips.

"*Shhh*," she shunned him, "Remember I told you that you would be going through a transformation?" he nodded a little. "You hair going white, is the first step to it."

"What's the next-?" he asked but her finger remained on his lips.

"We will deal with that when we get there," she shunned him again with a smile. She turned around and put the scissors away. With an easy swipe the old sheet around Kaos's neck was flung to the side and Kaos got up. "The next thing you should do is go down the hall and take a bath," she said and then dug further into the bag that she brought a pulled out some clothes, "I brought you some new clothes to change into, I hope they're your size." Kaos accepted them softly in his forearms arms. "Come on, Kay follow me." She had walked to the other side of the room and led him to a door and out into a hallway. The hallway, unlike the room, was wooden and welcoming to Kaos. It had a red Persian runner on the floor cover and chestnut colored wood with fine, but distinctive grains. The walls were tan and lit with yellow light from lamps. The bottom of his bare feet warmed against the fuzzy surface. They stopped at a chestnut door and Marina opened it and beckoned him inside with a bow. It was a bathroom was a large tub under a huge window. The walls and tile were white and a huge mirror covered the wall on the left, where there were also sinks. There were closets on the other side with long silver hardware carefully hand made. Marina walked over to the tub and started the water for him. "There's conditioner and shampoo over there," she pointed to the far end of the tub. Kaos peered his eyes a followed her every move. They stood there for a while and the water rose with bubbles. She turned the water off and pivoted around. "Condition the ends of your hair well, I will see you later today, I have to go do a few things." She walked out of the door and left him inside. He got into the bath, for there was little else he could do. The window though next to the bath was fogged, thank god, but it still made him uneasy. Suddenly the door opened. Kaos' eyes popped a rotund woman stepped in.

"Sorry son, I'll only be a minute," she went to the closest and took out what looked to be like bed linins. She stepped back and looked at him. His face flushed. "Oh, don't worry dear I can't see anything, that's why we use bubble baths. You must be Kaos, her eyes drew to his ears. Well now, she walked up to him and stared at him in the face. Her eyes floated into his. "I see that your hair has gone white," she said with ease in her voice, "Your ears are still round though, when did you arrive here?"

"I don't know?"

"Have you had anything to eat?" he gave her a look that said, 'No, nothing.' "Well then, save your appetite for dinner, I'll be sure to cook some of our elfin-specialties for you."

"Speaking of dinner," he said.

"Ah, the boy speaks," she smiled.

"Marina says that dinner is rather formal, may I ask why?" he said trying to seem polite.

"Yes, dear Prince Kaos," she said, "Dame Marina is having family over. There will be gleam in all their eyes when they finally see the 'ροψαλ δεμον' in their midst." She smiled at him.

"Will there be humans there?"

"No, your highness-"

"Please don't call me that, I was raised a farm boy, there is nothing for you to look up at."

"You are the first heir to the thrown of Ebony, there is much to look up at, but I shall call you by your first name if you would like?"

"Yes, please,"

"If you're worried that you'll be shunned away from during dinner, you are greatly mistaken. Since you are half-elf, those ears of yours will sharpen to a point soon enough after you've eaten and slept in these walls," She said with a dignified tone, "Even now you don't look much different than a elf, all but you ears." She smiled a turned from him.

"Oh," he said with worry and he felt the tip of his left ear.

"Meeting you reminds me, my mistress would like you to come down to her room after your bath. It's something like educate classes for tonight's dinner."

"Well," he smiled, "It's a pleaser meeting you, but could you please leave now?" Kaos said blushing.

"The pleaser is all mine, dear young Kaos." She bowed slightly and hurried out of the room. He sighed, finally a little more relaxed. "Your highness," he shivered, "Just doesn't sound right at all."

He slipped into the clothing his mother had given him. The hardest part was probably getting them on. It was a rather big top, which wrapped around like a kimono and was tied at the waste. It had short sleeves that jutted out from his shoulders. The pants were slightly formfitting but still rather large. He had also been given what looked to be like two pairs of shin guards and a pair of worn leather boots. He managed to get one set of shin guards on, but the other pair perplexed him. They were like long half-pipes that a strip of leather, not really, in the middle. He eyed them and there was a knock on the door.

"Kaos, are you alright?" he recognized the muffled voice as the voice belonging to the woman who had come in before. He walked to the door and opened it,

"Actually," he said with laughter, "I don't seem to understand what to do with this," he held up the strange pipe-like thing and she laughed.

"How old are you boy?"

"17," he said shutting his eyes with stupidity.

"Arg, let me enlighten you." She took the thing from Kaos's hand. "Now stick out your left arm." He obediently stuck out his arm. The woman folded the pipe down like an alligator's mouth, and slipped it up Kaos's arm. His finger fell through the tip. In-between his thumb and fore-finger lay the small piece of leather. She tied a few strings around to the top of it. Kaos noticed the small bends before, which now lay around his wrist and hand. He turned his palm up parallel to his face and stretched his fingers around.

"Not a bad little thing," he laughed. She smiled and he put on the other one. The woman turned to leave and he grabbed her shoulder. She flipped around in surprise.

"Sorry, but could you tell me where my mother's room is?"

"You are impossible," she smiled. He smiled too. "Just follow me." They walked down a series of corridors and stopped in front of a red door, with red trim. "Good Luck, I must get back to work," she scurried away and Kaos was left to stare at the door. "What should I do now?" he thought to himself staring at the door. The elves were full of strange customs. How would he know what to do in this kind of situation? He figured there was only one thing to do knock.

The room inside was a peach with white bottom trim. A fireplace lay on the far side of the room not to far from where Marina and an elfish man with green hair sat on old-fashioned couches. A glass coffee table sat in-between them. The two were in deep conversation when Kaos' knock reached inside. Marina turned to the man.

"I'm sorry, I'll be right back." She wore another outfit, this one much more prestigious than the last. A long silky-cream colored dress with beaded stands of more silky tied the dress to her thin body; the trail of the dress a foot behind her. Across her shoulders a transparent shimmery cape ran behind her fashioned with a gold engraved broach. She opened the door and to her surprise saw Kaos.

"Kaos, hello son," she said with some surprise. He looked into the room and saw the man sitting on the coach, "I'm surprised to see you so soon."

"Oh, I'm sorry, I guess I'm interrupting something," he said rather awkwardly he grabbed the tip of the door and started closing it.

"Boy!" the man on the couch exclaimed getting a good look at Kaos, "Come in, we were just finishing up anyways." Kaos look up at his mother for approval. She smiled and said, "I wouldn't want you wondering around too much." She left the door and went to sit down. Kaos slowly followed. The elf-man smiled at him as he slowly sat down on the couch. "So," he said with rather a want-a-be father deposition, "What's your name?"

"Kaos," Kaos answered. The conversation was slowing rather quickly and if the man hadn't stepped in than Kaos might have.

"Are you good at archery?" he asked.

"I guess so," Kaos said rather drily but he added in better tune; "But I mean, I have never matched up against an elf before so I really don't know good from bad." He laughed a little trying to lighten the mood a little.

"Well, I'm General Stirring," smiling, it seemed that Kaos' move worked, "We'll have to test that sometime. I, myself, have never faced against a human before, so it would be rather interesting."

"Well, it seems I'm going nowhere fast, so whenever you want we can square off. Speaking of which," he said worried now, "Mother what did happen to my horse?"

"Your horse?" she said.

"You know, the white-spotted gray horse … white mane, white tail, a diamond on her forehead."

"Did she have blue eyes?" the man said with his head in his hands.

"Yeah, how'd you know?" he asked the man.

"We picked up a stray horse about a month ago," he said laughing, "the girl was stubborn, we still haven't been able to tame her."

"Did you try a whistle?" Kaos smiled.

"Whistle?" he said shocked, Kaos smiled and shrugged, "Not many horses are taught to respond to whistles these days."

"Try it," Kaos smiled, "I can almost guarantee you she'll come."

"How bought you come down with me after I finish this talk with your mum so you can get your horse back…"

"I'm afraid, my son's a little busy this afternoon. We have to prepare for tonight's dinner."

"Educate lessons?" he laughed, "This boy seems to have fine educate." Kaos smiled a little happy that this man was accepting him.

"Maybe to you he does, but I have to tell him how to respond to my mother, grandfather, my sister…"

"Sh, Marina. As long as he can make conversation with people there he'll be fine. No one's going to jump down his throat if he makes a wrong move, not even her highness. We all were new once, we all know what it feels like to be introduced to new customs. Let the boy go get his horse and have a little fun…"

"Well, maybe I just want to talk to my son. I haven't seen him in thirteen years and I've hardly had any time to sit down and have a civil conversation with him." Kaos' eyes fell on her with care.

"General, thank you for your offer. " Kaos settled the feud, the general stared up at Kaos, "but I'm afraid that today isn't a good day, perhaps tomorrow I can take you up on that offer. In the meantime, please take good care of Cella for me she means quite a lot to me."

"Will do," he said, "It was nice meeting you Kaos," he stuck out his hand and Kaos shook it. He left the room. "If there is time after your lessons feel free to wonder down to the stables, she'll be around somewhere."

"Thank you," Kaos said as the man waved and left the room. He turned to his mother and smiled.

"You don't have to smile," she said quietly.

"Who says I'm doing it on purpose?" he asked.

"I know you probably want to go see your horse…" her voice softened.

"But I really ought to stay here and prepare." She shook her head.

"No, go with General Stirring, go have fun. We can check this out later this evening." She smiled to herself though frowning underneath, "the General is right when complimenting you, for a farm boy you know how to respect your elders. So go," she smiled.

rerouted|again

"General!" Kaos stuck his head out the door. Stirring wasn't far down the hall. After Kaos spotted him he ran up to meet him.

"She let you come?" he said with surprise.

"Yes," Kaos said smiling. His heart pounded, he would be able to see Cella, "I can't wait to see Cella again."

"Can you take up the offer of the shoot off?" Stirring, with an excited face turned to see Kaos' enthralled eyes.

"If there is a bow I could barrow, then sure," Kaos smiled, closed his eyes in laughter as he walked.

"Gees, I forgot. Then maybe we should wait till you get used to the bow then." Stirring said concerned that Kaos wouldn't be comfortable with the new bow and wouldn't know the "weight" to add to it.

"No, it won't take long, give me one practice shot and I'll be ready to go." He smiled and they walked down the hallway. They passed down a marble staircase into the front hall and headed outside. Kaos went silent as he watched his surroundings. They went at a fast pace and they turned around to the right side of the stone building and Kaos saw the large fields in front of him. Horses grazed about it and the general walked nearby to a black horse that was tied to a post and hopped up.

"Let's see if that horse is really yours?" he said cunning and whistled. They waited a few minutes. Cella was in the field, and Kaos immediately saw her head rise, yet then return to eating in her stubborn ways. "I'm s-" Kaos whistled before the man could finish his sentence. Cella was stubborn but eccentric when she wanted to be. A horse with treasure chests that were just hard to open. As soon as the lock was picked through carefully and with the right key, it would open to reveal the wondrous treasure deep within. His eyes fell on Cella in the field who looked up suddenly and started cantering towards the group. The general stared at Kaos smiling and at Cella who trotted up the hill to Kaos. Kaos patted her on the nose and rubbed her diamond.

"She is yours after all," he laughed. Cella rubbed him on the cheek affectionately and he smiled. Kaos using the fence nearby hopped up on her back. She was a welcoming familiarity to him with all these strange new things, she was what he had left to grasp on to his past. The memories and good feelings rushed past him just as the wind tossed at his body as he cantered into the field. The General kicked off his black stallion who whinnied and started up and cantering through the field "Think you can catch me?" the general teased Kaos as he rode up next to him. Narrowing his eyes he challenged Kaos. "You see that small hut up there? If you can beat me I'll tell you a secret," Kaos smiled and gave a look of sheer victory before it's even sought. "Ready, set, Go!" He shot out from besides Kaos a sprinted his horse. Kaos clicked his tongue and Cella me his pace, but didn't pass him.

"Come on Cella!" he yelled. Cella pushed forwards but still nothing. Kaos urged her on, but Cella remained the same distance away as before.

"Come, on we can do this," Kaos whispered to her. Suddenly Cella gained more traction and she caught up to the general's steed. He yelled out commands to his horse, yet slowly as they two approached the hut Cella caught a few feet on the stallion. Yet, as the brown blur of the hut went by, Kaos saw a black shadow stream in front of him. He had lost, "Good race," he said panting as he slowed Cella to a trot and then finally a walk.

"You two, for a war horse she's pretty fast," he said. Their horses stopped and soldiers ran up to the two.

"General!" on shouted.

"That was an amazing race you two had," one stepped out of the bunch and talked to Kaos, "What your name?"

"Kaos," he panted.

"General, is he a new solider?" another shouted from the crown.

"Kaos, is Marina's boy, he's challenged me to a dual." The crowd roared and Kaos smiled staring at him. He winked back at him. "Get on your horse's men, we're heading off to the archery range." The group spilt.

"Susano?" the general said quietly, "Could you bring an extra bow and arrows for Kaos. He stared up at Kaos then nodded and ran off. The group soon met and Kaos had gotten comfortable on Cella. The General started the move, to a walk. Kaos followed with the crowd. Soldiers whispered to one another.

"Look at the boy's hair," one said, "It's snow white. Do you think he's the heir?"

"The general did say that he was Marina's son."

"But Marina has a son named Argo, not Kaos." Kaos smiled in anticipation. The General smiled and spoke.

"I'll give you three practice shots boy,"

"No thanks, I'll only need one," Kaos said rather head strong.

"Little cocky, are we?" the general grin grew.

"Sorry, you just caught me in a good mood," Kaos smiled, "That's all."

"How so?"

"I want to shoot," he smiled, "I frankly, just want to shoot."

"Good boy good," he said jolly.

"Kaos," a solider stood up to him, "How old are you?"

"17," he responded.

"Ah, I see," he said, "Well my name is Lu-tenet Cerron."

"Pleasure to meet you Lu-tenet," Kaos said with an egger smirk on his face.

"When did you arrive at the castle? That horse your riding I'm presuming she's yours we've he her for a month at least."

"To tell you the truth, I don't know when I came and she is mine, so I guess I've been here for about a month."

"The boy woke up from a comma just this morning."

"You've been recovering from a comma for a month?"

"I guess," Kaos said.

"Aren't you worried?"

"Should I be?"

"I mean, you are the 'ροψαλ δεμον', are you not?"

"I've heard that before, but to tell you the truth I don't even know what the 'ροψαλ δεμον' is."

"It's what us elves call the boy to the heir of Ebony,"

"Then, from what Marina told me, I am," Kaos said, "But 'ροψαλ δεμον' is elvish, right?" 'ροψαλ ' means white, so what does ' δεμον' mean?"

"It means demon," the general said.

"So you call me the white demon." Kaos asked, "That's kind of strange."

"I don't know why, mind you, you're the first 'ροψαλ δεμον' I've ever met personally," the general added.

"That's because Strinning, used to be a solider like me, just recently he was promoted when a rebel spy killed General Daragon."

"That's interesting," Kaos shivered. And the name range more than a bell, but a blowhard: Daragon was master, he had killed him.

"Let the boy be at ease, spies murdering are unusual events. They're nearly impossible to rid of completely. People are bought out with money, promise of title and position in government. But they're usually lies. Dartawg wants to create a Republic that would send this new nation into Chaos. A republic would be poor and not meet those demands, and a republic can't grant titles of any meaning. As you can see having a group of people strong enough to create the government getting hasty that the government wasn't meeting their deals. Eventually these people would overthrow the government and create a new aristocratic government which would be far worse than the current monarchy government."

"So, you think that all the spies were out looking for money and power when challenging the government?"

"Do you think otherwise?"

"What if a spy joined the side, for the sake of getting back at the government for something they had done? I could see with the line of Ebony customs that you're bound to rally up enemies that don't feel like following those rules."

"You bring up a good point, but most of those people wouldn't have any power to give the Dartawg government because they are under those rules. No individual in the system would have power to corrupt it without supporters. And face it, most average people don't have friends in high places because of the system. If you look at the monarchy set up, it's set up to limit corruption in which a Republic is not."

"You're part of the system Kaos, in a rather high position, yet you question the government you're in line to inherit. I can see we have a lot of work to convince the 'ροψαλ δεμον' that his position is more than just a title in this monarchy." Cerron added into the conversation.

"So you think I'm oblivious."

"I just think that the farm-boy in you thinks the Empress does nothing," Cerron smirked.

"How would you know I was a farm boy?" Kaos smiled.

"The way you carry yourself," Cerron added.

"Well, enough of politics, we're here." Stirring laughed, "Kaos, the target in the bull's-eye drawn on that tree, here's a bow and two arrows." Kaos shifted Cella into a common position and drew the bow.

"Do you like your bows loose?" Kaos said as he yanked the wire back till the arrows tip barley lay on his thumb.

"I don't consider it louse." Stirring smiled. Kaos close his left eye and aimed. With a sigh let go and the arrow sprung forth. It easily grassed past the trees and landed on the center dot.

"Hey now!" Cerron exclaimed.

"The bow has got great balance though." Kaos handed it back to Stirring, "You're turn," he smiled.

"Boy, mine aren't just luck." He aimed and easily matched the bull's-eye.

"Now try the line between the yellow and blue." Kaos' was dead on, yet so was Stirrings. They did all the lines till they ran out of places to shoot.

"I think that the boy has more than just luck," Cerron added. Men nearby nodded.

"So do you think he has enough skill?"

"Yeah, boss," one spoke out, "He deserves it, especially if he didn't even use his own bow."

"Aw, you guys are so mean," Stirring.

"Γιωε ηιμ τηε Σψμβολ οφ Ωακιττα, (Give him the symbol of Wakitta.)" Cerron shouted. The group fell into shouts. Kaos sat in befuddlement. Stirring leaned over towards Kaos.

"Symbol?" Kaos interrupted.

"Want to know what that means?" Kaos just looked at him with some worry as Stirring leaned further over and cupped Kaos's ear. Kaos felt Stirring blow in his ear, which then gave a shock, from which he automatically rubbed his.

"What did you do that for?" Kaos exclaimed embarrassed. Solders around him laughed. His ear sting rang a little and he rubbed it until his fingers fell upon something. The thing was warm but far too smooth to be any skin. He sat in his earlobe, which he grabbed and then felt along; what he figured to be an earring that hung down in a thin and long up-side-down pyramid.

"It's an earring that means you're a high ranking official in the Wakitta Ebony Army."

"But I'm not in the army," Kaos stared at him worried, finally realizing that Stirring had one too.

"Then for you it means that you have been offered to be one," Stirring laughed. Kaos was a little shocked, "You don't have to give me an answer right away." The group cheered and clapped in applause. Torches were lit and the men's faces glowed with exuberance.

"Oh God, I didn't realize what time it was," Kaos interrupted looking at the sky which started to dot with stars, "I'll get back to you on that offer, I got to go." Kaos kicked Cella off and the soldiers parted for Cella cantered on through. Stirring smiled as he watched Kaos disappear down the trail they had come.

"Where is he running off to?" Cerron asked Stirring.

"Marina's having a family gathering tonight." Stirring smiled staring down the trail.

"At least we gave him something to talk about," Cerron added.

"We actually gave him more to worry about," Stirring sighed.

Kaos was crossing the field when he looked up and found Marina on the balcony staring at him. There was breeze across the valley, he finally noticed something about his mom: she looked quite young. He had heard that elves lived longer than humans, although they weren't immortal elves stay young for hundreds of years. It made him wonder what his life-span would be like. Would he lived longer than is father, but shorter than his mother? For the first time he finally saw one of the differences between him and an elf. He sighed and got off Cella, he rubbed her nose and started walking towards the stone structure. He shut the door quietly behind him and walked up the marble steps and to his mother's room. Kaos's hand hung over the door as he decided to knock or not? Yet, the door opened and his mother was behind.

"Come in," she said and turned away from him, "I'm glad that you came back in time, we have just enough time to go over everything quickly."

He walked in the room rather dazed. The earring that was in his ear was exactly like his master's. He had been yet again summoned into the Ebony Army.

"Okay then," she rose and turned away from him in thought. "Now what do you say when someone greets you,"

"How formal is this dinner again?"

"Very, think royalty." He rose and bowed in front of her.

"Pleasure to make your acquaintance," he said with ring of his tongue

"Not bad, but only do that when someone approaches." she said like a teacher, "When you greet someone at a formal gathering and they make first contact you respond simply and as fitting as you normally do as long as this is after or before the dinner. During dinner, I can guess that my sister will make a toast in your name and Argo's. There usually are only a few toasts maybe two at the most. The way we do toasts is you lightly tap your glass in fours. The person sitting next to you, across from you and diagonally. Do you understand?" Kaos sort of tuned out.

"Yeah, hopefully I'll remember it all."

"Well, then let's start over with a quick over view of dinner. You and I will greet the guests as they arrive. Don't worry, I'll do most of it, but since you are staying with me and attending the dinner you must be present. I can assume most will just ask who you are, you simply introduce yourself do your bow thing a keep quiet until you're asked something. Slowly the guests will come in, most will be chattering. Once all the guests arrive you can mingle as you please, or you can tag along with me if you wish. Eventually the servants will show them to their seats and dinner will start. I will say that the Empress will be sitting on the head seat of the table. My mother and I will be sitting next to her, then comes the heads of her Departments and their wives. You, my son, and his bride will probably be seated after that somewhere in the middle of the table, other important officials like generals will be sitting after you."

"What happens during dinner?"

"The   dinner   is   seven   courses:

_____

_____

_____

_____. You can talk, you cannot talk. All is up to you. Talking however would probably get you a few more friends among the group."

"After Dinner?"

"After Dinner, there is a mingling period and then they all leave. . We dismiss them." She said with some grace a smiled at him.

"Okay then," Kaos smiled, "I hope I'll remember it all."

"Now my mother, Dame Clara Johnamhold, I'm not sure how she will act around you. After all I never told her that I had a child before Argo until just this morning. But knowing my mother she'll be one of two extremes: harsh and judgmental, or inviting and jolly. My other son, Argo, he will be very jumpy around you, when I told him about you he got rather angry, how he will act around you I don't know, I'd try and stay clear of anything that might spark a fight, because I'm sure he would take you up on that offer. The Empress, she was the woman who came with me to find you. She is probably going to try and befriend you, seeing as she is your aunt you should respond in much the same way. Your grandfather, Dusaw Ebony, well, he's not exactly your grandfather, but he enjoys being called that. He is a very jolly man, his son's name is Drake, and he will probably be very glad to meet you. He can't have many sweats so if you see him reaching for some just try and veer him off course if Drake doesn't do anything. Am I losing you in all this?"

"Me?" Kaos sort of jumped, "No, don't worry I'll remember it all."

"Well, there's not much else to say then just be friendly and enjoy." She smiled and finally turned towards him. Her eyes immediately gleamed at the earring, "Ah, what did they do to you!" She went over and examined the earing closely.

"It is-"

"Oh, I know what it is, but why would they even think of giving you one?" she nagged.

"Stirring just blew in my ear," Kaos began, "I didn't ask for it."

"Stirring and his magic," she cursed.

"What's wrong with me having one," Kaos asked.

"It means that you're in the army, Kaos," she nagged, "And I won't be able to get that thing out because Stirring enchanted it with a seal."

"Why can't I be in the army," Kaos asked.

"Because, you'll have to go to war," she sighed, "I didn't want you going to war. As the Heir to the thrown you going onto a battlefield puts this entire country at risk. Stirring should have considered that before sticking this thing in your ear!"

"But it's noted that of high ranking soldier,"

"Which makes you even more of a bull's-eye for the rebels." She sighed, "If anything once they see your head you're going to be nailed. They will want to kill you. You're going to die on the battlefield or be assassinated if you step on a battle-field." She hugged him. "I wanted to keep you hidden from the Rebels for as long as possible, which is why I left you with your father. No one would expect the heir of the thrown a farm-boy." She grabbed her head and paced, "Now what do I do? I know, I'll send you back to your father's, Johnathan will keep you hidden."

"What about dinner?"

"No, you can't come to dinner, there's bound to be one spy among them, and now they will know that you'll be sent into an army and on the battle field, where we can't protect you." She concluded. "You should put on your old clothes, I have a cloak you can wear that should drape nicely over your head hiding your hair and that earing of yours."

"When will I be leaving?"

"Now, before any guests start arriving." She ordered, "Go to your room, your old clothes are on the bed. Come back to my room as soon as possible." Kaos didn't hinder and ran down to his room and changed. He didn't know what to think. He ran back up and Marina had another guest in the room. "Kaos meet, Yoki," the elf woman smiled and shook his hand. "She is my personal body guard, and she will escort you back to your father's house. "I also have a few weapons for you Kaos." She turned around and picked up a sheathed-sword. "This was mine, take it with you and if anyone should see who you are besides someone you know can't be a spy you must kill them."

"But, I've hardly used sword in my life." Kaos exclaimed.

"Soon, that fact will allude you," she said, "Anyways it's the best weapon that can be hid under your cloak. I know that killing not something that you could easily bring yourself to do, but you must; to save this country, and to save your own life. I also have some bows and arrows for you, yet you cannot carry them when wearing the cloak so keep them on your horse…which brings me to another point. You can't take Cella with you," his heart sunk with this, "she'll be an easy link for a spy to follow. Now put on the cloak," she handed him a brown worn cloak. He tied it around his shoulders, she kissed him on the forehead. She put on his hood.

"May you go with the God's," she whispered. Yoki turned to her,

"What will you do about dinner, you told the Empress that Kaos would be there,"

"I've personally sent her a message to remain quiet about him, I told her what happened," she said, "I sent Argo one, too. But, just go, there isn't much time." She pushed Kaos out the door. "I'll miss you Kay, but go back to your father's and hide. We'll have to catch up later" Yoki hustled out into the hall and dragged Kaos. Marina shut the door on Kaos and turned around a cried.

"You must hurry," Yoki hissed at him. Kaos was struggling with her hand.

"But-"

"No Buts, Dame Marina wants you to go, and you will go regardless of your personal opinions." She said defiantly. Kaos immediately did not like the woman much, but shut up and stopped fighting the woman's hand. They slipped down the stairs and out the front door. A carriage was rolling down the driveway. Yoki immediately pulled him down into the bushes. The carriage pulled up and stopped before the door. A elf-man hopped out and reached back into the carriage to a woman, who was ornately dressed in a yellow dress. The two had a conversation:

"Thank you, Argo," the woman said to the man.

"You're very welcome Sharon," he said politely.

"Are we going to get to meet that brother of yours today?"

"No, I'm afraid, not. He fell quite sick this afternoon."

"Oh, that's too bad," she said, "I hope he gets better, I've heard quite a bit about him from your mom and he seems quite interesting." The two walked hand and hand into the building. Yoki got up quickly and pulled Kaos. The skirted across the field and to the stables. The stable they entered was empty and dark. Kaos' eyes fell on Cella he approached her stall as Yoki went into deep action getting two bays tacked.

"I wish I could bring you with me, but I can't" a whispered and put his hand on her nose.

"Come on, Prince Kaos, get on you horse." She offered him a place to mount with her hands, but Kaos went around the other side and mounted the bay instead.

"From now on you should just call me Kaos," Kaos said to her. She got on her own horse and they walked out of the barn. They wrapped around the barn and headed into the thickness of the forest. Yoki tramped in front of him and quickened the pace as they grew further away from the castle. Kaos quickened and followed her. It was an endless scene of green for three hours until Yoki actually said something,

"We should really stop and set up camp for the night," she said worried. They stopped in a small ravine and dismounted their horses, "Kaos, set up a fire ring and hang here, I'm going to go hunt so there will be something to eat." Kaos nodded and got the stones nearby and set them in the ravine. A pleasant circle formed the hearth that a meal would soon be meandering. Yoki tramped away from the camp and searched.

She stayed out half-an-hour. There was a rustle in the bushes. Yoki drew her bow at it.

"Don't shoot oh elf!" a man exclaimed from the bush.

"Get up, identify yourself!" she ordered.

"Ruka, I'm the strongest in this forest, a Dartawg spy you could call me." She immediately shot him but he grabbed the arrow. He unsheathed a sword and she did the same.

"Forest nymph," she cursed. An arrow immediately went through Ruka's shoulder and pinned him on a tree. Four more appeared around his legs and arms.

"What kind of sorcery is this?" Ruka shot at Yoki who was in confusion.

"There is no sorcery here," Kaos' voice lingered in the trees. Buka stared off into the darkness.

"Archer, I demand you show yourself."

"You've been staring at me the whole time." Kaos met the man's eyes in the shadows.

"Name yourself,"

"Do I really need to name myself?" Kaos said with a smirk.

"Yes,"

"Do you not remember my voice, I was the young spy sent to investigate the Star of Thevies." Kaos stated.

"How do I know you're not lying?"

"Do you, or do you not recognize my voice?"

"I shall share no such thing, when I see your face I shall remember."

"May I remind you that you are pinned on a tree, and I still have arrows left?" Kaos hinted, "It would do you good to identify yourself as an acquaintance of mine so I don't have to shoot one more."

"If I must, then yes," he said, "I do recognize your voice, Kaos, you are tall, dark haired boy with brown eyes, if I remember correctly."

"If you knew what I looked like there was no need to ask." Kaos said in a rather calm and collected voice. The lie almost fell of his lips and though the nymph's ears.

"But why would you be dragging along an elf-woman? Using her to acquire some more author-?"

"Shut up," Kaos barked, "Need I remind you who's asking questions here." Kaos threatened and pulled back another arrow. What are you doing out here?"

"I was sent to learn the whereabouts of the 'ρоψαλ δεμον',"

"Have you learned anything?"

"The boy is sick in bed, Dartawg thought it to be the perfect time to go kill the boy in his sleep." He said, "Now if you know me why must threats be passed in between us, release me from this tree at once, after all I am your superior."

"Ruka, you will not complete those duties of yours," Kaos stepped towards the man his face in the shadows of the cloak - yet, Yoki took up her sword and stabbed the man in the stomach. His eyes fell in pain.

"It seems as though you've been corrupted Kaos, may you not remove your cloak so I may look upon my murderer?"

"For slime such as you, if it were not your final wish, it would not be granted, but yes I shall." Kaos flipped back his hood.

"You're…you're the 'ροψαλ δεμον'," he said shocked, "You were right under our nose, white demon…" he collapsed on the tree and Kaos put back up his hood.

"Why did you do that?"

"It's only honorable for when murder is committed to let the dying know who their killer is before they leave this realm, for rumors of haunting occur when the sprits unwary of their murderer go seeking the answer."

"Honorable or not you will not do that again!" she yelled at him. Kaos got down from his horse and retrieved his arrows, "You should have remained at camp and let me deal with him."

"You wouldn't have lasted long."

"What makes you so sure?"

"If I did not have the element of surprise on him, I might not have had the ability to bring him down either."

"So you're saying I'm week,"

"I'm saying the odds were stacked against you." Kaos said, "I know him, and he would have easily knocked away your sword. And anyways he had the element of surprise, which is something a spy is taught how to use to their advantage."

"Is it true then? You talk as though you really were a spy from Dawtag?"

"I am one," Kaos shot at her. She fell silent, "We should really go on without dinner. We need to cover as much ground as possible between Ruka and us. They're sure to have sent more of rebel soldiers.

"Fine," she said after thinking. They rode off into the night and finally escaped the trees. Yoki told Kaos he could fall sleep on horseback and she would lead them in the right direction.

Kaos was wakened by Yoki's soft voice. He now lay on the ground.

"Kaos," she whispered, "I'm going to go into town to get some provisions stay here." Kaos closed his eyes again and fell back asleep wishing that he hadn't been awoken. Yoki was around when he finally awoke.

"Did you sleep well?" he asked her.

"Me?" she said with some shock.

"Who else would I be talking to?"

"Oh, I slept fine," she said with disappointment.

"What did you get in town?"

"Some food: dried meat and canned fruit."

"So when do you think I'll get to go home?"

"In maybe a month, if we keep stopping."

"A month!" Kaos stood, "It won't be worth it."

"Why not,"

"I'll be eighteen by the time we get there and I'll be exiled." Kaos yelled at her, "I'll probably never live to see my family ever again!"

"You shouldn't be worried, if you pose as a eighteen-year-old in your home town no one would have to question your appearance."

"So, I'll see my father as an alias, will I?"

"Don't complain, at least you'll get to see him." She said with a sharp tongue annoyed with his attitude. The day's rolled by nothing happened they had stopped once a day for a meal, they hunted together now after the incident with the spy. Nearly a week had gone by since they had fled the castle, Kaos back in his cloak, looked towards the horizon and he spoke to himself.

"I wish my life was normal," he blurt out.

"Not everyone gets their wishes," she said rudely.

"Why do you hate me?" he asked her, "Every time I say something you manage to come back with a rude remark." She sighed.

"I don't hate *you* personally," she said with another sigh, "I hate what you represent."

"And what would that be?"

"You're the future of this Empire, you represent a world without war. Or this is the hope by the time you rule."

"I rule? Ha," Kaos laughed, "You must be joking; I don't care for this Emperor role my mother thinks she can place me in. Yes, it's nice to get to know the other side of my family, but to immediately put me in that position is rather irritating, it makes me wonder if she found me for the simple purpose of finding the heir, not to see if her son was still alive."

"You judge Dame Marina too high, she is only doing what is best for the empire regardless of her own feelings, you should have seen her when the Empress told her that she might have found you. That month couldn't have passed slower for her. The minute the Empress let her go, she went. She took you on a journey to the castle, where you woke up after passing out because of the drug overdose the detainment facility gave you," she laughed.

"What's so funny?" he asked.

"Oh, it's really nothing," she calmed down. Yoki looked up the road ahead of them with a smile which quickly changed to worry. Heavily armored and weaponed men was rushing towards them.

"What should we do?" He said ready to kick the bay into a sprint.

"Don't move until I say so," she said. They neared her.

"You two, in the road!" a man's voice shouted out from behind them.

"Now," Yoki yelled. Kaos stampeded his horse and the armed men and ran past them swiftly. Yoki had maneuvered her horse and was strides ahead of Kaos. The hood wouldn't stay on for long, and Kaos had to use a hand to keep it in position which slowed his horse. More men came in front of them and they both reared their horses back in hopes of switching. Kaos' teeth clenched as his neck almost met the silvery blade of a man.

"I said halt!" the man stated. Yoki seeing Kaos' neck less than an inch from the sword stopped. Men on horseback soon came to her and retrained her. The man's sword moved swiftly and removed Kaos' hood. And examined him.

"He's worth something," he said eying Kaos, "Boy unarm yourself." The man prodded. "Boy, I said unarm yourself!"

"I don't have any weapons on me," Kaos said seriously.

"You think I'm an idiot, I can smell the stain of blood all over your hands." Kaos didn't push his luck any more. He reached down, the blade still at his neck, and picked up the sword his mother had gave him and gave it to the man. "Good, bow?" Kaos reached behind him into the pocket of the horse's saddle and drew out the bows and arrows slowly and gave them to him. "Now put your hands up in the air." Kaos did as he was told.

"Soldier is the woman worth anything?"

"I would pay for her," he smiled perversely. Kaos glared at the man, 'What do you think you're sneering about?" The man's blade drew closer to his neck, "Bind their arms and ankles and load them in with the others. Kaos was edged off his horse and carried down to a board where lying on his back the tied his wrists, and ankles with rope to it. Yoki was done the same. A carriage appeared down the road and came up to the group. One at a time the men lifted the boards with Kaos and Yoki pinned on them. Kaos was placed on the bottom and Yoki's board lay in front of his nose; four more people were tied on boards next to him. The soldiers disappeared after a while and the carriage started moving.

refuted|past

Kaos glared at the board in front of him. The boy next to him stared at him then managed to say something.

"So how did they get you?" he asked. Kaos didn't really physically respond.

"The man had his sword to my neck," Kaos finally said teeth bared and voice trembling. He was so stupid to get himself caught like this, if only they had left the castle sooner, maybe they could have escaped. If he hadn't had to hold down the hood, he could have defended himself and Yoki better. His mine was still in this tavern of what if's and could haves that he could hardly wake up from his shocked-imposed daze as the boy continued talking.

"Better than me," he smiled and laughed, "I fell for the slave trader's first move, I halted and was immediately restrained. I was such a fool." He turned away for a moment and looked at Kaos again when he finally spoke with some prompt.

"The man's a slave trader?" Kaos' grim turned to worry. 'I don't want to be a slave! Hell, someone will surely recognize me as a slave!'

"Why you didn't know?" the boy said with shock, "He catches eighteen-year-olds that have just been exiled from their villages." Kaos turned away and sighed managing to think of one funny thing at the moment:

"I'm still seventeen," Kaos said disheartened hoping that the irony of the situation would better his mood/

"That sucks," he blatantly said, Kaos closed his eyes finding his plan failing, "when are you turning 18?" the boy asked again, rather inquisitive for a captive.

"In a few weeks," Kaos laughed sarcastically.

"Were you headed home to see your folks a last time?"

"Yeah," he said depressingly.

"Well, I'm sorry," he said apologetically, yet his very tone and babbled didn't make it sound worthy at all. He continued with his story as though something had made him so nervous that he could hardly stop talking. "I literally just left, I should have listened to my father had gotten married, I wouldn't have ever gotten into the mess in the first place. Did you have a bride in line, the woman you came with is it she?"

"Oh, no." Kaos said, "I didn't want to get married."

"What a coincidence! But don't worry, I know how you feel about that," he said exaggerating, "I can't think of how many times I fought with my father on the subject! He was always so persistent, it got me so mad."

"Yeah, I know," Kaos felt laughter coming on, the boy had really lighten his spirits a little.

"What's your name?"

"Kaos Bernedit, yours?"

"Micheal Shien," he said, "pleasure." He laughed and Kaos smiled, "So Kaos, where you from."

"The Patella Triangle," Kaos said.

"Whoa, what's a northerner doing all the way down here?"

"What do you mean?"

"Wow, what world do you live in, you're in Scorsa. I can't believe you were planning to make a trip all the way to Patella from here in less than a month! It'd take me nearly two to get there on horseback." He laughed.

"Well, where are you from?"

"I'm a local," he laughed. "Long journeys aren't really my thing." They were quiet for a while and the carriage continued.

"So where are they taking us?"

"Probably to a trader's market."

"What'll happen there?"

"Well, they'll give us bottom prices then auction us off to the highest bidder." Kaos eyed him with worry.

"Kaos," Kaos heard Yoki's voice muffled.

"Yoki?"

"Kaos, are you alright?"

"Yeah, I'm fine, you?"

"Yes, from what I can hear they're headed north to the Market of Squire's"

"Hey, at least it's on your way," Michael laughed.

"Shh," he shunned him.

"What are they planning to do with us when they get there?"

"I don't know, they haven't talked about that yet, but they are to arrive there a day before bidding takes place, so I can figure there really won't be too much time for us to make our escape."

"What should we do then?"

"I really don't know," she started weeping, "Oh, Marina will kill me if you get bought."

"Marina?" Michael gasped. "You mean Dame Marina?" Michael asked Yoki. Kaos and Yoki remained quiet. "Come on, tell me," he begged, "Tell me why Dame Marina would kill her if you were brought." He begged, "Come on, I'm going to be a slave and die all alone, please tell me."

"Well…"

"Kaos!" Yoki yelled.

"Hey, it's mine to tell, and I trust him!" Kaos yelled, "And anyways, I'm a captive slave, my future isn't too bright now. If I'm going to die, someone better be alive to tell my story!" He grumbled and met Michael's eyes. Michael stared at Kaos with gleam in his eyes, Kaos closed his eyes, "Well…to put it blankly I'm her son."

"That means you're the ρογαλ δεμον, ha, I knew it!" he laughed, "I wasn't going to say anything, but your hair was looking kind of white," he laughed.

"Yeah, I know." Kaos said rather flustered.

"Wow," Micheal said in aw staring at Kaos.

"What's all that racket back there, shut up!" Kaos and Michael heard a man's voice and they immediately shut up. The carriage stopped and the slaves in the back were quiet, a man hopped down on the ground and walked up to a stand on the side of the road. From what Kaos could see the slave-trader was asking a lot of questions Michael leaned over and whispered to Kaos:

"So you're part elf?"

"That's none of your business," Kaos shot at him.

"Oh, no, I think it's a good thing, which means that you have some of their magic, right?"

"I don't know?" Kaos whispered.

"You mean you haven't used any yet?"

Kaos bit his tongue for saying more.

"I mean, you got to have some," Micheal concluded, "Even if you were only part, it would only be logical, since the transformation is magic. So, can use magic to escape?"

"I can't," Kaos shouted finally, "I don't know any of *those* types of spells."

"What's your girl's name?"

"She's not my girl! Her name is Yoki,"

"Yoki" Micheal whispered louder.

"Yoki" Kaos whispered, and this time she responded.

"Yes, Kaos."

"Can you use magic to help us escape?"

"I could, it depends on how we would escape," Suddenly Kaos felt that his board was being wriggled out of position.

"Gently take the boy out so the skin doesn't peal from his bones." The slave trader yelled. Kaos turned his head to the side so his nose wouldn't slide on Yoki's board. He was brought down slowly. The air was crisp on his cheeks and his eyes remained closed until he was placed down on the ground. "The earring there, on the boy, is it worth anything?" Kaos opened his eyes to see the slave trader's face towered above him as he lay on the ground. A mid-twenties man, with an olive shirt and raggedy dark brown hair towered over him. He wore leather pants and boats and stood with a rather solid expression. His eye's ladened with interest crouched down intensely and stared at Kaos' ear. Using pale fingers he picked up the little dangling thing and examined it.

"Yes, indeed it is worth much," the man said, his voice was of a raggedy teenager and he sniggered, he got up and stared a Kaos more intently.

"How much will it gain in the market?"

"A fortune, if you can manage to remove it from his ear?"

"It's a simple earring, not much more force than a flick of a wrist should do the trick." The slaver trader said with pride.

"It is much more than a simple earring, the earring this boy wears is a magical item," the man said.

"A magical item you say, how might I remove it?"

"I will tell you on one condition,"

"That would be," the slave trader said tired of the boy's attitude already.

"That once the earring is removed that this boy becomes mine,"

"Pretty high price for a few words, he'd probably be the top sale. But yes, if the earring is worth as must as you say it is than you may have him."

"From the looks of it this boy has friends in high places. The earring is a war item, a present given to high ranked officers from Ebony's Elf General's."

"Do you know any specifics?"

"It was given to him by the General of the Wakitta Army, the highest ranked military force of Ebony. Probably given to him because of his abilities in battle."

"How might I remove it?"

"You cannot remove it, magic must defeat magic and the General's magic has locked this earring with a strong seal, which even I might not be able to remove. I will try,"

"Now hold on," he barked, "You mean to tell me that I've captured a warlord, with high skills of battle."

"Yes,"

"Then why would I want the earring in his ear when I can bid him off at the market for more." The magician stared into Kaos his eyes,

"This boy is worth nothing compared with the earring," he said glaring it into Kaos' mind.

"Why do you say that?"

"Because no one would buy him, he's far too skilled to allow himself to fall a slave to someone weaker than him. As a solider high in the ranks of the highest ranked army of all of Ebony finding someone weaker than him is very unlikely. The earring would sell for much more and at a quick pace. Such an item is rather hot in the black market for women."

"If he is a warlord, then how much would his sword go for?" The slaver trader took out Marina's sword and gave it to the magician to examine. He unsheathed it and sheathed it.

"The sword itself seems to be quite nice and well balanced, but it is old. The sheath is worn and the blade is dull. With the sheath in its current condition there is a lot of friction, the dullness of the sword attributes to that." He handed it back to the slave trader. "Considering that, at its present state it is worth perhaps 300 kars. If the blade and sheath were somehow fixed then 5000. The handle and sheath are decorated in silver accents, yet again of elfish make. Even in its current condition you would easily get buyers."

"Good, now if you would remove the earring and take your warlord," he smiled in his wealth. The Magician got down on his knees and hung both his hands over Kaos' ear.

"Σο τηε σταρ□σ μαψ ρετυρν, το μορταλ τηισ ορδαινεδ ση αλλ βε (Immortal magic may you release)" the man hummed the words and green sparks ran from his hand and hit the earring." Slowly, the lights grabbed the back and Kaos' eyes immediately shot open as pain was sent down his spine. The man crouched now in struggle. The Green lights making slow progress. Kaos wailed in pain. Yoki, lay still pinned by the ropes sighed. She knew what was happening. A few more minutes passed the pin was nearly out. Kaos' eyes glowed white and his body hovered, and hinder by the ropes, his back off the wood. His eyebrows narrowed down and he let out one defiant yell. A white ball of light erupted from his body and grew in radius pushing the magician back and sending the soldiers flying to the other side of the road. The magician rose up from his fallen position and held the earring in his hand. Kaos panted, his eyes still glowing. The magician walked over to the slave trader who just got up and rubbed his head.

"This is yours," he said and dropped it into the man's hand. He sighed once more. The soldiers were unconscious. The magician stumbled over to Kaos on the board and stared down at him. Kaos' eyes returned to normal and quickly fanned shut in exhaustion. The man cut Kaos's ropes with a small dagger he had gotten from his cloak and picked the boy up under the knees and shoulders. He carried him over to the small shack and put the boy in a cot just inside. He came back outside and using more magic woke the soldiers and helped them back to the carriage. He smiled as the carriage drove off into the sunset and walked back into the shack to find that Kaos had rolled over and was fast asleep.

Kaos woke to find the man in deep sleep as well in a fold up chair facing Kaos. Now that Kaos had a good look at the man, he was quite young. He was thinner than most, but still seemed quite strong. His small shack had a fireplace and pot above it, Kaos realized he lay in the only cot. He stayed awake as long as his body let him but fell asleep.

"Boy," a man's voice whispered in his ear, his shoulder was rocked back and forth, "Boy wake up," Kaos peeled his eyes opened and the man turned around and handed Kaos a bowl, "Eat something, it will make you feel better." The man's voice was kind and Kaos took the bowl. He felt quite shaken and weak for some reason. He felt the bowl in his hands but it slipped and nearly fell on the ground if the man didn't snatch it. He handed it back and Kaos took it in a far more secure grip. Kaos sat up and put his feet on the ground and sat on the side of the bed. The man plopped himself down next to Kaos and started eating. Kaos held the bowl on his lap and the spoon in the other hand and stared down at the bowl. He was almost too tired to move. Yet, he managed to scope a spoonful of what looked to be like soup. He placed it in his mouth. He swallowed reluctantly and put the spoon in the bowl. "It may not be good, but I put a spell on it to give you more strength, so eat it." Kaos stared at it again and slowly did another spoonful. Each time he put it back down he got faster at putting another in his mouth until he put is spoon in the bowl and it was empty. He placed the bowl and spoon on the floor and got up. Yet, his knees gave out and he fell back in the man's grip. "Whoa, don't try that so soon," he said with a laugh. Although the soup had made him more aware his body was still numb and he sat in the man's grip willingly. He moved Kaos back onto the cot. "Work on trying to sit up," he said softly and got off the cot quietly and took the dishes to a pot next to the fire. It was filled with water. Kaos just sat there like a doll just watching the man clean dishes then the pot. He wasn't much older than Kaos, maybe three years or so. He went outside a brought back a pile of wood and threw it on the fire. He smiled as he did so, but did not say a final word.

"Thank you," Kaos said quietly, to the man who stopped in shock and responded.

"It's not much," he said.

"You did me a big favor by removing the earring," Kaos managed to say quietly.

"I just started it, it was you who managed to destroy the seal."

"Me?"

"Yes," he smiled, "You launched a spell that nearly knocked us all over." Kaos smiled to himself

"Oh," Kaos whispered, "As soon as I am well, I must leave you though, a friend of mine still remains with the slave traders."

"Then we shall go in the morning," he smiled, "After all, you are mine."

"I'll dual you for that right," Kaos added.

"Even someone of your caliber wouldn't match against my magic," he said, "although your ways are rather interesting, your mana is weak compared to mine. It wouldn't be fair to fight with you."

"What's mana?"

"Spirit power," he said. "It's how much magic one possesses, it can grow when one uses more and more spells, I'll teach you some if you'd like." He smiled. Kaos stared at him, "ah, but don't get your mind worried over stuff like that yet, just rest up for tomorrow." He waved and walked out of the hut.

"I launched another spell today, mother, and the earrings out. I could come back to you but I'm sure that your secret is already sprung, considering how fast it flew to Ruka, soon Dartawg will send another and find Ruka dead. They'll storm the building with reinforcements and search the place high and low and not find me. Then they'll go after you demanding you speak about my whereabouts. You'll keep your mouth shut even if they kill you. My only option is to go to my father's, they won't find me there." Kaos sighed and put his head in his hand. "It's such a mess." The man caught what Kaos said to himself outside the door. When he came back in hours later he held with him nothing new but he sighed and stared at Kaos who laid back down on the bed.

"Today has been a long day," he sighed, "I'm beat." He yawned and stretched, "You should get to bed too, and you're going to need all your strength for tomorrow. Here could you get up for a minute."

"Yeah," Kaos said.

"It might be better to move you into the other room it's a little more private and secluded, I'd feel a little bit better if you slept there tonight."

"Sure,"

"Here let me help you up," He came over and Kaos put an arm around his shoulder for support and he hobbled over across the room and to the right towards a door. He opened the door and led Kaos into a small room. Kaos dropped himself quickly on the bed inside. "I can remember my first spell, I was nearly knocked out cold all day. But trust me it gets better, by the time you wake in the morning you'll barely even feel a thing." He smiled, "Well good night. I'll put up a barrier around this room. I tend to get wild animals this will prevent any from wondering in. Well good night, don't worry about anything, I'll protect you." He said and closed the door. The bed actually had a puff and sheets unlike the cot. Kaos sighed as he got under the puff and sheets. They were cold, but warmed him up in a matter of time. He hadn't slept in a bed for a while and he didn't want to waste its comfort by falling asleep so early. He stayed up pondering about the sorcerer in the other room. It puzzled him how he helped him, yet hadn't said a word about his hair or even the earring. He passed out later and the moon glowed outside.

"Get up," the man's voice was in his ear's. Kaos woke with a shock and rose with ease. "Feeling better?"

"Fine."

"Good, there's breakfast on the table," Kaos threw back covers and followed the man into the kitchen, "If you been wondering my name is Reion. Please sit down and eat." Kaos sat down in the two chair table and eyed the eggs that were set before him on the plate.

"Do these have an enchantment on them?" Kaos asked.

"What?"

"Did you enchant them?"

"Yes, I do it to all my food. I never know when there won't be any so it's good to get as much out of the food as possible." Kaos didn't make any more remarks. 'I'm surprised you even noticed. So, who are we going back to get?"

"Well, Yoki and I guess I have to snag Michael away too."

"So who's Yoki?"

"She's well," he paused, "she's an elf. She has long red hair and blue eyes. Micheal, he's ruff looking brown hair cut really short."

"You said there was one traveling with you, who's that?"

"Yoki," he said.

"Why are we picking up the other?"

"I told him some information that really shouldn't spread beyond his ears, and anyways he's a friend."

"Good then," Reion agreed. Kaos finished. "Stand up," Kaos stood up. Reion cracked his knuckles, "Now I have to disguise you."

"Let me guess, enchantments?" Kaos said.

"So, white boy knows something about magic, doesn't he?" Reion put his palms parallel to Kaos and closed his yes.

"Ever been a burnet?"

"No."

"You get to be one for a day," Reion said. Kaos was surprised when he saw the hair in front of his eyes go dark brown like Reion's. "I hope you don't mind me changing your eye color, too. You're supposed to be my brother so."

"This is just great," Kaos said sarcastically. He smiled and handed Kaos some clothes,

"They should fit you just fine."

"Could you teach me stuff like this?" Kaos asked him.

"Eventually, enchantments take more mana then spells," Reion said, "But yes, when you get there, I'll be glad to teach you." He turned away and walked outside. "Now hurry up and change, bidding starts at one." Kaos changed and went outside to meet him. "Okay then, we should head off." He beckoned Kaos to come closer. He did so. Reion put his hand on his shoulder and mutter a few words to himself. Kaos saw his scenery fall down before him into black. Then slowly new scenery fell from the sky. He found that he was behind a building in a busy market.

"Did *you* do that?"

"Yes, who do you take me to be? I can pull this stuff everywhere." He stood with pride and laughed. He walked from out behind the building into the crowd. Kaos caught up to him and they floated through the crowd.

"Good day, Reion," a shopkeeper yelled. They continued on past him, but a woman ran up to them.

"Oh, thank the gods, I found you" she panted, "I need your help."

"Please don't tell me you have broken glasses for me to fix again."

"Oh, I know but there was a brawl last night and I've nearly run out of decent glasses."

"You know what? I don't have time for such a little thing, but my brother, Siex, could help you out with that one," he jabbed Kaos in the stomach.

"You have a brother?" she stared at Kaos, "Oh, it's a pleasure to meet you," she stuck out her hand and he shock it. "I guess that magic of yours runs through the family." She smiled.

"Yes, it does," Reion said with a smile. Kaos coughed hinting, "May you excuse us for a moment," Reion said being dragged away by Kaos.

"What do you think you're doing? I can't do any repairing spell, I don't know the freakin' words!.."

"All the more reason you should,"

"What?"

"The words to say are: Τηε ωαψ ιτ ωασ (The way it was)" he smiled, "Now go follow her, then you can make your way to find Michael, I'm going to go get Yoki, because she probably is under more watch. Meet back in the ally we came here in," Reion walked away and Kaos finally walked over to the woman.

"You need some dishes to be repaired."

"Oh, thank you, you're very kind," she walked towards the edge of the road and into a bar. The door opened to reveal a busy and foggy place. Kaos coughed once between the laden of smoke but quickly stopped realizing that various people stared at him. The bar was wide a long, the table lay with circular stools. It had a very dark stain which was darkened with the thin layer of tobacco which lay on it. There were poker table's couches just in front of the bar. Men lounged with their feet up on coffee tables drinking, and occasionally chatting in cracking voices and about awkward topics. The woman flew around to the backside of the bar and Kaos went up in front and put his elbows down on the surface. A man sitting on a stool to his right stared at Kaos and as the woman was reaching down.

"I don't see you often," he said. Kaos turned and looked at the man.

"This is Reion's brother, Siex," the woman added. Kaos stuck out his hand and was met with a hearty and solid shake from the man.

"Jaken," he said. He didn't turn his head towards Kaos, only his eyes came down to star at him. A clever pair of eyes, which gave Kaos a tinge of worry, "Pleasure."

"He was so kind as to repair my glasses." She placed a bucket worth of glasses on the bar.

"Oh, so magic runs in his family, does it?"

Kaos reached inside the bucket and took the glasses out one at a time and stood them on the surface in a single file line. In all there were about fifteen. Kaos laughed and put his hands out, palms towards the glasses.

"Τηε ωαψ ιτ ωασ," he repeated the words and sounds Reion had done. Nearly immediately gravity release his body his hair flew about his head and his eyes glowed white. Light hovered around his body and it all slowly grew to his hands from where like a lightning bolt stuck each glass at a time making its way towards the last glass from which strangely flew behind the bar and hit an enclosed heater. The glasses melted and formed again. Kaos was released from the spell and slowly his eyes returned and he sat down in some exhaustion on a stool in front of the bar.

"You fixed my heater too," she said with glee, "I doesn't make the awful racket anymore. She came up and hugged him from across the bar, "Oh and these glasses are perfect, thank you so much." She said and admired the glasses, "would you like anything?"

"Oh, no thanks I must be going," Kaos sighed remembering what Reion had said.

"Oh no, stay for a little, let me treat you to a little something on the house." She said.

"If you insist," Kaos added and put an elbow on the bar, "I'll have a Shirley Temple." She hurried around and got the cherry drinks and seltzer.

"You're not much of a drinker?" Jaken asked him.

"No, not especially," he said.

"So how long have you been doing magic?"

"Not very," Kaos said, feeling a little dizzy.

"You did a pretty good job for a newbie."

"So it's that obvious,"

"You have a lot of mana for a newbie. What number was that?"

"What do you mean?"

'First, second…"

"Fourth," Kaos laughed.

"You are a newbie," he laughed, "Did you come visit your brother to learn."

"Well, originally no, but it seems he has taken me as his pupil."

"How old are you?"

"17,"

"Good, I was afraid the boy had taken a student older him," he sighed, "Reion is rash, but strong never the less. But you out of all people should know. If he ever gets rough on you just know that he does it in order to make you stronger." He stared at Kaos with intrigue.

"I know," Kaos lied.

"I was just reminding you," he winked. Kaos got a weird vibe from the man and tried to relax. "Does he know?" he said to himself. The man smiled and patted him on the head. "Come back whenever you want to talk," Kaos felt like a cat now, the man smiled.

"Sure," Kaos said awkwardly quickly dodging the next pat. He met Jaken's eyes with his own. His eyes were wise and he stared through Kaos in splendor. Kaos tested him to see if he could see through Reion's spell. He laughed,

"You are just precious," he laughed, "You better come back alive." Kaos met the Shirley Temple with his right hand as it was slid down the table.

"I plan to," Kaos said with suspicion, not quite knowing what he was answering to.

"You are hilarious boy," he chuckled, "I can't wait to see what you will aspire to."

"What are you chuckling over Jaken?" the bartender came back over to them.

"Oh, it's nothing," he laughed some more. Kaos got up from the table, rather perturbed by the man's actions.

"Thank you, but as I said must get going." Kaos said with a rude tone rose and headed out the bar.

"What did you say to the boy?" the bartender asked suspiciously. Jaken laughed. Kaos left the door without a second look. The streets were full and filled with tiny children being dragged along by their mother. Carts loaded with goods, donkeys straining under their weight. Young women balanced large baskets on the heads and the men were carrying around swords and bows. Kaos was about the only person not holding a weapon. He slip around people and curved his was along the road hopping to reach a point at which the crowd wasn't so enduring and he could figure out where he should go next to find Michael. He finally was able to sit down on a bench and think things over. Eventually he came to the conclusion that he should ask one of the store managers where he could buy a slave. He got up and strode calmly over to a man behind a small game stand.

"Want to play young man?" he asked with his salesperson tone, "Only 2 kars."

"I didn't come here to play, but for information. Could you tell me where I could find the slaves for the 1:00's auctions?"

"Play game," he smiled, "If you win, then I shall tell you." He turned around and gave Kaos a bow and one arrow, "You have one shot, if you get a bull's-eye you win." The man smiled in spite, probably thought that since Kaos didn't carry a bow that he didn't know how to use one. Kaos blankly strung the arrow and aimed. One release, the bow and the arrow flew dead into the target. The tail of the arrow was all that remained on the target. The arrow had taken out the center point and hung out the backside. The man walked up to the target and pulled out the arrow in shock.

"May I have my information please?" Kaos instructed him.

"Certainly, I am a man of my word." He said with shock.

"Could you tell me where the slaves are kept before the 1:00 pm auction, I want to get a preview."

"They are kept behind the store house down there," he pointed down the street.

"Well, sorry about your target, thank you." Kaos jogged away and the man was still in aw about how the arrow had protruded the target.

"I can't believe it," he stared at the target, "I swear that boy was human." He rubbed his head and then stared at the arrow in his right hand.

"That's what most untrained eyes would see," a man said from outside the both stood in a brown cloak.

"Hello?" he said still shocked of the figure.

"Do you know the name of the boy who shot that arrow?"

"No, I'm afraid not,"

"What did he look like?"

"Tall about 5 foot six, dark brown hair, green eyes."

"Anything different about him?"

"He smelt of smoke, probably just came out of one of the bars here."

"Here, let me fix that target, it's the least I can do for you." The man walked up to the target and put his hands over the target, he whispered, "Τηε ωαψ ιτ ωασ." The target glowed a gold for a moment then patched itself.

"You're just like Reion,"

"Reion?"

"Reion's a magician who lives just outside town. He comes here often."

"Do you know where I can find Reion?"

"Oh, the boy teleports everywhere, you got me where he goes. There are rumors that he helps out the slaver trader known as Sand-Plow, you might be able to ask him where his house is."

"Even though I have more questions I won't bother you with them-"

"No, feel free, I have nothing to hide. And anyways, I hadn't made any money to fix up the target."

"Well, where can I find Sand-Plow?"

"Behind that building there. Oh, and that boy you asked about, I sent him back there as well he was in some hurry."

"Thank You!" the man muttered and ran off as well. The game shop keeper watched him leave then met another customer.

Kaos ran behind the building quickly. In front of him were men and women wearing next to nothing. Kaos shot a hand over his eyes, "That's just sick." He had to open them to walk around. The men and women stared at him in shame. They each were tied to a poll, their wrists tied above their heads as they knelt on the ground. Kaos heard shouts coming near. He ducked down and started crawling.

"Boy?" a slave man whispered, "Come and untie these ropes, come on." Kaos eyed him in sorrow but he couldn't he had to find Micheal. He continued to crawl along the floor. The slaves looked at him strangely.

"Boy!"

"Shut up, I think he's trying not to get caught himself!" a woman whispered. The man cooled still pungent of Kaos' selfishness. He picked up his pace looking back and forth for Micheal. His eyes finally spotted him. He was out cold sitting on the ground. Kaos rushed over to him.

"Micheal," Kaos flipped to the back of the pole and worked on getting the ties undone. The boys tied next to him turned as much as they could.

"When you're done, could you untie ours?"

"Sorry I can't," Kaos said.

"Hey, that's not fair! You can't just bail one person out, and leave the rest of us here to be bought." He got Micheal's knees untied from the poll then his wrists. He ran around to the other side and caught him before he feel in the dirt. Flipping Micheal over on his back Kaos rocked him more.

"Micheal you have to wake up! Come on!" he shock the boy's shoulders and stopped. Slowly Micheal's eyes opened to Kaos's face.

"Who are you?"

"Come on," Kaos pulled him to his feet and tugged on his arm, "They're going to realize that your gone if we don't hurry up and get out of here." Micheal allowed himself to be tugged out of the field of slaves-to-be. The slaves yelled at them as they ran by throwing curses. Kaos ran back to the storage house and ran past the man in the cloak, who after a few minutes stopped and flipped back around.

"Kaos!" he yelled and ran after Kaos and Micheal. Kaos was running like mad, he turned a sharp corner down an ally and stopped. He panted and sat down on the ground.

"Oh, god," Kaos slumped. Micheal remained standing and was rather confused.

"Thank you," he said reluctantly, "And you are?"

"Look hard,"

"Kaos?"

"Yeah," Kaos smiled.

"Oh my god, your hair is brown!"

"Yeah, I know."

"What happened?"

"It's just an enchantment."

It's not mine, the sorcerer we met on the road, his name is Reion, and he's the one who did this to me."

"Why?"

"So that I could come into town with him and save you and Yoki."

"Where's Yoki?"

"Reion is off to get her, said she would be under heavier guard because she's an elf."

"Yeah, they took her away from the group as soon as we got here."

"Where are we going to meet up with him?"

"In this ally."

Reion crouched behind a barrel and listened in on a conversation of a few men around a fire.

"You should have kept the boy," one said to the slave trader.

"He would have been the top prize, you might have been able to give him to Dartawg, and there he would be useful."

"They're a republic," he cringed. "No republican would ever let a slave market run." He yelled at the other two.

"What about the Scarrows?"

"Scarrows?" he said in shock, "Like they'd take a boy?"

"You said he had white hair?" the man hinted.

"Ha, like the prince would wonder around unguarded!"

"So, the magician, he took him?"

"Yeah,"

"What's his story?"

"You mean the magicians?"

"Yes, what would a strong magician helping *you* with marketing?" on said and eyed the man across the fire.

"Reion, is a specific case. He bought his freedom from me by setting up a deal that for the rest of his life he would help me in marketing, in exchange for his freedom."

"I mean, aren't you worried? He's strong he could easily turn down his promise and betray you."

"Part of the deal was that if he ever betrayed me, everything he owned would be mine, including Reion himself."

"Wow, seems like a decent deal to me," one exclaimed.

"Yet, what with a sorcerer want with a boy?"

"Probably looking for a pupil," he laughed. Reion saw the perfect time to sneak by. He did so his feet making the slightest crinkle of paper beneath his feet. Yoki was tied up behind the group her eyes closed. Reion slowly moved in the shadows trying not to make any new ones of his own. He reached Yoki at last her eyes opened in shock as he touched her shoulders. Reion's hand was over her mouth.

"Just hold still and keep quiet, I'm a friend of Kaos'." Reion dropped his hand and Yoki remained quiet. Reion stuck his hands in front of the rope and moved his lips. The rope disappeared and Reion grabbed ahold of Yoki's wrist and said some more words. The scenery around them faded away and they were slowly brought into the ally where Micheal and Kaos sat. Reion's eyes widened as he stared at the entrance of the hallway. The man in the cloak stood there. He grabbed Yoki's wrist again before they were fully transmitted and transported across the street.

"Why did you do that?" Yoki asked.

"Look there," Reion pointed to the man at the entrance way.

"Who is he?"

"He's a sorcerer that's all I know."

"I can feel that," she said, "Do you think he's friend or foe?"

"I don't know, but I can't get in that ally way, he put up a barrier."

"But we were nearly transported."

"He put it up when we were transporting. If I had let the spell go on we would have blacked out of existence."

Kaos' eyes stared at where Reion and Yoki almost showed.

"What is it?"

"Reion nearly transported Yoki himself here."

"Nearly? What does that mean?"

"Means he redirected the spell for some reason," Kaos whispered.

"Wow, you've gotten better," a man's deep voice came from the entrance from the street. Kaos hopped up and met the man in the cloak.

"Who are you? Identify yourself!" Kaos yelled.

"You managed to see a spell halfway, and put an arrow straight through a target, your skills have sharpened Kaos. Not to mention that you've learned to use enchantments. It's been a while, seems that you've changed quite a bit, but I have stayed the same." Kaos recognized that voice but couldn't believe his ears.

"Daragon?"

"There you go," he said sweetly.

"But you're dead?"

"Dead, no," Daragon shunned, "I told you, I prepare for the rage of my students and that includes yours."

"Kaos, who is this?" Micheal said with shock.

"How do I know you're not just playing with me? Remove your hood." The man reached up and removed his hood. Kaos' eyes widened and he fell to his knees.

"But I killed you...I killed you with my own hands how can you still be alive?" Kaos was speechless. He had killed his own teacher in the blind rage of his conforming. Every inch of his soul had swallowed the man's heart in blood, yet he stood in defiance of all knowledge. Daragon stepped closer to Kaos. Kaos looked up with tears in his eyes.

"No!" Kaos stuck his hands out and set up a shield all around his body. He sat tearing his hands raised to hold the shield in place glowing a faint white. His eyes alit. "You're out to kill me, aren't you? Go back imposter!" Daragon continued to step closer to Kaos in a slow and steady motion. Micheal's eyes lay entranced by the situation and he was frozen stiff. Reion and Yoki saw the flash of white light through the crowd, yet they couldn't do anything to help him. (Because they could use magic they couldn't go through the barrier.) Reion grit his teeth, Yoki shoved him aside and walked towards the barrier. "Stay away!" Kaos yelled turned away from Daragon, who continued to walk. The bubble grew and hit Daragon, who stopped in his tracks.

"Kaos I mean you no harm," he said sternly.

"You liar!" Kaos formed balls of light in his hands and shot them with his mind at Daragon. Daragon's eyes glowed red and he brushed them out of the way into the buildings. Which blew up and burned. The street fell into chaos.

"Kaos, put down your shield." He said growling.

"I will not," Kaos yelled.

"Fine, then I'll just do it for you." He said and he put his hands together in a praying position and they grew redder. Taking them apart he knocked away the bubble around Kaos who sat with the lights in his hands. He threw them with all his might at Daragon and then ran towards the man his fists raised and made contact. Daragon has Kaos' fists in his own hands. "Are you a fool, Kaos?" Kaos felt his heart bond faster and the magic in him streamed from his body in flashes of white light running towards the sky. Kaos' eyes reverted to their green enchantment and his body went numb. He fell forward and Daragon caught him.

"I don't mean you any harm Kaos," Daragon said quietly, "I'm just frankly happy to see you alive." Daragon hugged him and Kaos couldn't do anything to stop him.

return | to

the | past

once | lived

"Kaos!" Yoki yelled as she ran towards Daragon and Kaos. Daragon quickly looked up and saw her.

"You're…" she said quietly, "general Daragon." Reion came quickly after and stopped when he saw Daragon.

"What are you doing here?" Reion said with grimace to Daragon walking over to Kaos.

"Come to get my pupil," he said with a smirk of almost grimace.

"Kaos?" Reion said shocked eyeing the boy who was dumbstruck and kneeling on the ground.

"Funny that I meet the traitor as his comrade."

"Just because I went to Jaken for training doesn't make me a traitor." Reion put his hands on his hips an scolded the man for saying such a thing.

"You were *my* student, and Jaken is a wicked man." Daragon emphasized.

"Wicked? You are the one who's wicked." Reion barked pointing his young finger at the formidable General.

"Yes," Daragon sighed in sarcasm.

"You should be happy that I never made a trip to Dartwg."

"You wouldn't have the nerve to," Daragon said.

"How would you know?-"

"I'm sorry to interrupt this reunion, but Kaos cannot go with you General."

"And why not?" Daragon said, "His apprenticeship under me is not complete."

"I don't think I have anything to say but just look at him. You can see through the enchantments, you know who he is."

"I knew from the start who he was," Daragon explained laughing.

'I've been sent to bring him to his father's house," Yoki ordered, "by his mother and I won't say neigh to it."

"Wasn't that because of the earring in his ear?" Reion said.

"How do you know?"

"I'm the one who removed it, you shouldn't be telling me what it is. Especially when put on the Queen's heir. I know what trouble it holds."

"But we can't bring him back to his mother's."

"Why not?"

"Dartawg has learned of the prince's existence. In the forests of Songham, I ended up murdering one of their spies."

"So, why can't he return to the city of Theives, the place is still safe from the rebels?"

"Umm," Michael interrupted.

"Oh, Micheal, I forgot about you."

"Who is this?"

"Micheal," Reion said, "A friend of Kaos's. Kaos' said he knew a secret about him that couldn't be spread."

"Micheal, did you know about Kaos' family heritage?"

"Yes, sir," he said quietly.

"So, we can take Kaos back to the city of Thevies. I'll have to send word to Marina-"

"Don't send word," Daragon said, "It is better if the information stays hidden between the four of us alone."

"So then we are taking Michael."

"We have no choice he knows of my pupil's where about." Daragon said and then stared up at Micheal who was shaken. He quickly grabbed a hold of Kaos's shoulders. "Reion, could you hold is body for me?"

"Me?"

"Yes, use the spell I taught you."

"I'm not *your* apprentice any more, do it yourself."

"Yoki?"

"Yes," she used blue to hold Kaos' body in a resting position floating in midair.

"We have to quickly get him back to the city. His body may not sustain much longer."

"What happened?" Micheal asked. "Why did Kaos' magic fly up into the sky?"

"When Kaos first took my apprenticeship he took part in a ceremony. As long as he was my student, if he ever were to channel his magic though mine. All the magic in his body would be stripped from him if he did so."

"So, as long as he was your apprentice, you could never dual each other?"

"We could dual each other with magic but with long range spells, such as the blasts Kaos was shooting at me. The rules are rather complicated."

"What's considered a close range spell?"

"When one uses magic to increase the strength of a kick or a punch."

"Oh," Michael concluded.

"Kaos lied to me," Reion said, "He had said he had never used a spell before in his life. Yet, I should have recognized the shield spell when he used it to protect himself from my magic."

"He probably didn't even realize he was using it."

"You mean he was that fresh?"

"I had taught him the basics of preparing to spell cast, the boy got egger and looked up a spell that I wasn't planning to receive nor teach him for that matter. I was dead for a time, yet the God's returned me to life."

"Wow," Reion said, "Yet, he was so fresh, how could he master a spell that would kill you?"

"He's quite special," Daragon interrupted, "Kaos is the 'αλυσ δεμον.' The fact that he's have elf makes me wonder how strong he would be if he was full."

"How can someone be half elf?" Micheal commented, "Well, I know *how* it could happen, yet what is it like, are you more elf than human or more human than elf?"

"It all depends on the individual," Yoki commented. They all stared at her. "The hybrid will slowly favor one side to the other and in a sense whichever one he or she favors more, the more they will be like." She said. So, everyone hold on tight." Reion stepped back.

"I won't be returning with you to Theives."

"I thought so," Daragon said, "Its good seeing you again, though you are a traitor. Good bye." Micheal, Yoki, Kaos, and Daragon disappeared with a transport spell. Reion walked back through the ally into the street and sighed, "There goes my pupil."

Daragon and the group appeared in front of the two large doors of Theives. He put his hand on the door and whispered:

"Τηεσε ωαλλσ βοω δοων βεφορε τηειρ Εμπρεσσ," he said calmly. The doors opened and he and Yoki didn't waste any time. Micheal not understanding a thing that was happening tried to keep up with the pace at which Daragon and Yoki were running. Kaos' body was being dragged in perfection, always remaining flat to the ground. His eyes were closed and the enchantments still remained.

"Take him down the street you'll see a library. Take him inside." Yoki, who ran faster that Daragon sped ahead and found the library. She opened the door and lugged Kaos in and put him in a chair.

"Hello?" She yelled. No one answered.

"Old man?" Daragon yelled throughout the library when he stepped into the room. A short stubby man stepped out from behind the shelves.

"Daragon? You're alive?" he said with shock.

"There's not enough time for hellos, we need your help. Kaos needs a place to hide out-"

"Kaos?" He stopped, "Where is the dear boy, I haven't seen him in ages it feels like." Daragon eyed the chair where Kaos sat.

"If you remove all the enchantments you will find that the boy sitting there is Kaos."

"He's changed I see." He said with dignity "Kaos may stay in my library, but you I still don't trust."

"Understood, where should we put him?"

"Hurry bring him in the back. The man used a spell to hover down the hall and Daragon carrying Kaos followed quickly after him. They reached a door in the back left hand corner. "Come in," he said and beckoned Daragon to come into the room. He shut the door behind them. There was a cot in the small room and Daragon placed Kaos down on it. The short stubby man came to Kaos side and held his hands over him.

"Σο τηε σταρ□σ μαψ ρετυρν, το μορταλ τηισ ορδαινεδ ση αλλ βε (Immortal magic may you release)" Kaos' hair immediately went white and his skin darkened. "My," he said staring at Kaos, "this boy is not who I thought him to be."

"You saw the white hairs on his head when we brought him here, aren't you not surprised?"

"Frankly, I never imagined him to be the ροψαλ δεμον," he said continuing to stare at Kaos. "How did he get in this state?"

"He touched me in battle," Daragon admitted.

"What? You let the boy nearly kill himself, you're his master, and you are supposed to watch out for the boy not kill him."

"Can you revive him?"

"Oh, the spell should be in one of my books, I can't remember it now." He shunned, "Get the elvish girl to help us search the texts, time is not on our side." Daragon immediately left the room and the librarian said another spell.

"Σανδ ηαυλτ, φαλλ φορτη νο μορε ον τηισ σουλ (Sand halt, fall forth no more on this soul)," Kaos's body glowed with light blue energy. "I have slowed time, but magic of that sort will soon overpower me." He said quietly and left the room. Daragon and Yoki had grabbed the elvish books off the shelves and were scanning through them. Micheal wandered nearby picking up books and looking at them.

"Boy, what is your name?"

"Michael,"

"Michael, go sit by Kaos and yell if anything happens." The man didn't stay any longer and hurried past and picked up books and started scanning as well. Michael in confusion walked down to the small room and sat in a fold up chair across from Kaos' glowing body.

Daragon and Yoki search through the shelves ravenously, and the librarian search the shelves for books for them to read.

"I found it!" Yoki yelled and then turned and ran down to the room. She held the page between her hands. Daragon dropped the book he was holding and ran after her. The librarian jumped down from his latter and followed. The three filed into Kaos' room.

"Micheal, go back outside," Michael who was sick of the orders did as he was told and quickly left the room.

"Release the spell," Yoki yelled at the librarian. He quickly disabled the spell that halted time. "Daragon because you're his master you have to do the spell," Yoki instructed him. "Now put both you hands over Kaos' face." He did so. "Now repeat after me." Daragon nodded. "Ρεπρεηεντιον δο νοτ τακε τηε σουλ οφ μψ μισριβλε στυδεντ, (Reprehension do not take the soul of my miserable student)

"Ρεπρεηεντιον δο νοτ τακε τηε σουλ οφ μψ μισριβλε στυδεντ," he said.

"Ψουκι, γοδδεσσ οφ θυστιχε, (Youki, goddess of Justice)"

"Ψουκι, γοδδεσσ οφ θυστιχε,"

"Λετ τηε σουλ λιϖε, (let the soul live)"

"Λετ τηε σουλ λιϖε,"

"Λετ ιτ βρεατη ανδ ηυμ, (let it breath and hum,)"

"Λετ ιτ βρεατη ανδ ηυμ,"

"Λεαρν φρομ μιστακεσ ανδ παρδον ηισ μορτουσ. (learn from mistakes and pardon his death.)

"Λεαρν φρομ μιστακεσ ανδ παρδον ηισ μορτουσ." Daragon finished. Nothing had changed, there were no lights. Kaos still lay on the bed, the concerned eyes of all three stared at him. The librarian commented:

"Perhaps, we are just too late,"

"No!" Daragon shot, "My student will not die on my behalf! I φοργιϖε ηιμ, λετ ηιμ γο (I forgive him, let him go)." Daragon whispered. There was a gasp. Kaos' eyes flew open with a shock. Daragon removed his hands quickly and smiled. Kaos coughed as he rose; Yoki came up a hugged him.

"Thank the gods, you're alive!" Kaos fell back on the bed in her weight, Yoki on top of him crying.

"Yeah," Kaos said to clam her nerves. He was alive again, he had felt his body slip from him when he attacked Daragon. His eyes fell on

Daragon's face and he immediately lost all emotion. Daragon, he would soon punish him for all that he had done. He had attacked Daragon only to finish the job he had been sent from Dartwag to do, what he started was a rather complicated situation and he knew he should have died from using magic against Daragon.

"Don't look so grim," Daragon whispered. Kaos turned away and raised Yoki off him to sit on the side of the bed. He sat himself on the side as well. He put wrists on his knees to support himself a little.

"Be happy Kaos," the librarian interrupted. Kaos slowly lifted up his eyes to the man's kind eyes.

"Iori," Kaos said monotone with a little grimace to his voice, "Thank you." Kaos picked up his body off the bed. "I know it's your magic that kept me alive." He said quietly and walked to the door and put his arm on the door frame, "Daragon for what it's worth, thank you too."

"Yoki found the spell you should be thanking her, without her we might not have revived you in time."

"Well," Kaos said staring into the library, "then I guess I should give thanks all around." He remarked. He dropped his head.

"Kaos…" Daragon spoke.

"Yes, master," he said with grimace.

"Kaos, I must tell you something-"

"Then tell me later, I really don't want to hear it." Kaos said closing his eyes. He dropped his hand from the door and walked into the library out of the room.

"Kaos-" Daragon started rudely and Iori grabbed his shoulder.

"Let the boy go,"

"It's easy enough for you to say so," he cursed at the man, "He's my only pupil."

"He's only a boy," Iroi commented, showing his foresight.

"This boy is going to run away like he always does," Daragon commented.

"He's a boy trapped in walls only opened by magic,"

"His magic has been stripped from his body, he won't be getting any back." Iroi commented. Daragon sighed. Yoki sat on the bed.

"Marina…" Yoki said in the silence.

"Yoki?"

"The transformation is not complete," Yoki said softly, "Kaos can't lose all his magic now!" she yelled. Ebony's faulter was on my shoulders and now I've let everything fall apart." She punched the cot.

"You mean to tell me that Kaos is still 17?"

"Yes, he turns 18 in 13 days," Yoki said tearing.

"Kaos brought it upon himself," Daragon said, "He knew it would be stripped from his body when he attacked me…I just don't think he thought that he would be brought back to life."

"The god's control his fate now," Iori said. "They alone have the power to restore the 'ροψαλ δεμον' powers or not. Time will tell whether his sentence will pardoned or not."

"The first heir to the thrown who's a fugitive; a young, murderous spy form Dartawg who's a high ranking officer in the Ebony Army; Prince Kaos Bernidict: only apprentice to the sorcerer known as Daragon. Both known and unknown; relative and contradictory; a boy who's full of chaos himself." Yoki said in silence.

Glowing in residence of the solitude and lonesomeness of being lost: a firefly lights signaling for his family and friends to remember him. Sat resting from weariness in Kaos' hand. The grass blew in the valley's belly as he sat in the field.

"The first firefly of the night," Kaos said quietly. Cold air crept down the U-shaped valley and settled on the ground. Mist of warm vapor rose towards the sky, floating higher till it reached Aria's Limestone ball in the sky somewhere beyond the stone that entrapped the city. The vapor formed droplets, freezing cold. Kaos shivered as it fell on his body. He hugged his knees and bared the pain to repent for all his mistakes and wrongs. His shoulder's stung and were red where there was not sleeve. Yet he said to himself:

Τηοσε ωηο εξχιταωερυντ ανιμυμ αδ δεασ, Λετ δεατη ωε νιβυντ ινωιτα, Αωακεν τηειρ ηεαρτ σ, βυντ αδ αμαρε ετ χα ωερε, Λετ εαχη νεω λιγητ βυρν βριγητερ ιν αγε, Δυξ τηειρ το υχη αδ φυτυρμ,Μαψ τηε ηοπε ανδ λυξ εξχιπιεντ τυ χυντι"

"What a fitting prayer," Daragon's voice was behind him. Kaos flipped around in surprise. Daragon was smiling and holding an umbrella above his head. Yellow boots on his feet. Kaos turned back around.

"I thought so too," he said.

"Come out of the rain," he said like a father.

"I like the rain," Kaos lied and sat, he was drenched now as the rain pummeled down from the sky.

"I brought two umbrellas let's go take a walk in the rain," Daragon laughed.

"Then you wasted your energy bring that extra all the way out here," Kaos said. He just wanted to be alone, if that meant getting sick then so be it, he would get sick a hundred times just to be alone.

"Wasted one, why not waste two," Daragon smiled and closed the umbrella over his own head and went down to sit next to Kaos. Kaos aggravated that he had to be near the man as well as stay stuck in the freezing rain, got up and grabbed an umbrella and opened it over him.

"Come on, if you insist to be near me than we might as well be dry." He judged the situation. Daragon got up happily and put the other umbrella over his head.

"Good, because it's rather nippy tonight."

"Let's just go and get this walk of yours over with." Kaos whined, closed his eyes and turned toward a path. He started walking than turned back to Daragon, "Well, did you want to talk or not?"

"Yes, let's talk," and he walked to his side. The path was muddy and slippery, but it was the usual for them both.

"So," Kaos interrupted the silence, "Why do you still care about me, I lost all my magic so what good am I as your apprentice?"

"You are more than my apprentice, Kaos," he said staring warmly into Kaos' eyes, "You are much more of a son than you know. Even if the Gods don't give you back your magic, than I still have the duty of celebrating your birthday with you, don't I?"

"How do you know?"

"I wouldn't forget such a thing." He smiled, "the big eighteen, must be excited?"

"No, not really," Kaos said quietly, "When I turn eighteen I'm banished from my home. I can never go see my hometown again for another year. I don't find *that* anything to celebrate about."

"Oh?" Daragon commented. "It makes me wonder why?"

"Why what?"

"Why you never listened to your father in the first place."

"Something as feudal as that? My father and I are simply not friends, he hates what I love, and I love what he hates you could say that it's just one of those teenager things," Kaos commented.

"Oh, in that case the Gods might tip in your favor…" Daragon said.

"Why? All I've done is betray people again and again."

"You are still a child, and children must make mistakes in order to learn from them. There is the decided factor that you are the 'ροψαλ δεμον' your soul has magic that intertwines with the God's themselves."

"There's no more jumping in surprise over that," Kaos mumbled and needlessly reminded himself of his white hair. "Marina never told me what the next step to my transformation was…" Kaos said in disappointment.

"Your eyes will go gold," Daragon interrupted.

"My eyes?" Kaos said staring at him.

"When you turn eighteen, many strange things happen to the 'ροψαλ δεμον'." Daragon exasperated.

"Do you think that there are any books Iori has on the 'ροψαλ δεμον'?" Kaos asked him.

"Kaos, you must trust me when I say this," Daragon said, "Don't read them."

"What'll happen if I do?"

"Nothing. But just don't read them."

"Why-"

"If you read the books nothing will happen, you'll be you, and your future will remain the same. But I don't want you to burry yourself in those books…" he held his tongue.

"Is something bad going to happen?"

"…no, nothing bad will happen to you I promise." Kaos turned away.

"Your word is good enough for me," Kaos said. "And master?"

"Master? That's something you haven't said that in a while. Yes, young Kaos?"

"I would like to apologize for everything I've done to you," Kaos said truthfully, "Words cannot ever tell how horrible I felt the day that I thought I killed you. My mind went back to the past that day, and all the times that you had helped me through and the things that you had taught me. They were more than just spells and attacks, but values and moral lessons. And as much as I hated the little tasks you had me do daily, and as much as I whined and nagged, the fact that you never let me win just showed how much you cared for me and my future. So, thank you Daragon, my master for all that you have taught me about life." Kaos said with a smile. Daragon smiled as well and a grin spilled across his face.

"That's just what they wanted to hear," he laughed.

"What?"

"Dear apprentice of mine, you are more naive than I ever thought possible for a seventeen-year-old to be." Kaos stared at him with a confused expression, "Just try to do a spell dear boy." Kaos put his hand towards a tree he was nearly leaning on.

"Ωηισπερ ιν τηε ωινδ βε γονε (Whisper in the wind be gone)" Kaos said. He felt nothing. "Nothing happened."

"Gees, just turn around," Daragon smirked. Kaos turned around and the tree wasn't there. He smiled and felt where the tree had been. The tree's presence was there put you couldn't see it.

"Holy crap, it worked!" Kaos yelled and he felt along the tree's ruff surface.

"Kaos!,"

"Sorry," he said apologetically and prayed in penance. He stared up with a apologetic eyes to Daragon, but with a grin on his face. He was almost laughing. For some strange reason he just jumped. He jumped and put the umbrella over his head as the water turned to hail.

"Whoa, we better get home, before they turn into golf balls." Daragon ran down the path holding his umbrella.

"Oh thank you gods, thank you, thank you," his mumbled to himself as he ran behind Daragon.

The two raced back to the library. Where Yoki immediately greeted them at the door.

"Daragon you're back, oh and Kaos, you're soaking wet!" she said like Kaos' mother always had and rushed towards him. Daragon took of his boots and closed the umbrella, Kaos closed his umbrella and put it next to Daragon's. "Kaos go take a shower and warm up, you're going to get a cold if you stay in those wet clothes I'll got ask Iori if he has anything your size." She left.

"She didn't even tell me where the shower was," he laughed turning towards Daragon.

"That's because you had her so worried that it nearly drove her insane." Daragon laughed, "Come on, I'll show you." He laughed and led Kaos into an odd section of the library. "You came here to save the man's research not to use his utilities." He laughed. Just inside there he pointed to the door. "You should know how to work the thing. It's not the greatest thing, but it does have hot water. Kaos went down the hall and opened the door. Inside it was much like schools bathroom, except with much smaller proportions. The showers were just separated by curtains and they each had their own temperature gauge which was the nice thing about it.

He took his time and got out a good half-an-hour later and found some clothes on the floor just inside. He got changed in them and walked back outside. He went back to the endurance hallway looking around for anyone who could be there.

"Hello," he said, and there was an echo throughout the library. "Any one still here?"

"Oh, I'm sorry dear boy," the librarian appeared down the hallway of books. "Daragon, Yoki, and that Micheal kid. Have went to stay at an inn in town."

"You mean you actually won't let them stay here?"

"I mean what I say," he said rather harshly. "I don't trust magic folk, the only reason why I trust you is because I owe you for saving my research." Kaos sat down in a chair.

"For once, it's kind of nice to be rid of them for a time," Kaos said.

"Yes, everyone needs room to think," he smiled. Kaos thought to himself, he couldn't pass anytime reading through elfish books, Iori would probably get suspicious and lock him in his room; for now he could read some novels, I'm sure that that wouldn't do any harm. Kaos got up and walked down the first isle just looking across the spines to catch and interesting title or cover. He hands fell on one that read: "<u>The Light of Other Days</u>" by Arthur C. Clarke and Stephen Baxter. He read the inside flap and then the first page and decided that it was worth sitting down and reading. He sat in the inlet of the front entrance, his feet up on a tabled and his back on the front window. The book was good, the first chapter was about *(Get/read the first chapter and write summary, very brief)* Kaos didn't realize that snow was piling up behind him and it was nearly nine. Yet there was a tiny bell.

"Hello?' a woman's voice hung in the doorway, she cradled in her hands two shopping bags that she must have collected throughout the day. "Excuse me?" She stared at Kaos who looked up in shock at her.

a ride home

"Yes?" he said not knowing how else to respond.

"Is this your library?" she said in shock looking at him.

"Oh, mine, no," Kaos laughed. He got up and walked up to the hallway. "Iori, you've got a customer."

"Not really," she said laughing. "I was wondering if anyone had a horse or carriage I could get a ride home in?" Iori appeared and watched the two of them.

"What do you think you're doing," he shouted at Kaos, "Go to the back and stay in your room." He shoved him down the hallway and whispered in his ear, "The whole point of you staying here was so that you could hide here."

"Excuse me?" the girl said again.

"Yes, madam?"

"Is there and horse I could barrow, I need to get home and my feet are nearly numb." She nearly begged.

"Kaos," he said again. Kaos who was nearly stomping down the hall, came back with a snarl on his face. "Be so kind as to take this young girl home."

"How do you expect me to do that?" Kaos yelled at him, finding the perfect opportunity to get back at him.

"I have a horse in the back," he laughed, "I'm far too old to ride her, so you may use her."

"Fine," Kaos grumbled. The girl with her wet boots followed Kaos out the back door of the library.

"Are you two related?" She asked him as they walked to the barn.

"Related? No," Kaos barked.

"You seem to be,"

"That old man, just knows me too well," Kaos said.

"Oh? I never see you around here a lot?" she said. Kaos stopped. "I'm one of the regulars around here, which is why I would dare enter this library."

"So," Kaos veered away from the subject, "Iori's made himself a name to be feared has he?"

"Everyone admires him for he's the only human in town that can perform magic. Some of the villagers fear him for this, I don't" she smiled.

"Is that so?" Kaos laughed in his own competence. "I know a few people in town who can do magic."

"So, what are their names?"

"Well, Daragon…no he's an elf, Yoki- up elf too. Well there's me, I can do a little."

"You boy!" she exclaimed in disbelief. Kaos stopped and flipped around.

"Hey, I'm probably older than you so don't be calling me boy,"

"Really?" she said with laughter. "How old *are* you?" She laughed and ran a finger under his chin.

"17," Kaos said stepping back and he crossed his arms.

"What a coincidence, me too," she laughed. "So, you say you can do magic, what can you do?" She smiled with some laughter still alit in her eyes. Kaos stared at her with a playful eye and raised his hand. His eyes glowed and the girl's face grew in enlightenment, yet she soon whipped it off not wanting to seem amazed by his abilities. He gathered light in his palm and grasped it in his hand. "Fancy light show." She commented cleverly.

"Light Show?" Kaos smirked and tossed the ball with the flick of a wrist over his shoulder and into a barrel. As soon as the ball hit the wood there was an amazing explosion. Wood smashed and wrenched into shards few by and smoke came from the spot where there used to be a barrel. "I'd call it more than just a light show." His ego shown brighter than his eyes at this point as her eyes fell on the indiscernible remains of the barrel. The girl stared up at him with a bit of disappointment since he had proven her wrong. But the laden grim on her face quickly turned and flipped over into a smile with a laugh.

"Let's go magician boy, I would love to see your tricks but I must get home." She laughed. Kaos waited for the girl to walk past him till he turned and found the barn. The courtyard in back was something of an ally. Yet, the buildings beside it were short and stumpy. The ground was wet and slushy as the snow fell softly from above. Creaking of a door was what the girl heard as she jumped from her idle stance and met Kaos opening the barn door.

"Sorry," Kaos whispered.

"No, its okay. It's the first time I've ever been in town this late. It's so peaceful." She whispered and shook her head in her frailness. Kaos walked into the barn his boots echoing on the wooden floor boards.

"She hasn't been out this late either," Kaos inferred, staring at a brown and white pinto.

"She's gorgeous," the girl whispered coming up beside him, "Is she yours?"

"No," Kaos said truthfully. He opened the gate to the stall and the pinto eagerly stepped out before Kaos or the girl even knew what was happening. The pinto stepped towards the girl who stood shocked, Kaos grabbed her by the shoulders and pulled her out of the way. Abruptly the pinto stopped in the middle of the barn, flicked its tail in glory, and peered behind at Kaos' and the girl's crept-out expressions. "Well, I've never had a horse that did that." Kaos said and dropped the girl's tense shoulders.

"Thank you," she whispered to him as he passed. He walked up to the horse calmly and grabbed the reigns and saddle and set her up. The Pinto was rather regal as she stood there letting Kaos busily set her up for a ride.

"Are we really going to ride her?" the girl's voice trembled.

"She's not a wild animal," Kaos stared at her.

"But she's not even your horse, don't you think that she'll be difficult to ride?" she said and slowly walked towards Kaos, making sure to stay a safe distance away from the horse. He plopped the saddle on top and fastened it underneath.

"Nope, come here," he beckoned her to come close to him. She walked up. Kaos knelt down and put his palms out. "Here, I'll be so kinds as to give you a boost."

"What about my things?"

"Just put those down I'll attach them to the horse." She placed her belongings down and set one foot in Kaos' hand and grabbed the top of the saddle with her hands. "One, two, three," Kaos said as he pushed up on the girls foot. She was surprised and hung by the side for a while. "Hurry up and put the other leg over, I can't hold you all day." Kaos said with a grunt as he bared her weight. She scrounged up on the horse as best she could but slipped out of the stirrup and fell back on Kaos. Kaos collapsed back on the ground, the girl sitting on top of him. "Sorry," she said.

"Could you just get off me," Kaos groaned. She shifted her weight and got up off him. He rubbed the sawdust off his pants and got up.

"I've never ridden a horse before," she said grabbing the back of her neck.

"I think I guessed that one." Kaos groaned, "Just try again, this time when I push up on your foot throw the other foot over." Kaos got down on his knees and put out his palms once more. She stepped on and Kaos pushed up again. The girl quickly hopped one not wanting to upset him anymore. Kaos grabbed her things and latched them to the saddle.

"How are you going to get up here?" she said staring at him. He placed his foot of the stirrup and pushed up, easily grazing the saddle. He stood in the stirrup until the girl slid back in the saddle and let him on.

"Thank you," he said as he sat down.

"Just make it look so easy," she said under her breath.

"I'm taller than you," Kaos said and urged the horse into motion. The girl let out a yell and grabbed Kaos by the waist as the pinto shifted weight and strut out of the stable. Kaos didn't care at this point if she was frighten to death or not, he wasn't about to comfort her for such a minor thing. They walked outside the girl was shaking, she realized that her hands were tight around Kaos waist and quickly removed them.

"Sorry," she said quietly and shoved them behind her back.

"Where do you live?" Kaos said, ignoring her words.

"Yagon Township," she said her voice weary as she blushed.

"Okay then," he said and turned the horse. The girl let out some nervous noises but refused herself to move an inch. Kaos walked the bay out of the ally into the street. Slowly she grew used to the pace and brought her nerves to say something.

"Thank you for taking me home," she said.

"No problem," Kaos said trying to brush away his nerves after all this was the girl's first time on a horse. The pinto was steady and didn't make sharp nor sudden turns. "I had nothing better to do."

"You were reading <u>The Light of Other Days</u> were you not?"

"Yeah," he said, "But I was growing tired of sitting in that library and reading." He managed a laugh and the girl's body relaxed.

"Where did you learn magic?"

"In this town," Kaos said, "Daragon took me as his apprentice, and since then I've been taught by him."

"Daragon?" she said, "As in General Daragon?" she said with shock, "You're in the army?"

"Not anymore," Kaos laughed, "I quit before I ever had to step onto a battle field."

"Were you drafted?"

"Yeah," Kaos' voice went soft.

"I'm sorry," she said.

"Why should you be sorry?" Kaos said, "It's not your fault I was drafted, heck it was mine."

"It's just that it isn't right for people to be drafted and taken away from their homes, it seems that if Ebony is such a strong Empire that it should be able to win this war without the need for drafts." She said.

"Wow," he said awkwardly.

"Wow?"

"It's the first time that I've found someone who agrees with me." Kaos exasperated.

"Really? I can name a bunch of people who agree as well."

"Well, hey it just goes to show that I haven't met the right people." Kaos laughed.

"Well you've met me," she smiled.

"Yeah," he smiled, "I guess I have." The pinto walked off and they reached the edge of town without a sound.

"Now, refresh my memory, Yagon is…" he started.

"That way," she pointed left towards a forest and small homes dotted the hills nearby.

"Are you comfortable if I go a little faster?"

"Faster? How much faster?"

"Well, considering it's your first ride I suggest you grab my waist." He laughed and the girl's hand clasped around his stomach wearily. "Okay then, here we go," he clicked his tongue and the horse reared back and then kicked off into a sprint. The grip tightened and the girl cling to his back. Her eyes were clamped tight and she grid her teeth. "Come on, open your eyes it's the best part." He said gently. The girl's eyes opened though she remained tense and she stared out over the plain. Kaos felt the girl fall into a trance as the scene of the rolling horizon of glittery snow faded into fog into the distance. He didn't say a word for it would interrupt the girl's vision and guided the horse across the fields. They reached the first hut and the girl said:

"I live just over there, she pointed to a farmhouse in the middle of the fields. The two story white building freshly painted and fashioned with flower pots under every sill. The somewhat mounding fields were covered over in tents, like green houses. The snow quickly building on top. They walked down a narrow street, two field tents ending on either side. A small open sided tent appeared on a corner where there was a second street intersection. "Turn down that street." She said and he turned the reins and horse did so. Just make your next left. Kaos made the next left into an enclosed driveway. It was shady inside for three sides were banked with the actual house itself. The pinto's clunks on the cement inlet were loud and Kaos brought her to a stop. "Well thank you Kaos," she said and hopped off the horse. A window upstairs opened and yellow light streamed down onto the driveway. The picture of an thin aging woman stuck her head out the window and looked down on the driveway.

"Enna, is that you?" she said with a worried voice.

"Yes, mom," Enna waved up gleefully and smiled.

"Good, dear, the door is unlocked." The woman stared down with a smile at the two of them then wondered back into the room.

"Thanks again, Kaos." She grabbed her stuff off the horse and turned.

"You're welcome Enna," he said softly and watched her head into the house. He smiled and laughed and headed back the way he came.

"Dear, dear, you must be soaking wet!" the blond haired woman shunned as she approached her daughter, who was plucking her soak-soaked feet from her water resistant boots. "Here are some new socks you can put those directly into the washing machine." The girl delicately peeled off her socks and handed them to her mother, received the new ones and put them on. She plopped down her bags and sat down on a stool and sighed.

"Have a busy day?"

"Yes, it took me forever just to find a good gift for Suzy," she sighed once more and rested her head.

"Who was the boy?" her mother said.

"Mom…" she said like every girl says to her mother when they intrude to learn secrets.

"Come on, tell me," she smiled.

"His name is Kaos," she said at last knowing that her mother would not be satisfied if she didn't speak up.

"Kaos," she let out a squeal, "How old is he?"

"Mom, why are you asking all these questions?" Enna rose and walked out of the room. Her mother smiled as she walked up the stairs and into her room. She sat down on her bed and fell back and sighed.

strange ceremonies

Enna woke suddenly and rose out of bed. Her red hair a bob on her head she went to her vanity and brushed it until in ran flat down her head. She dabbed concealer on her few pimples and covered her freckled filled face with a skin tone base. She put one a little mascara, walked downstairs into the kitchen, and sat down on a stool in the island.

"Heard that you came home with a boy yesterday," a man's voice came from nearby. She looked up and smiled to find that her dad was standing in front of the toaster waiting for his toast to pop up.

"He simply gave me a ride home, father, that's all." She smiled in a girlish faddish that made father's nervous.

"That was quite nice of him." He smiled and reached for his toast as it finished crisping in the toaster.

"So, when do we have to be ready for church?" Enna asked him, straying the subject away from her evening. She placed her hands calming on the table as her father turned around with plate in hand.

"As soon as we're finished eating we should leave and head into town." He smiled as he buttered his toast and sat down across from each other. Enna got herself a piece of toast and they ate in silence. Enna ran upstairs first and got dressed, not only to escape her father's close eyes but the strange silence that had fallen between them. She wore a pale blue knee length dress that was simple a black leather long tailed coat on top. She let her hair down and drew half of it up behind into a bun. She put on some lipstick and left the vanity. On her feet, she wore satrapy black stilettos. She left the room and walked down the stairs carefully the clunk of the heels a womanly gesture in her more girlish appearance.

"Hurry up Enna," she walked through the kitchen and out the door to see that a carriage was waiting in the driveway. Her Father, Mother and older sister, Suzy, and herself got up into the carriage and started into town. Enna stared out the window and kept recalling the night before.

When they reached the church in town it was crawling with people. They all got out and headed into church. *(The ceremony and church service.)*

At the end of the service, a group of girls rushed over to Enna.

"I heard that you got a ride home with a boy last night," one whispered to her, cupping her mouth towards Enna like she held some vast and important secret the world could not have imagined to have ever happened.

"So," Enna said and rose an eyebrow at the girl in her faddish of common.

"Well come on, you know. You're turning eighteen, you'll have to get married." the girl nearly jumped up in down in excitement, although at the question Enna stayed quiet, "Is he cute?" As the silence grew she smiled, and slowly Enna smiled too.

"Okay, yes, I'll admit he is cute." She said her face wildly red laughter, was nearly burst from her lips. She couldn't hide it, all morning she had spent thinking about him, this was yet another loop that she nearly choked to swallow.

"Oh, someone has a crush." The girl squealed

"Shut up!" Enna said embarrassed.

"Well, describe him," the girl questioned her further trying to find out the juicy details of the mystery man.

"Tall, tan, light-brown eyes, with long shaggy silver hair."

"He has silver hair!"

"Oh, I love guys who have silver hair." Another added.

"Hey, he's Enna's." the other slightly tapped the girl on the shoulder, who shrugged in innocence and responded:

"It's whoever snags him first, there are only so many eligible guys around with silver hair."

"Anything more?" the original asked.

"He's a sorcerer, well an apprentice of one." Enna added.

"What?"

"You mean he knows elvish too!"

"He must, in order to be a sorcerer you have to know the language. But why would that matter?"

"Oh, you must have heard some elvish!" The girl squealed, "It's so romantic."

"Does he have an accent?"

"An accent?"

"Elvish has accents?"

"She hasn't heard any!" the other scolded her for asking such a stupid irresponsible question.

"Wait, how old is he?" worry fell over the crowd as the tension grew. Enna's answer would really be the deciding point to whether he was eligible or not.

"Seventeen," Enna said with a smile and immediately burst into laughter

"It's so perfect!" the group harmonized and jumped.

"Oh, what is his personality like?"

"He's so sweat in his own little way." Enna could just remember him the night before. Her mind of dreamy times turning every movement he made into some thoughtful gesture or expression of love.

"What do you mean?"

"He brought me all the way home. We watch the horizon as we cantered through the fields. I've only known him for a few hours but it feels like more."

"Sounds too perfect to me,"

"True, he can be a little sarcastic at times, but he sweat at the heart I just know it!"

"There we go, now we know she's not just making it up" she smiled, hearing a thorn among petals. "So, what's his last name?"

"Last name? Oh no!" Enna's heart dropped. "I didn't ask him."

"You mean to tell us that you're falling head-over-heels over some guy you don't even know what his last name is, How can you even tell your father you've found a man!"

"Hey, it was late at night and it was the first time that I had ever ridden a horse, I just forgot."

"Well where did you meet him?"

"In the library."

"Library?"

"From how the librarian was talking to him it seemed that he was spending the night in one of the rooms there."

"We should go see him after church," "I'm dying to see what he's really like."

"Oh, I can't,"

"Why not?"

"Suzy's wedding," she sighed, "I have to go and help prepare."

"Oh gees," "Well we'll go see him anyways, just to get his last name." She laughed. "Then we'll see you there. Who, knows we could bring him along."

The library was far rowdier today than the other days. Iroi had been so rushed with requests that he had drawn up the courage to get Kaos helping file the returns on the shelves as he helped the people find books.

"Now here another cart," Iroi rolled him a bin full of books.

"Another?" Kaos stared at the bin. "I swear you never used to get so many customers when I was here last."

"Oh, just stop complaining, you're getting free house and board, the least you could do it help me file books here and there."

"This is more than here and there," Kaos said under his breath and picked up the first book and wheeled the cart down the hallway. The doorbell rang for the fifth time and three girls filed in with shopping bags over their shoulders. The tallest put down her bags and took out a small crinkled piece of paper, "Yep, this is the place." She said and looked around.

"I never knew that libraries could be so crowded." She said as people filed by her.

"I think some of these people have to learn about Television." One said with a high and city-girl slang talk.

"Quiet, we're here to acquire not accuse. Let's just ask someone who works here to see if they know a Kaos."

"Oh, that man over there looks like a librarian go ask him-" she started saying but the other put a hand on her shoulder and quietly said.

"I don't think we need to ask," she said in awe and then pointed to Kaos shoving a book on a shelf down the hall.

"Holy crap!" tall one exasperated, "That's him." She sat down and watched him as he shoved yet another book on the shelf. "He is really cute."

"But why would he be working in a library?"

"Maybe he has to pay for room and board?"

"It doesn't matter if he's poor or not, he's hot. Anyways that's not your average librarian."

"You got that right,"

"Well, are we going to sit here and admire him from a far or are we going to take action. We promised Enna that we would get a last name. So Chearie, just go over there and introduce yourself or something, ask for a book and see if he has it."

"Me?"

"Yes, you're the one who said that you liked guys with silver hair, well?"

"Fine." She got up and walked down the hallway as Kaos turned a corner. She flipped and around and ran into him as he came out. He caught her by the shoulders.

"Sorry," she said. She blushed and got back up.

"No, really its my fault," he said and turned to the cart. Chearie stuck out her hand.

"My names Chearie While, You-,"

"Pleasure to meet you, Chearie," he said and turned. Chearie was confused he was supposed to be a gentleman and say his full name back.

"I need to find a book," she said to him. However, he continued to turn.

"I'm no librarian go ask Iori, he's the old man behind the counter up there, you really can't miss him." Kaos exclaimed in a haphazard tone, as he waved and pushed the cart down the hall. Chearie was not about to give up. She stomped past the cart and turned about-face to block his path.

"Can't *you* help me?" she said and grabbed the other side of his cart.

"Sorry, I can't" he said with a sharp tongue leaning over the basket to get in her face.

"Come on," she said begging. "If you can put them away you should be able to find one."

"If you know the author just look alphabetically their last name." He said to her frankly.

"Thank you…" she started hoping that he would say his name.

"You're welcome," Kaos said and left her. Her face went in shock and then she flipped around.

"I need to find a non-fiction book," she said with horror.

"Just go ask Iori. " Kaos said getting uncomfortable and rather irritated. Figures that first person that he ends up having to talk to is a total ditz.

"You're putting books away. Why wouldn't you know?"

"I'm doing this because Iori wants me to. Okay, it's not my job to help you find books in this huge place." Kaos said clearly. He quickly grabbed the chart and wheeled it past her.

"So you *can* help me!"

"You know what? Fine. I'll help you." Kaos let go of the chart. "What are you looking for?"

"Um…" she said. She did not know what to say, "I'm looking for…the history of Thieves." She laughed remembering her project her father had requested her to do.

"Can you be a little more specific?"

"Specific?" she said and gave an expression of surprise on her face.

"Like what time period?" Kaos hinted.

"Mythological," her lips moved slowly enunciating. She couldn't think of anything else."

"Gees," Kaos rubbed his head. He stopped, "Fine." He said and walked away from the cart. Chearie sighed with relief and followed him. They walked down the hallway quickly, and Kaos didn't slow for Chearie to catch up.

"So, how long have you worked here?"

"As I said, I don't work here. Iori's an old friend I'm doing this so I can make up for him giving me free room and board." Kaos turned "Here, you go all the books on this side are about the mythological state of Thieves." Chearie walked to a shelf and took out a book.

"But these are all in elfish," she stared at the pages, "I can't read elfish."

"God, damn it!" Kaos cursed under his breath. "You-"

"Oh," she stared at the page closer, "Could you read this, I think it would help." She shoved the book in Kaos' hands, quickly stood next to him, peered over his shoulder with a smile. "That's one," she pointed to the middle of the page:

"Ἱτ τακεσ τηε ποισον βαχκ το τηε νεστ ανδ κιλλσ τηεμ ωη ερε τηεψ λιϖε– (t takes the poison back to the nest and kills them where they live)" Kaos read the elvish but was cut off when suddenly the girl moved towards him and he slammed his body back against the bookshelf out of fright. She smiled at him with an awkward glance. A book falls down from the high shelf and lands nearby.

"I think we both know that we're not here to find any books." She stared at him and fluttered her eyes. She moved her face closed to his and closed her eyes. Her lips hovered just in front of his - suddenly the gears in Kaos' head moved. He pushed back and pushed her away. She stumbled on the floor. He wiped his lips and yelled.

"What was that?" He narrowed his eyes at her, "I don't even know you! Don't you dare try a kiss me!" Kaos stood fixed.

"Kaos?" she said quietly. Kaos' temper rose as he heard his name.

"Get Out!" he yelled, "How the hell you know my name, I don't know, I don't care!" He glared at her, "Get the fuck out!" He was panicking now. The fact that she knew his name scared him half to death, was she part of Dartawg's army, a spy? "Do you hear me?" Iori floated down the aisle and found the two, Kaos raging, Chearie quite frightened.

"Kaos don't make another move!" He yelled at Kaos, went up to him, and grabbed his wrists. With force, he pulled them down and twisted Kaos' wrists. "Don't ever hurt a woman!"

"She knows my name," Kaos mumbled in pain, "I never told her it." He let him go and turned to Chearie.

"My dear," he said, "Do you know this boy's name?"

"Kaos?"

"Where did you learn it?" He said with worry.

"Enna, Enna told me she got a ride home last night with a boy named Kaos." Chearie said, "I'm sorry," she said, "I came here to see if Kaos was all that she said he was." She said with a discerned heart, "Don't hate Enna because of what I did." Chearie said staring at Kaos, "I simply came here to find out your last name, but I got a little carried away."

"Chearie, I think you should leave," Iori said.

"Serves you right," Kaos mumbled rubbing his lips again.

"Kaos!" Iori turned on him.

"She tried to kiss me!" Kaos yelled at him.

"Kaos, go to your room," he said defiantly. Kaos glared at him once more in the eyes and then stomped out of the hallway."

"Did you try to kiss him without his consent?"

"Yes," she said and shrunk against the walls.

"Will you promise me something?" Iori said. She looked up at him. "I know Enna well, if she wants to know Kaos' last name it is Bernidict. But next time, for Kaos' sake, have her come and ask. He is not one who trusts everyone he meets." She smiled at him.

"Thank you," she said. She walked back to the front. The two other girls sat worried and they showed it with their expressions. Yet, immediately when she saw them she put on a smile and did a thumbs-up.

"His full name is Kaos Bernidict." She said with glory. The girls sat in a little circle.

"What took you so long, we were getting worried."

"I'll just say this:" she smiled, "I wish I had found him first. Then I wouldn't have to have been so pushy."

"So, learn anything else?"

"He staying here for free, Enna was right."

"You only learned that!"

"Well, he can speak and read elfish." She put a finger on her chin. "God, he's got the dreamiest accent I've heard!' she exclaimed her eyes sparkling. One grabbed her shoulder and shock her from her daze.

"What did you learn?"

"He was rather reluctant to give me any information. I practically had to beat it out of him."

The book cart still lay in the middle of the hallway where Kaos had dropped it. Iori walked up to it and brought it back over to the counter.

A rat was he. A trapped rat. Unbelievable was his story, trapped in a maze with only one path to take. It was useless to look for another, but he kept searching for it. Happiness laid at its entrance and hatred the exit. The maze has to have a week point the point of neutral emotion, in mid-maze he would find a way to blank out of this existence. He walked to the back of the library and used the door to leave it. He walked out in the open ally and into the small barn.

The more he thought about his life the more he hated it. He didn't believe in Ebony's ways, but Dartawg wasn't any better. Stirring was right. A republic would be weak and soon turn into an aristocracy; he, a Prince of Ebony, was the next in line to receive the power as an emperor. He didn't want the power of an emperor. He didn't want anything to do with it. He wanted to simply be, be what he wanted. Do what he wanted to do, when he wanted to do it. Getting caught up in politics would just add more hassle in his life and slow him down.

His white hair blew in the wind rolling across the plains looking at the scene of impeccable beauty. Splendor of the moment caught him and he let the wind blow on his face and lift his hair behind him. He closed his eyes and tilted his head up at star of Thieves. He opened his eyes and watch a red balloon float up to the stone ceiling. With surprise, he looked down and found Enna's house littered with balloons. The green tents pulled back and kids ran across the fields. He sat firmly on top of the pinto and gazed at them with a smile. Whatever it was, it hit him like a doornail. He clicked his tongue and twice and headed down the hill. The pinto was tall in the fenced in passageways. As he neared the house, he grew a little nervous. Should he really go into such a populated place without any kind of disguise? The corner at which he turned left was a small canopy. He stopped before it and got off the pinto. The place was filled with kids and women. Father's had gathered off somewhere he was sure. The canopy was dark green and a man sat down underneath it. Kaos just walked off in the crowed.

"Hey, young man!" a man's voice called out to him. The jolly voice came from desk. Kaos walked over a little befuddled. "You look lost, need help?" Kaos laughed.

"Yeah, do you know where Enna is?"

"Enna Berk?"

"Well," Kaos paused, "yes." He said at last.

"She's somewhere," he laughed, "She was walking around with her friends the last time I saw her. Why do you need to see her?" Kaos paused.

"I just wanted to talk to her," Kaos said to the man.

"Your name is..."

"Kaos,"

"Kaos..." he signaled for a last name.

"Bernidict." Kaos said.

"Well, Kaos Bernidict, if I see her I'll tell her you're looking for her."

"Thank you," he said and walked off into the crowd.

Enna wore a white spaghetti silk dress, with blue ribbon accents. Baby blue ribbons were braided into her hair. Her counterparts were dressed just as well, but different colors.

"Oh, Enna," the man sitting down underneath the reception table yelled to her, waving a hand for her to come. Enna, who was in the middle of all the commotion, turned towards the man and smiled. Like she led the entire group, they all turned around and watched him. "A boy named Kaos Bernidict. He came by just recently, he wanted to talk to you." He said smiling at her and winked.

"Ooo," one of the girl's to her right said. "He came by to talk."

"Shut up," she snapped at her blushing. "Thank you." She said and turned back to her friends. The five of them all huddled in a group.

"Does someone have a crush that she didn't tell us about?" the fourth girl said. (She hadn't gone into the library.)

"Yes, and I don't blame her," Chearie said and knocked Enna in the side.

"You've met him!"

"He's quite cute."

"Considering what you did to him yesterday, I'm surprised that he would even come a talk to me."

"Whoa, what happened yesterday?"

"Well, Chearie, Claire, and Uxoi. Went to find out more about him yesterday at the library."

"Library?"

"Don't worry about it, he's no librarian."

"He's a magician!" one of them commented.

"Well anyways, it turns out that they were a little pushy and got kicked out of the library."

"A Magician?" She exclaimed. "Really- what am I saying? Let's get down to the real point. You should find him. He could be your date for your sister's wedding."

"My date?"

"Hey, all of us have one and it's not even our sister's wedding."

"And anyways, it's not too personal an occasion all he needs to do is write his name down next to yours on a sheet."

"But I've known him for only a day!"

"You said that it felt like you knew him for more," Chearie commented.

"But that was-"

"Come on," the girls smiled. "Claire, Uxoi, Chearie, spilt up since you all know what he looks like. Enna and I will do our own search. In fifteen minutes come back here, even if you found him."

"Guys, this is absurd!"

"You're seventeen honey and there's a eligible guy who's looking for you? I'd take him in a heartbeat if I wasn't already hooked up." Chearie commented. "Let's go." The girls split up.

Kaos had walked around so much he was so bored, he should have just not come at all. Meanwhile Iori was probably searching for him, worried to death that he was kidnapped or something. Kaos walked up to the balcony on the far side of their house, which had been opened up to the public. The large balcony was empty, all but a company of a couple which sat in the back corner. Trees shaded it and the stone was gorgeous. It hung over in an arch a path way to the back pastures. Kaos stared out over the fields in thought.

The girl was pulling Enna quickly; they ran along the stone pathway, dodging people.

"Wait, Saria!" Enna said like a whisper as she stared upwards.

"What is it?" She said and stood next to her.

"That's him," Enna said as she pointed up at Kaos who was still on the balcony. Saria smiled and pulled her away.

"Its perfect, let's go talk to him silly."

"What about meeting them back in the tent?"

"Oh, who cares," "We wanted you to talk to him so you go talk to him and I'll run back and tell them that you found him." They went inside and up the stairs. The door onto the balcony was a double and white paned. Enna stared out and watched him. Saria stared at her, at him, and then back.

"That's defiantly a crush." She laughed, "Now go," she pushed her friend onto the balcony and closed the door behind her. With her hands nervously fidgeting in front of her, she managed to say:

"Kaos?" her voice was sweat. Kaos flipped around in surprise.

"Oh, Enna," he panted, "You scared me."

"I'm sure not as much as my friends, Sorry," she said and walked up to the balcony banister next to him. He smiled warmly.

"It's alright," he said and rubbed the back of his neck. "With random people coming to visit me, I figured I should come and ask you up front. What did you want to talk to me about?"

"Well…" she paused. She wanted to get engaged, right then and there, but Kaos wasn't about to propose. "I was wondering if well what your last name was."

"Bernidict. If you really wanted to know, you should have just asked." He laughed ending the awkward silence.

"I didn't ask them to go and interrogate you," Enna shook her head in emphasis.

"It's alright, just next time…" Kaos stared over her shoulder at the girl at the door. She quickly moved.

"This might seem a little awkward, but Kaos, would you be my date to my sister's wedding?" she bit her lip. Kaos stared at her with some shock. "I know it's rather sudden," she said.

"You know what?" he laughed, "Why not?" he smiled. "I'm already in enough trouble as it is."

"Really?" she asked him second-guessing his action.

"I would much rather attend a party than go help Iori stack books. But do you really think that I'm fit for a wedding?" Kaos laughed.

"We can find you something to wear, my family has enough clothes." She smiled at him, and he returned it. "Oh, I have to introduce you to everyone!" she smiled suddenly and pulled him out. He stopped placing his feet down firmly, "Could you tell me your last name?"

"Oh, gees, I'm sorry. It's Berk." He smiled.

"Then let us go." He laughed and walked next to her. She couldn't help but smile and blush a little. He laughed some more when she did as he looked down at her slightly. "First, you should meet the rest of my friends." She said, "I know you've met Chearie, but there are three more people you should know." The two walked off into the room inside. It was crowded with people, but they went by them, receiving a few smiles from guests. They walked down the stone gateway in full conversation.

"So, it's your sister's wedding?"

"Yes, how did you know?" Kaos didn't even know why. He had certainty that he was right, yet didn't know where it came from.

"Just an intuition," Kaos laughed, brushing off the uneasy feeling he got from it. Somehow, he was able to read her mind or something. How? When?

"You better not be using any of the magic or stuff to read my mind." She said back to him with a smile.

"Trust me, if I do, it's not intentional."

"Intentional?" she questioned. "Why would you do it by accident?"

"Magic isn't just something that is controllable," Kaos laughed in embarrassment, "We can try and make it do certain things, but some things in life are just magical all together."

"I don't quite understand."

"People who finish each other's sentences off," he laughed, "friendship, the love in a first kiss." Kaos laughed, "Its all magic," he said. She stared at him with integument.

"Oh, Enna," a girl ran up to her side, a few more followed. They huddled nearby and quickly scurried her away to the other side of the path. Kaos eyed them, as every now and again he would be stared at.

"So..." Claire said.

"Did you ask him to be your date?"

"Yes,"

"Yes! What did he say?"

"Yes," she said blushing. They all picked their heads up and stared at him. Jumping over to him in a burst of joy, they stood admiring him. He got a little flustered and blushed a little.

"Hello?" he said, "Am I supposed to know all of you?"

"These four ladies are my friends," Enna commented from behind the group.

"I hope so, otherwise they're all stalkers." Kaos commented, "Weren't you three in the library?"

"Claire," the girl on the far left said.

"Uxoi," the girl nest to her said, moving right.

"Chearie, nice to see ya again." She winked and smiled, Kaos gave her a look.

"Saria," the last one said.

"And your name is?" Saria asked him.

"Kaos," he said plainly.

"Nice to meet you Kaos." Claire stuck a hand out and her met it out of kindness. "We hear that you're Enna's date." She said with a finger on her chin and an eyebrow raised. "Do you really think that you can go looking like that?"

"No-" Kaos said but his shirt was quickly grabbed by the girl's hand and he was being dragged and herded away from the crowds. Enna watched them as they went laughing a little. They ran inside a house, to a brick house with a white door and they stopped just inside. "Okay," he said with dignity and stood fixed, "And you dragged me here because?" he hinted with some anger.

"Well, you need some proper clothes." Claire said. She walked over to him and with a kind voice said. "Come with me, for a moment." She grabbed his arm and walked him into another room. Kaos saw that the room was filled with men chatting around by a snack table. Kaos grit his teeth as they neared a group.

"Father?" Claire said plainly. A man turned around and stared at her with a smile.

"Yes, dear."

"I would like you to meet Kaos," she said and suavely introduced him.

"Pleasure to meet you," Kaos said, not wanting to be impolite he took his hand and smiled.

"He's Enna's date for tonight, and he doesn't have anything to wear for the wedding." She said.

"You don't?" he stared awkwardly at Kaos.

"Sorry sir," Kaos bowed his head slightly. It was a gesture that he often did to Charad's father when he did something wrong or faltered.

"Well, I'm sure we could find something for you to wear." He said smiling, especially if your Enna's date." He smiled at him. "Here, come with me." He put an arm around Kaos' shoulders and slightly dragged him into another room.

"I can tell you're not from around here," he said quietly as he closed the sliding doors. The room was now empty and the lights were almost completely off. "Where is your home town?"

"In the Patella Triangle," Kaos commented.

"Where the Scarrows flew over the walls of Ebony and took down the Raging Rebel Fleet that could have taken the north." He commented.

"Were you in the army?" Kaos asked him.

"Me?" he whispered, "Yes, I was in a small army, the Surgaraessa. It was our job to monitor the wall. It's a very peaceful countryside," the man smiled at him.

"During that time it wasn't so," Kaos smiled.

"Have you lived there all your life?"

"Yes," Kaos laughed. He wanted to say from the day he was born, but his mother was Marina, so he didn't quite know what to say. "Ever since I can remember."

"How old are you?" he asked his eyes peeled on Kaos.

"I'm seventeen right now," Kaos laughed, "Yet in a week or two I'll be eighteen."

"When's your birthday?"

"October 17," Kaos told him.

"My, only 2 weeks!" He said with shock, "Are you excited?"

"No, not really," Kaos said gloomily.

"How come?"

"I haven't seen my family in three months, I've traipsed everywhere else."

"Why are you in Thieves?" Kaos had to stop before he said anything. He needed a good excuse, but he hated lying.

"I'm an apprentice," Kaos said Daragon's order finally coming into his mind.

"Apprentice, a magician's apprentice?" he said shocked and stared at Kaos with some puzzlement.

"Yes," Kaos confirmed, hoping to force it to end at that.

"Whose?"

"General Daragon's,"

"That would explain something," the man laughed.

"Explain what?" Kaos asked.

"The earring in your left ear," he said. "You are a high ranking officer in the army...if Daragon... then the Wakita, I presume," he said with some doubt, Kaos stared at him with some shock. "Am I right?" Kaos stared at him.

"Yes," he said.

"Well, I'm honored to have someone like you in my presence he said. I was just a measly solider." Kaos walked over and bowed down before him.

"But I honor that fact that you stepped on the battle field and saved my home town." He said.

"Northerner, your customs are appreciated, but lighten up and relax a little." He smiled and patted Kaos on the head, "There is no need to bow General." Kaos got up. "You seem quite young for any General that I've ever worked under, but for your age you are wise beyond your years. So I honor that and we are even."

"Thank you sir," Kaos commented with a smile.

"When did you meet Enna, Kaos?"

"I gave her a ride home last night, and I just stopped by to see her again." Kaos laughed.

"You never planned to become a part of a wedding," the man laughed.

"You're right," Kaos rubbed the back of his neck.

"There was a rumor about Enna falling head over heels for a magician boy with silver hair." He laughed, "I can imagine that you must be he."

"I guess so," Kaos smiled awkwardly.

"Well, son, shall we got a get you fitted for a suite?"

"A suite?" Kaos said, "No, you don't have to do that. I can't ask you to make a new suit for me..."

"I insist." He said, "It is the least I can do." He said quietly, "I'm not a poor man. I want everyone to look perfect on my son's wedding day." He didn't take no for an answer and quickly brought Kaos into another room. "Riory," he said with a smile. A plump woman wrenched her head up from a ball of fabric and stared at them.

"Yes, Master," she said wearily put tried to put on a decent face.

"Could you make a suit for this young man, for the wedding tonight. He's Enna's date."

"Oh, Enna," she said and her mood immediately changed, "Certainly, she is quite a nice girl." She smiled and moved about a small circle of tables and found a tap measure. She walked up to Kaos and smiled. The man moved to the other side of the room and waited. "Lift up your arms." She said so and did more measurements. "So what is your name?"

"Kaos," he said.

"Kaos?" She repeated and busily did more measurements taking the occasional minutes to stop and turn to the table to write down numbers. She drew the tap from his waist down to the floor. "You can put your arms down now," she laughed as she turned down and took the last measurements. "All done."

"Thank you," he did a little head bow.

"You are quite tall," she said, "Taller, than most boys your age." She said to Kaos, and then turned to the man in the other side of the room, "I'll have it ready by seven."

"Fine." He said, "Kaos you are free to go wherever you like, meet me back here at six."

"Okay, thanks for guiding me through this." Kaos laughed.

"No problem at all," he turned, "And Kaos, don't be late, its three now." Kaos' eyes fell on the clock. Time had flew. Last time he had checked it was only noon. Kaos walked outside. The streets had grown in population as those who had gone eating were soon. He walked slowly, not knowing anyone nearby and not knowing what to do either. His glance fell on behind all the commotion to a field, its gates wide open. Two horses strode through them in a slow walk and headed into the forest. Kaos slightly ran back to the pinto where he had tied her up. He undid her and hopped on her back.

"Boy, did you find her?" The man behind the table asked him once more. Kaos shocked to see him eyed him from atop the pinto.

"Oh," Kaos laughed at his own fright. "Yeah, I found her."

"So…" he said leading the question on. Kaos felt a little awkward talking to the man about it so he simply got the pinto into a walking mode.

"I'll see ya later, then," Kaos eyes him as he walked past the tent. The man had a wide grin on as he watched Kaos leave. When he did, he turned around.

"Score," he pulled his forearm back in glee. Kaos was a little bit nervous because of the man's response. Yet, he just walked down the dirt path towards the gate.

"Halt," a man wearing armor stepped in front of Kaos. Kaos peered around the pinto's massive head with a rather perplexed look on his face.

"What?" He said.

"No, one is allowed into the forest at this time." Another man stepped forward holding a staff.

"I just saw two people enter it just now?" Kaos said his finger pointed lazily up the path.

"No one can enter," he said.

"Come on," Kaos whined. "Don't make me go all the way around!" He acted as though he was using the forest path as a shortcut. "Come on, won't you just let me through."

"No one attending the party can enter!" The man shouted at Kaos.

"Party?" Kaos lied, rather well, "I'm just passing through." He said pretending to be befuddled.

"Passing through?"

"Yeah, so could you just let me though so I don't have to walk all the way around the forest?" Kaos pleaded.

"Well," he put a finger on his chin, "What do you think?"

"Fine, young man, you may enter." He said, "But if it turns out you're lying you're going to face my wrath." It wasn't much of a threat to Kaos but he bowed his head, "Thank you, sirs."

"Yeah, you're not from around here," one whispered as Kaos walked by. The difference between a lie and the truth is the simple matter of if you are caught. Sure, you can lie, but no one knows that it's a lie until someone proves you otherwise. Therefore, in someway, fantasy can be fact until it is proven impossible. Dreams can be the future until they are the present. Kaos thought as he walked into the forest. The trees mostly condensed pines and soft needles of clay brown made a good muffler of the hooves of the pinto. Kaos smiled. The forest was much cooler. The needles made a soft glow beneath their canopy and the haze added by the smell of pine and sap made the place irresistible. The forest was old, old and mysterious. Filled with animals untamed and unharmed: its ecosystem intact to the very last mushroom. Kaos walked the path and stopped. To his right just behind a huge tree trunk, behind a door of loose and moveable vines was a stone. Kaos with interest got off the pinto and walked up to side of the path. With a delicate hand, he moved aside the vines and walked behind the tree. A rock slab, with three gems and a handprint just below. Kaos in thought, subconsciously his hand grew towards the handprint as though it wanted to fall upon the engraved stone. With a jolt, and realizing what was happening Kaos drew his hand back and shook his head a little. He grabbed his wrist in his other hand and stared at it.

"Help!" a woman's voice met his ears. Kaos looked up in shock, then befuddlement, of if he heard anything at all. When it sounded again, he got up and stood in the middle of the road, the pinto's reigns in his hand. He looked down both sides of the path, until he heard it a third time, now with a large *thump* after it. Kaos got on the pinto, and waited for it again. With a little uneasiness of what he would find Kaos followed the yells and thumps until he saw it. A young woman raced across a foyer, a short stubby creature lingered slowly with bloody claws, arching back, bony, his head short and blood shot eyes grazed upon the woman in sheer murderous nature. The woman back up against the small bench standing grasping onto it hoping that maybe it wound spring to life a save her. Kaos looked quickly down searching perhaps for something that he could use to throw at it. His hands fell on a log. A short, but five-inch-in-diameter log. Grabbing it in two hands, he charged from the bushes straight up to the thing. With a yell, he swung downwards on the thing. As it hit the stone floor, it cracked and stone unleveled and deformed under the pressure. To full of adrenalin, Kaos didn't notice but looked up to find the creature perched now on a nearby boulder staring down at him.

"Now, now," it said in a dingy voice, "another soul dare to ruin my love for vengeance." He sneered at Kaos and crawled along the face of the rock like a frog. "Pretty must me my dessert." He jumped and lunged at Kaos. Its nails grew nearly double in size as he neared Kaos.

Locking his knuckles, he swiped them horizontal at Kaos. Kaos' eyes popped he jumped back, but the thing came back for more. He swiped with his right hand, missed, then with his left. A rhythmic patterned got Kaos in a momentum. Suddenly the left jab came to soon Kaos slammed forth on the ground four parallel gashes on his body. Kaos' eyes closed. His impact had cracked the stone below him. His breath was knocked out of him, yet soon he panted. He opened his eyes as the thing lunged forward aiming for his neck. Kaos whispered a few words a white bubble extended from his body and pushed the thing back. Kaos slowly got up, his chest drenched in blood.

"Boy," the woman said behind him. Kaos didn't care. Kaos glared at the thing. At this point, his only goal was to kill that thing. To smash in into tiny bits.

"Wizard, do ye dare conjure up more trouble?" it hissed at him and nursed its hand. Kaos put a smirk on his face, stuck a hand up and gathered light in his palm.

"Let's go nymph," Kaos said still panting. The thing lunged at him he threw two balls of light at the thing; it quickly dodged the first but was hit by the next. Stunned but not damaged he fell to the ground. Kaos ran up to it and jumped on it. It cringed once on first impact then met Kaos' eyes and smiled. Kaos flipped back. He didn't know what else to do…he could. It clicked in his mind. He could use the spell…

"You're a fool," he said. Kaos closed his eyes and slammed his fists together.

"Slayer's   sacristies,
πονο μενδαμ χαστι, περφυνδο ρεχτυε πεχχατυμ χαστι
(Slayer's Sacristies: I place fault in the faultless, drench sin directly on the sinless/ pono mendam casti, perfundo rectue peccatum casti.) Kaos exclaimed the words. The nymph's eyes widened. Kaos' body rose and glowed an eerie black. The raging black fire roared into his hands as it had done when he first used the spell. He held his palm towards the nymph who sat stunned. "χαδετε (Fall!/Cadete)" The fire immediately sprang up at the nymph's feet. Kaos stared at him as he wailed in pain. Soon enough he slowed and fell on the ground, his body still burning. Kaos held the flames and just stared. The fire burnt out on his hands and he sighed as he fell to his knees. He was drenched in blood and too weak to move much. He knelt on the ground. The

woman who was standing behind him ran past him. She stopped near the edge of the platform and knelt down.

"Oh, hold on," she whispered kneeling over a man, who bled all over. Kaos on eye squinting watched the two of them. She tore some of her dress and wiped his forehead. Kaos rose and stumbled over to them. She didn't look up at him until he said something.

"Let me heal him," Kaos said quietly, "I'll use what manna I have left to help him." Kaos whispered to her. She stared at him in some shock, and then nodded. Kaos put his hand on the man's chest, it glowed a white. He sat there for a few minutes, slowly feeling his body grow weaker and weaker as the manna drained from his body. The cuts stopped bleeding and slowly they came together, healing before their very eyes. Kaos' vision was poor now, the man on the ground swayed in his eyes. Kaos, though in pain brought his other hand down next to him to hold his position steady. He could feel the magic ending; he met the end and fell down on the stone unable to keep himself steady. His hand slid off the man's chest as he fell to the side. The man's eyes opened as his slowed and he sat up. He looked at his hands in astonishment, no scars or cuts, just dry blood. He then looked at the woman whose tears turn to joy. She hugged him. The man turned around and saw Kaos sprawled on the ground, bleeding and panting. Kaos was now semi-conscious; his vision was dark all he could feel was his body. Pressure on his arms and legs occurred as the man picked Kaos up. His shirt was torn off and he felt a large once of pain fill him as a bandage was tied tightly around the gashes in his chest. He cringed and snatched the man's arm with an entire hand. He couldn't control his body; it just did what it did. He gripped harder when the bandage was tightened. Slowly he just let go and lay in the man's arms. He then was placed in a saddle; someone got in behind him and held him upright. Every moment of the horse shot through his body, made him cringe and nearly fall. They rode for a short period of time, when finally Kaos heard the voices of the two spear-carriers at the gate he had entered.

"Close the gates to the forest, they aren't safe enough for anyone." The woman's voice yelled from behind him.

"Ah," they gasped. There was a clanging and the gate must have closed. The horses moved swiftly up to the house and under the archway.

"Father!" the man yelled the horses came to a halt and gates opened. There were footsteps running towards them.

"Oh my word," the came to us, "Get the boy down here." They yelled. There was movement all around Kaos. Suddenly he felt his body being lifted down onto a stretcher. "Bring him inside and get a doctor as soon as possible." Another yelled. Kaos' stretcher must have been moving swiftly his body jumped up and down a little. Everything stopped and he was heaved onto another bed.

"Where is he?" A door swung open. In addition, a man's voice came nearby, "Nurse, get that cloth off him." He turned, "What happened?"

"He saved me from a forest nymph," the woman said. "He burnt the thing, but got scared in the process. Then he was healing my fiancé when he just all of a sudden collapsed and he hasn't awakened since."

"How did he create the fire to burn the nymph?"

"He's a wizard," she mumbled, "He cast a spell, incantation, something like that."

"Get me some alcohol, a needle and some surgical string." Kaos groaned and slammed a fist down on the bed. The man jumped. Soon Kaos found the cuts stinging far more than before as a cool liquid was poured into them. A towel, something patted them dry. Then he was stitched up. They wrapped gauze around his body. Kaos lay in the bed, panting still his body weak.

"Can't you do more?" The woman asked her.

"What he's suffering from is a sever-lack of manna," she said.

"Manna?"

"Manna is the magic everything living thing needs to live on." He said defiantly "This boy has just enough to keep his body alive. He probably can't see at this point, even though his eyes are open. The problem with sorcerers is they're so arrogant that they end up using too much of their manna and end up in such a state. There is nothing I can do to restore manna, his body just has to build it up on his own."

"How long till that happens?' she asked him.

"It fluctuates between the individual, if we keep him quiet for two hours or so he might build up enough to see and speak."

"I feel so horrible," the woman said, "He used all his strength to save my fiancé and I; but there's nothing I can do for him."

"Don't fret, be thankful that he stumbled by. Your wedding is tonight, is it not?"

"Yes," she said quietly. "But,"

"Don't worry about me," Kaos said quietly and hoarsely on the bed. He coughed, "I've lived through worse."

"You're able to talk!" The man turned around and looked at him on the bed. He rose and walked over to Kaos. He waved his hands in front of Kaos' eyes. "Can you see that?"

"I see the blur," Kaos said.

"Good. Could you tell me your name?"

"Kaos," he said.

"Good, how old are you?"

"Seventeen," Kaos said.

"Now, just relax and rest a little. You're safe, so don't worry." The doctor said. "Suzanne, let's let Kaos rest a little, we can talk outside." He walked up to her and lead her out the rooms door, it sounded like. His hand was on her shoulder. There were footsteps running down the hall.

"Is everyone alright," a man approached the doctor worried, "Oh, Suzy you're alright," he hugged woman and released her. "Oh, is Frederic alright?" eh said worried.

"He's fine father," she said.

"Oh, I'm so glad," he hugged her once more.

"I heard about the nymph; how did you escape?"

"A magician named Kaos, saved me, and then healed Fredric."

"Kaos?" he said shocked.

"You know him?"

"Yes, he's Enna's date," He said with shock. "Where is he?"

"The boy has a number of gashes on his chest I had to sew up. He's recovering in that room." The doctor said.

"Is he alright?"

"He'll be just fine, with some rest." He smiled.

"Ah, that's great." He said, "Suzy, you have to go get ready for the wedding, come with me." He grabbed around her shoulders. "I'll tell Enna about Kaos, you go get ready for your big day." He smiled and gave her a slight push down the hallway.

Kaos coughed hoarsely, the back of his neck stung. "I can't believe I used it again, that same spell." Kaos sighed and closed his eyes. Deep in slumber, nothing but his family came to him. His vision zoomed on his house, yet, not the house that he knew of it when he left. Something had seemed to pass there long ago, up and left what stood now before him. Windows broken and shattered doors knocked in, and dust laden the scene. It was as though its own very character represented his past.

Kaos walked through the empty corridors; there was no one waiting for him to come home. Now eyes peered around the corners and stared at him. Desolate, and feeling now quarries of being watched upon he went further on. He entered his living room. He walked to the center of it and slowly with sparks of light furniture was back in its place, mirrors and old paintings. The fireplace had logs burning it and pictures were on the fireplace. Kaos walked up to the fire and put his hands out to it. Nothing, his hands remained numb to any true feeling. Among the many arrayed pictures, Kaos picked out one that he didn't really remember. It wasn't a family photo and one that Kaos didn't remember taking part of, but it was of him and Marina. He had an elbow around her neck smiling in laughter and she shown a smile too. He put the photo down among the main more and looked at them. He thought another awkward. He picked it up in its old fashioned frame. A family photo that was photographed by a lake. He looked at Tako, Sharle, and John. They all had aged. Tako was looking more like John had grown several inches was standing next to Kaos, although he still was a few inches short. John whose hair was thinning and his face more wrinkly sat on a box below. Sharle's hair was streaking with gray but her face was as rosy as ever. Kaos fell upon himself. His reflection hadn't changed a bit. He looked much like he did now.

Yet, a third picture, this one he remembered: A July day in town. In the middle of the celebration Kaos, Tako, and a bunch of Kaos' friends had gone away from the group to play with some paintball guns. Kaos naturally, as any brother should, made it a point not to be on the same team as his little brother. He snagged Charad seeing he was Kaos' closest friend; Tenkin, who was a muscular boy with good aim, but not much else; and Phao, or 'the speed demon' as he was referred to during that game. Tako wasn't much of a leader like Kaos, so he was simply part of the team. Anyways, Clide, had a natural rivalry against Kaos and clearly took a hold of the other team wanting badly to whip it in Kaos' face. The two had competed against each other ever since they were kids, whether archery, soccer, stick ball, even tic-tac-toe. Clide pulled together three other boys, seeing as there was an odd number: Keinda, who was a year older than Kaos was probably the strongest player out of all of them; then there was Duku, the rather 'skittish' Duku, who was nearly dead frightened of Kaos. Now, that was all because of a certain shot Kaos took on the boy that day. Last, but not least, Kargo, who was Tenkin's cousin, though you couldn't tell.

The picture was taken at the end of course. All of them with rainbow colored paint blotches all over their bodies. In the middle Clyde and Keinda were back-to-back; posed. Clyde held his gun vertically and smirked. Keinda, though in the picture you could hardly see, had brought his gun slowly to Clyde's side and was resting his finger on the trigger with a smile. Phao on Keinda's side was sniggering at him. Next to Phao were Kaos and Tako. Kaos smacked on the cheek with a blue dot, held onto the barrel of his gun and had an arm around Tako's shoulders. Tako had a look of cringing on his face out of the sores on his body. On the far side, Duku and Kargo had jumped into the picture, in it still mid-air. Kaos' mom had come fetch them that afternoon had taken the pictures. Kaos remembers some nicer ones, but remembered that this was the funniest moment. Well, actually, the funniest moment was when Keinda pulled the trigger on Clide, but for that they all ended up cleaning up the festival. In his dream, Kaos put down the frame. The dream went on, as dreams always do. The pigments of his imagination played with his eyes until he knew neither what nor when everything had truly taken place.

Slowly threads of reality kicked in and he opened his eyes to the unfamiliar ceiling of his consciousness. The clarity in his eyes was refreshing and showed that his room was quite dark. Shades of black, blue, and gray, browns and pea-greens were thrown astray, with his motions as the snow from outside-reflected touch light from outside. He sat up in his bed. His chest bandaged heavily, restricted his movement. He put a hand on his chest,

"Should I?" he asked himself whether he should test his manna to see if he could heal the wound on his chest, but thought less of it. The last thing he would want to do was fall back in bed helpless once more.

He sighed. Just then colored light shown through the window, Kaos crawled towards the window and look outside onto the fields, where the wedding ceremony appeared to be taking place. Fireworks sprang from the horizon as love blossomed between Suzy and Friedrich. Their lips locked in a kiss. When done, they stared at each other. The crowd roared with glee and rice was thrown up into the air. The Dawning sun rose on the horizon and made the entire area sparkle with falling, glittering, rice.

Suzy and Friedrich hand and hand turned towards the crowd. The Priest stood behind them.

"I present to you, Mr. and Mrs. Cunningham!" he smiled. The two stared at each other with embarrassment, but glee. Kaos with shock immediately got out of the bed and scurried down the hallway. Following his ears, he opened a door underneath the archway. He peered around the door and saw Suzy and Fredrick making there way down the isle greet a few people. He stepped out from behind the door and watched them.

"Congratulations dear," an old woman said to Suzy as she walked by. Suzy grabbed the woman's hand and smiled. "Good luck on your journey, come back in a year."

"Thank you," she said kindly and moved on.

"Suzy, this is for you," a young girl held in her hands a ring of flowers that must have been picked. Suzy knelt down and the girl strung it around her head.

"It's quite lovely," Suzy said kindly to the girl and smiled. The girl blushed and ran behind the crowd.

"I don't have a gift for you," Kaos said with a smile. Suzy looked up in shock of hearing his voice. "So I'll just say this," Kaos extended his hand with a smile. She shook it, "Congratulations, Suzy!" Kaos said. "May you live a *long* and happy life."

"Thank you, Kaos," she said with a warm smile and got up off the ground. "I hope that someday you'll find true love, as well." She said to him. He smiled, in laughter. Kaos put his hands in his pocket as she left. It made Kaos wonder what might have happened in his life if Daragon hadn't summoned him. What would have he said to his father about his mother? What would he say back? How would Tako act to the news?

His mother, he friends, and everyone in town? It was shameful to be motherless. Fatherless happened frequently because of the war. The hype among the village had calmed down as they realized that it was no happy matter. Yet, Kaos would be the first to be considered 'motherless' in town.

"Kaos!" Chearie came running towards him. Down behind all the spectators, she weaved. Kaos turned his head lazily as she came up to him. "Kaos," she panted, her hair frayed and her face slightly red. "Where were you?" she looked up at him. He gave her no response. "Kaos-"

"Shh," Kaos said, "Have a little respect," Kaos shot at her. She shut her mouth quickly. The rest of the procession walked past them and out of view. Spectators moved on, Kaos didn't.

"Why did you run all the way here?" Kaos asked her. His tone wasn't that surprising. Chearie had not left a good impression on him, and frankly he trusted her rather slimly.

"Well," Chearie started and fixed her image by brushing her hair a little and brushing off her dress, "Because you broke Enna's heart! You jerk!"

"I didn't mean too," Kaos said honestly.

"Well? Then where were you?" she said.

"Where does it look like I've been? Recovering," Kaos told her.

"Recovering from what?" she said with shock, but some concern.

"I got slashed across the chest by a nymph," Kaos said and turned to face her.

"How did that happen?" she asked him.

"I was careless, that's all," Kaos mumbled to himself.

"I've rarely seen nymphs wonder the forests," she said, "I've lived here my whole life."

"Well, I didn't mean to stand Enna up," Kaos said.

"She totally thinks that you hate her," Chearie told him.

"Hate her!" Kaos asked shocked, "Why would I hate her?"

"Enna's a little self-conscious sometimes. She makes so many assumptions, that aren't even true!" Kaos sighed and stepped towards the door.

"Hey!" Chearie yelled at him, "Where do you think you're going?"

"I'm going back to bed," Kaos said and opened the door. Chearie ran over and shut it, yanking his hand from the door handle.

"No," she shot at him, "you're not just going to leave Enna upset."

"Here, let me spell it out to you," Kaos said, "I go back to bed, and we pretend that this conversation never happened. She comes looking for me, I'm asleep in the 'doctors' room or something then she'll blow it off as an assumption. You see, therefore, she's fine and I don't have to feel awkward."

"You can't just do that!" Chearie yelled at him. "I don't care if you feel awkward or not, you're going to talk to her before this wedding celebration is over! You don't have to say anything monumental, just tell her what you told me. The bandages are good enough."

"There's no point," Kaos mumbled. "Why the hell would she care if I showed up or not? It's not like we knew each other all *that* well."

"Enna is..." Chearie shut her mouth quickly.

"Well? She is what?" Kaos asked her placing his hands on his hips.

"Enna is seventeen..." Chearie started and fidgeted with her hands "...she's never really dated all that much."

"Aw," Kaos said staring frankly at her in shock. "You can't be serious," Kaos looked at her in disbelief and horror.

"Be serious about what!" Chearie yelled at him.

"You want to set me and Enna up so that when I turn eighteen she'll marry me," Kaos said with disgust on his face.

"Yes, and what's so wrong with that?" Chearie yelled at him. "It's common practice!"

"Common Practice! I hardly even know her!" Kaos yelled, "How dare you mess around with my life! Who do you think you are?"

"She has a crush on you, Kaos!" Chearie yelled, "You have a crush on her too." Kaos blushed for a second, but the feeling was to hot to handle within all his lies.

"Do not tell me, what I believe!" Kaos growled, "You don't know me, Chearie. You don't even know the half of what I've been through, so don't start putting words in my mouth."

"Then why did you come to the wedding?" Chearie remarked, "Why did you even come back to see her, to talk to her? If you hadn't come back she would have blown you off as just another crush. Yet, know you come back and break her heart!" Kaos moved towards her teeth bared.

"Shut up!" Kaos yelled, "I'm not here to get hooked up with some brawn, raise a fuckin family, and die a meaningless death!" His words hit here like a flaw in a diamond. Crack, the unbreakable jewel crawled tenderly across the surface.

"Get out!" she yelled at him, "Get out!" Kaos stared at her and didn't move. "Did you hear me? Get your ass off this property and never come back! Enna doesn't need to know anyone like you!" Kaos narrowed his eyes and flipped around. "Now go!" Chearie watched him leave. He went down the path in silence, staring at the ground.

"Kaos," the man from before came up next to him to meet his walking pace. "Just the man I wanted to see." He said with a smile. Kaos didn't meet the man's eyes nor slow his agitated pace. "Kaos, could I talk to you for a moment?"

"Sorry, sir," Kaos sped up a little, "I must be going," Kaos said and finally looked at the man.

"Oh, then I take it you feel much better?" he said. Kaos put a foot down gently and stopped.

"Thank you Mr. Berk for your kindness," Kaos turned to him and bowed his head, but the man stopped it.

"I told you not to do that," he moved his finger from underneath Kaos' chin after he rose it in the air.

"Thank you for the medical treatment, you have showed me exquisite kindness today. If there is anything I can do to repay you, don't be shy to ask." Kaos said politely and turned in aggravation.

"There is something you could do," the man said. Kaos stared over his shoulders. "Marry my daughter," he said with a smile. Kaos sighed.

"I'm sorry Mr. Berk," Kaos started to say but he couldn't get it out.

"You're sorry son?" he laughed a little and put a hand on Kaos shoulder. "For what? All you have done is the best you can do, you saved my eldest daughter's life and enchanted my youngest heart." Kaos wanted to say he wouldn't ever consider marrying, but he was so happy. The man was joyful extravagant. His eldest daughter had just gotten married and was leaving the house; Kaos just couldn't put him down now?

"I..." he stumbled in the silence, then grabbed his head trying to think of what he could say, "I really...I really must be going." Kaos turned away and walked steadily away.

"So I'll see you tomorrow?" he asked to Kaos back. Kaos stopped and rubbed his head. "Two days?"

"Sure," Kaos no longer cared to hear him, and walked away.

Kaos shivered as the pinto clopped up in front of the Library. It was freezing. He stared up at the Star of Thieves seeing just a thin sphere of flames just beginning to spring all around it. The surroundings looked like a fiery ice cream cone surrounded by whipped cream. Kaos Hopped down on the ground and stumbled. He fell down on his side and cringed as the wound he received from the imp stung. The pinto stepped back and whinnied.

"Shit," Kaos cursed to himself and got off the ground. He rubbed his elbow and brushed off his pants of the snow that littered the frost-bitten ground. He looked towards the Pinto who couldn't help but give him the sure sense of mockery. He lowered his eyes and her ridicule ceased. Snapped her reigns in his hand, he lead her down the side ally and into the back. The door creaked loudly in the barn as he opened and guided the pinto in.

Kaos walked into the back door of the library and shut the door quietly behind him.

"He's such a fool, how does he just think that wandering out unguarded or disguised is a good thing!" Daragon cursed.

"It's all your fault!" Yoki took a finger up to Iori. "If you had just let me take care of him, he wouldn't have been able to just walk off!"

"It's not my fault that the boy got tired of shelving books!"

"You had him shelving books! Why you-" Yoki grabbed him by the collar of his tiny shirt. There was a quiet click of a door.

"What was that?" Daragon interrupted. The two stopped quarreling to pay attention to the heels echoing across the library's aging floor.

"Is that?" Yoki looked down the hall. Kaos figure charged through her eyeshot and behind shelves once more. "Kaos?" She gasped and ran down the hall after him. Hearing her footsteps Kaos stopped and turned around. She reached him and her face was in shock. Her eyes wide and jaw dropped, her eyes just stared at the bloody bandages around his chest.

"Kaos!" Daragon appeared behind her. "What happened?"

"A forest imp attacked a woman and husband in the woods, so I stepped in." Kaos confessed.

"Oh, my gods," Yoki approached him and examined the wounds. "I taught you the healing spell, why the hell didn't you heal this, you're going to end up with a scar." She put her hand across it. Kaos cringed.

"So you got medical attention, from someone! You really got yourself in a fix, didn't you?" Daragon reprehended him.

"What? Kaos, you didn't wrap this yourself?"

"How could he? He used up all his manna," Iroi commented. "It's not even fully recovered yet, you can see it in his body; the way he's carrying himself."

"You used that vicious spell again didn't you?" Daragon stormed up to Kaos. Kaos couldn't meet his eyes. "That- that Slayer Sacristies of yours!" Yoki's eyes popped. Kaos continued to look down at the ground. "How many times have a told you the spells of the ancients are not to be toyed with!"

"Oh, just… shut up!" Kaos barked, "I sick of hearing it. To hell with the rule, the ancients were the only people who knew how to conquer a spell."

"You could have been killed!" Daragon scolded.

"What?"

"You didn't even have enough manna to heal that little wound."

"That's cause I healed Fredrick's first!" Kaos yelled back.

"Fredrick? Now you're exposing yourself more!" Daragon yelled, Kaos' moment of assertiveness failed him and he was submissive once more. He shouldn't have gone out, but it was Iori's idea to send him out on the ride in the first place.

"Now, now," Iori hushed and moved up to Kaos. "Let's tend to what is most important first, which would be the slash on your chest, and the sores on your back."

"Sores?" Yoki went around and started at Kaos back, redden with blotches from where he was slammed on to concrete. She touched them slightly. Kaos cringed instantly and rocked his shoulders back forth.

"I'm sorry," she said.

"Whatever," Kaos mumbled. Iori beckoned him down to his room and he followed. Daragon started after him, but Yoki stopped him.

"Where did he learn Slayers Sacristies?" Yoki asked, not curtly, but honestly. Daragon's temper did not settle so easily.

"Sure to hell it wasn't me, he taught the fuckin' thing to himself."

"Sit down boy, before you collapse," Iori said with a warm jolly tone. Kaos kept his head down, as though being a wounded puppy. He should have known better, known that exposing himself was the wrong thing to do. To help and interfere with the Imp, Fredrick, and Suzy's affair was dangerous; yet, it had to be done. He also couldn't stand Yoki's mothering issues. Daragon was so strict and insanely critical. "So things didn't quite go as you planned, did they?"

"What?" Kaos' voice turned a little harsh, "You're the one who sent me as a taxi, then make me shelve books."

"And what does any of that have to do with what's wrong now?"

"All that made me go see her again! If you had simply been more critical, I wouldn't have had to deal with any of it!"

"Deal with what exactly? Real life?" Iori said wisely. Kaos just stared at him with hatred, and disgust. Iori put him through all that for just the sake of living! When he had almost died! "Now, turn around so I can remove the bandages." Iori indicated to him as he finished soaking a washcloth. Kaos was reluctant to say the least but managed just out of the stinging pain he had received from the bitter cold. Iori cleaned the wound in silence and tactful ways. "As much as I see the risk of you going out in your current state, I don't think its fitting for a boy to be sheltered under careful eyes when trying to grow up into a man."

"It's because I'm the Prince, right?"

"It's your mentality that worries us the most." Iori sighed. "You just can't play it safe."

"You were the one who put me up as a taxi!"

"I know her very well, I know she leads a sheltered life in this place. I knew she couldn't have made a connection between your white hair and the Prince of Ebony."

"But the people I might have passed?"

"What time was it? If anyone saw you and knew who you were, they would have thought it all a dream."

"But why do it in the first place?"

"You were bored, and you need to get out and live a little." Kaos sighed. Iori smirked. "Don't expect all your answers on a silver platter, Kaos. Just-"

"Is the convict wrapped up yet?" Daragon's voice harked from outside the door.

"Up. Looks like your master would like to talk to you." Iori smirked, but Kaos grit. "I'll let him in, then take my leave." He walked up wisely and opened the door to revel and reddened faced Daragon. Iori passed and Daragon stood by the door in silence. Kaos must his head in his hand and his elbow on his knee.

"What was running through your mind?" Daragon growled as he stepped into the room and closed the door. "To leave without any note as to where you were going?"

"You would have never let me go if I had told you."

"So where did you go."

"To a farm house by the woods."

"To see who?"

"A girl I had taken home the night before. She wanted to know my last name." Daragon pondered the thought.

"You know what that really meant?" Daragon sighed.

"Yes," Kaos barked, "Why do you think I came home?"

"You do understand why though, right?" he asked Kaos who couldn't help but give him a stare.

"Why? I don't want to get married that's why!" Daragon immediately put a hand on his forehead and Kaos leaned over towards him. "What did you have in mind?" Kaos growled.

"Marina wouldn't want you taking a bride just yet," he said softly.

"What?" Kaos cut him short, "I'm nearly eighteen, my mother will not dictate what I do!"

"Just calm down," Daragon motioned, "I think by your little action today we learned that she won't dictate everything you do."

"Well, she won't," Kaos leaned back and crossed his arms in front of his chest, agitated by the simple thought of his mother controlling the idea of whether he would marry or not. All it did was remind him of the time when his father had tried to set him up with Lural. The idea simply made him sick, arranged marriages!

"Now, let's change the subject," he started. "How did you get tied up with the Imp?"

"The girl's sister, her name is Suzy, was having her wedding tonight to her fiancé Fredrick. The girl I gone to see was named Enna. When I talked with Enna this morning she asked me if I would be her date to her sister's wedding… I agreed to it." Daragon sighed. "…Just shut up!" Kaos barked and continued. "So after that I wondered off by myself into the woods hoping to find something to do. I heard the cries of Suzy and rushed to the rescue so to say."

"During the battle…why did you use *that* spell?" Daragon asked.

"It was the only thing that I could think of at the time. I had tried others, but nothing was working so I launched it."

"The reason why I don't like you using that spell-"

"Is because it was the spell that nearly killed you, right?" Kaos added.

"Not quite," Daragon snapped at his pupil's curt tongue, "as a growing boy your manna is every changing, there will be points in your time where you'll have no manna in your body to do spells for no apparent reason. Cause that spell takes a lot of manna, it worries me when you choose to use it because your body might not catch up with your brain."

"Did I die?" Kaos asked.

"That's not the point," Daragon said, "The Slayers Sacristies is a black level spell and is forbidden by any unregistered under-trained spell caster to perform." Kaos looked away. "God, I wish there was a way I could make you understand this."

"I don't see why it wasn't appropriate, I was going to die!" Kaos yelled, "The thing was out to murder me as well. I took the chance, either I would kill myself with my own spell or I would kill it. Either way it looked better than being slaughtered helplessly by a forest Imp."

"They're slimy and vicious in their own way, and I'm glad that you live through it. Really I am. I just don't want you at this moment in time to take anymore of those dangerous risks, especially at the state in which your body is. I know you are sick of hearing it, but as the Price, you are the 'white demon' and your body is using much of its own manna just undergoing the huge transformation. You may had even hindered you transformation by using that spell and zapping the manna from your body. That also means that your transformation might never be complete and if you stay in this constant adolescence, not only will it take a huge toll on your body but your mind will never be able to get past much."

"What? You think I like doing it?"

"Yes," Daragon nodded. Kaos was quiet. In a way he felt pride in knowing such a spell and being able to use it when he felt the need. True, maybe he could have worked harder and used a different spell and saved his manna. Yet, the Slayer's Sacristies was such an exhilarating spell. It made his blood boil and simmer in its own thoughts and hatred. He felt almost lifted after he launched the spell, like Kaos for a moment was free of everything that had happened. Kaos had finally broken away from the white demon and he had felt like his old self again. Daragon started to laugh a little bit at Kaos' dismay.   There was a light tap on the door.

"Hello?" Michael's voice was softer than usual.

"It seems like you are wanted by everyone today."

"Michael? Michael's here?" Kaos started to panic. His mind quickly flew to the door.

"We couldn't just leave him back at the Inn," Daragon laughed, "And besides, he insisted that he would be allowed to come thank you for saving him."

"Hello, can come in already?" Michael whined from behind the door.

"Sure," Daragon cried. Kaos bit his tongue as Michael walked in and laid eyes on him.

"Hey, Kaos-," he started. Kaos was nervous now, what made him stop. "Can I call you that?"

"What?"

"Kaos, is that too informal?"

"It's my name," Kaos laughed, "That's all it its."

"Cool," Michael cheered up and jumped on the bed next to Kaos since there was a lack of an empty chair. "So where did you disappear to all day. Daragon and Yoki rushed me back to the Inn, and asked the Innkeeper to give me a tiny job as a cook."

"I went to a wedding," Kaos commented.

"A wedding? Whose?" he said with enthusiasm.

"A girl I met in the library asked me to be her date, it was her sister's wedding."

"What? You already got a girl! It's been only a day!" Michael exclaimed, "Wait…are you allowed to do that?" he asked Kaos who could hardly understand a word that was flying out of Michael's mouth. "Are Princes allowed to choose their wives?" Michael turned to Daragon who bit his lip.

"Good, she's only a friend!" Kaos shouted at Michael, who immediately coward.

"Sorry, sorry. I didn't mean it in that way, don't worry, you can marry who ever you'd like." He sighed as Kaos rubbed the back of his neck.

"Whoa! What the hell happened to you?" he asked catching sight of the bandages.

"Just got into a fight?"

"At a wedding?" Michael asked shocked.

"No, this was before the wedding! … Well I guess it technically was. I never really attended the wedding; I was unconscious through the main thing. I only woke up for the final processions."

"What happened?"

"There was a forest Imp who had attacked the couple, I stepped in when he fell."

"What happened to the Imp? Did you beat it up?"

"Yeah." Kaos laughed and rubbed the back of his shoulder, "It's gone."

"That's amazing! You were like a super hero! I wish I had the power you must possess, being have elf and all." There was long silence as the conversation finally took a breather.

"So who was your date?"

"Her name is Enna Berk," Kaos said.

"She cute?" Kaos blushed in silence. "I bet she is. What's her personality like?"

"She's timid at first, but she's real. If you know what I mean."

"What?"

"She doesn't take crap from anyone, and she doesn't take the spotlight either."

"Enna, did you get to say goodbye to her?"

"Goodbye?" Kaos stopped, "No. The last time I had seen her was before my fight with the Imp."

"What?"

"What made you leave?"

"Her father approached me after the final procession and gave me permission to marry his daughter." Kaos confessed.

"He just proposed the idea?"

"Yes," Kaos emphasized.

"Kaos?" Yoki cried as she stood outside his door.

"What?"

"Good morning," Yoki said with a strange tone, "Please come on out it's already 10:00."

"Go away!" Kaos groaned and rolled over in bed.

"Come out here this instant!" she put her foot down.

"I feel like shit, can you just come back in another hour," he continued to groan.

"This is the third time I've done that today, you need to get up! Eat! Study! Do something other than sleep!" he groaned loudly inside and rolled over. "Kaos!"

"Hold on, I'm coming." His door slowly opened Kaos stepped out and sneezed and whipped a finger just under his noise. All over his face, neck, arms, and legs was this brown moist seaweed. Yoki's jaw suddenly dropped and she was baffled staring at him.

"What?" he asked impatiently. She caught herself quickly and grabbed his wrist. "Come with me," she said and tugged him down the hallway in a light run. She ran ahead of him and opened the two large heavy wooden doors that lead into the private study of the library. The room was square tall bookshelves filled with aged books far too holy and too important to lie around on the floor. Three ornate olive green love-seats were set in the middle of the room with reading lamps behind them. Daragon sat on the couch towards the left legs crossed reading a book.

"Iori!" Yoki yelled in desperation. Kaos stared around the room and didn't find Iori among the sofas. In seconds however the old man slide down one of the four tall letters and speaking from the foot of it said:

"What is it Yoki?" he said almost tired.

"Something very strange has happened," she said.

"What did you put all over my pupil?" Daragon said looking from his book. He rose and walked over to the two of them.

"It's just some water-nymph seaweed that I had received as a gift a while back. I was told it would restore Elvin manna quickly."

"Turgo!" Daragon shouted. Kaos took a deep breath in and suddenly sneezed again.

"I think I'm allergic to this stuff," Kaos said his head full.

"Sure as hell you probably are," he said and came over to Kaos and peeled a strip off his forehead. The skin where the seaweed was raw and red. Kaos yelped. "Yeah, it's gonna sting. Now just hold still while I remove it." He did as he was told, and it was painstaking. Daragon peeled them of quickly as though waxing. Kaos cringed at the first few, but his body grew used to the stinging.

"Who gave you Turgo?" Iori asked.

"More importantly why would you use it on my pupil?"

"I apologize, I felt that he had sevied his chances for a complete transformation. I was hoping that the seaweed would bring back his manna sooner as to continue to allow his body to mature."

"I'm sure you never thought that Turgo can only be used on elves, and is nearly deadly to humans." Daragon commented.

"All I thought it did was redeem Elvin manna, that's all."

"Well," Daragon barked, "Look what your mistake has done to him, he's blistered all over. His body is probably using more manna to try and heal itself now than his transformation."

"Daragon," Kaos whispered. Daragon stopped. "Stop arguing."

"How can I? She's supposed to be protecting you, while she's doing more harm than good; what do you expect me to do?" He said.

"So she messed up," Kaos barked, "So what?"

"So what?" he said.

"I made the mistake of using that spell," Kaos argue, "So now it's all even."

"No, it's not," Daragon said, "She's more experienced than you, you shouldn't have you deal with this when you already have much to deal with." Iori walked over to the group. "If she is Marina's body guard, I would like to know how she managed to get the job." Daragon scolded. Yoki was quiet.

"Kaos, I asked Yoki to go get you, because I wanted to tell you something, and I don't think that it can wait any longer," Iori said. "This morning I received a telegram from a Richard Berk addressed to you." Iori commented reaching into his pocket and taking out a small slip of paper. He handed it over to Kaos and Kaos opened it up and read it.

"Shit," Kaos muttered.

"Now, Kaos," Irori said, "What did you say to this Richard person?"

"I wasn't thinking, the guy wouldn't let me leave, so I just agreed so suddenly, I didn't even bother to worry cause I thought after the fight I had with Chearie, he wouldn't dare come after me." Kaos sighed and fell back onto the couch then cringed in response to his wounds.

"You don't have to go," Yoki stated.

"Yes, I do," Kaos, "I promised the man I would come back in two days."

"What time does he want to see you tomorrow?" Kaos looked at the sheet, "5:00 pm."

"Is that for dinner?"

"My guess is that it is," Iori said.

"We'll just enchant you,"

"They already know," Kaos complained.

"Then just decline, say that you're busy or something."

"Besides, I have to start training you again," Daragon added, "You know what the second day of training feels like." Kaos sighed.

"Yeah, that would probably be the best thing,"

"Well, get dressed and take a shower," Irori said. "The library will be opening, and I would like you to shelve a bunch of the elfish books that have been sitting around on the return shelf."

"More book shelving?" Kaos complained.

"I've agreed to it," Daragon said, "and after you do that it's off to training with me."

It was a cumbersome task, that's all that shelving Elvin books could be considered. Kaos stared at the small leather bound book in his hand. It was blank on the cover, dented and had scrapes all the way down one side of the book. He sighed, it was the third book he had found with not a single reference word on the cover. Each of the books was just so bare and beaten it seemed as though they would fall apart in the palm of his hand. There were then footsteps coming down to this secluded portion of the library. To be more specific one pair of high heels and a second a pair of worn in sneakers so that the sole of the shoe it very softly and almost muted on the ground. Kaos lifted a book that blocked the view into the hallway as he looked through the bookshelves. A flash of brilliant pink walked by, then a flash of bright blue.

"We really shouldn't do this," a sweat girl's voice echoed through the bare shelves of the secluded bookshelves. Kaos grabbed the edge of the cart and as quietly as a squeaky cart could go walked deeper into the elvish section of the library. He had been told by Iori to stay in the elvish section; giving him a less likelihood to run into anyone he didn't know. Daragon and Yoki, being elves themselves wouldn't seem strange walking into the section, and Iori was the bookkeeper so it was publicly acceptable for him to wander into them. Kaos turned down a corner and looked back around to see that two aisles down stood a faulty Chearie and being dragged behind; a very nervous-looking Enna. Kaos peeled back behind the shelves with worry. Chearie walked down the aisle nearing his hiding place on the end of the shelf to her left. He couldn't move the cart now, so as she turned her head down his hallway, he slipped into the next. She looked down and found his cart.

"Hey, here's the book cart," she said and picked up a book and opened the pages to the Elvin text. "They're elvish. Then he's got to be around here somewhere. Kaos started to breathe a little heavy and he sneaked down the aisle away from her very slowly as not to draw her attention. He walked backward very slowly. He came up to the intersection and Enna was still there.

"He probably left it to put a book on the shelf or something."

"Chearie this is ridiculous!" Enna said blushing.

"It is not," Chearie demanded. "You realize how hard it is to find a good boy, Enna?" she stopped and looked back at Chearie, "You like him, and I have a feeling he likes you too. Yet your both too damn polite for your own good neither of you will make another move." Kaos stepped back as Chearie moved down into the aisle. It was a simultaneous moment. Enna shouted, so did Chearie, and a book fell flat off the shelf just behind Kaos.

"There he is!" Chearie's voice was most prominent. She stomped up to him. "How long have you been there?" she asked, "Are you trying to escape us or something?" she asked and narrowed her eyes at him.

"No, not at all," Kaos covered.

"Hey, you look different," she said and walked up to him.

"Different?" he asked.

"Did you cut your hair or something?"

"No," Kaos said as the back of his neck sweat.

"How are you?" Enna asked quietly in her normal voice. Kaos bent down to pick up the book. He laughed staring at the torn cover of the small brown leather book.

"I'm just fine," Kaos said with the smile he had with the book that haunted him.

"Oh, that makes me so happy," Enna, jumping to put her wrists around his neck, hugged him. He was taken off guard and he stood stiffly. Chearie eyed Kaos with a slight foxy-look. Enna came down and stared at him in the eyes and was quiet admiring them. Kaos blushed rather uncomfortable with her deep stare into them. "So can you make the dinner tomorrow?"

"Tomorrow?" Kaos repeated.

"Did you get my father's telegram?" she asked.

"Oh ... yeah," Kaos said softly rather disheartened to tell her face to face.

"What's wrong?" she said and looked at him.

"Enna ... I" he started. He felt so bad, he had promised. He bit his lip.

"What?"

"I'll be a little late, that's all," Kaos said rather solemnly. She shrieked in glee and jumped on him again, it made him smile at bit. Her playfulness reminded him of Tako. Yet quickly she jumped off and neatened her dress and said in a dignified tone.

"I mean," she laughed, "That makes me very pleased." She twitted with the tip of his left shoe on the ground behind her.

"Enna, we should really be off," Chearie interrupted.

"Oh," she said and turned to Kaos and bowed her head slightly like he had done to her father. He was a little shocked. "I heard its one of your customs from my father, did I do it right?" she asked worried she had done something horribly wrong with the look on his face that was one of perplexity. She bit the tip of the nail of her right-index finger.

"Well…" Kaos rubbed the back of his neck, "Yeah, but I'm just not used to receiving it I guess."

"Should I do that?"

"To be honest, I don't really care." Kaos added and dropped his hand to the side lazily, "I usually only do it to people profoundly older than me." Kaos looked at her apologetically.

"Okay then," she said and ran up to him. She motioned him to come closer, like they were about to whisper. He rose an eyebrow and she grabbed his head closer. Suddenly she puts a kiss on his cheek then jogs over to Chearie's side.

"One of our customs," she laughed. The two left and that was when Kaos bolted from the elvish section past Iori who was behind the desk. The old man peeked out of a trading offer to see Kaos dash off down the hall into his room. He apologized to the woman and followed Kaos down.

"Kaos?" he asked and knocked on the door. It flew open and Kaos very distressed asked him disparately.

"Iori, do I look any different?" he asked. Iori was quiet and clam.

"Besides the bug eyed gold eyes and the bitten-raw lip I see no difference," Iori said like a judge monotone, with his eyelids half-closed. Kaos sighed.

"Thank you," he sighed.

"Why do you ask?"

"Chearie said I looked different than the last time she saw me,"

"Chearie?"

"A girl I met at the wedding," Kaos filled in the necessary information.

"Well, from my eyes you look know different," Iori rose. "Relax."

"It's just this stupid transformation doesn't like to warn me about things, not to mention from this morning with the seaweed."

"Did you just see her?" he asked strangely.

"Yeah," Kaos sighed, "she and Enna sought me out."

"You saw Enna? Did you tell her about the dinner?"

"I couldn't say no," Kaos sighed. He fell back on his bed and cover his head with a pillow. "I said I would be late."

"Oh, Kaos…" Iori sighed. "Well, there's nothing we can do about that, we'll just have to send Yoki with you."

"Yoki?" Kaos whined.

"What's wrong with her, she is supposed to be your guardian."

"She's an elf," Kaos sighed. "How am I supposed to explain how I got in touch with her?"

"Daragon?"

"The General of the Wakita, her father already knows I'm a General too, he'll expect the Wakita to stand around the house or something having two Generals of the same faction in the same building."

"He's your master, also."

"Yet, why would I *bring* him there?"

"Extermination?"

"That's just too awkward."

"Would you rather me go with you?"

"…Yes!" Kaos said excitingly. Iori raised an eyebrow at his excitement. "That will work, I can pretend that I brought you along because you were kind enough to give me shelter here that will work."

"Well, I guess I'll just have to close early that day." Kaos sighed. "You know you're going to have to learn to be mean."

"I just could say no to her…" Kaos sighed.

"But you're doing her no good saying yes, Kaos. You can't marry her, you're the Prince of Ebony."

"I know that!" Kaos exclaimed. "I know that too well. It's not like I'd like to marry her anyways," he added quietly. Iori yawned.

"Well, if this is decided get back to work, I left a woman with a great book at the front desk." He rose and left the room. Kaos walked up to the mirror one more time and said it to himself.

"You look just like you did this morning," He rose, "At least after the fuckin seaweed!" Kaos walked out and down the aisles back to his cart. There he picked up the book that caused it and opened to the first page.

"Αν σο ιτ ωασ δεστινψ τηατ γαϖε α περσον τηε ριγητ το λ
ιϖε (And so it was destiny that gave person the right to live.)" it read
and Kaos read it aloud.

"Pardon?" there was a voice from the far side of the shelves. A girl's
voice and a girl peeked her head around the corner and laid eyes on Kaos
who had dropped the book in shock. Their eyes locked and Kaos
breathed heavy.

"Hey did you say that?" she asked him. He was quiet as she
approached him and looked closer to his golden eyes. Her eyes lit up
with shock and she opened her mouth. "Are you-" she started to ask yet,
then Kaos' hand flew over her mouth.

"Don't say it!" Kaos ordered. She struggled in his grip and looked
at him angrily. His eyebrows narrowed, "Be quiet!" he whispered
decisively. He looked down the aisle and dragged her down into his
room around the shelves. He dragged her inside and slammed the door
shut and let her go!

"What is your problem!" she shouted at him immediately and
emphasized it with hand motions. "I was going to ask you if you were
the librarian's assistant! That's all!" she sighed and went for the door,
Kaos stepped in front.

"That's all?" Kaos interrogated.

"What is your problem?"

"Is that all!" Kaos asked in a higher tone.

"God, I didn't want to do this fuckin research project," she muttered
to herself and reached for the doorknob again. "I should have simply
been sick today."

"Research project?" Kaos asked weakly. He sighed.

"Yeah, you freak! I was assigned to a research project from stupid
mistress!" She exclaimed and crossed her arms, "Now, let me go." She
demanded. He stepped in front of the door.

"You didn't recognize me?" Kaos asked.

"No, why would I recognize a freak like you!" she exclaimed. "Let
me go!" she stuck her hands out in threat to do a spell. Kaos looked
quickly over her and found pointed ears.

"You're an elf?" he asked.

"Yeah, you human, and I can do magic too, so let me pass or I'll cast you into a toad." Kaos put his hands up worried about what could really be done.

"There's no need for fights, I think we just had a misunderstanding," Kaos laughed off. Yet, he bit his tongue as she stepped closer suddenly. "Hey, could you put your hands down already."

"Why? Frightened?" she hesitated, "Now move!"

"I feel like I have do some damage control here," he said to her.

"I'll do damage if you don't move."

"I can't-"

"Λιγητэσ οφ τηε ωορλδ λιγητ ανδ βριγητεν α πατηωαψ (Lights of the world light and brighten a pathway)" she said in elvish and her palms lit. Kaos covered his face for a direct impact. He was blown from his room and she ran out over him. He rolled up and put out his hand.

"Χομε το με, (Come to me!)" he hissed, his eyes were bright white and his palm grew white. Suddenly the girl, still running was moving back to Kaos who grabbed her by the shoulder. "This is not over!" Kaos said, "I can't have you running outta here like that!" Kaos moved her into the back office of the library.

"I swear I thought you were human!" she gasped, then looked at his ears again.

"I'm sorry to do that, but Iori would have my head if you ran out like that," Kaos said rather stressed. She was quiet in fright. "I'm sorry to have dragged you off like that, I've been a little paranoid thanks to the war." He said sadly, "I'm sorry, I'm truly sorry." He sighed. She stared at him quietly.

"You mean the war of the outside?" she asked.

"Yes," he added. "I'm so worried they'll send assassins and spies…" he didn't say anymore loud enough for her to hear. But he found himself just relaying everything so quietly to himself that he talked himself into tears. She stared at him with a sudden pity that he hardly expected from her.

"I don't know much of the war," she started softly, "My mistress said that Dartawg threatens to turn this world to an anarchy where only the fittest survive."

"That's a part of the conflict," Kaos sighed and whipped his eyes. He rose and walked over to the door. He opened it, "You can go now, I'm sorry to have frightened you like that." He said and she walked slowly out of the door and past him. He turned away from her and leaned on the door. She looked back at him once then continued down the hall.

"Oh General Daragon!" the girl cried from down the hall. "It's so good to see you well!" she shouted with glee. She had stopped in the hall next to Daragon's tall figure.

"Good to see you Pheonie," he said welcoming.

"You here to pick up a book for class or something?" she asked like a little kid.

"No, I'm actually here for a lesson."

"A Lesson?" she said shocked. "A lesson, that must mean you've taken on an apprentice, I would love to meet them?" she asked excitingly.

"Yes, but I don't know if you could meet him," Daragon asked. Her face was suddenly shocked and she looked back at the door and saw Kaos still lying there. 'No,' she said in her head. She remembered the spell he had launched, 'it's him. Shit. That boy was Daragon's new apprentice.'

"What are you-" Daragon stopped and saw Kaos at the door. "It's a pleasure Pheonie to see you again." He asked and walked away from her. She stood and watched him approach Kaos.

"Hey, you all right?" he asked. Kaos sighed and fell heavily on his right foot as he stepped into the back room. His cheeks were still red from his babbling and he was soft-spoken.

"Sort of," he said and sighed.

"Sit down," Daragon motioned him to sit. He didn't argue and sat, Daragon sat beside him like a worried parent. "What happened?" he asked.

"It's so stupid," Kaos shook his head.

"Kaos-"

"Let's just get the training over with," Kaos said argumentative. "I just want to get off my mind."

"It's not good to just throw things aside." Daragon hushed, "If you don't want to talk, then let me charm you." Daragon hushed and moved his head to Kaos' forehead. Kaos stopped and was in some thought.

"It will allow me to see what your mind was on recently," Daragon said, "That's all I can get at Kaos, don't worry." His cold hand fell on Kaos' forehead.

"I won't go any deeper," he said as Kaos saw his hand glow. Daragon closed his eyes and the two sat in silence. Kaos saw all the images flash through his mind as he knew that Daragon was scanning them. Tears overwhelmed him again and impulsively shock Daragon's hand off him. Daragon was a little shocked but saw his state.

"Kaos…"

"Let's just get started," Kaos said and placed his hands parallel to one another on his lap. They glowed, but his hands shock as fright ran though him. He tried to steady them but they only got worse. "Ah!" he yelled in frustration and almost immediately he rose and sent a magic white glow beneath him that quaked the library for a few moments. The floor was crushed own in and the dirt could be seen in the basement of the building.

Iori held onto the small pencil cup on his desk and stared around quickly at the bookshelves worried. They all stood though, the books in the end had fallen over, but other than that no harm was done. The habitants of the library were shaken.

"AN earthquake?" one question holding onto her daughter.

"Is everyone all right?" Iori asked over the crowd. No one said anything. Iori got down from his high seat chair and went around to the front of the desk, "Is anyone injured he asked.

"I don't think so Iori," a man commented to him.

Kaos sank to his knees and his lungs heaved up and down slowly and he teared.

"Let it all out," Daragon whispered. Kaos rose his hands and gathered up another blast and screamed as he threw it down in the hole. The books on the shelf hopped and settled once more.

"Damn you Marina!" He scream and launch another one, "You had to have me as the fuckin heir! I didn't want any of this royalty crap! I didn't want your motherhood! I didn't want a family! Damn everyone in this empire! You're all so stupid!" as he continued each blast went with a word and the books started falling from the shelves. "All…I…wanted…was…to…become…a first level spy!" he stopped as the light bulb exploded and the glass glitter on the way down to the hole. He stared at it as it disappeared to the ground and panted. "To prove Ijae wrong," Kaos said panting. Daragon sat on the sofa eyes closed. He stood up.

"Feel any better," Daragon said regally. Kaos dropped to his hands and knees as the manna drain hit him. He looked at his hole.

"Yeah," Kaos panted. Daragon rose and patted him on the shoulder.

"Good." Daragon said quietly. "Sit back." He pulled him back on his knees.

"I think that was enough for tonight," he put his hand to the hole in the floor, "Τηε ωαψ ιτ ωασ (The way it was.)" the hole was patched and Kaos still sat there. "You should keep more strength for tomorrow's dinner so you don't look like you were hit by a train." Daragon spoke softly. He went to the door and looked back at Kaos.

"Regardless of what happens, I'll be here for you Kaos, no matter what state you'll be in." Daragon stepped out. Kaos sat there for a while and eventually found the strength to raise himself to his feet. He walked to his room and collapsed on his bed.

disease of the heart

(October 5th) Kaos woke in the morning to a head full of splinters. As he raise his head slowly from the pillow black hair laid on top his face making him groan for more than just being ill. The pillow, although soft on his head, did not ease his suffering. He was still dizzy from the night before and presently in no position to transform. So, with lack of anything better he closed his eyes and prayed that the Empress would just remain quiet. He drifted off again down somewhere we he couldn't be found.

Yoki poked her mousey noise around the door. She stopped with some shock and the door halted ajar. Kaos was lying in bed just as he had fallen to bed; with his hair a elegant jet black. It was in this moment that her heart skipped in tune with her scurrying feet as she quickly retraced her steps down the library hallway to get Iori.

"What is it, Yoki?" Iori was in the library staring at a book as he normally did. His voice was agitated, whether it was from Yoki's constant pestering or the troubles of locating a book, would save her from his wrath.

"Iori…" she peeped quietly at the door.

"You know what time it is?" he asked and brought a sturdy hand up to his glasses. Removing them with the grace of a philosopher he paused before his wrath. "It's almost three in the morning and I have work to be done before I open the store at six! How you manage to be up at this hour is a feets in of itself-" he stopped when her cry came in again.

"Iori!" she said a bit more forcefully. He stopped and waited for her to continue, "Kaos..." Iori sat still and just looked at her shaking eyes.

"Oh," he commented more seriously and closed his book.

"Kaos," Yoki whispered quietly. She stood beside his bed with a frail finger just about his shoulder. "Kaos?" she insisted again on his unconscious body to wake up. She looked over her shoulder at Iori and then back and Kaos. She gulped and spook louder this time rocking his shoulder side to side a bit. "Kaos," he voice echoed. Immediately she jerk her hand from his shoulder suddenly as he rolled over with a yawn. When he rolled over with his eyes closed, her tense body relaxed and she sighed. "Oh, Kaos," she spoke in her normal tone. His eyes remained closed and he rolled back into his original position.

"Come back later," Kaos mumbled into the sheet still exhausted.

"But, your hair is black," she said concerned and tapped his shoulder. He took one of his free hands and slapped it off like a fly. Yoki shook his shoulder determined to wake him. "Kaos, your hair is black, you really must get up!" His eyebrows lowered and he wacked her harder. At this she reviled in disgust.

"Kayoron!" she put her hand on her hip.

"I know," Kaos whined, pulling on his sheets in his frustration. What was she thinking? "Daragon," Kaos voice was surprisingly firm for speaking through a pillow and in sleepiness and lack of energy he added, ", bitch." Iori, with her sensitive ears and regal moral values broken with Kaos' single word, gasped in direct insult. She rose a palm towards Kaos when Iori intervened.

"Yoki," Iori interrupted another attempt on her part to wake him. "Let's let him sleep."

"Let me go!" she whispered in aggravation of the old man's firm grip on her wrist,

"What good will it due him?" Iori tried reckoning with her.

"It will tell him to keep his mouth shut that's what!"

"Shh, here come with me," he pulled her wrist away and her body could not help but turn with his persuasion. "He beckoned her out of the room.

"But-" she said. He gently guided her out and Kaos sighed.

The two walked down the hall.

"But what if the Empress calls?"

"I think that he doesn't have the strength to transform," Iori said, "The only way he can gain any back is sleeping."

"I'll go heal him," she said with a sudden burst of energy.

"No!" Iori said," I think he needs the time," he said, "Let the boy have some peace."

"You think I'm too strict don't you?" she asked.

"You're just too worried," he said, "You won't let nature take its course, even though nature knows best."

"Iori?" Kaos said weakly as he leaned against the doorway of the office. His shadow was draping into the small study and Iori, in his usual spot from a desk on the far left of the room look up first at the shadow, and then at the doorway where Kaos stood buckling at the knees. His eyes were half lit, and his very voice was forced.

"Kaos?" Iori said shocked and saw a limping boy at the doorway and, alarmed, rose quickly, pushed his chair back under the table and shuffled in his normal fashion over to Kaos. He smiled in good intentions as Iori neared with concern. The man's face was struck with a look of an old grandfather chasing his old dream. Kaos suddenly felt a cold chill run up his body from his feet.

The next thing felt was the soft fabric of Iori's old green blazer against his nose. He lifted himself up quickly realizing that the man was probably struggling being caught off guard. Kaos tried to stand but his knees fell in and Iori's old wrinkled hands could barely catch him. Kaos then stuck his hands out for the wall again as Iori's arms gave.

"Iori, something's wrong with me," Kaos was kneeling, softly as he rolled back to a leaning position on the wall panting.

"Go back to bed," Iori's eyes were worried. Kaos' chest heaved after the shock of waking up, he must have blacked out for a moment there.

He was quiet, "It's the only thing that I can do for you right now, and you certainly shouldn't be walking around if you can hardly stand." He shook his head and knelt beside Kaos and put a hand on his forehead. He removed it from the cold, sweat-struck face.

"I went…to bed," Kaos explained, "I feel worse than this morning…" Kaos said seriously. "Something's…wrong." Kaos closed his eyes and gravity pulled his chin down slowly. Iori placed his hand on Kaos' chest, and Kaos jumped back.

"Then come on and lie down in here, I have work to attend to but I'll keep an eye on you." Iori said softly. "You really need your sleep. Now get a hold of yourself, I can't bring you around too far, after all I'm just an old man." Kaos nodded and Iori grabbed Kaos under the arm and helped him over to the couch. "Lay down, and hold on while I get you a blanket," Iori commented, while Kaos fell back on the couch panting. Iori gave him a blanket and felt his again forehead. Shaking his head it was ice cold, he was drenched in a cold sweat. Iori rose and went to the shelves and took down a book. He went to the other couch, put on his reading glasses and fell deep into a book.

Awaking from the seam of two rather boring pages, Iori slowly put on his bifocals and rubbed his cheeks from the paper's touch. His gaze wandered up from the word to the subtitle, eventually on to the table and finally just over the edge of the table, so that his view was just on the couch Kaos was laying on. As he sat in the stillness of the room something rather odd seemed all of a sudden apparent. He though he saw movement in the blanket. He shook his head, figuring that Kaos might have moved, or his own confusion was making him start to imagine moving spots on walls and false indoor breezes. He shook his head and looked down at the book. He recalled that a client had asked him to do more research on the herbs of the native areas. He shook his head

"There's no need for herbs during this time," although it seemed trivial he went back to his book.

It must have been an hour after that when Kaos rolled suddenly over then back. Iori looked up and saw Kaos' lips moving. He took his glasses off and looked closer and saw the feint glow of the earring. He stared at the earring then at Kaos' mute words. He reached towards Kaos and slapped at hand on the bottom of his jaw. Suddenly a loud screech ran through Iori's mind and Kaos bolted up and pinned Iori on the ground. Iori stared into his face. His pupils had triangulated like a cat's and his teeth had sharpened into points. There seemed to be magic flying around him constantly. Suddenly Iori caught the earing glowing a bright red, and then went back to Kaos' disarranged face. His mouth opened like a predatory animal, but on his forehead a green insignia glowed. Iori in defense used his only free hand and slashed Kaos across the eyes. Kaos like a wild animals released him to tend to his eyes. Iori struggled to his feet and picked up the lamp on the table in one hand. Kaos rubbed his eyes, then a ear piercing screech ran through the room again. Iori dropped the lamp in sheer pain from his ears. Kaos was on his feet now stepping towards Iori. Iori backed slowly and his foot hit the bookshelves of the room. Kaos inched forward, his paced started to retard. One step fell and he came to the step up in the floor, at this the animal fell and went silent. Iori panted and waited a few minutes. He walked up to the body slowly and went down slowly. He put his hand down almost touching it, but he pulled his back. Yet, when nothing happened his pulled back the dark hair and revealed Kaos' sweat barn face. Iori slowly cleared his face and rubbed his forehead where the insignia had been, he jumped as a shock ran through his fingers. He lifted Kaos body and struggled to put him back on the couch. Iori fell down on the couch wiped blood trickling from his ears. They both fell asleep, and Iori left Kaos be. Iori's eyes fluttered when he was Yoki bent over Kaos about to touch him.

"No! Don't touch him!" Iori screamed at Yoki, who drew back immediately and stared at Iori.

"What happened?" she asked and came over to him seeing the lamp on the ground and blood.

"I don't know?" Iori stated and looked over at Kaos, whose lips move slowly.

"He's just muttering in his sleep," Yoki said.

"No, that's not muttering," Iori said threatening. "That's not muttering." He was shaking his head. "That's what I know. It has to be more than muttering." He said and rose and went to a shelf.

"Iori you should lie down." He was flipping through a small elvish book that. It sat in his hands, its small brown leather cover scraped down one side.

"Oh, no," Iori said laughing, "Sleeping? No my dear, with him in the room I don't know if I can."

"What happened?" His eyes soared through text and Yoki walked up to him slowly. He slammed the book shut severely.

"He's sick, something..." Iori said frightened looking up at Kaos.

"Iori?"

"I saw the 'ροψαλ δεμον" he words were shaking. He pointed to Kaos, "Kaos..."

"Yes, Kaos is the 'ροψαλ δεμον" we know this," she said slowly.

"Oh, no, Kaos...troublesome Kaos is not the 'ροψαλ δεμον"."

"What?" she said shocked.

"I think the 'ροψαλ δεμον" is inside Kaos,"

"What did he do?"

"He suddenly awoke when I tried to stop him from his muttering, he jumped on top of me and I saw in his face that of an animal's." He shook. "There was this shriek that was so high." He peeled out another book.

"Do you think we should get Daragon?" Yoki asked.

"Yes, get him in as soon as possible. I'm going to go looking through some books to see if there were any reports of behavior like this."

Yoki approached Daragon in a room. Daragon had his hand to his ear, where his earing was glowing purple. His eyes were wide with horror. He looked up in worry at Yoki.

"Kaos!" Daragon jogged into the room with his ear still glowing. Iori looked up.

"What?" Iori commented, "She's sending a signal?" he said worried then looked at Kaos.

"No," Daragon reached Kaos, "He is." Daragon stared at Kaos. "What to do? I can't touch him."

"He attacked Iori," Yoki added.

"That's because he was transmitting," Daragon explained, "The Royal Family tongue is the only way to communicate through the earrings. He's using White magic, if we attempt to stir him he's going to defend himself."

"Iori said he turned into an animal."

"Aysil has to go into a room by herself when she transmits, with the Royal Family tongue comes a curse. Since to use it they are the closest to the original elves they can cross between an elv, which is a primitive elf, and themselves."

"What?" Yoki questioned.

"Why do you think every member of the Royal Family has a stone on their forehead?"

"He had an insignia on his forehead," Iori jumped in.

"That's the curse," Daragon said. "But what can we do? We have to get him to stop transmitting." Daragon said seriously, "Otherwise he's going to drive Ebony crazy." Iori grabbed a book.

"Would a silencing spell work?" Iori asked.

"Silencing?" Daragon stared at Kaos.

"Let's try it," Yoki asked.

"I'll need both of your help," Daragon indicated.

"Σηριεκσ ανδ λαυγητερ, χεασε βεφορε τηε ηανδσ οφ τηοσ ε ωηο πρεσσ φορ σιλενχε (Shrieks and laughter, cease before the hands of those who press for silence)" They all said. Kaos's body jerk and instantaneously Daragon's earring halted and Kaos was back to muttering in regular elfish. Daragon sighed and wiped the sweat from his forehead staring at Kaos. He walked up slowly and shook him. Kaos woke with a slow rising of eyes lids.

"Daragon?" he said softly eyelids have closed.

"Kaos," he said concerned.

"Something's wrong with me, Daragon," Kaos whispered.

"Yeah, we know," he said and felt his forehead, "It's okay Kaos, we'll get you better. I did say that I would be there, no matter what state."

"Thanks…" Kaos' voice droned off.

"I know it's hard Kaos, please try and stay conscious." Yet it was to late, Kaos had fallen back to sleep in his arms. He placed him back on the couch. "He probably can't hear me. We'll take shifts," Daragon commented, "He's too exhausted to stay conscious, so we'll just have to stay on shifts to monitor his muttering. We should contact Aysil, and explain the situation to her, Yoki could you do that?"

"Yes," she said.

"Iori, you read up on the insignia, find out specifically what it is since you have seen it."

"Okay."

"I'll take the first shift." HE said and Yoki left the room. Iori was quiet and looked at Daragon, who sat down on the couch across from Kaos.

"Why do you need to know what kind of insignia?"

"The curse is placed on the royal family by a certain god, its different for every member. The insignia that flashes on his forehead will of the God or goddess that cursed him. When we find that we can get a stone and cure his curse, until then we have to be on guard."

(October 6ᵗʰ) The night was uneventful and Yoki came back gravely.

"Daragon," she sighed, "Marina's on her way."

"Marina?" he shouted, "Why is she coming?"

"She overheard my conversation with the Empress and insisted upon coming and helping."

"At least Aysil knows," Daragon sighed.

"She wants to address the situation, but Kaos' ears in his human state won't be able to endure the transmission."

"I forgot about that." Daragon said quietly.

"How did he survive his own?" Iori asked.

"I can only guess cause it's his own tongue, and he was in elv state." He looked at Kaos. "I don't know if Marina will bring any help to this situation," Daragon said.

"She is his mother," Yoki said.

"You didn't hear him last night Yoki," Daragon sighed. "Kaos resents his mother."

"Well, I can't do anything about her." Yoki sighed, "She insisted."

Shattered and splintering the night reflected in a small piece of glass. Its sky a marvelous deep blue dotted with diamonds. Yet it started as a crackle, as a small fly buzzing around a fire. Growing in magnitude like the tendency of growing velocity of a penny falling down a skyscraper. With a slash, mounds of red fire reigned down from the heavens. Like a stampede of leaping dear bounding away from a gunshot. The vision turned towards a sun of great fire, burning the entire horizon to its knees. Fireflies of ash nature spiraled up over the cries and shrieks, over the grass blades of house rooftops and dark green pines, over everything. Fires roared over the plains and helmeted men marched in kismet.

"Παττελα, δον□τ φαλλ, δον□τ βυρν. Φατηερ, σαωε τηεμ πλεασε λετ με γο σαωε τηεμ (Pattela, don't fall, don't burn. Father, save them please let me go save them)," Kaos was whispering. The group looked at him.

"What did he say through the earring?" Yoki asked.

"Daragon?"

"He said that Dartawg lay in quiet in the east hoping to burn the wall of Pattela and invade the east. He ordered troops to douse fires ... "

"That's can't happen,"

"I don't know ... " Daragon whispered.

"What? You think he's right?"

"He spoke the name Ijae, last night." Daragon said.

"Ijae! He's the master mind of the Dartawg forces."

"My rival," Daragon said quietly. "Kaos spoke as though he was denied the status of first level spy by Ijae himself, even though he passed the test with flying colors."

"You think Kaos knows the movements of the Dartawg forces?"

"I don't know," Daragon spoke. "I knew he was trained as a spy and sent here to collect information, but I never asked him what kind. If he knows Ijae personally, he must have been sent on something important."

"When he first came to my libaray, he was looking for the Carta and Mortion Spell," Iori added.

"What?"

"I kicked him out when I heard spell, but before he had asked if I had any books that explained the Star of Theives."

"You don't think that Dartwag would want to steal the Star of Theives?" Yoki asked.

"It could be possible," Daragon spoke with concern.

They sat for a few hours waiting in the afternoon as the night approached. There was a knock at the door of the office.

"That must be Marina," Yoki stood up quickly and swung the door open to not find Marina, but Enna.

"Where's Kaos?" she said firmly.

"Who are you!" Yoki demanded.

"Where is Kaos!" she said. Iori stood and looked at her at the door.

"Enna?" he asked shocked. She stopped and stared into the room the three strong figures sat stiffly all looking at her. "What are you doing here?" Enna barged passed Yoki and ran up to Iori.

"Where's Kaos? Is he alright Iori?" she asked pleadingly. Iori's eyes fell instinctively on Kaos, on the couch. They didn't want to wake him or touch in fear of him jumping and having another elv explosion. Daragon saw Iori's troubles with Kaos out in the open. Enna suddenly turned around and saw the heaving lump on the couch. Her eyes were wide in shock and she ran up to him and crouch down to see his face. Yoki closed the door. "Oh my gods," she exclaimed and then looked at him she made a move to wake him.

"Don't wake him," Iroi jumped frightened.

"What happened to him?" she asked worried.

"He's really sick," Iori said gravely.

"I saw him just yesterday, he looked a little different, but not like this!" she wept. "Call a doctor!" she yelled. "Why don't you have a doctor here!" she exclaimed in tears yelling at Yoki. "Why do you have these elves around him, Iori!" she said spitefully towards Yoki and Daragon." Yoki bit her lip as her fist clench.

"Enna," Iori said softly, "There is something that you should know about Kaos." Iori started slowly. She stared at him. "He's half-elf." Iori said softly. Enna's head turned sharply on Kaos with some worry. Tears wheeled deep in her eyes.

"He can't be!" she yelled, "He can't be half-elf, it's just not possible!" Iori was quiet, "I don't care!" she yelled and ran up to Iori, "Half-elf or not he needs a doctor this is what happened at the wedding, he'll die!"

"Then you know there's nothing we can do, but wait." Iori calmed down. She slammed his fists in his chest.

"Iroi this always happens!" She screamed, "The guy I fall in love with dies on me! He always does!"

"Calm down, Enna," Iori spoke.

"How can I be calm at a time like this?"

"Do you think I like this anymore, that my pupils on the verge of death?" Daragon hissed at her. "He can't get any better cause he's cursed?" Daragon looked shroud over at Enna. She hushed.

"So you're his master?" she asked strangely.

"Yes, Enna Berk," he said decisively, "My name is Daragon, the woman over there is Yoki." Daragon hinted to Yoki.

"I'm sorry," Enna spoke softly, "I didn't mean to be rude. Can you accept my apologies?"

"It's hard to say with deaf ears."

"Don't be hard on the girl, Daragon," Iori commented, "The girl is much like I was, you know what its like around these parts."

"Oh, I know." Daragon rose and walked over to Kaos. He bent down and put his hand on his forehead and sighed. "His mum will be coming shortly, you should take her to the other room."

"Kaos' mother?" Enna said surprisingly.

"Enna come with me," Iori eased her.

"Why do I have to leave!" she asked she was nearly crying, she glared at Daragon.

"Enna, it'd be best," Iori said softly.

"Why do I have to do what he says?" She put her foot down. Daragon looked up at her. "How do I know that you're not out to kill him!" she spoke tearing. There was a loud rapping on the libraries front door.

"Iori!" Marina's muffled voice was on the far side of the library.

"Enna come with me," Iori grabbed her forearm forcefully. He dragged her down the hall, she was still in protest.

"He's gonna kill him!" she screamed. "Let me go!" Irori opened Kaos' bedroom's door and dragged her inside. He closed the door and locked her inside. She screamed and pounded on the door. She quieted as Iori went and unlocked the library's' door. Iori swung the door and found a most distressed Marina on the other side.

"My lady," Iori tilted his head.

"Where is my son, Iori?" she asked panting.

"Follow me." He led her down the aisle into the back room.

"My Lady," Yoki bowed as she enter the room.

"Yoki," Marina said gratefully and took her hand, "Thank you."

"It's a honor," Yoki said softly.

"General Daragon?" she said shocked. He got on one knee and bowed his head.

"My Lady," he spoke.

"I thought Kaos had killed you," she said.

"My dear Marina, I am prepared for all my students," Daragon said. He looked at Kaos, Marina walked slowly towards the couch and saw Kaos unconscious on the couch.

"How is he?" she asked gravely.

"He's been in a cold sweat for several hours now," Daragon spoke, "Frankly, I'm frightened. He can only gain energy if he sleeps, yet he'll lose it if he starts using white magic. Then Aysil is stuck because he's trapped in his human state.

"What happened?"

"He crossed the barrio to elv when Iori tried to stop him from whispering the incantations," Daragon said.

"Was he transformed at that point?" she questioned and put a hand on his forehead.

"No, at least I don't think he had,"

"To be honest, Marina," Daragon spoke casually.

"Yes?" she said.

"I think the next thing that should be done is that we attack the curse."

"It still won't stop the fact he's still transmitting," she shook her head, "Was that the first time you heard his voice over the intercom?"

"There had been a male voice that transmitted a very strange signal a few days ago." She knelt down and ran a finger around her son's face. "But it was much quieter, almost inaudible through the earrings."

"I've never seen him so drained," Marina said quietly, "I've never before seen him in his human state." She whispered softly. She was nearly tearing.

"Marina, would you like to go down the hall and rest?" Yoki asked Marina who was about to fall asleep sitting at her son's bed side.

"No," she wiped her eyes, "I'm fine."

"My Lady," Daragon spoke softly, "You really should rest, and you need your rest."

"I couldn't sleep even if I wanted to." She said, "Not with him like this."

"Daragon!" Iori ran into the room, "I think I've found it!" Iori ran in holding a thick book.

"You've found the insignia?" he said hopping. Iori brought the book over and pointed to a sketched picture in a scrawled journal.

"That's the one." Daragon tried to read the sprawled handwriting of the journal.

"Peainie, goddess of love," Daragon said softly, "You sure that that is the right one?" he asked seriously.

"Positive," Iori commented.

"That's pretty funny," Daragon smiled.

"I'm sure that was it."

"The poor boy was cursed with love." He smiled, "Well, in that case, the stone we need to get our hands is a piece of Riche," Daragon spoke quietly.

"He's so young," Marina commented, "To get his stone, already?" she shook her head.

"It'll be the only way we can assure he won't do harm when we try and wake him."

"I know," Marina was quiet, "I don't think he'll like the idea, Daragon."

"He's got no other choice," Daragon said seriously. "He's a danger."

"Perhaps we can hold off with it for a little while longer," Marina spoke.

"A little while longer?" Daragon roared, "He'll murder us all!"

"How do you know that?" Marina said stiffly.

"You've haven't seen the damage your son can do when he's normal let alone when his elvin half gets the better of him." Daragon spoke, "As his master, I highly suggest that we ease his curse as soon as possible before his elv transformations appear more frequently."

"Let us think on the matter," Marina spoke.

"I'll go find the stone," Daragon crossed his arms. He left the room quickly and Marina sighed.

"Yoki?" she asked. He looked up at her, "Can you understand that Kaos won't accept the idea of a Yoko." Marina asked. Yoki sighed and nodded.

Kaos' eyes opened quietly and he stared at the ceiling for a little time. Marina's face peered over him in a short while.

"Kaos?" she said softly.

"Mother?" he whispered, "When?-"

"Shh," she hushed him. "Kaos, do you remember anything strange?" Kaos rocked his head side to side. "Then I should explain this to you."

"I attacked Iori?" Kaos questioned.

"Yes, you haven't been able to recover because you've been using white magic in your sleep," she said quietly.

"Then what do I need to do?" Kaos asked her, "If I stay like this, then…"

"yes, my dear, you could very well die," she said disheartened. "There is a way that we can insure that you won't transform into an elv and attack us when we try and stir you from mutter incantations in your sleep…"

"What?"

"To give you a Yoko," she said softly. "It's a small stone that would be placed on your forehead to dissemble the curse." She touched his forehead.

"Is it like yours?" he asked.

"Yes, it would be like mine and my sisters."

"Have you ever turned into an elv?"

"Me?" she asked. "No, Kaos. I received this the day I was married to Crag, to insure that I wouldn't transform."

"I've found the stone," Daragon said.

"Daragon held in his hand a beaten brown paper bag, and at this Kaos recognized it.

"That's the bag you had when you summoned me," Kaos said quietly. Daragon looked down.

"I suppose that it is." Daragon said.

"Were you looking over me then?" he asked Daragon, "To keep those things around in case I transformed?" Daragon smiled.

"I said I had my reasons,"

"I should have known," Kaos smiled slightly in drowsiness. "You knew everything all along," he said and closed his eyes and laid on his side.

"Kaos?" Marina interrupted. He looked up. "Son, do you allow us to give you one?"

"You're actually telling me I have a choice?" he asked.

"No," Daragon directed, "She's just being kind." He said and walked closer. He peeled out of the bag a orange-yellow stone with veins of red and white. It was about the half the size of a fingernail and molded into a elongated rhombus rounded on all sides. "Lay on your back, Kaos," he spoke. Kaos rolled over and waited. He closed his eyes. Daragon spoke an incantation and rubbed the stone. "If this is the correct stone then there shouldn't be pain, Kaos." Daragon moved it down slowly to Kaos' forehead and with a soft handed placed it directly in the middle of his forehead. Instantaneously the insignia appeared and flashed on his forehead. The stone move slightly and settled in Kaos' skin, the insignia still glowed and Daragon removed his hand and patted Kaos' cheek with a little laugh. "Good boy." There was a shriek that slowly muted. "That's a good boy Kaos." Kaos peeled apart his eyes lids and saw Daragon's smile. Daragon reached behind his head and undid the tie about his forehead. He came back down to Kaos and tied it about his head over the stone. "There we go," Daragon spoke rather kindly. "Now you're all settled." Kaos rolled back on his side and fell into sleep.

"That was quite kind of you Daragon," Marina said to him.

"He's a good pupil," Daragon said honestly, "Troublesome, but the best I've had in years." He smiled.

"Yoki, you're rather quiet," Daragon commented. She bit her lip. "Are you alright?"

"I need to apologize My Lady," she sighed, "My presence with him was not for the better at times."

"Yoki," Marina said quietly, "You did all that you could, and there's only so much we can do in this physical world." Suddenly Daragon jumped as his earring lit up. He looked over at Kaos, and Marina's ears pricked.

"My?" she clipped in shock. He walked over swiftly and stirred Kaos who opened his eyes slowly in mid-word.

"What?" Kaos said in English drowsy.

"You started transmitting," Daragon explained. Kaos acknowledged this by closing his eyes again. Daragon came back over and stood around with Marina and Yoki.

"He sounds so much like my father," Marina was quiet, "The sound of his voice."

"You'd be right," Daragon added, "As frightening as that is."

"Would somebody please open this door?" Enna shouted once more at the still door of Kaos' back room. She sighed and walked over to his bed a plopped down. It was nearly mid-night and she hadn't been let out of the room. She fell down on her side. "I hope he's alright, I hope he's okay." She said. "Iori, I hate you so much, you're such a fool to let that Daragon control him in such a state. He's going to die, half-elf or not, he's still half human and thus he'll still be able to die like a human."

"Would you like anything to eat?" Yoki asked Kaos after the third time he was woken up after starting to chant.

"I don't know,"

"It would be best my dear, you haven't eaten since breakfast." He was brought food and he didn't deny it. It was scarfed down and he fell back asleep.

"He's looking a bit better," Daragon commented, "He's a bit warmer, which is a sign that his manna is starting to return to him."

"That's wonderful," Marina said and sighed.

"Enna?" Iori's voice was outside the door. Enna's eyes burst open and she dashed over to the door.

"Iori? Is that you? Let me out!" she said.

"I brought you some dinner, would you like it?" Iori asked. She stopped talking and the door opened.

"How is he?" Enna asked him as soon as he stepped into the room. Iori was a little baffled then answered.

"He's getting better, slowly."

"That's wonderful," she said just like Marina. "Could I see him?" she asked. Iori stopped and pondered her question

"He's still with his mother," he said, "Perhaps when she is gone, and he's stronger you can, but for now, it is better that you remain here. Unless of course you would like to go home."

"No," she answered quickly.

"Then you're welcome to come and take a book off the shelf to read while you wait." He said and opened the door for her. She walked out slowly and Iori followed her about the shelves as she found a book. Iori led her back to Kaos' room. After he left the door she walked and jiggled the handle; it was locked. He came into the small office and found Kaos sitting up talking with Daragon.

"Thank you," Kaos spoke softly, his words still lingered with effort in his voice. Daragon nodded.

"You're welcome. I'm glad to see you're looking better." Kaos smiled,

"I feel much better."

:I'm not surprised, white magic drains a lot out of you, and you've had quite a night," he said.

"So yet again, no training." Kaos asked. Daragon laughed.

"No, I think you've used enough magic for one night. Yet as soon as you feel ready, I urge you to transform. In your elvin state you'll mass manna much faster and Aysil will be able to transmit and fix all of what you have said."

"What have I been saying?" Kaos asked.

"Don't you know?"

"No," Kaos said

"You talked about how Dartwag was going to storm the Pattella wall and burn it to the ground." Dragon asked. Kaos looked down.

"I've been getting nightmares about that recently."

"Nightmares?" he asked.

"I've seen the great wall surround by flames and blue-sailed ships coming across the harbor filled with soldiers."

"Was there anything else?" Daragon asked.

"No, I always woke up at that time," Kaos said, "I never got any further I n it than that constant scene." Marina had been sitting next to him on the couch. She reached around his shoulders and hugged him so that his head rest on her shoulders.

"Oh, my son," she said and kissed him on the forehead, "You've made me worry so."

"I'm sorry mom," he said.

"Hopefully now the only things we need to worry about is the incantations." Daragon said

"Don't forget the Berks," Kaos spoke quietly.

"Yes, I forgot about her."

"Who re the Berks. "They are a family I met few days ago, I attended their eldest daughter's wedding and her younger sister was my invitee.

"Why would you go there in the first place Kaos? " Marina said worried and looked at him

"Iori sent me on a mission to drive Enna home and I do believe that she fell in love with me."

"She is in deep love with you Kaos, "Yoki said and sighed, "It's horrible to break hearts. But I must confess on behalf of the group, she came in while you were sleeping and presently ... " she bowed to Iori.

"She's locked in your room." He said. "I'm sorry to stay that I told her of your half-Elvin kind in hopes that it would scare her off. Yet, it seems from me the way she speaks she could care less."

"Enna's here?" Kaos said softly in his strange state.

"Did she him?" Marina asked Iori.

"Yes, my lady," Iori nodded.

"What are you going to do then?" Marina asked, "You know how much a danger haven't knowledge like that is in the public."

"She doesn't have a clue he is the Prince, Dame Marina," he spoke. "I simply said that he was part-elf in hopes her prejudges of elves would kick and she would leave him be."

"Don't worry about Enna," Kaos sighed and cracked his back stretching. He closed his eyes and concentrated. His entire body glowed for a time, white hair sprouted the roots, and all eyes were on him. Kaos stopped and his chest heaved.

"Kaos ... " Daragon tried to stop him.

"It's done," Kaos said, "Aysil can undue my orders." Kaos panted. Marina closed her eyes. Almost immediately Kaos' earring sparked. Daragon closed his eyes as Aysil's voice came through the item.

"Just in time," Kaos sighed.

"I'm glad you did it when you did," Marina said, "My sister was rather impenitent. You have to understand that even she has never transformed to elv as you have."

"Then how do you even know about it?' Kaos asked.

"It was my father who transformed once on my birthday," Marina sighed and pulled Kaos' hair away from his face. "Have I ever told you how much you resemble him?" Kaos was quiet; Iori and Yoki were both listening intensely. "By the Gods," she muttered and leaned into him and whispered, "If I didn't know better, Kay, I would have thought Charles had come back to me." She fell into a hug, "I love you, my son, how much I love you." She whispered and let go. Kaos was quiet and the room was motionless. "Perhaps, then it's time that I take my leave." She said. "After all my dear, this is your hiding place and I will be missed at the castle if I dare to stay much longer."

"Mom?" Kaos said slowly.

"I love you." She kissed him once more and left the room. Kaos still sat on the couch rather bewildered by her first comment.

"Good journeys, my Lady," Yoki bowed as she leaved. Daragon looked at Kaos.

"Kaos?" Iori questioned him.

"Yoki could I see your sword?" he asked her. She was a little bewildered.

"Why?"

"I'd like to cut my hair if you don't mind," he said aggravated and eyes closed. He had his hand stuck out. She took the sheathed blade from her belt and handed it to him. He unsheathed it and cut his hair. Holding it in his hands he whispered.

"βε γονε," the hair glowed white then disintegrated.

"Kaos!" Daragon scolded.

"That's nothing," Kaos commented and re-sheathed the blade. He held it out to Yoki who snatched it from his hands rather scolding.

"You shouldn't be using any more magic for at least two days after all that!" Daragon walked up to him on the couch. "And you need to rest, your body has to recuperate!"

"That tiny spell, won't do a thing, Master!" he exclaimed in his normal tone. The two argued, and Yoki smiled.

"Kaos, do you wish to see Enna?" Iori commented, "She's still locked in your room."

"What?" Kaos questioned. "You locked her in my room!" he said abhorred.

"I told her she could leave," Iori claimed, "She didn't want to leave, she wanted to see you."

"Well, the least you could do is let her out, yeah, bring her in." Kaos said rather forcefully. Daragon rose.

"I think I'll take my leave then," Daragon spoke. "That girl doesn't sit well with me." Daragon left and took Yoki with him.

"Kaos!" Enna ran up and knelt on the ground close to him. "How are you?" she looked at him and he smiled.

"Why did you wait so long?" Kaos laughed.

"I'm so happy to see you, as yourself."

"Who else would I be?"

"Oh, I don't know, you had black hair and you were half-dead!" She suddenly threw her arms around him.

"Enna," Kaos said softly.

"What?"

"I guess I would like to say thank you," Kaos said sweetly.

"Thank you for not dying on me!" she said happily and plopped down in relief next to him. She smiled and laughed. "I really thought that I was destined to destroy everyone I loved."

"What?"

"I was told by a fortune teller as a young child that all the boy's that I fell in love with die," she laughed, "Something like that anyways, our translator was new at elvish."

"You had your fortune read?" Kaos said strangely, "That's kind of odd."

"Odd?" she said, "Its common practice here, at every birthday an elvin priestess from the Raika Shrine comes and tells the fortune of the child."

"What was your fortune on you seventeenth birthday?" Kaos asked excited. Yet at this her laughter ceased. "What's wrong?" Kaos asked, "I'm sorry if I asked anything I shouldn't have."

"No, it's just on my seventeenth birthday I was told that Τηε λοϖε τηατ ωονϑτ φαδε αωαψ ισ α λοϖε υνηυμαν ον τηισ ωορλδ, υταμαβλε ιν ηισ οων ριγητ, ηεϑλλ βε λατε (The love that won't fade away is a love inhuman on this world, untamable in his own right, he'll be late for sure.)" Kaos translated in his mind. She was quiet, "That's why I'm doomed to be alone for the rest of my life." Kaos was quiet. As they sat in silence Kaos opened his mouth to be kind.

"I know what it's like," he said softly, her ears turned on although she didn't look at him, "I'm in a position where I'd rather not wish to be in. Sometimes I wish I could just run away and have it all disappear, but it will never disappear from me." Kaos said solemnly.

"I really wish that what she said to me that day would just go away, and I would fall into true love." She was rather intrepid.

"Then don't believe it," Kaos said, "If you don't believe her, my guess is that it won't come true."

"It's fate!" she cried.

"How can it be fate?" Kaos grabbed her by the shoulders, "How can that be your fate if you fell in love with me?" he said and she blushed.

"How did you know?" she said.

"It doesn't matter, Enna you fell in love with me and I didn't die!" Kaos exclaimed trying to cheer her up, "And I don't plan on dying for a long time." He shook his head, that's when it hit him, the true meaning of the fortune. He stopped and let go of her shoulders shocked.

"Kaos?" she asked. He stared at her bewildered and blushing. "Kaos are you alright?" she said and moved closer to him. She put a hand on his forehead and he scurried back. "Kaos what's wrong?"

"Nothing," Kaos shook his head quickly.

"You're bright red," she exclaimed.

"What?" he choked.

"Kaos!" she ordered and put a hand on her hip. Her expression grew tainted and her force more forceful, "Kaos, spit it out!" she exclaimed.

"Didn't Iori already tell you?" Kaos didn't look at her.

"Tell me what?"

"That I'm half-elf," he said and grabbed his knees.

"And what about it?" she asked as though it meant nothing.

"I'm not human," Kaos said. "Don't you get it?" he asked and stared at her, she didn't respond. "I didn't die, I'm inhuman…" Kaos lead her. "You love me, inhuman, undying me." He looked away from her.

"The fortune," she said softly with shock. She stared at him.

"I think I'm the one in your fortune," Kaos said softly. She was quiet then a rush went through her.

"Then could you do something for me?" she asked. He looked up.

"What?"

"Kiss me," she said. Kaos looked at her with some worry, "There was another part of the fortune, it said that when I kissed the man I was meant to be with something amazing would happen, and at that moment I would know it was him." Kaos gulped. He sat still and she approached him slowly staring into his eyes. Their noses touched and Kaos felt her warm breath, they were nearly touching hen Kaos snapped back.

"I can't,' He shook his head, "I just can't Enna. It's not that I don't want to, I just can't." he blushed far redder than before and he couldn't meet her eyes. Enna came and jumped around his shoulders pushing him back on the couch. She lay on top of him hugging him.

"It's all right," she comforted him, "It was a really stupid question," she sounded true to her word, "It wasn't right for me to expect you to do such a thing on the spot like that." She softened. "Could you ever forgive me?" she asked so sweetly. She lay on his chest.

"How could I not?" Kaos said warmly. He looked down at her with a sense of comfort that he never saw before. She was a little child sweet and innocent. They stayed like that for a time.

"Kaos?" Enna asked, although he didn't respond. She looked and found him sleeping so angelically. She rose off him slowly not to wake him. She slipped out of the room.

(*October 7ᵗʰ*) Kaos rose about two hours after she left and found Iori sitting in the room reading. He rose and rubbed his head looking for Enna.

"How long was I out?"

"About two hours since I came in," Iori said looking down at his book. "You didn't say a single word," he said finally.

"Really?" Kaos said quietly.

"Yep," he said short and sweet.

"Where did Daragon and Yoki go?"

"Daragon took Yoki to the Elvin School with him. He teaches a class there, he said he would come back later tonight to check on you." Kaos rose.

"How is our Prince doing?' Daragon asked Iori who still sat in the office. Daragon stood leaning with one hand on the table that Iori had a book open looking studiously.

"He seems to be doing quite well, he slept for about three hours this afternoon and I do believe that after that he took a shower and he's be in his room since."

"He slept?"

"Yep, after Enna left I found him sleeping soundly on the couch."

"He didn't transmit?" Daragon asked

"Nope," Iori said. Daragon walked across the room in pursuit of Kaos. He opened the door to his bed room and found Kaos dazed on his bed. He was quiet, the band still about his forehead. Yet, his hair was cut and still damp.

"Hey Kaos," Daragon said.

"Hey," Kaos said serenely.

"How was your day?"

"It was okay," he said distantly.

"Could you take off the band for a moment," Daragon asked and walked over. Kaos sat upright and undid the knot and peeled off the band. Daragon knelt down and brushed aside pieces of hair to look at the Yoko. He felt it and rubbed his hand on Kaos' forehead. "Okay, you can put it back on." Kaos knotted it tight on the back of his head and let the tails fall down just past his shoulders. "So I hear you slept soundly this afternoon, that's great. Your body probably needed that." Daragon claimed.

"I feel much better," Kaos spoke.

"I need to take you to the Raika Shrine in a few days," Daragon said, "You need to be blessed by a high parable, and the safest bet for you would be from the high parable at that Shrine."

"Cunti?" Kaos asked.

'Yes," Daragon said a little surprised. "How did you know that?"

"I knew him as a child, every now and then my father would take me to see him." Kaos added. "I thought he was some crazy old man making strange comments to himself when he saw me, but ha! Now I think I'm crazy." Kaos smiled.

"That's even better," Daragon smiled, "We'll need all the friends we can."

"So how did your class go?' Kaos asked him.

"My class?"

"Don't you teach at an elvin school?" Kaos asked, "That's what Iori told me."

"Oh, yes, it went quite well. Although…" he started, "Yesterday, did you encounter a girl in the library?" Kaos sighed.

"Yeah," he laughed, "That was a horrible miss understanding."

"She came up to me today after class and asked if I could bring you to class, as my apprentice."

"She knew I was your apprentice?"

"I think she figured it out while she was here and met me. What did happen between you, she said you locked her in your room?"

"I thought she recognized me as the Prince so I didn't want her to go spreading it around so I kept her in my room, but then I found that she was simply asking if I was Iori assistant so I let her go, but she was defensive and we both ended up using magic and she finally calmed down and I let her go." I didn't want her running out in her state."

"You left quite an impression on her, she claimed to the other's today in class that I had found a superhuman as an apprentice!" he laughed.

"I didn't do that much," Kaos claimed.

"Well," Daragon laughed, "I'm glad to see you well Kaos."

(*October 10th*) "So has he completed?" a man with grey hair pulled back in a low long ponytail. He wore long red wrap around robe. The sleeves fell down over his wrinkled calm hands. A shall with elvin characters hung loosely around his neck. Underneath a white robe. Prayer beads were run around his chest going under his arms then around his neck. They met in back where they were tied in a knot. His voice was wise and soft. Yet there was something about him that made you listen closely. Among his large wrinkled features a small green dot on his forehead, where a small extravagant hat was placed.

"Not fully high parable Cunti," Daragon bowed. Cunti smiled and lifted his hand on Daragon's head.

"I have not seen young Kaos for several months now, it's always a pleasure to see the dear boy," his smile was warm, Daragon looked at it. "You may rise, and bring him in." Daragon rose and went back to the front room where Kaos sat. Daragon stopped when he found Kaos with a large bird clasped to his wrist.

"Yeah, it's been a while," Kaos commented to the bird who coed and tilted its head. Kaos brought a hand out and stroked its head. "You seem to be quite relaxed today." Kaos said the bird cawed softly and Kaos smiled.

"Kaos?" Daragon said in the silence.

"Oh?" Kaos jumped. "You ready for me?" Daragon walked up to them.

"What type of bird is this?" Daragon asked Kaos.

"I don't know," Kaos questioned. Daragon reached out to pet it, but the bird jumped in aggravation and squawked at him. Retreating to Kaos' shoulder it barked at Daragon again.

"Hey," Daragon crossed his arms.

"I guess he doesn't like you," Kaos commented. Kaos tried to coax the bird back on to his hand, but the bird would go and just stared coldly at Daragon. "Hey, I got to go." Kaos said to it. It took its head and rubbed it against Kaos' affectionately. "I really got to go see Cunti." The bird wouldn't budge. Cunti peeked around the corner.

"That *Sharae* seems to have taken kind to you, dear Kaos," Cunti smiled   and   stared   at   Kaos, "Σηαραε ηε□λλ βε βαχκ, I μυστ σεε ηιμ. (Sharae he'll be back, I must see him.)" The bird hopped off and Kaos rose from the bench. Kaos walked over to Cunti.

"That's the first time it has done that," Kaos said staring as it soared back to its roost.

"That Sharae is very picky when it comes to deciding who its likes. It likes something about you Kaos." Cunti spoke, "Well, come with me Kaos, Daragon could you wait here for a little," he directed Daragon who sat down. The two walked into the other room.

"So, I'm sure you have much to say," Cunti said to Kaos, "But before we get deep into anything I must asked you to remove that band." Cunti commented. Kaos undid Daragon's head band and tied it around his wrist. Cunti walked up to it and it started glowing Kaos felt slightly dizzy. Cunti's hand hovered over the Yoko and Kaos sat very still.

He whispers and blesses it. Strangely Kaos jumped, the crest on his forehead lit up and the stone glowed a white. It stopped and Kaos felt like he had been drained. Cunti bent down and took the time to grab Kaos chin. The old man's eyes stared down into Kaos' eyes, then he took Kaos' chin turned it sideways to look at his profile. Then he took his old fingers and ran up the edge of his ears and halt on the tips. He rubbed them in his fingers and then told Kaos to stand. Kaos did and Cunt moved around behind him and looked at his back. He came back around.

"You may sit now," Cunti spoke. Kaos sat down and stared at Cunti. "I'm sure you know this, but you're in the midst of a transformation."

"It's not finished?" Kaos asked disappointed.

"No," Cunti shook his head.

"Damn it," Kaos muttered to himself.

"How have you been holding up?" Cunti asked.

"You should have been a little more forewarning when it came to my mother," Kaos growled still in a foul mood.

"Perhaps," Cunti said. "You're more interesting when you're agitated."

"What?" Kaos raised his voice.

"That bird, *Sharae* has taken to no one since I received it as a gift from the Shrine in Mesodow. They tend to like elves but that one doesn't seem to like anyone, anyone but you. So, I'd like you to take it with you."

"Look," Kaos spoke, "Why did you see me all those years monthly, then weekly, what were you looking for?"

"Your father was worried about the transformation and wanted to know when it might take place. HE had you come see me so I could check your progress."

"You…"Kaos bit his tongue, "You knew all along and you didn't prepare me?"

"There's nothing I could do, my hands were tied. Marina had explicitly said that it was to remain a secret till the time was required, even from you."

"Transforming to…" he stopped, "I don't even know what to call it!"

"Ηαλφωαψ," he said, "You should call the transformation to you current state: "Ηαλφωαψ,""

"Halfway?" Kaos was questioning, "I'm only halfway?" he said shocked.

"Yes, you're still half human, hence half-way." Cunti eased.

"But then that must mean…" Kaos said worried.

"Kaos, don't worry over such things…"

"How can I not worry over that?" Kaos yelled. "I can hardly handle being half-elf, let alone full!" Kaos rose from his seat.

"Kaos, calm down."

"How can I be at ease, something in me is happening and I can't do anything to stop it!" Kaos spoke clearly. He walked over to Cunti. "They've stripped me of everything, Cunti!" he said sadly. He grabbed the man's shoulders and shook them, "They've taken it all away, Cunti!" Cunti didn't look at Kaos then laughed. "What's so funny?" Kaos growled, he felt a prickle up his spine. He kept laughing and it exploded, "Shut up to fuckin old man!" Kaos yelled. The man looked once more at Kaos.

"How I love to see you frustrated," he said.

"What?" Kaos said disgusted.

"You seemed to be able to pick things almost instantly it's refreshing to see you struggle,"

"You sick old man!" Kaos shoved him back in his seat and started to leave the Shrine. He pushed the door open in the waiting room with a glare on his face.

"Sharae come with me," Kaos walked up to Daragon. The bird swooped down and landed on Kaos' shoulder.

"You don't have the band I gave you,"

"Oh," Kaos said and stuck his hand out to the side. "Χομε το με" he whispered and the thing slew into his hand he tied it around his forehead.

"Daragon, may I speak with you before you two leave."

"What gonna tell him that I'm only halfway to my doom?" Kaos said and opened the door. He stepped out into the cold night and let his breath make puffs at the edge of a rolling hillside.

"Kaos!" Daragon yelled.

He is only half-way transformed Daragon…it's not wise to let the boy get in a state of little manna anymore…his full transformation is late.

"Kaos wait up!"

He'll be oblivious for only so long until he goes and looks for the answers himself, we should expect nothing less from dear young but clever Kaos.

"Kaos…" Daragon yelled at him but he was already walking down the path.

We can expect that he will surely try to tire his own body to prevent his full transformation; all we can do is try to ease his internal struggle and guide him. I fear that the god's grow impatient for their messenger, so take care. Goodbye my friend, I hope for the boy's safety from the world around him and himself most of all. The Sharae will protect his soul, that's all I can give him, I hope it serves him well.

Daragon ran up and grabbed his free shoulder, the Sharae squawked at him and Daragon immediately removed his hand. Kaos didn't argue with its decision.

"Hey, keep that thing under control."

"He is under control," Kaos said to Daragon sternly and stroked it on the head. Daragon stared at Kaos.

"Hey," Daragon said softly, "Kaos, as I said before, whatever state you're in I'll be there for you."

"Yeah, I know," Kaos said softly turned away from him.

"You should really cover up," Daragon said softly and handed him a cloak. The sharae floated around Kaos as he tied it around his shoulders and put the hood up. The bird settled again on his shoulder and the two walked into the darkness down the snowy path.

Kaos walked his head hung low towards the ground as he bared the frigid air placing his wet boots one foot at a time in the snow that seemed to never dissipate. Puffs of smoke soared from his mouth into the wind of the snowy woods. He heard a crackled in the wood in front and he lifted his head in shock. The Sharae fluttered its wings startled as Kaos stared into the dark. He stopped still and Daragon did also.

"What's wrong?" Daragon asked.

"Something's here," Kaos whispered.   Daragon moved close to Kaos and looked behind his shoulder.

"Are you sure, Kaos?" Daragon asked him, "It's wicked cold, no one would be stupid to go ambushing in this weather."

"I'm sure," Kaos said. He stared out in the darkness and the fiend of its wood lay hidden in disguise. Daragon turned around and they faced back to back. There was another crackle. Daragon must have heard it because he suddenly tensed and dropped an arm in front of Kaos.

"I want you to stay out of it," Daragon claimed.

"If you *can* get the thing by yourself," Kaos claimed. There was a shrill woman's laugh that broke the wind breeze. Daragon whipped around behind Kaos. Kaos' heart pounded, and Daragon's in tune. She laughed again and the snow swirled. Daragon covered Kaos' head, clutching both of the capes over each other. There trill of a twitter of a bird. Kaos wrenched up and yelled:

"Sharae!" he yelled. The bird had shrieked and dashed away from them.

"Don't worry about it Kaos," Daragon said softly, "I think I know why our friend took off." Kaos looked down and in the middle of the path was a black wolf with a shimmering white chest. Kaos felt something deep in his stomach give staring into its eyes as it stared back. "Kaos, you should move back very slowly," Daragon hinted stepping slowly back. The eyes of the wolf hopped on him like prey. He slyly took a few steps closer. Daragon stopped in sheer shock. Suddenly the wolf walked slowly up to Kaos, it was then that Daragon saw something he had not expected. Kaos where he was standing fell into a daze the wolf twirled around him and rubbed his leg affectionately. From the wolf's shoulders sprang back and it stood up in awkward motions. Its body jerked back and forth until in its aftermath a charcoal skinned woman appeared amidst the snow. Her long silver swooping hair blew in the breeze, the elaborate dress glimmered. Daragon fell to his knees as he saw the snowflakes stopped in their tracks. The faces of the woman shown with eerie darkness and the pupil-less eye whites gazed their large blind glare at Kaos. She walked up to him and spoke in a strange tongue at him with a lovely tone that Daragon could barely hear. She suddenly caught Kaos frail figure as his knees dropped. She brought him down on her lap and stroked his chin. Suddenly her hand was deep inside his chest, blood spattered and she yanked out his heart. She stood and blood dripped from her fingers, Kaos lay limp on the ground. She stared at him and out of the darkness the black wolf appeared once more and walked up to the figure. She rose and sat on top the wolf holding

Kaos' heart in her hand. Daragon blinked and it was all gone; the blood and the woman, all that was left was Kaos' body lying on the ground. Daragon ran up to Kaos and grabbed his shoulders.

"Kaos!" he yelled. Kaos didn't' wake, suddenly Daragon stopped and noticed something about Kaos had changes. He peeled away Kaos' head and found razor sharp elf ears sat upon Kaos' head.

He slammed the door to the library open panting and shivering, the limp figure that hardly resembled Kaos draped in his arms.

"Iori! Yoki!" he yelled in the hallway. Yoki came dashing up to them.

"Kaos?" Iori patted him on the cheek. Kaos didn't react and Iori's face grew grave. His body had been placed in his bed. The three adults in the room hovering in silence. The winter air sped by outside a small window of the back room.

(October 12th) Rapp rapp. There was a tap on the window. Kaos' eyes snapped up, although they still held a zombie feel to them. He rose thematically and sauntered over to the window stumbling. He grabbed the slider and with two hands yanked it open and collapsed on the ground. The wind blew ice cold flakes through the window and through the mist came the Sharae. It swirled down to him and snuggled under his arm as he lay unconscious on the ground. Yoki opened the door suddenly, the bird ferociously hopped from under Kaos arm and squawked at her viciously. She retraced the few steps she had taken into the room as the bird advanced on her. Upon the foot-an-a-half long body, every feather stood on end.

"You!" she yelled and picked up her strength. She picked out her sheath and drew the sword. The bird squawked more retreating on top of Kaos' body. "Get away from him you vial thing!' she yelled and advanced with the sword. As she grew a few close to it the bird hopped into the air and with its talons scrapped after her. She dodges the first few in the midst of the scurrying she knock down a side table. She lifted the sword and swung. It vooshed by the great bird's side. She rose it again swinging it with speed just missing the bird. Iori hearing the crash dashed in.

"Yoki!" he yelled. Yoki lifted her sword again and Iori dashed to restrain her.

"Let me go! It has done something to Kaos!" she yelled and pulled with her strength against Iori. She easily knocked him off and rose the sword again.

"Σο τηε σταρ□σ μαψ ρετυρν, το μορταλ τηισ ορδαινεδ ση αλλ βε," Iori whispered and the sword feel from Yoki's hand.

"Iori," she warned. Iori walked up to her side and stared at the bird atop now Kaos' body squawking like a mother guarding her chicks.

"Πλεασε βε ατ εασε," Iori spoke to it. It stopped and tilted its head for a moment then gave a loud squawk once more returning to its defending. "Ωε ωονϵτ ηαρμ Καοσ. Βε ατ πεαχε μαγιχαλ βεαστ. (We won't harm Kaos. Be at peace magical beast.)" The bird stopped and Iori walked closer to Kaos. The bird didn't take any actions. Iori crawled slowly toward Kaos look at the bird carefully. He stopped and the bird stared coldly at him. He stared once more and the bird rotated to watch him more closely. Daragon was next to Kaos' head upon the ground. He reached out and touched Kaos shoulder. The bird seemed at that point to restrict an instinct to squawk. Iori came close to Kaos and placed his hands under Kaos' shoulder preparing to lift his head off the ground. At this the instinct boil up once more and the bird squawked and reached a great talon in the direction of Iori's hands. Iori decide to quickly snatch up Kaos' shoulder. The bird roared and scrapped at his arm with its talons flying about wildly. Iori dragged Kaos back to the bed and heaved him in it. As soon as Kaos was back on the bed, Iori popped off Kaos and the bird retreated back on top of him. Iori rose his bleeding and scraped hands and stepped away from the predatory bird.

"Ι϶μ σορρψ βεαστ οφ τηε σκιεσ," Iori bowed. The bird actually quieted, but didn't not get off Kaos.

"What is that thing?" Yoki asked quietly. The bird didn't keep his eyes off Iori. Iori moved slowly to his left towards the door and Yoki in side step.

"I don't know," Iori commented now behind Yoki still staring at the bird. "But I think if it is doing anything, its guarding Kaos from us." Iori spoke. "Come out of the room, Yoki." He instructed her grabbing her arm. He pulled her into the hallway.

"What should we do?"

"I'm going to go see if I have anything in this library on such a beast. I need you to look with me."

"Yoki!" he cried. "I have found it I think. Come!" he beckoned her over to the table he was reading on. He pointed to a picture and started reading the passage beneath. "Sharae, a magical beast found exclusively in region containing Raider's Cavern. They take on the form of a hawk ranging from a foot to a meter in body length. Sharae are known for their motherly nature, and are usually friendly with elves."

"Well, this one isn't."

"...Sharae's are usually given to Shrines as guardians as they are rumored to embody the spirits of the gods. Unlike affectionate animals that are known for their helpfulness to all of society, each bird tends to pick a 'master' or mother. They'll guard and die for the protection of this person. Abilities that one should be careful of is the magical capability the bird has been reported to at times pray on elves and humans in defense. The bird is very territorial; one should act in severe care around these animals. Magical abilities: uninvestigated. Physical attributes: long feathers, bright colors, and talons.

"I bet you it has chosen Kaos as its master," Iori said.

"But where did Kaos ever meet such a creature?" Iori stopped at thought for moment.

"The only place could be at the Rakia Shrine."

"Was it the bird that did this to Kaos?" she asked.

"No," Iori said calmly, "Remember what Daragon said he saw. There was a woman riding a wolf who stole Kaos' heart, literately..."

"Please, spare the details," Yoki said rather awkwardly. Iori looked at her.

"Yes, the very thought is bone chilling." He said. "Kaos, what happened to you? What will happen with you when you wake up?"

(*October 15th*) "I'm guessing he still has not awoke?" Daragon asked.

"No, the boy is still in that unconscious state."

"What about the bird?"

"Still there," Ioir said. "That's bird still sits there watching."

"I still can't believe my eyes," Daragon said strangely, "that woman…"

"It sounds just so strange, the snow literally stopped in midair?"

"Yes, and…oh god it was so beautiful but horrid."

"Have you seen Kaos?" Iori asked him. "Seen his ears?"

"Yes," Daragon closed his eyes, "It makes me nervous after speaking with Cunti."

"What did Cunti say?"

"Kaos, transformation is half-way through," Daragon sighed. "With this development I'm worried that the god's pushed him too far too fast."

"The gods?" he said.

"Cunti said that he felt the gods had been growing impatient and Kaos' transformation was late.."

"He has pushed his body to the limit far too many times than even a normal sorcerer should."

"And that's all my fault." Daragon sighed.

"No, its Kaos fault!" Iori shouted, "I think that if he feels like draining himself, he's the only one who can prevent it." Daragon's earring lit up. He rose with shock and held it. His mouth somewhat open.

"What is it?"

"Patella has been burned…" Daragon whispered. Daragon sat down with a plop and the two were silent. "…Water Nymphs have betrayed the Empress' call and the east has been invaded…"

"By blue ships," Iori said quietly. "Kaos was right." He said and looked at Daragon. Daragon's face grew in sheer horror. It stopped glowing.

"What will become of us now?" Daragon said and rubbed the back of his neck. Suddenly there was a huge scream from the room besides the office. Daragon sat still. Iori stood up.

"Sounds that Kaos is up," Iori said.

"Do you think he heard Aysil?" Daragon asked in pain. There was then a loud thumping crash from inside the bedroom followed by silence.

"That didn't sound too good."

"God, I really don't want to go in there," Daragon spoke shaking his head.

"And you think I want to," Iori sighed and the two remained at the table. The door to the office slammed open. Kaos held a single fist out. The doors hinges had snapped and the door smoked on the floor.

"What the fuck is happening!" Kaos had appeared in the doorway, eye brows low and voice defiant. He stared at the two men for some sort of response that he didn't get. He stomped up to them.

"Kaos, you should go back to bed," Iori commented. Kaos turned to Daragon.

"What the hell is happening? I know you know!" Kaos stormed. "What the fuck was that transmission about!" Kaos stormed. Daragon covered his head. The Sharae flew in and scraped at Kaos' shoulders. "What?" Kaos barked at it. It snagged his shirt and attempted to drag him away. Kaos didn't budge and shook it off. "Daragon…" he hissed. Daragon was quiet. "It was something about Patella! I heard Patella!" Kaos yelled. Suddenly the bird dived again. "Leave me the hell alone!" It squawked and snatched his shirt and yanked him back.

"Kaos…" Daragon started. Kaos furious and anxious grabbed Daragon from his chair in two hands a rim of white around his whole body. As the two went nose to nose the bird made a strange noise. The glow immediately ceased and Kaos' pupils shrank. His grips on Daragon's shirt loosened and almost in order his head, neck, shoulders, knees dropped till he collapsed eyes opened on the floor. Iori rose and found the bird's eyes glowing and stared down at Kaos; paralyzed on the ground.

"Kaos?" Daragon said questioning. He looked down at Kaos.

"The bird paralyzed him I think," Iori spoke. Daragon rubbed his head, "I guess that solves the problem. I think I'm starting to like this bird." The bird took roost on the couch. Daragon reached down and grabbed Kaos' shoulders. Immediately the bird clawed him. "Maybe not," Daragon back off.

"At least it solves the problem of Kaos using magic," Iori said.

"It doesn't solve the fact that Kaos must have heard part of the transmission, and you'll be sure he'll wake up pissed." Daragon put a hand on his head.

Kaos woke up a few hours later, with a built up stomach rage as he saw the bird roosting on th couch watching him.

"Damn you!" he cursed at it. It squawked very regally as though his anger fed its pride. Kaos rose and walked out of the office quickly looking for Daragon. The bird flew nearby constantly. He saw Iori coming out of an isle and ran up to him

"Iori!" Kaos yelled.

"You're up," Iori said looking at Kaos face.

"Where is Daragon?" Kaos said decisively.

"At the Elvin School, he won't be around to talk with you until late this evening." Iori stated firmly. Kaos stopped and formed another plan. "Where is this school?"

"He told me not to tell you," Iori said.

"What?"

"He said that you were to remain here under the watch of your friend," Iori said and eyed the bird on top of the bookshelves.

"You can't be serious!" Kaos exclaimed.

"Not only am I going through this horrible crappy transformation into a fuckin elf! But Daragon can't even tell me what is happening in Patella! This is a piece of crap! I'm stuck in this fuckin library all by self with this parent of a bird and not a thing to do but flip out over my family and my future and all my friends! If they even will recognize me anymore!" Kaos yelled at him.

"Don't start taking your frustrations out on me!" Iori said and put a finger on Kaos' chest. "You've caused me nothing but trouble! You can't shelve books and you can't just suck it up and stop complaining! I'm not the one who put you in this position so don't dare start yelling at me, when all I've done is try to help you!" Iori turned abruptly and slammed a book on the shelf. Kaos stood silent, Iori's words sinking into him. He looked down to the ground and back at Iori in guilt. He had been such a horrid person.

"I'm sorry Iori," Kaos said softly and began to turn.

"You can make yourself useful if you help me shelve books." Iori said. Kaos jumped and buried himself in the work.

interrupted

"Hey I thought I shelved this one," Kaos stopped with the small leather brown book with the scrape down the side.

"What?"

"This book," Kaos held it up and at that moment the Sharae swooped down and snatched it from his hands in its great talons. "Hey! You!" The Sharae took the book up to his roost and it claw hung to it. Iori laughed.

"It certainly doesn't want you reading that one," he chuckled.

"Well, who said I was going to read it."

"That thing is sure a good parent," Iori laughed remembered what the book contained. Kaos went up to the book shelf and tested its strength

"What do you think you're doing?" Iori asked as Kaos placed a foot on the bookcase.

"Getting that book," Kaos spoke and moved up the shelving. Iori laughed and watched the bird. Kaos was nearly in arm's length when the bird hopped back and took off to another shelving grouping. Iori was laughing now.

"You're never going to get your hands on that book," Iori said.

"Oh, we'll see," Kaos said and jumped on top of the shelves. "I'll get that fuckin book even if it means becoming paralyzed a few more times."

"It's just a book,"

"No, it's a book which *that thing* has to demonstrate its leash on me!" Iori laughed at watched Kaos' trapeze act as he kept getting so close to snatching it, but failing.

"What's up all?" Michael's voice rang through the library and he walked down the aisle. Kaos jumped across the shelving above him and the bird squawked as Kaos wrestled with it. He rolled and snapped him on the wrist. It wriggled free and Kaos lay half-falling off the shelf.

"Kaos?" Michael yelled up at him. Kaos jumped in shocked and his balance was thrown off.

"Whoa," Kaos yelled when all of a sudden he slipped off the shelf and landed on top of Michael.

"Ow," Kaos groaned and rose his head. "Sorry," Kaos said looking at Michael. He got off and helped Michael up. Michael brushed himself off.

"Gees, what were you doing up there?"

"Trying to get a book that bird stole from me," Kaos pointed to the Sharae.

"Holy fucker!" Michel exclaimed staring at the thing. "What the heck is it?"

"It's my stupid Sharae!" Kaos mooned.

"Where did you get it?"

"It was given to me by the high parable of the Raika Shrine."

"It's fuckin awesome!" Michael said.

"No," Kaos rubbed his wrist, "The thing is worse than my dad."

"Owch," Michael said and turned to Kaos.

"Whoa!" Michael exclaimed and walked up to Kaos. He grabbed the tips of Kaos' ears suddenly and awkwardly. "You really look like an elf!" Kaos cringed and held his tongue. "I heard you had fallen ill, but that?" he exclaimed astonished. "You should really see the places around here!" Michael exclaimed, "God there are some many really cool shops and things to do, hey, they even have a wizard dueling shop, he jabbed Kaos in the side. I'm sure you could kick everyone's asses."

"Funny," Kaos said sarcastically.

"Hey, I'm sure it's true."

"Yeah," Kaos sighed.

"Well I'm glad to see you well, and well enough to jump after that bird." He laughed and grabbed Kaos around the shoulders as if Kaos hadn't changed.

"So what brings you around if there is so much to do in this town?" Kaos asked.

"I wanted to talk to you, my friend, heard your birthday was coming up in a few days," he said and poked Kaos in the nose.

"It is?"

"Two days? October 15th stupid, it's the 13th" Kaos couldn't believe it he had two days till he was officially eighteen. Michael grabbed at his to give him a noogie and bit his lower lip in playfulness.

"Hey!"

"You're such a rebel!" Michael laughed. "Just like me! We can sing in our single selves!" he yelled throughout the library. "Although, I'll admit, there sure are some cute girls round here!" Michael said on the side note. "Yet, I'm sure you already know that hot stuff." Michael jabbed him in the shoulder.

"What?" Kaos asked defensively.

"Enna?" he asked. "Not to mention the girls in her little crowd!" he said like the typical guy.

"Why did you want to remain single?" Kaos said wary.

"What?" Michael laughed, "God, am I scaring little o' Kaos" Kaos raised an eyebrow, "Oh, it's alright!" he claimed. "But what are you doing for your birthday?" he asked. Kaos was quiet.

"I don't know, I suppose nothing special like always."

"Come on! It's your *eighteenth* birthday!" he exclaimed, "Kids usually have weddings and wedding parties for god's sake, why can't we do something instead. It should sure cost a whole lot less."

"That is if I'm let out of this library," Kaos said.

"You're stuck here?"

"Yeah," Kaos claimed, "'I'm safe here', or that's at least what they claim."

"Well that's a piece of crap ain't it? Enna, curses, massive birds; Instead of meeting trouble you're bring it in." Michael stated.

"You're right about that," Kaos said and eyed over his shoulder on Iori who was eavesdropping on their conversation. Iori looked away but didn't move.

"Then I'll come up something," Michael said winking, "Even if it is small."

Michael left soon after that, Iori found Kaos again, perusing the bird.

"Kaos!" Iori yelled at him as he was in mid-air between the "I" and "H" shelves of the English books. Kaos caught himself on the far shelf and nearly stumbled while replying.

"Yes?" he yelled.

"Come down here," Iori said, "Enough is enough. You still need to save your strength." At this Kaos was not pleased, but he got down never the less grumbling.

"Gees, you guys are all so damn worry, 'oh no, he might never finish his transformation!' "He taunted in a high pitched voice as he stormed by Iori.

"Oh, we just love you." Iori said and laughed as Kaos walked down to his room. The bird followed him of course it now perched itself just on top of his desk chair staring at him and then fluffing its feathers.

"Sure, you all love me," he said. "Yet here I am, changing into to someone I don't want to be." He said and looked at his reflection. If he ever looked like Marina, he looked even more like her now. "So Charles," Kaos said, "I look like Charles, whoever he might be." Kaos sighed and fell back on his bed. "Why? Oh why am I tortured like this? What did I do to anyone to deserve all of this unnecessary crap? …I actually…" he said it astonished, "…I actually just want to go home."

"Daragon?" Iori said shocked as Daragon walked through the front door of the library at quarter-to-nine. "What are you doing back?"

"I think I can do it," Daragon breathed deep. Iori was quiet. "Is he in any of a better mood?"

"After I did some barking, I do believe he calmed down." Iori said stiffly.

"You yelled at him?"

"Yes, it was about time someone did," Iori said.

"I just never would have thought you out of all people."

"Oh, just go ease it to him, I won't say he won't be upset. Yet it's better to tell him, it's a large step in the war that he's so tangled in."

Daragon walked down the hall and halted at the door and put his ear to it. He heard whimpering from the other side so he knocked very softly on the door.

"Kaos?"

Inside Kaos jumped, and whipped his tear-stained face. He spoke.

"Come in," Kaos sat on his bed as Daragon entered. Daragon looked at Kaos who clearly was trying to hide the fact he had been crying just moments before.

"Kaos you alright?" he asked. Kaos gave a strange response however compared to his normally concealing self.

"I'm just a little home sick," Kaos sighed. "It's kind of funny," Kaos laughed, "I never like to be home, yet here I am crying over the fact I can't be home."

"Speaking on the subject, I now am ready to tell you what your aunt said over the transmission this morning." Kaos wasn't angry or agitated. He just sat there and stared at the cot. "What she said was-"

"Daragon," Kaos stopped him, "I'm sorry. I'm sorry for being so damn stubborn and agitated all the time. And so, if you don't think I should know, then you don't have to tell me."

"I think that you should know, Kaos," Daragon said, "I just could barely bring myself to say it knowing what kind of effect it will have on you."

"Well then…" Kaos said, "I've worn myself down all day on the idea of the worst idea, so the feeling won't be new."

"Kaos," he paused, "This morning the Patella Triangle was invaded by Dartawg. They burnt the wall…" Daragon trailed off but the first idea hit him hard.

"So that's what it was," Kaos said softly.

"I'm sorry Kaos," Daragon said, "I really am."

"It's not your fault," Kaos claimed.

"But you saw it coming," Daragon reminded him. Kaos looked up remembering all his dreams.

"Still, Daragon, there's nothing that you can do about it." Kaos said gravely.

(*October 14th*) Kaos heard chirping from the birds outside his window, it must have been noon at least but Kaos still didn't want to rise out of bed. He lay there his stomach growling and his eyes still tear-stuck with his cheeks red.

"Kaos, please come out," Yoki begged him from behind his door. Kaos was quiet and the Sharae eyed the door.

"Go away!" he yelled, "Just leave me alone. " he mumbled on his pillow. He didn't want to do anything, everything just felt so meaningless and empty. All he could think of was Charad, Gorath, Sharle, and the rest of his friends back home being burned and kidnapped by Dartawg back to slavery camps as Prisoners of War. There in camps Kaos knew they would be asked to claim disloyalty to the Empress. Kaos knew neither Sharle nor his poor father would knowing that their son sat near to her. He kept thinking of his father, how distraught he was in all this. He knew of it and he knows that Marina is in danger and his own son.

There was tap on his window and Kaos looked up to see Michael's smiling face beckoning him to the window. Kaos got up and opened it.

"Come on, Kaos," Michael said. "Get dressed, and get out here, its time to have some fun." Michael said. Kaos stared at him and knew that staying in the library would only make him feel worse. So he got dressed and climbed out of the window. The Sharae squawked but Kaos turned on it quickly and stuck his hand out to it. Suddenly with little or no response on the bird's side it collapsed to the ground paralyzed.

"Sweet!" Michael exclaimed.

"Let's just get going before Yoki finds it." Kaos said. The two snuck around into the Pinto's barn where a second horse stood; presumably it was Michael's.

"Get on the Pinto, we're going to go see someone," Michael stated as he mounted a black horse. Kaos raised an eyebrow but did as he said. The two on horseback rode swiftly away from the library and into the streets where they were forced to walk.

"So where are we going?" Kaos questioned.

"You're going to go see Enna," Michael said.

"What? What are you going to do?" Kaos said shocked. "I'm going to go see her friends." He said.

"But?" Kaos stopped.

"But what?"

"A…" he stopped reluctantly blushing, "I mean, I don't know if she want to see me, well like this."

"Like what?"

"Do I have to spell it out?" Kaos said. "My ears, you dumbass! What else?"

"Oh, god, you're so self-conscious, anyways they make you look more dignified, if I can say anything."

"And the Yoko?" Kaos asked.

"Yoko?" Michael questioned and stared at Kaos. "What's a Yoko?" Kaos reached up and removed the head band and came closer to him. He pulled back his lng bangs and Michael smirked.

"Whoa!" he said and rubbed it, "Is that in there for good?"

"Yes, that's what a Yoko is?"

"Doesn't the Empress have one like that?" Michael claimed.

"Yes,"

"Wow, you're becoming more official by the day here." He laughed.

"But what about Enna?"

"If it's in there for good, I would not worry about what she thinks,"

"Should I wear the band?"

"Personally I wouldn't," Michael said, "I think you look better without it."

"I thought you would do something." Kaos added as they headed through town. The air was brisk and the streets were chanting with their normal mid-morning laughter and chatter. Men stared at the two on horseback. Their eyes fixed not only with warning at Kaos, with wary and terror at the same time. His eyes rolled strangely upon each face growing nervous. It was interrupted though by Micheal who looked over his shoulder and winked.

"Did I not spell it out in the library yesterday?" he sniggered and smirked probably red evil horns curling on top his head.

"Mister know it all, how did you managed to tell Enna on such short notice?" Kaos laughed and poked fun at him. Suddenly a man carrying a basket of fruit walked in front of the Pinto. Kaos reared him back with effort and she shared her distress. The man stumbled and the fruit fell on the ground.

"Smart one," Michael cheered. Kaos hopped down off the horse and helped the man pick up the apples. He reached towards the closest one and handed it to him with an apology.

"Sorry about that?"

"Oh, keep you hands to yourself you beast!" he said and snagged it from his hand. Michael was silent, passerbys didn't argue with the man's commented and Kaos was horrified. The man quickly gathered the rest of the apples and scurried away muttering to himself curses. Kaos looked up and a child nearby with its pumped hands sank deeper into the pleats of his mother's skirt.

"They don't know what they're talking bout'" Michael tried to ease his pain. Kaos lowered his gaze and like a criminal mounted the pinto. He walked on in front of Michael's horse his head low and eyes cast at the reigns placed very loosely in his lap.

"Kaos, don't listen to him, he doesn't know you." Micheal tried to say trotting up to his side. "You're not a monster."

"Yes I am," Kaos muttered, "I look like a monster."

"What? Kaos?"

"If I didn't have this Yoko I would be a monster," Kaos teared. He stopped his horse and turned around.

"Kaos? Where are you going?" Michael claimed.

"I'm going back," Kaos grumbled.

"No!" Michael grabbed the reigns from Kaos' hands. "You're not going back and hiding in your room."

"Patella's gone, I'm an elf, it's like the gods never wanted Kaos to exist."

"Enna wants to see you."

"Enna?" he said suddenly. "He dove for the reigns. "No! She can't" he dove but Micheal swayed.

"You're going to go visit her, you want to, I know Kaos does."

The sun sat high in the west by the time Enna's house appeared before them. Kaos followed by Micheal walked up the driveway and dismounted. Kaos slowly and reluctantly went up to the door, his fist hovered just over the door. Michael knocked suddenly, Kaos turned with a grim face and Michael shrugged. The door opened in this process and a thin wrinkled faced woman appeared at the door.

"Hello, good afternoon, can I help you?" she asked looking at the two of them.

"Is Enna around?" Kaos asked, at his voice the woman jumped.

"Enna?" she said excited, "You want to see Enna?"

"If it is possible," Michael added, Kaos jabbed him in the side.

"Who might be asking?" she said with interest.

"He is," Michael pointed to Kaos like a little kid. "My name is Michael."

"Any you are?' she stared at Kaos.

"Kaos," he said plainly. She finally grew sincere and real hearing his name.

"Oh my dear, it's so good to finally meet you." She said warmly and escorted him in. "I've heard so much about you for my daughter…and I must say thank you for the pedals at the wedding, Enna said you were the one who exchanged it."

"You're welcome…" Kaos said smiling.

"[Enna's Father]," She said.

"Is Enna home?" Kaos asked.

"Um…yes, she is," the woman said rather strangely all of a sudden.

"I would really like to see her," Kaos said.

"Well, she's a little busy, if you wait a half-an-hour or so she should be free…" she said yet again in that strange tone.

"What is she up to? Does she need any help?" Kaos asked a little reluctant, unsure of the strange tone and what it might mean.

"No," she said, "She doesn't need your help." At that moment Enna came through the kitchen doors under the arm most uncomfortably of a large well-built man with a pressed lack shirt half buttoned up, showing thick dark chest hair. His hair, atop his head, fell around his shoulders in dark curls and his cheeks high and defined, like every other muscle of his body.

"My sweet, you and I are meant to be," he said his voice deep and majestic. Enna looked horribly miserable under the man's grip. She seemed to be dressed quite up, her hair done is sausage curls like Lural's always was when she came over. She wore a beautiful simple dress that flattered all her beauty. Kaos didn't realize it but his mouth had dropped and he had rose instantly upon her entry.

Enna looked up from her dismal gaze to see him. Immediately her frown grew to a grin. She tossed off the man's bulky arm and ran across the kitchen to Kaos.

"Oh, Kaos!" she yelled in delight. She dived into Kaos in a great hug and at this Kaos met the bulky man's razor-sharp eyes. The man glared at him with pure jealousy. At this Kaos snagged his arms around Enna and hugged her back. She was innocent, this man certainly was not.

"Oh Kaos, I'm so glad to see you!" she exclaimed with glee.

"Enna," Kaos said, "I really am glad to see you too." He was surprised but the words didn't fall out with a lie. He felt most rattled by this man, the kind he felt with Chet, his rival back in Patella.

"Enna, introduce your friend to Hugal." Her mother instructed. Enna let go of Kaos most reluctantly and stared down at her hands.

"Kaos," she said and indicated to Hugal by raising a hand in his direction, "This is Sir Hugal of Dramet," she said solemnly. "Hugal," she pointed to Kaos now. "This is Kaos Bernedict of…" she stopped.

"The Patella Triangle," Kaos finished it for her. Kaos walked up to the man and put out a hand. "Pleasure to meet you, Sir Hugal." He said out of politeness. Hugal hesitated and looked Kaos up and down deductively.

"A northerner are you?" Hugal commented rudely, "What brings you down here?" Hugal asked.

"Darmet, is not exactly inline either," Kaos commented cleverly.

"My father owns a mill down here. I'm sent to check on its production monthly."

"How is production, if I may ask?" Kaos created small talk trying to investigate his foe.

"Decent," Hugal gave a rather ambiguous response. "Enna, I'll see you tomorrow, I have much to do." He said, "It's a pleasure meeting you, Kaos. Good day." He left clearly distastefully. Enna's mother was distressed, but the look on Enna's face at Kaos was priceless.

"Oh Kaos!" she cried again in glee. Immediately her mother slammed down a pan on the table.

"Enna!" she halted. Kaos jumped. "You!" she pointed at Kaos, "You half-beast you! " She came from behind the counter waving in her hand a kitchen knife. "You bastard! Stay away from my little girl! You here!

She's finally met someone decent, so you should keep your kind clear!" Kaos was pushed out the door by the woman.

"Mother!" Enna cried and tried to help him from her onslaught.

"I'm doing this for your own good, dear, he's nothing but trouble, he's their kind, them devils should go rot in hell, wherever hell is for those beasts!" Kaos was shocked. Enna grabbed her mother's shoulder.

"Kaos!" she screamed holding the knife back "Kaos! Run!" she yelled, "Get out of here!" she said.

"I can't" Kaos said, "I can't let you marry with that bastard!" Kaos said firmly.

"Bastard?" her mother yelled, "Bastard! His father is the most revered statesmen in all of the south," he owns all the mills in a 400 mile area, he can offer so much. True, he's a bastard, but he's a rich bastard and can take good care of my sweet daughter. Not some half-breed who has to work as a librarian's assistant just to get room and board!" she yelled at Kaos. Kaos' mouth dropped.

"For your information Mrs. Berk, I don't have to work to get a room there, nor am I a poor dirt bag, as for the half-breed, yeah, you're right." He declared, "But you know what? I don't think your sweet innocent daughter deserved to live her life unhappy under some arbitrary title!"

"You don't understand!" she yelled, "I know my daughter deserved all that! She deserves the best, that's why Hugal was selected!"

"She is far better than him!" he yelled.

"Do I hear General Kaos' voice in my house?" Mr. Berk asked as he stepped into the room and looked at Kaos.

"General?" Mrs. Berk asked herself, "you're a General?" she looked at him with shock.

"Yes, I suppose that is technically what I'm called," he spoke still agitated.

"Of the Wakita, my dear, can you believe it?" he said with pride in his voice. Mrs. Berk stared at Kaos strangely. Kaos didn't like it at all. "How about you two go in the back and talk?" her father signaled to Kaos and Enna. Enna grabbed Kaos' forearm gently and led him outside, as a quarrel began in the kitchen. The air was fresh and Kaos sighed as it fell on his face.

"Kaos, I'm really sorry," Enna walked besides him.

"Why should you be sorry? It's true, I am a half-breed." Kaos claimed and sighed.

"But that was never your choice," Enna said. "I remember you told me two days ago that you had been placed in a position where you didn't to be, thank you."

"Huh?" he said and stopped. She suddenly hugged him.

"Thank you," she said again, "no one has ever stuck up for me like that or talked to me on such a level."

"Well," he started laughing, "You know me and my philosophy about marriage ... " he laughed.

"What *did* you come here for?" she asked.

"Nothing major I suppose, I guess I just wanted to see you."

"You've done more than that!" she exclaimed.

"I'm sorry, I just think men like Hugal who flaunt around titles are absolute bastards!" Kaos claimed.

"That's what I love about you," Enna said warmly and grabbed his hands in hers.

"You deserve better," Kaos spoke staring at her, "You're so beautiful." Kaos said.

"Kaos?" she said, "Not as pretty as my sister<" she said putting herself down.

"You're more beautiful than your sister." Kaos said and warmly put and hand on her cheek, she blushed.

"God? Are you pulling off more magic on me?" she yelled playfully.

"Magic?" he blushed now.

"You all googly-eyed like that?"

"What?" he raised back, "Do I have to be drunk for you to believe that I think you're beautiful?" he asked her and she stopped her heart racing in adrenaline. "If you want I'll go get drunk right no if that will make you believe me/" she smiled and turned around to stare at him.

"Why you ... " she growled playfully and tackled him, as he was laughing. "You have to go be all cute and charming on me don't you?" she said laying on top of him. He was laughing and smiling. Suddenly he arched his neck and pecked her on the cheek. She immediately stopped moving and looked down in shock at him. He smiled waiting for her response.

"You just kissed me?" she said shocked. Kaos laughed.

"Yes, sweet innocent Enna, I just kissed you." She stared at him lovingly when suddenly her face dropped.

"Hey, what was that?" she said and brought her hands to Kaos' forehead. She attempted to lift his bangs, but he rose and sniggered tickling her on the lower ribs. She fell back in laughter and he sat on the grass staring at her. "No, really... there's something on your forehead." She crawled over and parted his bangs. She stared at the Yoko strangely and the tried to brush it off. It didn't budge. At this Kaos tried to distract her again, but she shrugged it off and held his head. "Hey, Kaos, there's something stuck in your forehead," she said worried, "it won't come off."

"Don't worry about it," Kaos said leaning into her and placed his head on her shoulder, and his arms hung at her sides.

"But..." she said and the sat nearly in a kiss. She learned in ready to kiss him, yet when there should have been warmth on her lips, her cheek felt his lips. She opened her eyes feeling his body lift away.

"Hey, where are you going?" she yelled after him, as he walked back to house.

"I doubt your parents or mine would want for this to go any farther." Kaos said with a smile.

"Kaos?" Enna asked him. He stopped, "Please don't listen to them," she said but he walked away. "Kaos!" she got up and dashed after him. "Kaos! Stay a while," she insisted.

"It was stupid of me! I'm such a jerk!"

"Kaos? What are you talking about? How are you a jerk?"

"I've led you on too far," Kaos sighed, "I've opened a doorway that should have stayed locked!"

"Kaos?" Enna questioned.

"You and I can never work out," Kaos shook his head.

"I won't marry Hugal, even if my parents beat me, if that's what the problem is."

"It's my mother," Kaos said softly. Enna remembered what Iori had said about Kaos' mother.

"She came to see you the night you fell ill, did she not?"

"Yes," Kaos said, "She did come. But she..."

"You're turning eighteen soon, you must be married!" Enna claimed and ran up to him, "Your mother should surely approve of that, its law."

"Enna…" he started and look solemnly at her.

"Unless you've been arranged to marry someone else," she said slowly with great disheartenment.

"No," Kaos shook his head, and Enna was relived.

"Then what?"

"I'm nothing but trouble, Enna," Kaos sighed unable to say more, "I'm too deep in the war for you to be safe around me."

"What?" she didn't really believe it.

"I put you in danger every time I come here, and the last think I want is to see your innocent eyes to be drenched with tears." Kaos sighed, "You're much to good for my dirty hands."

"Then I'll soil mine too!" she screamed. Kaos was taken back, "I know that you don't want this war! Whatever you have done, you have done it with causes of not your own heart!" she yelled tearing, I love you, Kaos Bernedict, whether your mom approves of me or not! She slowed, "My one, undying, unearthly love, Kaos!" she hugged him, "I will let you leave, but I won't let you leave my heart."

"Enna…" Kaos sighed.

"Kaos!" Mr. Berk called from the back door that lead into the kitchen. Kaos turned. "Please, may I have a word with you?" he asked. Kaos sighed.

"He probably wants to apologize for my mother," Enna claimed, "You can go, Kaos," Enna whispered Kaos turned and did walk towards the house. He was let in by a smiling Mr. Berk.

"I must apologize for my wife, she does not know of what she speaks of, and has been a mess with Enna's loss of love."

"It's alright," Kaos sighed.

"No," Mr. Berk claimed, "it's not, after all you did for us, there is more debt to be paid to you than owed from you."

"Don't think that I have the complete judge of character," Kaos sighed, "I should not speak of betrayal."

"Hugal is the son of a close business partner of mine, no way is he a man of as dignified and self-confident rights as you!" he claimed.

"You give me far too much credit," Kaos said, "I'm simply trouble for the Empire."

"Enna, when she was younger, had a fortune told of her life. It was that every boy she fell in love with would die, but there you stand, and how long have you known her?" he continued. "I remember that your birthday is tomorrow, with no home to go to do you have a place to stay for a while?" he asked, Kaos nodded.

"Yes."

"Well my door is always open."

"Thank you," Kaos thanked him.

"I have heard to the tragedies of Pattla from an old-army friend of mine, I'm sorry for your home."

"It's not something one wishes to hear wen one known he could have made the difference." I should be off," Kaos sighed. He rose.

"Do come back tomorrow," he said.

"I don't know,"

"You must! I have never seen my daughter so happy, as when you are around. About 9 in the morning I would like you to show up."

"I don't know if I can get away for that long."

"From work?"

"Yes,"

"It's your birthday tomorrow, you should be allowed a few hours of free time!"

"Mr. Berk, I don't know,"

"You owe me one favor, so this is what I ask of you. Kaos met the man's eyes. "If not for me; Enna." He said, "She hasn't had smiles for days until now," Kaos smiled to comfort the man's heart, but his heart and the thought of home wouldn't allow it to continue.

"I'll see what I can do," Kaos said as he said goodbye. Mr. Berk led him out and wade as he trotted down the road on the Pinto. Apparently Micheal had disappeared somewhere.

Kaos approached the back of the library cautiously. The hooves on the cold ground were almost completely muffled. He managed into the barn when he jumped.

"Kayoron Ebony!" Daragon's voice was scolding. Kaos jumped when suddenly Daragon's strong hand grabbed his right ear. Daragon's body appeared and Kaos was yanked downward so that he bed down. "Kaos, what were you thinking! He muttered, shaking his head, "Out of all the days to disappear! The eve of you eighteenth birthday! How could you think of this?" Kaos cringed under the man's wrath. "You don't have any idea how dangerous this day is, for everyone! You have worried the hell out of Iori, Yoki and me. And that bird! Hat bird, when it woke up through a fit and charred an entire shelving of Elvin Encyclopedias." Daragon started at Kaos! Well Pupil? What do you have to say for yourself?" he tossed Kaos back. Kaos held his tongue. Daragon walked up to him and punched him on the right cheek. Kaos bit his lip, which bled. "You will go in there and apologize to Iroi and Yoki, then you will come to me for some training!" he paused. Kaos looked at him. "You go that?" Daragon hissed.

"Yes, master," Kaos said. Kaos stomped out of the barn into the library, where he immediately went to the back office. Opening the office door suddenly, he curtly spoke in the silence. "Iori, Yoki, I'm sorry for running out and for my bird's fit." He said and closed the door on the two befuddled faces.

"[Floating-bubble]" Daragon's voice chanted. Kaos suddenly felt the pressure of his body dissipate, as he started floating in mid-air in a bubble of Daragon's magic. "Try and get down…" Daragon said and Kaos' training started immediately.

Kaos collapsed on top of his bed or cot rather panting.

"Holy shit," he muttered.

"You tired?" Daragon asked calmly. Kaos actually panted heavily. "Good tomorrow we'll do the same thing until you are able to get down in one shot. Eat this!" Daragon stuck out what looked like a biscuit of shredded wheat. Kaos felt sick to his stomach. "Eat it, Kaos!"

"Why?" Kaos exclaimed after silence, "I feel like I'm going to hurl!" Kaos whined and turned away.

"You'll eat it or I'll make you do thirty more charges!" Kaos rolled up and snagged the thing out of his hand. He took a bite and nearly gagged. "All of it!" he emphasized. Kaos bit back all reflux to gag and struggled the biscuit down. He fell back on his bed, still coughing.

"What is that thing for anyways?" he asked.

"It's to absorb the remaining manna in your body," Daragon explained.

"What?" Kaos said a little shocked, "I thought that you wanted me to build it up?"

"That piece shouldn't hit you till tomorrow morning. Tonight, as your birthday officially passes there's a chance your transformation will finally finish. Without the transformation eating your manna, your body won't be able to get rid of it fast enough on its own.

"So you're saying that I could be a full elf by the morning?" Kaos whimpered.

"Kaos…" Daragon sighed at Kaos' tone, "…there are many more important things you need to think about right now than that! Don't try and focus on things that cannot be avoided."

"Thank you!" Kaos grabbed his head and exclaimed, "That you for reminding me of the stupid thing!"

"Just go to bed," Daragon eased, "We'll see what the morning brings if it brings anything at all." Daragon left him with that. Kaos was tired after the training session, his body was completely exhausted. Even if he truly wished to get up and look in the mirror one last time, he doubted he could. All he could do was weep, and so he cried himself to sleep.

"Stand up straight!" Aysil's voice ordered as she sat atop a white horse, caped and decked with metal scales. A battalion of soldiers stood in front o her, their faces soiled and weapon's blood stained. They stood with experience although the dead lay among their feet.

"We cannot greave at this hour!" she yelled, "You all are brave and true, this act of courage is more than worthy of this nation's name. I give you all honors to face such peril. Patella has fallen, but it will not lay down for long! Its wall may have been burned by Dartawg fire, but they have not seen what Ebony Fire can do!" the crowd roared in spirit. Aysil turned about behind her and faced a bay. She stopped her face monotone.

"The crowds love you," a familiar man's voice stated.

"Have you received word General Daragon?" Aysil asked.

"No, my informant should be arriving soon with word, he is a few minutes late I can only hope he has not been seen by the enemy." Daragon concluded.

"This new informant of yours…his deeds have even reached my ears yet his name has not." Aysil said.

"I'm sure you have met him," Daragon said, "His name need not be spread around."

It was then that suddenly a boy phased besides Daragon. One knee on the ground and one hand on the ground. His head bent down towards the ground, causing a fire-red head band's tails to fall before his face alongside snow white hair.

"Master, the Dartawg's have formed just on the edge of town. They should move in approximately 3:00 hours." The boy's voice was precise and dignified. His eyes were shut, but his very presence demanded warning. His sharp ears on end for every sound, hung on one a golden upside down pyramid – more notably the same as the General's own.

"Good," Daragon said stately. Aysil stood silent, staring and gawking at the boy who had just appeared. After a few moments,

"Kaos?" she said quietly. The boy's lean muscular body stood up – only looking at Daragon and ignoring the Empress and her remark.

"Why are you late?" Daragon questioned.

"I'm afraid I ran into an old acquaintance of mine," Kaos said.

"Is he taken care of?" Daragon looked at Kaos worried.

"Yes," Kaos dropped his head. Daragon saw some blood spatters on Kaos' shirt – fresh ones.

"You aren't hurt, are you?" Daragon asked but Aysil interrupted seeing as her nephew ignored her completely. She stepped forward towards them and Kaos' eyes flashed on her with warning. She stopped.

"I'm fine," Kaos answered, "He uses arrows mostly so close-range fighting with him didn't endanger me." Kaos explained.

"Kaos, Nephew!" she called again. Kaos didn't turn to look at her.

"Kaos, please converse with the lady – she insists." Kaos didn't feel like it, but turned towards Aysil out of orders.

"What is it, Empress," Kaos spoke reluctantly.

"How can you do this? To yourself? The country?" she asked frantic, "If I had known it had finished I would have called you home immediately!" she exclaimed.

"I'm the best there is," Kaos finished, "No one else can do the type of work I do because no one else knows Dartawg as well as I do."

"You don't know Dartawg well,"

"I have had their training and I know their officials, besides this is my home town – I'm not going to go and sit idle while my family is captured or my house destroyed!"

"Kaos, I order you to go to my castle this instant!" she shrieked finally. Kaos didn't move but kept the same apathetic and unresponsive glare in her direction. She lowered her eyes, [transportation spell]" she muttered. The spark of white lightning was aimed right at him but within a yard or so of hitting its target. It's clearly veered off its target and was sent spiraling away into a tree nearby which shuttered then disappeared. Kaos gave no outright refusal but his unwillingness to conform to even her order was a blatant response.

"Kaos, return to your post," He stated, "We'll talk about this later and I'll summon you when needed." Daragon instructed him. Kaos continued to look at his master.

"Yes, master," Kaos bowed his head and he immediately disappeared.

"Daragon!" Aysil exclaimed in frustration, "How can you let the Prince do this! He should be with my sister since he is apparently fully transformed!"

"So you noticed have you?"

"Daragon? How can you not? He's the twin of Charles, I nearly fainted!"

"I know," Daragon smirked.

"This is not funny! He's going to get killed!"

"He's the strongest being, a great Dartawg spy, and with the teachings of my magic, he is almost needed."

"No, he is needed to succeed me on the thrown not in death on a battlefield?"

"For your information Kaos does not fight on an open battlefield?"

"Then the blood? Is he going off on assignations?"

"That is what he does best with – it is the safest place for him!" Daragon charged. She reared up and could hardly speak.

"How dare you directly charge me! You're the one who's gone underhandedly and made him a murderer! The secret of the Wakita's success. Here I thought it was your men – no it's Kaos!"

"I did not make him the murderer!"

"What happened on his birthday?" she asked suddenly.

"Nothing," Daragon stated with a hint of a lie.

"Something huge happened, where's his Sharae, and Yoki?" she asked, "She too is supposed to be looking after him."

"His Sharae is still around, I do believe he likes to roost it on his shoulder."

"And what about Yoki! That bird doesn't seem to have Kaos' best in mind."

"Well for your information it's the fucking bird that saved Kaos' life!" Daragon charged, "Yoki nearly killed him!" Aysil was quiet. She wanted to ask more, but Daragon interrupted, "There is too much to tell for us to talk about it right now. We only have three hours and there's an entire army to prepare."

"I make myself very clear, you and I will sit down and *have* this conversation."

"Yes, my lady, you have my word, but now we must prepare." The turned and walked up to the small hill where they met Kaos leaning against a tree with the Sharae, which now held dark brown feathers.

"I thought I told you to return to your post?" Daragon queried him. Kaos struck out a very vivid answer.

"Our men need to be prepared, Master," Kaos claimed, "Besides, our guest needs to be escorted to her safe position-"

"If there's anyone who needs to get to a safe place it is you!" she said and walked and laughed.

"My lady, you need not worry about my safety during this battle. I've done this thousands of times – it is you who has never seen the Wakita fight." Kaos smirked.

"I have too," she exclaimed. The Sharae did a little cooing and rubbed his cheek. Kaos patted it and then it took off from his shoulder to a nearby branch.

"Not after what I've taught them," he explained and walked up to Daragon. She looked at him with frustration.

"Kaos escort your troops to their positions, I will bring out guest to the rear, after that I expect you in your keep, do I make myself clear?" Daragon order.

"Crystal, Master," Kaos did a slight bow again. He walked past Aysil, "Good Luck, your highness." Kaos spoke haughtily and disappeared down the hill towards an Appalachian, which he mounted.

"All troops proceed to positions, hold your strike till orders!" Kaos yelled again and again. He would halt at certain groups and give information to the leaders to hand out key movements and procedures for certain calls. He trotted up in down the lines and the crowd cheered as he passed.

"Why do you men listen to him?" Aysil asked.

"They know what he is capable of doing." Daragon added, "They respect him because he does what he isi told to do at the greatest he can. At eighteen he has gained and earned the respect a General earns over a lifetime – this boy can rule an army – I imagine he can do the same with a country." Daragon smirked.

"Where is his keep?"

"I found him a small place to live, a tent near mine to put it blankly. It allows me to make sure his mouth stays shut during the nights and his mind at ease."

"His transmissions come now and again, in short bouts," she exclaimed, "I would imagine that you have not gotten much sleep."

"No, I've been using nightly silencing spells that turns his white magic into elvish muttering – at times it works and at others he overpowers them. I've also been giving him limiters, and today he's up to nearly eight in one sitting. In many ways Kaos should be grateful to his spying abilities, they relieve some of his excess manna that would otherwise ill him."

[This missing segment was actually written by hand and will not be available in this edition because it wasn't available to the hackers either.]

"It was nothing," Kaos explained.

"Well, it's the nicest thing anyone has ever done for me," she finally admitted. Kaos paused. "I never liked the guy, but he was in line to marry with me so he assumed that he could just kiss me up and down, and well, you know…" she struggled, "…he had made plans later this night, for him to take me to his place…and…" she was a little nervous, "Well what you did pissed him off so much that he left without remembering his plans with me." She smiled and looked at Kaos. Kaos sighed and looked away from her.

"I must tell you," he stated, "I'm not who you think I am."

"What?"

"I'm not available," Kaos informed. She blushed a little,

"Why do you think that I would do that?"

"Well, I just wanted to cover all the basis while we're exchanging stories," he stated. She laughed, "You're certainly different." Kaos couldn't help but blush a little. "May I ask who the lucky lady is?"

"Her name is Enna Berk, and she and I are already married," Kaos explained.

"I've never heard of her before," she stated puzzled, "Aren't you only allowed to marry within the family?"

"That's why I'm on house-arrest," Kaos explained, "My family refuses to acknowledge her or allow us to be together."

"Wow," she stated after a long silence, "You're not who I thought you were. So this gathering," she indicated slowly, "This gathering is your family's attempt to get you remarried?" Kaos nodded.

"Did you and Enna have a formal Elvin wedding?" Kaos shook his head, "Then you're not married yet!" she exclaimed, "You must have a formal Elvin wedding otherwise the union isn't legal."

"We can't have one, you see Enna is human," Kaos admitted. The young elf looked at him and then laughed. "What what's so funny?"

"You just said that you tried to marry a human?"

"I did marry a human!" Kaos forced.

"What?" she cried, "You can't marry a human! It's not fair to either one of you!" Kaos was quiet, "She die and grow older as you remain young and alive for centuries. From you're point of view it's going to last as long as a friendship or an engagement, not a wife." She exclaimed, "By the time you're 20, she'll be in her forties and two years later she'll be dead and you're nearly different from where you are now!" she stated, "It's not equal."

"So you're saying that I shouldn't marry a human?"

"I don't think it's wise even for her, even for love." She exclaimed, "Besides, with the laws it's impossible. You must be wed under Elvin-law and she cannot be a part of that union no matter if your parents like her or not." She laughed a little. "Now come close to me," she stated and he trusted her enough and came and sat down beside her. "Now close your eyes." He did so. She bent over and kissed him. Kaos eyes flashed open. She sat back and smiled at him.

"You'll find many good elvin women to pick as a wife – you shouldn't look towards a human it's not fair." She stated. Kaos flushed and he got nervous. She rose and went towards the door, "I'm going back inside to hopefully have a little fun – you should too."

Kaos managed to go back inside. His grandmother nearly knocked him over on her rush to query his where-about.

"Where the hell did you go off to? I sent guards looking all over trying to find you!" she exclaimed. Kaos sighed.

"I just stepped out for a bit," Kaos couldn't take her relenting.

"A bit? It was an hour!"

"You were counting?"

"Yes, and you left with the darling Charleston girl, and then she came back in thirty minutes ago!" he pushed her away.

"Are you watching my every move!" he exclaimed and started to walk away from her.

"Oh, dear, I'm sorry," she stated, "Really, Kaos I am."

"Then you won't spy on me?" Kaos exclaimed, "Tell me you won't spy on me anymore."

"Kaos, how can I trust you?"

"Have *I* done anything against you since I arrive here, since I was younger?"

"You disappeared and never reported to the castle when your transformation was complete!"

"I didn't know that anyone cared if it was complete or not! Besides the whole mess is crap and no one would appreciate any of that happening in their face during a war!"

"Crap?" she asked.

"My transformation, was a shit-hole grandmother, that's the nice way of putting it." He stated.

"Well, that is the past, and you need to start thinking about your future!" she exclaimed, "It's not so much that humans are bad – they're not – it's with them comes heartbreak for elves. We live a lot longer than any human.

"Yes, I know," he said rather weak. He was shocked to believe that he was finally questioning Enna's relationship. She appeared not to want to fight this as much as he did and it was a fact that they could never really get married and he would live longer, much longer. He muddled over the fact that "the Charleston's girl" commented on, she would be 80 when he would be 20 and it seemed unthinkable for even Enna to feel the same about him when they were of such different ages." He found himself sitting on a couch beginning to cry. He didn't know what he was doing or what the right thing was. A large part of him wanted to just fuck the whole system to just be with Enna – but the thought of staying young when she grew old. They would clash on opinions and she would no longer be able to do all the young-hearted things that they could do now because her body wouldn't be able to handle it. If he didn't marry her he would be appeasing his family, which he hated conforming to because it wasn't him. There was no way to stop time, not even in magic terms not for that long. Kaos abruptly headed towards the door, and Marina caught him by the arm.

"You're not disappearing again," she stated. Kaos immediately turned his head, still tearing and looked at Marina. His strife was written all over his face.

"Kaos, what's wrong?" she asked worried.

"I want to leave, I don't want to be here," Kaos mumbled.

"Why are you crying?"

"I can't talk about it!" he exclaimed.

"Kaos, this is about Enna, right?" he nodded.

"You love her, but you can't be with her." Kaos paused, he didn't want to admit it, and he gulped.

"I had to do this with your father, Kaos," she confessed, "I had to leave him because of the solid fact that's making you cry." She began crying herself and then hugged him. "I loved your father, and we couldn't be together and it wasn't just the system – it was Mother Nature!" she exclaimed. "You can't beat mother nature no matter how strong you are!" she exclaimed. Kaos couldn't help but look at the scenery. They were hugging and sharing all this amongst a crowd of elves dancing, with shadow lights. Kaos eventually hugged her back.

"I'm sorry I did that to Enna, really Kaos," she mumbled, "I am sorry. I would rather be the cause of that strife than see you beat yourself up over it." She confessed. "I would rather murder than have you face this heart-ache." She exclaimed.

"You have me,"

"Yes, Kaos, you are my Jonathan," she commented and wiped his tears and brushed the hair from his eyes, "And you are my son, our son – which makes you so special to me."

"What are you two tearing about?" a jolly man came up and put two gentle hands on both of their shoulders.

"Nothing," Marina commented and wiped her eyes.

"Ah, so you are Kayoron?" the man asked. "Your mother here has been telling me all about you and we have never met!"

"Kaos, this Clara's brother – Dusaw." Kaos looked at him.

"You do honestly look like Charles to a dime!" he smiled and shook feverishly. "He'd laugh his head off to think his grandson is his twin! So have you found anyone you're interested it?" he asked and jabbed Kaos in the side, "There are plenty of nice girls around." Kaos faltered,

"Dusaw, my son and I need to take a little walk outside if you don't mind."

"And have more crying? This is a happy day – you just returned didn't you and you serve the Wakita am I not mistaken, with Daragon?" he asked and put an arm around Marina. Then he saw the earring and quickly checked it with his hands, "my, my, my, you're quite the General from what I've heard. You know Charles' specialty was war also-" Marina cut him off.

"Now Uncle Dusaw," she stated, "Please."

"Oh, don't get so fussy," he exclaimed, "Your father was impressive and if Kaos is following in his footsteps he best know where to plant them." Kaos sighed.

"Mother, may I just go," he stated, "The guards won't let me leave and I don't want to stay here anymore," he confessed. Marina was placed in such an awkward position.

"Why do you want to go?" Dusaw asked. Kaos faltered again. He didn't want to look irresponsible in front of his grandfather.

"Well…"

"Now listen here Kaos, I think I know what this is all about," Dusaw stated seriously and let go of Marina. "Well I've heard this from many people now as they talk about you." Kaos cringed and so did Marina. "So you must no it's not a shame to not know how to dance!" He stated firmly and both Kaos and Marina nearly fell over.

"Thank you uncle," Marina stated, "Perhaps a lesson or two will cheer him up." Kaos looked at her with question.

"Mother?" he growled.

"No, son. Let's not get grumpy about it, it's not your fault," Dusaw was falling right through the lie and Kaos was painted as a poor soul who was too embarrassed to dance, "Yes, when we don't know how to do things the first thing we think of is fight and flight." Dusaw said and grabbed him kindly around the shoulders. Kaos looked at his mother as he passed into the crowd towards the side of the room. He was led into one of the side rooms and told to wait in the corner.

"Now, Kaos, you stay right here." He warned, "and if you slip out I'll just have to expose your little secret to the world." He smiled and Kaos smiled weakly.

"Yes, grandfather," he said and he patted him on the head. As he went off into the crowd Kaos looked around. He was surrounded by random guests, none of which were generals or army-men or people who he had met previously. He quickly returned and there was a girl about Kaos' age at his side. She had strawberry-blond hair and a long sleek silk dress. Around her shoulders were a delicate translucent sheet shrug and a blue flower in her dun-up hair. Two small diamonds were at the corner of her eyes, which were so delicately outlined in eyeliner. She had a red jewel in the middle of her forehead and smiled sweetly at Kaos.

"Kaos, this is Tuta – she would be happy to teach you how to dance." She slowly came up to him and held out a hand. He took it reluctantly.

"Pleasure to meet you," she said. She taught him how to dance using the step-and-follow technique until he got the patterned.

"Thank you, I suppose-" Kaos cut it suddenly when she took his other hand in hers and took a few steps closer.

"Now you just put your hand on my waist and continue," she said. "Now there's something called slow-dance. I'm sure you know what it is. How you do it is you get very close to your partner, and take small steps." She did so and Kaos blushed. She found herself resting against his chest and he didn't really think that this was part of the lesson. Suddenly at some point afterward she realized what was happening and jumped up.

"Oh, I'm sorry," she stated red as a dime, "I'm sorry, I didn't mean-"

"It's okay really," Kaos didn't want to make this something big, "It's fine."

"It's fine?" she questioned looking at him.

"No big deal, okay?" he stated.

"I should have more control," she shook her head, "Anyways that's how you do it, there's nothing more to it." She stated and bowed her head. Tuta bit her lip as though she was wanting to do something else. Kaos was well aware of something – she wanted to ask him to dance and it was blatant from the way that she "lost control" that she had wanted to.

"Tuta, I don't suppose you can allow me a test run," Kaos stated. There was something in him that didn't want to say it because it could be leading her on. They went out into the dance floor and started.

"You know I've never really ballroom-danced before," Kaos admitted, "This is really awkward for me."

"What did you used to do during dances?" she asked. Kaos didn't know how to say a mosh pit or an ogre and still remain dignity in this place.

"Well, things were…less formal and a bit more intimate," he stated roughly although part of him didn't want to categorize it as "intimate."

"What do you call your dancing?"

"Well, you don't want to know about it," Kaos laughed, "It's really not anything to be saying out loud."

"Wait, wait," she stopped with a smile, "You know dirty-dancing?" she smiled. "You don't have to censor it with me."

"Well, I'm used to clubs," Kaos finally admitted quietly, "This hole formal thing is giving me the creeps," he stated. She laughed and they stopped dancing. "What so funny?"

"You're just not who I was expecting, that's all."

"What were you expecting?"

"Some snot-nose rich and stupid Prince," she smiled, "You're certainly not as innocent as I expected. My father told me you were a General and I thought you would be some hard ass stringent military man."

"Well I'm not that, that's just my job." Kaos informed her.

"Well you still do sort of show it," she swaggered.

"Oh yeah?" he asked, "How do I look like a general?" she flicked his earing.

"One," she smiled and he knew what it meant.

"Besides that?"

"No stay-at-home boy has a body like yours. You're too strong for you not to be actively involved." She exclaimed. "Besides the Prince is supposed to be a ruler, right? You go through all sorts of random training for that, right?"

"No," Kaos stated flatly, "No one has told me how to rule a country – and frankly I don't want to." He stated. She laughed again. "You know you're the second person who has just laughed at me. Why does everyone think I'm so funny?"

"You're not funny? It's just when we think of the men in your family we relate them to hard-asses." She exclaimed, "Argo's a completely nut." She exclaimed. Kaos looked at her.

"Come," she put her hand out, "Let me introduce you to a few good people."

She brought Kaos over to a group of elves, two boys and two girls.

"Hey," she said.

"Tuta, please take him back where you found him," one of the boys exclaimed looking at Kaos. "I don't feel like hearing another lecture. Kaos looked at him with question.

"Terk, He's not going to give you a lecture, besides he's into clubs," she smiled. The boy looked at Kaos, who didn't really understand why this all was so important.

"I can't believe that!" the other one laughed, "He's the Prince, he hasn't been to a club in his life."

"You don't know that!" she fought.

"Shida is right," the girl looked up and down Kaos, "He's way to sheltered."

"Sheltered?" Kaos remarked.   The group was shocked at his outburst.

"Fine, then lets prove it," Terk stated, "Dance dirty with Tuta, Kaos?"

"Right here?" Kaos questioned.

"Yes, are you deaf?" Shida remarked. Tuta came up to him and started swaggering and putting her arms around him. The group sort of laughed a little.

"Tuta…" he stated.

"Come on, Kaos – don't listen to them." She stated and Kaos just ran with it. He was frozen for the moment because all he had was ballroom music and absolutely nothing to work with – plus the fact that he was married made the entire situation awkward. He found himself having to forget about Enna. After a few moments, the girls had their mouths drop as Kaos continued with Tuta with some rather provocative moves. The two boys' moods seemed soiled.

"Fine, fine that's enough," Kaos and Tuta were laughing as they stopped.

"Not good enough for you?" Kaos exclaimed.

"You dance like a fuckin northerner!" the boy exclaimed. "The wakitas been in the South all the time!"

"I don't have to justify myself, now do I? Apparently that doesn't make me very sheltered?" Kaos smiled and held Tuta around the shoulders with a smirk. She smiled knowing Kaos was taunting the boy.

"Your mother know about this?"

"About what?" he stated.

"The whole club-thing?"

"Why the hell should she know about it?" at the curse the group paused.

"Did you just curse?" Terk questioned from the table. Kaos looked at him,

"I'm sorry," Kaos questioned, "It's just sort of natural – that's all."

"No, it's okay Kaos," Shida stated with disturbance, "Really, it's just really weird to here you say it." Kaos looked at him oddly.

"So can he come with us?" Tuta asked.

"Well it seems so," he exclaimed. Terk tossed her two bracelets, "Wear those and come at ten," he stated and the group left.

"What's that?"

"Entrance Bracelets."

"To what exactly?"

"A club," she smiled. She turned around and handed him his.

"This is going to be my first Elvin-club," he laughed.

"Don't tell me you don't know what to wear?" she exclaimed with some glee.

Kaos snuck her to Clara's room, making sure that she was still at the party. He used some magic to go invisibly and Tuta was laughing nearly the whole time.

"Gods, I can't make your laughter invisible also," he complained in fun. They were inside Clara's bedroom and Tuta was amazed.

"Wow, this is Clara's room?" she went over and felt the bed.

"Yes, and don't touch too much, I don't want her to think we've been in here." He stated. He went over to the walk in closet and pulled it open. Tuta walked over and besides him.

"So this is where your clothing is?" she questioned awkwardly.

"I don't have any clothing," Kaos exclaimed, "I have to used Charles's stuff. It's the only clothing that we have that fits."

"Whoa!" she exclaimed, "You're saying you fit into Charles stuff!"

"Yes," he said irritated.

"And I thought you two were just look-alikes, but you must be his replica!"

"Well I inherited only my mother's genes, so I would imagine..." he stated and went over to the closet. "Here, I don't have any idea what would be appropriate, so go right ahead and look." He motioned for her to go and she hesitated.

"Now I'm going through a ruler's closet," she mumbled in glee, "This is so wild." She looked and gasped at all of the pieces. "Oh my word, Charles had excellent taste! He has Gibona?" she exclaimed and stopped at a piece, "He no longer is making anything! Shit he has several!"

"Is that some maker?"

"Gibona is only the hottest fashion designer around. He stopped factory-produced work years ago and now only makes things by hand." Kaos looked at her. "So you can fit into all of this?" she asked and looked up and down him.

"That's only Clara's estimate."

"And she knew Charles to a dime," she looked back into the closest than at Kaos.

"Well, I want you to try a few things on for me," she stated, "before I make a decision." She pulled out all of the pieces that were made by Gibona along with others. He stood a little flabbergasted about the number of outfits.

Kaos came out in the seventh he had tried on and she looked at him a blushed. It was a Dark leather piece that was strappy and revealed around his neck. (black outfit). She paused,

"That's the one," she commented.

"I don't even know if I have this on properly," he exclaimed.

"What do you mean?"

"There are these straps everywhere, and they have latches on them…" she got up and moved the buckles on them and tightened them.

"There," she said.

"So this is it?"

"Yeah, it's a Gibona piece – I can't believe that your grandfather would own this sort of stuff." She looked at him.

Kaos walked up with her, he was wearing the clothing and some long arm socks with the fingers and palm cut out. It was cold outside and she led him across the grounds of the castle and to the small village below. Tuta was much more revealing, and Kaos had first blushed on her appearance. They slunk behind buildings and then down an ally where they saw two men.

"Name and purpose," they stated firmly.

"Tuta and Kaos Ebony we're here for the party," they looked at them and then they passed. Kaos slowly began to be familiar with the routine – it was like any club and he eased once they reached the basement staircase. On the way down a few girls passed by.

"Hey cutie," one stated and looked Kaos in the eyes. They continued down the stairs and Terk was standing taking names and cash. He saw both of them come.

"So you actually came," he exclaimed at Kaos.

"Yeah," Kaos smiled.

"Nice outfit," he stated, "Tuta, did you bring those bracelets?"

"Yeah," she lifted up her wrist. They had already put them on.

"Then, please enter," he laughed.

Kaos loved it, he danced with a whole bunch of random girls and drank – stuff which he didn't really recognize. He never got drunk although some of his friends did.

"Poor Kaos is too elvin to get any side effects!"

"I bet he could drink us all clean and still run a marathon!" one yelled. "Kaos?"

"Well, I'd rather not try," he stated, "I'm going to go dancing again," he left and rose. Tuta came over and they danced probably for a good three hours. They were on the dance floor when she grabbed him and led him off.

"Do you want to go lay down for a bit?" she asked. He looked at her and she took his hand laughing. That's when Kaos remembered Enna. She led him into a side room with a bed in it and quietly came up to him.

"Tuta I-" he mumbled.

"Now," she put a finger to his mouth, "It's okay Kaos, it's all okay." She smiled and then kissed him on the lips and Kaos kissed back. He couldn't help it. It seemed as though all his body wanted was to be with her. He thought of Enna and pulled away. She looked at him, "Kaos, its okay. Why are you fighting me?" he shook his head.

"This is not right," Kaos continued, "I should have never done this."

"Kaos is this because of Enna?" she asked.

"What?" Kaos looked at her with shocked, "How do you know about Enna?"

"Kaos," she sat down on the bed, "There's something you must know about me. I am wed to you." She stated and looked at him, "And I honestly want to be." She looked at him and came up to his face. "I love *you*, not because of Ebony law Kaos. You are the most honest thing that I have ever met in my life and I just know that you and I should be together."

"But I'm in love with Enna," he stated and pulled away.

"I'm not saying you are not," she confessed with tears, "Enna is human, she'll die and you'll be alone. I don't want that to happen!" Tuta cried, "I want to see you happy to be with you!" she dove into him, "You don't deserve any more sadness. I know what you have been through – I know it all Kaos down to your father and Dartawg." She cried and hugged him, "You're the strongest soul I have ever met, I love you, and you don't deserve to have your heart broken again!" she yelled. She wept and Kaos put his arms around her. "That's why I want to be your wife, Kaos." She wept, "That is why I want to be with you."

"I can't just let Enna go," Kaos explained.

"I don't care if she does stay with us Kaos," she explained, "I know that you are worried about her, I'm offering you a way out Kaos." She explained, "A way out of this war of traditions." Kaos didn't understand.

"Marry me and I'll keep you safe. I respect Enna and your relationship with her – I can understand how she feels. I'll keep you both safe."

"I can't have two wives," he stated honestly, "Its not fair to either of you."

"Well none of this is fair to you!" she looked him dead in the face. "You've been fooled for your entire life, and you've gone with your heart the whole way!" she sobbed, "Please consent, Kaos. They will wed you within the hour: to me or to someone else." She stated.

"Why would they do that?"

"Because you are to be king," she stated, "you need an heir, so you need a wife fit to produce an heir." She mumbled and cried. "A human cannot birth a half-elf or and elf." Kaos, only a elf can do that. Enna will die in childbirth if you are to attempt to have children." Kaos stood still. They had already made love and thrown away protection because of the marriage. Kaos suddenly felt ill, he never asked Enna. "Enna is pregnant," Tuta confessed, "She was checked when your mother found you." Kaos began to cry, "She *will* die because of it." She stated.

"You're lying to me, it's not true," Kaos stated weary.

"Kaos, why would I lie to you!" she yelled, "Please, I'm telling the truth – in all honesty! I don't want to hurt you!"

"Enna!" Kaos yelled and pulled away from her. She let him go and looked at him crying herself.

Kaos burst into the castle, the guards were shocked to see him run into it. He was screaming Enna's name and running down the hall towards Clara's room. He burst in and found Enna sitting on her bed looking down at the floor at her lap. Kaos looked at her.

"Enna," he mumbled. He ran up to her and knelt before her. Clara, his mother, Aysil were all present in the room. "Enna please, look at me!"

"Kaos I'm pregnant," she stated holding back tears.

"Enna, look at me!" he pleaded with her, and she couldn't.

"I might die because of it," she nearly cried.

"Abort it," Kaos exclaimed, "Terminate the pregnancy!" Kaos yelled, "Enna please, I don't want to lose you." She shook her head.

"We've tried to reason with her," Aysil explained, "She refuses our aid."

"Enna, please listen to them," he stated, "You must."

"I don't believe it," she stated, "They just want us apart!" she yelled.

"Enna this isn't about them! Look at me! I wouldn't be on my knees following them around!"

"This baby means that you and I are together," she looked at him, "Otherwise how can I know that we are husband and wife – because as far as their law is concerned I'm nothing!" she yelled.

"Enna you're going to die!" he yelled, "Don't die over your pride! Please!"

"Look at you, you're alive and you're half."

"Enna that's because my mother is an elf," he stated, "You are human, you can't carry an elf!" he cried. "Your body can't handle it." He explained. She looked at him unable to respond back. She started to bawl and he held her.

"I'm sorry. It was my mistake. I was the one who said not to use protection! I got you pregnant!" he stated.

"Will you take our abortion, or not?" she asked. Enna nodded.

She lay in Kaos' bed and he kissed her on the forehead.

"Kaos, I-"

"Shh," he mumbled, "It's okay."

"Kaos, I've been doing a lot of thinking," she mumbled, "I don't think I can do this anymore." She confessed.

"I'm afraid to say that I have been having those thoughts also."

"So then?" she said, "You feel the same?"

"I don't think that we should be together," he stated. "I can't take any more of this. I love you but I can't be with you, I can't have children with you, and the world is trying to tear us apart. We don't have a future together we don't even have death."

"As much as I love you we can't be happy together," he stated.

"I think that this is for the best," she stated with tears. He pulled his arm from around her.

"I'm sorry," he stated honestly, upset.

"It's okay," she cried into him.

Kaos road her back to Theives and saw her parents and explained the entire situation. He sat very still, Marina a few feet off. The Berks were very shocked.

"I'm sorry," he stated, "I'm so very sorry about all of this," Kaos stated.

"Well, this was not something in your control or anything you deliberately caused," Mr. Berk intervened.

"I'm sorry, I cannot forgive you," Mrs. Berk exclaimed, "I cannot forgive you for the pain my daughter has endured. No man can understand how that must feel. Every man that she has ever had a relationship has died, and then you keep living but bring with her a pain because she can never have you," She was tearing. Kaos didn't argue.

"She will always be close to my heart," he closed his eyes, "and always welcome to see me. Please tell her that."

"Yes, Kaos," Mr. Berk nodded, "I will tell her the message."

"You can always come and speak with me, and don't hesitate to reach out to me. I am in the greatest debt of all and I love your daughter so dearly." He stated.

They left and Kaos had kissed Enna on the forehead for one last time. He was holding back tears as they went back into the carriage. When they got in Marina didn't signal for the coach to go.

"Kaos," she put her arms out and he crawled right into them and bawled. "It's okay to cry," she stated, "It's okay."

Marina told the coach to drive and held Kaos all the way back to the castle.

beginnings

Kaos couldn't get up for days. He lay in bed sobbing, not even stopping to eat or go to the bathroom. He just laid in his bed crying Marina came in hopes of cheering him up but he was so fragile.

"He needs to be married," Clara insisted, "Aysil is not settled with him just laying around all day and wallowing, enough is enough!" she yelled.

"Kaos is not ready to get married," Marina yelled, "He's hardly even capable to hold a conversation with!"

"When is he going to get over this?" Clara yelled.

"He was married to her!" Mairna yelled, "You're so insensitive!" she cried. "This is the type of stuff that people kill themselves over!"

"Tuta has put in a marriage request," Clara remarked, "Kaos has already signed his name to it!" she yelled. Marina was shocked, "When?"

"He signed it before the abortion took place," she remarked, "Tuta was aware of the situation and told him that it would be a last-measure procedure." She stated.

Tuta came into Kaos room and gently went to him. Kaos cried and she rubbed his shoulder.

"It's okay Kaos, you have every right to be crying," she stated.

"Please, just stay with me," he cried. She sat down on the bed and he cried in her lap, he stopped and she rested a hand on his head.

"Do you feel any better?" she asked. He had stopped crying and Tuta bent down and kissed him. "It's alright. I'm not going anywhere." He closed his eyes and curled in slightly.

"Thank you," he mumbled. She smiled. They sat for a few minutes and Kaos finally got up.

"How did you know?" he asked her, "How did you know that Enna was pregnant or about me at all?"

"I spoke with your mother frequently," she commented somewhat ashamed, "Then I spoke with Daragon after I heard that you had refused to come to the castle." She explained. He didn't say anything.

"So you know *everything*." He emphasized.

"Yes, Kaos – and I still love you," she commented. "Kaos, I know that you hardly know who I am," she explained, "and that you have just lost someone very close to you in your life," she paused, "but I promise you that you and I will make a wonderful couple – I wouldn't have wanted to marry anyone who couldn't dance," she laughed and he did slightly.

"Well, I can only dance because of you," he laughed a little.

"No, you could dance before that," she laughed, "Just not ballroom." He smiled remembering the club. "Ballroom really isn't my thing, perhaps you grow into it or something like that."

He got up a day later and move slowly and went down into the dining room. Upon entry some faces looked at him, yet his eyes didn't look at any of them.

"Hey, Kaos," the chef smiled, "You look like you've been ran over by a carriage," he smiled, "Can I get you anything?" At that Kaos stopped and stared at the ground. "I did some research, I don't suppose you'd like some Oatmeal?" Kaos paused.

"Sure, _____" Kaos stated. It was human-food something of which the poor man didn't feel comfortable serving, but Kaos knew that he was doing it to cheer him up. Kaos went over to a free table nearby and sat down. He had taken a bath and dressed in the outfit that he originally wore. He pushed back the chair legs and played with a glass of water that had been set on the table. He had been a father, but he could never be. He was still upset about it, he couldn't get over Enna –

they were separated by Mother Nature not by any cultural divide. It was brought before him and he ate it in complete silence, and afterwards went down into the library and fingered over the books. When he was upset he read – for some reason it was what kept his mind off of it. Sadly it was the type of skill that only delayed the inevitable feeling of distress the entire situation brought him.

Marina came down in a few hours and went towards him.

"Hey," she smiled, "I have an idea," she smiled, "Daragon is coming back to the castle for recuperation and I thought that you would want to go and see him." She smiled, but Kaos was just looking into a book. "Kay?"

"I would like to go see him," Kaos explained, "I'm just-" she saw the look in his face and he didn't have to explain it. "I just need my space, that's all."

"Yep," she smiled, "I know it's hard, but you can get over it." She stated. She left and when Daragon came a few hours later Kaos walked Cella down with him. He approached the tent and the soldiers greeted him with hugs and cheers. He stood outside the flap waiting for the personal guard to open it. When he did the guard just stared at him.

"Hello, may I speak with Daragon?"

"Yes, General," the man bowed and let him in. Daragon was waiting and watching him enter.

"Kaos," Daragon stated, "I heard what happened. I'm so sorry." He stated.

"No, its alright," Kaos exclaimed, "It wasn't anyone's fault, what happened between Enna and I. We just weren't meant to be."

"Kaos," Daragon sighed, "I must say that I wish that things would have been different," he stated.

"Thank you, master," Kaos stated, "If you don't mind, I would rather not dwell on the subject."

"Well, then, everyone around here has missed you. My men have become wosses in battle and training without you."

"No one died did they?"

"I'm afraid that Irop lost a leg due to his carelessness and was sent back home, but I have managed to keep everyone alive since. The men have begun to be nervous, which is why we requested a recuperation period. They miss you dearly, I miss you dearly." He looked at him.

"I will try and train them while they remain here, but I doubt that I will get permission to leave home." Kaos informed him.

"I heard that you are getting married?" he stated. Kaos halted.

"Yes," Kaos admitted, "I am getting married."

"To whom may I ask?"

"Tuta," Kaos explained, "I have heard that she and you have been speaking."

"Yes," he admitted, "She was greatly worried about you when she heard that you had fully transformed."

"You've hardly met her though," he stated.

"Yes," Kaos admitted, "Clara was going to wed me if I didn't make a choice so after meeting her she explained to me what was going on with Enna and I. She said that she was okay with what happened between us. That's why I consented."

"She's not your average elf," he smiled, "I bet you two will find you have a great deal in common." He smiled.

"Do you really think so?"

"Trust me, when I spoke with her she quivered once when I told her what happened on your birthday." He looked at him shocked.

"She knows?"

"That was the first thing she inquired about. I saw no harm in telling her." He stated, "Marina was nervous about it and apparently the two have been close for some time. I figured that she would deliver it to Marina better than I ever could."

"Yeah," he laughed at himself.

"Well you will always have us," Daragon explained, "I will always be here, and my men love you to pieces so if you ever need us just give us a call." He laughed, "Just try not to use white magic," he indicated to his ears. Kaos laughed a little.

"I'll try," he smiled.

"I don't suppose you could give swordsmanship lessons to a few new recruits?" he asked. Kaos nodded, "I'd be happy to."

Kaos wandered out into the battled field and produced the sword that he had given to Enna. As he turned the corner he suddenly stopped.

Standing before him in a small group was Sharle, Jonathan, and Tako. Kaos could hardly speak, tears came down his face and Yatako ran up to him and hugged him.

"Tako," he whimpered and went down on his knees to look at his brother in his eyes. "My gods," he hugged him again and was crying. Jonathan and Sharle came up to him and he rose and hugged his mother.

"Mom," he started sobbing. She patted him on the back,

"It's okay son, it's okay,"

"I thought you guys were dead!" he muttered into her.

"Kaos," Jonathan opened his arms and Kaos looked at him, "I heard what happened." Kaos froze as Jonathan came up and hugged him, "Marina told me the whole thing when Daragon brought us here. I had never been so proud to here that my own son was fighting the same war I did." He smiled, "You've made me so proud Kaos. You really have." After a few minutes they parted and Daragon came out smiling.

"I picked them up on the outskirts of Lbonon," he laughed, "You're father had escaped before the wall fell."

"Where are you guys staying?" Kaos asked.

"Daragon gave us a small place in the barracks, Marina said that she would send us into the country house once affairs in the castle settled down," Jonathan smiled.

"Good," Kaos explained.

"I was told you are getting married," Sharle smiled. Kaos reddened a bit, then smiled.

"You can come!" he explained, "Father, I want you to come!" Jonathan sighed and shook his head.

"Kaos, I can't," he stated, "Marina's mother knows me too well, its not safe for me to go into that temple," he stated, "I would really love to, Kaos."

"You're father is right, there are more enemies in that temple that still can't get over what Marina and Jonathan have had," Daragon interluded, "It's not personal." They smiled,

"Still, my Kaos is finally getting married," she smiled.

"Now I still want to meet this Tuta of yours," Jonathan laughed, "I can't have a daughter-in-law I don't approve of," Kaos laughed and he smiled.

"Yes, father," he smiled. That night he brought Tuta down for dinner and the group had a simple and glorious time.

"I've heard all about you Jonathan!" Tuta exclaimed, "You're quite charming in person." She smiled.

"Charming?" Sharle defended, "Looky here, old Jonathan is my husband, ain't that right dear?" Jonathan laughed and.

"Of course, I'm more so," Kaos cradled her and kissed her on the forehead.

"Certainly," She rested in her arms and kiss him back.

"Get a room!" Yatako yelled. Kaos laughed and Tuta smiled. The two parents cracked up and Tako blushed like mad.

"You shouldn't be complaining match-maker."

"Match-maker?" Tuta asked.

"Tako's the little pimp of Patella."

extra

She gathered the white strands behind her head, and dressed in a long tunic. Tuta would go see her would-be-husband, who was being coronated tomorrow as the heir, then married to her – of course in succession. She stepped outside and turned around. At that moment a hand came over her mouth and grabbed her throat.

Kaos stared at the mirror. His hair was longer, back to where it was before, but longer on one side where Marina hadn't buzzed it.

"You have to cut it this time," Marina stated. "I won't cut your hair forever."

"Okay," he hesitated and picked up the electric shaver – he had to buzz one side of his head.

"You're the princes betrothed!" he exclaimed. "You were supposed to get Kaos!" Ijae appeared around the corner. She had been taken away, "This bitch is not my apprentice – how could you make that mistake!"

"White hair, golden eyes," he stopped.

"Don't you think that a shock from behind wouldn't be enough to take him?" The man cowered. "*She*," he emphasized, "This elf is female for gods' sake, Kaos is by no means female, even from behind!"

"That's all a matter of opinion," the youth stated. The group laughed.

"Or Lucky wasn't really large if you know what I mean."

"Well, then you believe after all these years, that he's the little thirteen-year-old that came here?" Ijae warned. "He's grown up, boys!"

"Are you saying Lucky is a force?"

"He's half-elven and what are you? He's drastically different from when we last saw him. My guess is hat he's been through a process of transfiguration by now – which made him a full elf. You must imagine the physical changes for that to occur."

"We're looking for an elf?" one questioned.

"Yes!" Ijae yelled, "A *male* elf!" The magician stood calm

"Sir – we don't' have the means," on solider commented.

"I'll take him," the magician commented.

"No!" Ijae ordered, "You out of all people are weak against Kaos! Chard!"

"Yes?" a man slim in stature answered out to him.

"You will get my apprentice!"

"What?" the magician commented, "Chard has no experience with mann or sorcery! He'll be a sitting duck for Kaos!"

"Exactly," he commented, "He's so ignorant Kaos may just believe him."

"If I go I can make sure he'll come with us!" the magician complained, "How can a boy bring him here! Even if he were to befriend Kaos – that's not enough to tear him from the coronation tomorrow!"

"If you go, Kaos will just manipulate you in killing yourself!" Ijae exclaimed, "He's a master of shadow magic, not to mention a current general of the Wakita, or the 'white demon!" Ijae exploded.

"I-"

"He's *my* apprentice, boy, do you take me lightly?" Ijae stood in eh silence of the group that dared to talk to him.

"Hello?" a guard had opened the door and looked at Chard," May I help you?"

"I wanted to see –" at that moment Kaos came into the scene with a heated conversation.

"Mother, I swear, if you make me cut my hair again, I'll take those scissors and cut yours!"

"Kaos," Marina laughed, "We have to make sure you don't seem like a fledgling!" he shook his head and glanced at the door and saw Chard, thinking that it was Tako.

"Pardon," Kaos pushed the solider aside. Chard stared at Kaos shocked for a few minutes. Currently his hair was buzzed on his right side and the rest was cleanly layered to his chin on the other side.

"Prince Kaos?" he asked.

"I would prefer just Kaos," Kaos explained, "but yes."

"I was wondering if you could spare a few minutes for an interview?"

"An interview?" he questioned.

"Kay, who is at the door?" Marina question. Kaos looked at Chard closely.

"Some press-person." He stated the boy looked at Kaos with astonishment. "I'm sorry," Kaos stated disappointed, "I don't do interviews." He began to shut the door, when Marina stopped him.

"Now Kay," she stated, "He'll accept, young man." She smiled.

"What?" Kaos exclaimed.

"Come one, you're being coronated tomorrow! It's a big deal!" she proclaimed with a smile. Kaos sighed.

"If I do this – can you just stop with this coronation thing?"

Kaos took the boy out into the courtyard.

"So what do you want to know?" Kaos grumbled.

"Where were you for seventeen years?"

"Patella, and around the empire," Kaos explained.

"What do you mean by 'around the empire'?"

"Well just- around," Kaos stated.

"What do you think about Dartawg?"

"It's got a good cause," Kaos stated, "However its leaders are unrealistic and extremists." Kaos grumbled.

"So you don't like Ijae?"

"He's a bastard-" Kaos looked down at the boy with sharp eyes. His entire demeanor changed and Chard took fright. The boy jumped.

"Do you plan on crushing the Dartawg forces?" He paused and Kaos stood silent, "Did you hear me?"

"I have no intention of crushing anyone who seeks peace – but I don't see how an aristocracy can ever expect to deliver democracy."

Kaos paused and stood for a bit. "I have no intention of killing anyone unless they threaten me."

"What of the recent assassination attempts?"

"You know, I don't know who you are, but you can go back to Ijae and tell him to suck my balls!" Kaos stated and closed his eyes, crossed his arms. The boy dropped the clipboard and jumped aside.

"What?"

"He's an ass because you have no idea of what I am capable of, and I could kill you in an instant." The boy drew out a dagger and picked a stance. Kaos mumbled something and suddenly there were four of him surrounding the boy.

"Nice trick, but I have tricks too," Kaos commented. Chard dropped the knife in fear.

"What? What are you to do? Kill me?"

"I won't kill so long as you do something for me?"

"For you?"

Chard came back to the camp and Ijae was waiting.

"So where is he?"

"He told me to give you this," he handed Ijae a note.

"I will not meet you one your terms – if you wish to see me I will wait beyond the castle borders at noon tomorrow. This will not be a blood bath, I have no intention of murder – however if you feel so inclined – I will be more than happy to murder those with that intention." After reading it Ijae laughed.

"Caught you, did he?" he looked at the boy, who was shaken, "Normally you would be condemned for failing, but this may be profitable."

"Ijae," Kaos commented as Ijae came towards him.

"Kaos," he stated, "You should still address me as master." Kaos laughed.

"You're not a master!" he stated, "And you want to kill me."

"You'll always be my apprentice," he commented, "as well as my son, I have never wanted to kill you." Kaos stood silent, he wasn't mad. Ijae looked earnest. He came closed and hugged Kaos awkwardly, and began crying.

"You are the closest thing I have to a son, Kaos. Please forgive me, I wish to save you from this curse." He stated. Kaos felt a dart in his back. Ijae hugged him again. "You are the best student I have – I will not have them take you." There was a dimming of light. Kaos looked down at his hands, and his hair which was black. Ijae drew his shoulders back and then smiled at Kaos and put a hand on Kaos' cheek.

"I'm not transformed," Kaos mumbled with shock.

"With injections you can suppress your elvin half," Ijae commented, "Each should last approximately two hours." Kaos plucked out the dart from his back.

"Why?"

"There's just suppressants," he stated.

"Why did you do this?" he stated.

"I promise not to hurt you Kaos," he stated, "Please come back with me."

"Come back?" Kaos questioned.

"I know you don't want to be the heir and you don't have to."

"I can't just leave," Kaos commented, "This isn't about me."

"Then just come for a little – for a little sojourn before you return." He commented, "Get a chance to be Kaos for a few last minutes." Kaos had tears on the end of his eyes.

Kaos came walking into the camp beside Ijae.

"I heard that you were given a master's diploma." Ijae stated.

"Yes," Kaos stated, "I'm a full member of the Circle of Master's now."

"It means that you're the only shadow master in the entire empire – you're a better sorcerer than I'll ever be – you managed to get that book from the box beneath my bed." Kaos looked a little shocked that he had noticed.

"Well, that day you made me very angry," Kaos commented.

"You have always been a little thief," he laughed, "but I never thought that we would end up like this."

"Kaos?" a man stormed into the tent while Kaos had his arms crossed. The man paused and stared at Kaos.

"Oh, General Watson, you know Kaos,"

"Little Lucky?" he stated, and witnessed Kaos' height and stature, "You're not so little anymore."

"As you know, Kaos, Watson, is a fellow dark sorcerer – Watson our Lucky is an official Circle Master!" he stated and put an arm around the man's solider. He then looked at Kaos with a stink eye. "He has a master's Dipolma is Shaddow magic!"

"You continued your studies?" Watson questioned Kaos, "That's unbelievable."

"Yes, and by-gods, he managed to squirm out our old-man's book!" he exclaimed. Kaos was a little shocked.

"You didn't know it was me?" Kaos interjected.

"How the hell was I supposed to know that it was you out of all people?" Ijae laughed. Watson stared at Kaos with question.

"You can read the ancient language?"

"Yes," Kaos stated. He walked up and took Kaos' hand with shock, "A fellow scholar! It's good to have you back!" he exclaimed, "I have some other ancient texts you should find to your interest."

"Well, Kaos is going back to the castle after this," Ijae stated in correction. Kaos was puzzled by the whole interaction.

"Oh, yes," he laughed, "I should have noticed. Your hair," he laughed, "It means that you are engaged – correct?" he indicated to Kaos head. Kaos flushed.

"Yes," Kaos stated beat red. Ijae laughed.

"Well it seems that you are all flustered by that!" he stated.

"It's not as if I want to get married," Kaos stressed.

"Do you know her?" Watson questioned.

"Yes," Kaos questioned.

"Well that's good," he stated, "You'll be together for a very long time – I would imagine that you would want to make sure that you marry the right person." Kaos looked a little ill and he looked away from the man. He couldn't help but think of Tara at this moment.

"Yes, I wanted to ask you," Ijae stated, "Who is the lucky girl?"

"I am not dumb enough to state her name," he declared.

"Tuta?" he asked. Kaos looked at him with ponder. "I'm right."

"How would you know?"

"She began communicating with me to learn about you."

"That's bullshit she communicated with Daragon, my master, not you," he stated.

"So Daragon is your master, is he?" Ijae questioned and went up to Kaos.

"He's taught me light magic," Kaos stated.

"Light magic isn't worth anything for a human," he stated. Kaos remember his transformation. "Now do you still have the insignia?" he stated. "Turn around!" Kaos did so and he allowed his neck to be inspected. Ijae took his finger and pushed on the insignia. It burned and Kaos pulled away.

"What?" Kaos growled, "What did you do?" Ijae laughed. Watson suddenly grabbed him, and the youth came in and snagged him from behind. Kaos pulled him foreward and flipped the boy. He stumbled back and was restrained by Watson.

"Hold still, my dear apprentice," Ijae stated and took out a needle. Kaos pulled at his arms, but his strength had left him.

"Hurry up and inject him!" the youth cried.

"Let me go!" Kaos yelled as the youth jumped him and pulled him a position so that he bent over. Ijae came around behind Kaos who shuffled his feet.

"Someone get him to be still! Hold down him on his right!" another solider cam and grabbed him on the other side so that he couldn't shift. Watson was on his left, the solider on the right. The youth had him in a head lock and Ijae was behind him filling up the needle with a clear liquid.

"Now you hold still, and do as you're told or this might sting a bit," he explained.

"Make sure you give him enough for 24 hours!" the youth stated.

"Oh, yes, he's going to get enough for a week" Ijae smiled and put a hand on Kaos' neck to steady it, "Okay, Kaos, here we go." Within a few seconds Kaos felt a pinch on the back of his neck and a rush of cold liquid into his body." He jumped, but the youth restrained him. Kaos felt his body go numb and the group eased their grip. "Good, now one more," he stated and he switched vials. This one was a translucent red – at which Kaos suddenly felt his body start to shake. They held him down and Ijae removed the need and attached a bandage firmly.

"Thank gods," the youth exasperated.

"Is it taking effect?" Ijae asked. Kaos body fell cold and his hair grew in black.

"Yes," Watson stated, "Just a few minutes longer and he should be reverted to a full human." Kaos' eyes turned auburn and his skin lightened further. Kaos yelled and pushed although he couldn't feel his body.

"Don't pull!" Ijae screamed and held him in a fixed position. "You'll hurt yourself!" Kaos finally fell to his knees after several minutes – his strength had left him and he felt nearly unconscious. The group no longer need to hold him – even if he was loose, his body was so weak that he could hardly manage a run. Ijae caught him, and felt his body trembling. He kissed him.

"Dose 1," he laughed, "You made it."

"What did you do to me?" Kaos mumbled.

"You're going to need a haircut," Ijae laughed.

"Remember I said that you would remain human for two hours – this should last you a whole week!" he exclaimed. Kaos felt his eyes drooping.

"I'll take him to his courters," Ijae commented, "Youri," he looked at the youth.

"Yes, sir?"

"Could you help me transport him?"

"With magic?"

"No, silly, your two hands."

Kaos was lifted and carried up a bunch of stairs into a cottage. Kaos knew it all too well – it was Ijae's homestead. He had a wife, but no children. Years ago he had a son, but he was killed by Ebony Soldiers. Kaos was laid in bed and stripped of his clothing. Ijae laid a hand on Kaos' back, where the tattoo lay and he was shocked at its size. He laid in bed and Ijae rested his hands on Kaos shoulder. Kaos was crying. He felt so violated and out of control.

"Shh," Ijae hushed, "It's all right now, no one will harm you anymore."

"You don't have to worry anymore," he stated, "You don't have to be king." Kaos was scared, frightened, "You can be here, live with us, marry whomever you wish to." He stated. Kaos felt his body come back to him hours later. He woke and had a flashback of what had occurred the night before. Ijae walked it pleasantly.

"Gods, you've been out for nearly eight hours!" he exclaimed holding a tray, "I brought you some food." He put the tray down and came over to Kaos. He pulled the sheet off and Kaos covered his head. "Come now," he laughed, "You're not going to sleep forever!"

"Leave me alone," Kaos grumbled to himself.

"Lease you alone?" Ijae laughed, "Now why would I do that? You're needed out in the camp – I need to see what I've missed all these years!"

"Shut up," Kaos growled.

"What?" Ijae stopped.

"Shut up and leave me alone – you've already done enough damage as it is!"

"Damage?" he questioned again in a friendly tone, "I don't think that I damaged you at all. What's wrong with you?"

"This is all because of the coronation!" Kaos exclaimed.

"And you want to be king?" he asked. Kaos was silent, "I didn't think so."

Ijae moved him into a chair and his wife cut his hair. She cut it short and trim so that it conformed to the shape of his face. The front however fell over his face – far enough so that it hung near his chin.

"Your life must be very difficult," she commented. "I hope that you like this, I don't know what you would want. Ijae said that it had to be short so as to stay out of the way, but I know that you don't like it short so I hope that the compromise for length in the front is all right."

"It's fine," Kaos commented. "My hair is constantly cut."

"I hear that it grows out whenever you transform," she smiled.

"Yes," he sighed.

"Must get frustrating since you can never have a style for too long." Kaos sighed. She took out a electric shaver and neatened up his neck line and trimmed the hair there. "You should take a shower and condition it – you'll probably have this one for quite some time." He sighed and was led towards a shower, which he took. She smiled to try and comfort him, but the severity of his situation was weighing heavily on him. He recalled that she was always very nice to him – something that Sharle never was. When he came out she had laid out some clothing for him. They were simple, a pair of jeans and a tank-top. He had jewelry still in his ears and he looked in the mirror. His Ears were round, but they still had loops in the cartilage. He sighed and changed. He sat down on the bed.

Fifteen minutes later there was a knock on the door.

"May I come in?" Ijae's voice was there. Kaos sat on the bed,

"Come in," Kaos stated. Ijae came in and looked him up and down with shock. Kaos stared at him.

"What?"

"You just look surprisingly-" he stopped.

"What?"

"Good," he stated. Kaos sighed,

"Thanks," he stated.

"Are you up to coming out with me?" he asked with a smile.

"I suppose."

Kaos walked besides him as they entered the camp. One of the soldiers was holding a coffee cup nearly dropped it in shock when they caught sight of him.

"Is that?" he muttered. Kaos walked along. Waton approached warily.

"Commander Ijae?" he stated and walked specifically to Ijae.

"Yes?" Ijae asked. "I have gathered up the students," he stated. Ijae smiled.

"Good," Ijae turned to Kaos, "You'll get to see the new shadow sorcerers," he smiled, "They've been looking forward to meeting you."

Kaos followed him into a clearing where a group of boys and girls were sitting, a few years younger than himself. They all wore uniforms and insignias were on their arms. They all watched and then suddenly formed a neat line in solute to Ijae.

"Welcome back master," a girl commented as he walked down the line.

"It is very good to be back," he smiled back at her. Kaos waited nearby and a few of the students took interest in him.

"At ease," he stated and then smiled and let down their guard, "I have a surprise for all of you."

"Really?" one commented with excitement. Kaos couldn't believe how happy these kids were.

"Yes, my apprentice, Kaos, has returned with me," he smiled, "He'll be around the camp for a while." The group smiled.

"Can he teach us?" one asked. Kaos was flabbergasted.

"Well, that's all up to him, he's a very powerful sorcerer – he received his Master's Diploma a few months ago." He stated. The group was dazzled over this, "So don't push his buttons!" the group laughed. Kaos turned away.

"Kaos, why are you being shy?" Ijae asked him.

"What?" Kaos looked at him.

"Come over here, you don't have to stand there like a parent," he commented. Kaos walked towards Ijae who put an arm around his shoulder and kissed him. Kaos blushed. The group laughed, "I'm so happy you're back!" Kaos just sat there and watched Ijae teach them something in the Shadow Arts. He sat cross-legged on the ground and sighed.

"Lucky?" there was a girl's voice behind him, and he flipped around. He saw a young woman standing in a uniform, she stared at him with shock. "My words, it is you!" she was shocked. Kaos looked at her, but could not remember who she was. She same up and held his cheeks, "My gods, puberty did you wonders!" Kaos blushed.

"Um…"

"Last time I saw you, you were some soiled-up skin-and-bone boy," she stated. Kaos pulled his head out of her grips.

"Pardon," Kaos stated, "I'm afraid I don't remember you." She looked a little shocked.

"It's Claire, Calre Turchow, you're study-buddy." She commented. Kaos looked at her again. "Oh," he stated with some disappointment. He recalled that she always made fun of him.

"'oh'?" she stated again, "What does that mean?"

"Nothing," Kaos shook his head.

"So where have you been all this time?" he was surprised that she didn't know, "Well, I don't mean recently, we know where you have been recently – but before that." He laughed depressingly.

"Around," he added ambiguously.

"Oh, come on!" she exclaimed, "*around* as an answer doesn't cut it!"

"You're a general, a spy, a prince, and a farm boy, what other roles have you played?" she nagged. He punched her and she fell on the ground. Everyone in vicinity turned around. She picked herself up and held her chin. She looked at him with shock. He held his fist out and was crying.

"You keep your fucking nose out of my business!" he exclaimed.

"Kaos, I-"

"You want to know what I have been through! Do you?" he yelled, "The shit that I have been through!" She looked at him. Ijae came over and put a hand on his shoulder.

"Lay off me!" Kaos pulled away and continued at her, "You relentless bitch! You have the nerve to pick up right where you left off!" She looked at him and began to tear as well, "Don't you dare cry-!"

"Kaos that's enough," Ijae caught his arm in mid-air. Kaos looked at her.

"I would slap you-"

"Kayoron!" he proclaimed. Kaos hesitated at the name. It was what he was called in elvish. He put his hand down and started walking away.

"Are you alright, Claire?" he asked her. She rose and revealed her cheek was black and blue already and she had some blood in her mouth.

"I just bit my tongue," she commented.

"Let me see," he stated and she opened her mouth. Her tooth was knocked out in the back.

"You lost a tooth," he stated.

"What?" she reached in and found it. She held it and looked sick. Kaos strode step by step with a furious look on his face, but after a few minutes he was crying again and he ran and hid behind a building and cried. Ijae found him several minutes later.

"Kaos?"

"Leave me alone, Ijae," he mumbled.

"Now, I can't do that," he shook his head and came down and sat next to Kaos. "Shh," he stated and gently guided Kaos' head to rest on his shoulder.

"Chard told me that you thought that I was a bastard,"

"You can be one," he stated.

"So you don't hate me,"

"I don't hate you, I hate your judgment," Kaos stated, "That's two different things."

"What about my judgment?"

"I don't want to talk politics, Ijae," Kaos grumbled.

"Fine, we'll save that for later."

"Why did you call me Kayoron?" Kaos stated.

"It's your name," he stated.

"My elvish name,"

"You are still half-elf," he explained, "no serum will ever make you completely human, or any transfiguration make you completely elvin." Kaos turned into him and collapsed on his lap.

"My grandmother called me Kayoron," Kaos stated, "She refused to call me anything but." He laughed.

"She wanted to make you elvin."

"She dressed me up in Charles clothing too, as though I was her husband," he stated.

"What?" he stated shocked.

"Ijae," he started but began to cry, "I would be forced to see her for three hours every day."

"What did she do to you?" Ijae asked with shock. Kaos closed his eyes and cried more. "Kaos, you can tell me."

"She would raped me then dress me up to look like Charles," Kaos stated and they cried more, "Every fucking time!"

"Kaos," he stated and hugged him.

"She was the one who gave me the tattoo on my back, and the piercings,"

"Do you want to take them out?" he stated.

"I'm scared that if I do she'll put them back in," Kaos shook his head with tears, "That fucking piercing gun! Fucking haircuts! Formal parties! Damn marriage and coronation!"

"And you're mother?"

"She's no longer my legal guardian!" Kaos proclaimed, "Marina is my mother, and she was forced by Ebony Law to hand me over to her father's friend and their family!"

"There's a lot of fuss in the castle I see," he stated.

"And your stupid attack on Patella!" Kaos yelled, "You want to know how scared I was about that! That you would kill my father, Tako and Sharle!" Kaos roared. "I had nightmares before the darn thing even took place."

"I'm sorry, but Patella was a strategic location," he stated, "We took in a lot of prisoners."

"Yeah," Kaos sighed.

Kaos returned to the house with him and went up into his room to lay down.

"That poor boy," his wife stated.

"Ruth, he's been through a lot," Ijae commented and sighed.

"You can tell, he's a very bright an articulate man for a boy his age," she commented with a smile, "but he's as arrogant as ever." She laughed. Ijae sighed.

"Don't tell him this that I told you, but apparently he was raped by his grandmother," Ijae stated seriously.

"What?" she stopped shocked.

"He was forced to see her every day for three hours and Clara would rape him then dress him up like Charles," he stated, "I can't imagine what that is like."

"They say that growing up too fast can do damage to one's soul," she stated.

"I never imagined," he stated, "It makes me want to destroy them even more!" he growled.

"There are those who are tainted, but those who are not. Many claim that Kaos would make a good ruler because of his history." She stated, "Those are the rumors in the elvin community."

"It doesn't matter, he won't be in control of it – his family will," he stated, "Kaos cannot stand up against the Ebony family no matter how arrogant he may be. Marina failed – and so didn't Charles."

"Quite a pickle," she stated, "if you ask me."

"That's why its war," he stated. "If the elves can't rule, and neither can the humans – then there is no solution."

"What of his fiancé? Have you told him that you have restrained her?"

"No," he stated.

"What?"

"I don't know what he may do, I don't want him to think that we betrayed him by doing such a thing."

"What are you going to do with her then? Let her go?"

"I don't know," he stated, "If I let her go then she will know that Kaos has been taken by us and the Royal Family will do anything to get him back."

"They'll do that regardless."

"I don't want to bring the war *here* of all places. Not when he's like this," Ijae stated, "He's too frail right now to go into any sort of family brawl."

"You can't keep her here forever!" she stated, "She's going to be missed just as much as Kaos."

"You want me to kill her?" he asked. She looked down at the food she was making.

"I don't want to kill her either, but Kaos has no intention of marrying her! He's traumatized!"

"You need to ask him that," she stated.

After a few days, Ijae confessed what had happened.

"What?" Kaos claimed, "Where is she? What did you do to her?"

"She was held in the dungeons, it wasn't my decision," he stated, "the consul believed it wise. Kaos was led down and saw her. She looked at him,

"Kaos?" she questioned and took his head in her hands. She was exhausted, beat, and her hair had been cut savagely and she dressed in rags. It had returned to its normal color and she was crying.

"Oh Tuta," Kaos hugged her. She was crying and he was.

"Why are you human?" she asked.

"I'm under suppressants, Tuta," he stated.

"But you're coronation," she stated and brushed his hair out of his eyes, "our wedding. Why?"

"Tuta, I'm going to get you some food and proper clothing okay, you can come with me." Ijae looked down at them.

"Kaos, I don't-"

"She's getting a decent place to stay!" he exclaimed. "I can ask for that much, can't I?"

Kaos bathed her and brushed her hair out and Ruth lent her some clothing. She was shocked and traumatized and hardly said a word throughout the entire process. Ijae watched them from the doorway with his hands crossed. He cut her hair so that it was even and even used some of the techniques he had witnessed.

"There," he smiled and brushed her off, "Feel better?" he laughed.

"Thank you," she blushed.

"Now you know how I feel," he smiled and took her around the shoulders. Her hair was only slightly longer than his and they stared in the mirror. "You look good in short hair." She blushed,

"Thank you," she stated.

"Now would you like something to eat?" he asked. She looked at Ijae and stopped.

"Tuta?"

"Why does he have to be here?"

"Because I don't want you doing anything to Kaos," Ijae stated sternly. "Kaos, she can stay in Watson's house tonight – I won't have her in the same vicinity as you without watch." She looked at him with frustration, "You should really take her over there shortly."

"Yes, Ijae," Kaos agreed.

"Kaos?" she questioned suddenly, "You're going to just listen to him?"

"Hey!" Ijae harked up, "I'm looking out for him, not telling him what to do!"

"Did you forget that he is the leader of the Dartawg forces!" she yelled and Ijae grabbed her arm.

"That's enough!" he proclaimed.

"Ijae!" Kaos yelled at him. Ijae eased up and released her arm. "If you harm her, I'll harm you." Kaos took her arm and led her outside. It was dark as they walked and she had little to say.

"Are you going to take the thrown?" she asked. Kaos was silent. "Kaos, you're the prince!"

"I don't want to!" Kaos exclaimed, "I don't want to, Tuta!" he started crying, "I would rather be here than go back to the castle!"

"Then you're a dartawg!" she was horrified.

"I'm not a Dartawg," he stated. She pulled away from him.

"You *are* a Dartawg if you are not with Ebony!" she exclaimed. "And I want nothing to do with you!" she looked at him firecly. He grabbed her arm forcefully and pulled her to Watson's house."

"Kaos," he was startled.

"Keep her safe," Kaos stated and pushed Tuta inside. He took her abruptly and Kaos shut the door on them.

"Dame Tuta, I believe," he stated. "I'm Watson, a scholar. Please I'll show you the room we have prepared."

Kaos hardly slept that night, and when Ruth came in to wake him he was already sitting on the vanity and crying as he looked in the mirror.

"Kaos?" she came up to him and held his shoulders. "Kaos, what's wrong?" He cried and dropped his head further.

"…I can't win…" Kaos mumbled, "…no matter what someone will hate me…"

"Kaos we don't hate you," she stated.

"…I have to give up everything to make her happy…and I have to take shots to make myself happy…"

"Kaos, shh," she stated and hugged him, he turned and went into her arms. "Please stop this, we accept you – please don't beat yourself up over this girl."

"Kaos is a good boy,"

"Are you affiliated with Dartawg?" she questioned.

"No, I am independent," he stated, "A personal friend of Kaos'," he stated. "You have no crude judgments here." She was shocked.

Kaos went out with Ijae again, if only to get out of the house. He saw Tuta walking in the street and buying groceries. Their eyes met and he turned away.

"Kaos!" she yelled and ran up to him, "I'm sorry," she stated, "I'm sorry for yesterday."

"You're not sorry," he stated.

"I spoke with Watson, he told me-"

"Told you what? That I made myself an independent?" he asked. "What would you know about life outside of Ebony!"

"Kaos, I-"

"You're just a stuck up elf!" he proclaimed, "I want nothing to do with you, too."

"Kaos I'm sorry! Please!" she stated.

"Give me one good reason too," he stated.

"I want to be your friend at least," she stated, "I love you, Kaos! I know you better than anyone else!"

"Than why could you find it so hard to believe that I would make myself an Independent?"

"I don't find it hard to believe," she stated, "It's just hard to believe such things exist," she stated.

"I want to live my life outside of war, of politics. Ijae was the closest thing I had to a father and he's willing to accept that I don't wish to get involved in the war any longer!" he exclaimed, "He can offer me sanctuary from my curse!"

"By taking those injections!" she yelled, "Do you even know what might happen to you? What the hell they're doing inside your body?"

"My body isn't going to die!"

"Are you so sure?!" she yelled, he was then uneasy. "You weren't meant to be human, Kaos. If you were than Marina wouldn't be your mother! I can respect your decision to not get involved, but you have birthright, and you can't just ignore it! You have a chance to make a difference in the world, are you just going to let the world pass you by!" she ordered. Kaos looked down. She took his head and kissed him, they locked for a time and he kissed her back. "Look I love you for you! For the fool who couldn't dance!" she stated. "I don't care what you do with the empire when you're king – but you must go there or it will follow you forever."

"Kaos!" Ijae yelled. Kaos looked at him, he ran up beside them, "Is everything all right here?" he asked.

"It's fine."